The Singular Six

J. S. Volpe

Peridor Press

For Betsy

CONTENTS

Chapter 1

Sweetwater

1

A hush fell over the Sweetwater market as an RV pulled by eight draft horses rattled to a stop in front of the Quartered Orc Tavern.

The RV was thirty feet long and had been adapted for travel in this mostly pavement- and fossil fuel-free post-Cataclysm world: The engine, exhaust system, and all other now-useless components had been removed; a draw pole and swingletrees attached; the windshield taken out so the horses' reins could pass through to the front seat; and the old axles and wheels replaced with sturdy oaken ones reinforced with iron bands.

But no one spared the RV more than a passing glance. Instead, all eyes were fixed on the horses. Horses had been rare in these parts ever since the orc invasion a few years back, during which the orcs had seized every horse they could find (not to ride, but to eat). Nowadays, owning one was seen as a sign of either blessedness or bastardliness.

Heads craned as the RV's doors opened. The dust and mud that covered the vehicle indicated it had come a long way, and given how dangerous the roads were, with beasts and bandits as common as sparrows, everyone expected the RV's occupants to be mighty warriors, or mages, or mutants with fantastic powers.

Thus everyone was surprised when two young women who at first glance appeared perfectly normal climbed out. A second glance, however, showed they weren't perfectly normal after all, for while the women were dressed somewhat differently—one with a green cloak, one with a black one; one with white sneakers, one with black leather boots—they were otherwise identical: same brown hair, same brown eyes, same face, same physique. Whether this marked them as twins, clones, robots, or something else, no one knew. But it was intriguing. Or worrying, depending on one's basic temperament.

While the black-cloaked woman reached back into the RV and pulled out an olive messenger bag, the green-cloaked one turned and eyed the crowd that filled the market in the town square. Not wanting to be caught staring by this possibly puissant entity, everyone swiftly returned to their business.

The black-cloaked woman slung the bag over her shoulder, and the women entered the market. They examined each seller's wares in turn, making no move to trade until they had seen the whole range of goods on display, most of which had been scrounged from the countless pre-Cataclysm ruins that dotted the landscape. The low wooden tables were crowded with clothes, toys, wishing stones, canteens, dentures, holocubes, cookware, books. Here and there were rarer, and thus much pricier, items. On one table otherwise occupied by grimy dolls was a broken Chen-Chen X55 Laser Pistol that could probably be fixed by someone with the right knowledge. One old woman had a plastic replica of a human head that spoke an unknown language in a deep, resonant voice when you pressed a button behind its right ear. Fat Harvey, the shrewdest trader around, had a pair of ornamental daggers, one's hilt set with a large ruby, the other's with an emerald. Bingo Burberry, one of Sweetwater's small halfling community, was offering, in addition to his usual selection of delicious home-made cheeses and top-quality home-grown pipeweed, a black leather doctor's bag containing various medical supplies: a stethoscope, band-aids, gauze, a syringe, antibiotic ointment, and, most precious of all, Cipro.

It was this last table and this last item to which the two women returned after their circuit of the market. Practically everyone in the area had had their eyes on the doctor's bag ever since Bingo first offered it for trade three months ago, after he found it in some weeds next to a cluster of thriving tanglevines in the depths of which could be seen a modest black coat, a pair of spectacles, and a grinning skull. But Bingo's asking price was far too high: Seven sacks of grain was something no one could afford to part with. As time passed and it remained untraded, everyone figured he would lower his price, but he didn't, insisting that someday some-one would need it badly enough to pay up. Now, it seemed, that day had come.

"How much for the bag and its contents?" asked the woman in the green cloak.

"Seven sacks of the best grain or the like," Bingo said in a cool, even voice that made it clear the price was non-negotiable.

The women looked at each other. The one in the green cloak nodded. The black-cloaked one reached into her bag and pulled out a shiny silver cylinder.

"We can give you an atomic flashlight," she said.

Those nearby, who had been surreptitiously watching this exchange, now gasped. Though few had ever seen one, word had it that atomic flashlights worked forever, unlike the battery-operated ones, which were now no more than fancy clubs, their batteries having gone dead in the fifteen years since the Cataclysm.

Bingo, though equally awestruck, maintained a mask of professional cool.

"Let me see it," he said.

She gave it to him. He pressed a button halfway up its shaft, squinted into the bright light that shone from the clear plastic head, then switched it off and examined it closely, turning it this way and that. Unlike most of those present, he *had* seen an atomic flashlight before.

When he had determined to his satisfaction that it was the real thing, he smiled and said, "Well, now. I think we have a—"

Somewhere in the distance a woman let out a long, shrill scream. It stopped with jarring suddenness, and a cacophony of hoofbeats flooded into the silence where it had been. Shouts rose up from the next street over.

"What's going on?" said the woman in the black cloak.

Bingo shook his head. "I don't know. Probably more—"

A mechanical whir rose above the shouts and hoofbeats. Bingo's eyes went wide.

"It's *them!*"

"What? Who?"

Before he could answer, two young men on hover-boards—large metal antigravity skateboards—shot out from behind the one-room schoolhouse on the west side of the square. The taller of the two men was skinny and pale, with wide rubbery lips and spiky black hair. He wore scruffy blue jeans, sneakers, and a black T-shirt with a white A in a circle on it. The other man, who was dressed much more conservatively in black shoes, gray slacks, and a white shirt with even the collar buttoned, had lank greasy hair, glasses thicker than Coke-bottle bottoms, and a perpetual scowl. They streaked toward the crowd, their boards glinting silver in the sun and kicking up clouds of dust as they glided a foot above the ground.

"Who are they?" asked the woman in the black cloak.

"Skippy and Oscar, two of the Marauders," said the halfling, his voice cracking with panic. "We must flee."

He snatched the atomic flashlight and, leaving everything else, dashed away.

Behind him, dozens more Marauders poured into the square, some on foot, some on horseback, all of them brandishing swords, or knives, or spears, or other weapons. Their ranks included Johnny Circumcision, a bug-eyed, bristle-haired psychopath with shiny silver coveralls and a pair of hedge-clippers in place of hands; Klaus von Klaus, who wore full Nazi regalia...and full make-up, including rouge, eyeliner, and Cherry Alive lipstick; the Cardiac Kid, a hooting, hollering, constantly drunk young man who always wore a Cleveland Browns helmet and a jersey numbered 8; Droke, a leathery-skinned creature with vestigial wings on its back and a pair of large white bull-horns sprouting from the sides of its misshapen head; Tricky Dick, a short wiry fellow in a black three-piece suit and a rubber Richard Nixon mask, the nose of which was shaped like a long, thick, upturned penis; Hairy Harry, a grizzled biker whose hirsute beer belly ballooned out between his black leather vest and his winged skull belt buckle; Schweeliski, a tall, blonde, rail-thin spaz in an Izod shirt and Dockers who had a thing for knives and kittens; Big Red, a massive, mead-soaked Viking, complete with horned helmet, two-headed battle-axe, and lice-ridden beard; and then there was the Grottle...

Seven-and-a-half feet of solid muscle, with completely hairless skin the yellow of rich butter and teeth so stained and pitted they looked like chunks of pumice, the Grottle resembled no known species or type of monster. It wore gray pants and a gray shirt both of which were so filthy and tattered they looked as if it had crawled out of its grave in them. Its "boots" were strips of similarly filthy and tattered gray cloth wound round and round its huge, splayed feet until they were so thickly padded the Grottle could stalk across a sheet-metal floor without a sound. Unlike the rest of the Marauders, it never used a horse or a hoverboard or any other mode of transport; instead it loped along on its thick legs, never tiring, keeping perfect pace with the galloping horses. When the Marauders attacked a town, it beheaded men left and right with mighty sweeps of the long-handled shovel it carried everywhere it went. And as it committed its slaughter, its mammoth frame shuddered with its terrible laughter—"hurr hurr hurr!"—the only sound it ever made.

And so when the people of Sweetwater saw this gang of nightmares descending upon them, they ran. And when the severed heads started flying and the air shivered with screams, their run became a stampede.

The two women fled for their RV, but before they could travel far, Skippy and Oscar veered toward them, having singled them out as good breeding-stock. Oscar reached them first and with the ease born of much practice pulled the black-cloaked one into his arms, his board wobbling a moment with the excess weight then steadying itself.

The other woman crouched down as Skippy raced toward her, and then leaped to the side at the last moment, avoiding his groping hands by centimeters. He whirred past, casting a hateful glance over his shoulder at her as he went. Then he banked the board around for a second pass.

While he did that, she sprinted after her companion, who thrashed about in Oscar's grasp as his board carried them toward the edge of town, where several Marauders were opening the wheeled, horse-drawn cages in which they transported the women and loot they captured back to their base.

The woman writhed free of his grip and thudded to the dusty street.

"Bitch," Oscar said. He jerked his board to a halt, then backed up quickly before she could get to her feet. Instead of trying to bring her onto the board with him again, he grabbed the collar of her cloak and took off at full speed down the street, dragging her through the dust behind him.

"Maggie!" she called out to the other woman. "Help!"

"Anna!" cried Maggie.

A whir behind her heralded Skippy's return. She stopped in the middle of the street and waited, listening to the approaching hoverboard, calculating its speed, its distance, all her possible responses, and once again she dodged at the last possible instant, only this time she threw out a leg, clipping Skippy across the shins and flinging him from his board. The board continued speeding down the street until it slammed into the side of a building that resembled a giant teapot, at which point its whir ceased and it clattered to the ground. Skippy rolled back and forth in the dust, groaning.

Maggie started to resume her pursuit of Anna, but skidded to a halt when Hairy Harry and the Cardiac Kid stepped into her path. Harry held a switchblade in one hand and a length of chain in the other. The Kid gripped a baseball bat with foot-long spikes driven through the end. They strode toward her, grinning, while behind them Oscar reached the edge of town. A pair of Marauders grabbed Anna and threw her into one of the cages, where she joined half a dozen other frightened young women.

Her eyes never straying from the two swiftly approaching Marauders, Maggie turned her head partway toward the RV, which stood about fifty feet behind her and to her left.

"Adam!" she shouted as loud as she could. "We could use a little help here!"

Immediately the vehicle wobbled, the rear end dipped slightly, and the back door flew open.

The being that emerged from the RV was so tall he had to bend nearly double to get through the doorway, and when he stood up to his full height and looked around for Maggie, the top of his head was nearly parallel with the RV's roof. But it wasn't just his height that made both the villagers and the Marauders gawp at him in awe and terror. His bulk was equally great: His broad chest strained against his gray cloak, and his fists were the size of hams. His skin was yellow—not the buttery yellow of the Grottle's, but the dirty yellow of old parchment. A pair of watery, jaundiced eyes glistened in the midst of a face almost as wrinkled as a mummy's. His narrow black lips were squeezed into a thin line. His hair was long and black and tied back with an incongruously dainty blue ribbon.

Most of the villagers saw only another monster, no different from the Grottle. A more well-read few recognized this being, and their terror was worse, for this was none other than Frankenstein's Monster, the infamous creature cobbled together from bits of corpses and brought to life to wreak havoc on the innocent.

The Monster—Adam—looked around in search of Maggie, eyes skimming quickly over the horrified villagers as if he were inured to such reactions. When he spotted her, he stormed forward.

Seeing him as the primary threat, Hairy Harry and the Kid swerved past Maggie and ran to confront him. Once they had passed, Maggie squatted down and whipped a dagger from a sheath strapped to her calf. She charged after the duo.

"Look out, guys! Behind you!" It was Skippy. He had risen to his knees and was pointing a finger at Maggie as she closed in on them.

The Kid spun around, swinging his bat. Maggie barely leapt back in time. As it was, she felt the breeze of the bat's passage on her face.

Meanwhile Hairy Harry confronted Adam. With a fierce cry, he thrust his knife at Adam's stomach. Dodging back, Adam slapped Hairy Harry's hand so hard it not only broke the biker's wrist but sent the back of his hand smacking against his forearm. The knife clattered away.

Hairy Harry gaped at his ruined hand a moment. Then, snarling with rage and pain, he swung the chain at Adam. Before it could travel far, Adam's fist shot out and smashed into Harry's throat, collapsing his windpipe and fracturing two vertebrae.

Adam stepped over Hairy Harry's dying, twitching body and stalked toward the Kid. The Kid glanced back over his shoulder, saw Adam approaching, and mumbled, "Fuckin' Modell."

The Kid lunged forward as if to attack Maggie. The moment she backed away, he spun around and swung the bat at Adam. With no time for finesse, Adam raised his left arm into the bat's path, letting the spikes punch into the thick meat of his forearm. He swept his arm to the side, wrenching the bat from the Kid's grasp, then sent his right fist hurtling into the Kid's face.

The Browns helmet and the skull beneath it shattered like china under a steamroller. The Kid's lifeless corpse sank to the dust.

"Decerebrate scum," Adam said as he wiggled the

spike-studded bat out of his forearm. He flung it away with a sneer of distaste.

"Are you all right?" he asked Maggie.

"They got Anna!" She pointed at the cages, which were now nearly full.

With a low growl, Adam charged past Maggie, past the corpses, past the overturned tables and the scattered wares.

Most of the battles and bloodshed in the street had ended, and the majority of the Marauders were now converging on the cages at the edge of town, their job done. One of them saw Adam coming and alerted the others gathered there.

As Adam ran, his growl swelled into a roar. Even though he was still a good four hundred feet away, many of the Marauders unconsciously backed up. Those with more presence of mind locked the cages and drew their weapons.

As Adam passed a blacksmith's shop, the Grottle burst from the front door and barreled toward Adam, shovel raised. Adam skidded to a halt and crouched down, arms spread, hands open, ready for the impending attack.

The Grottle swung the shovel so hard even Maggie, half a block away, heard the whistle as it streaked through the air straight at Adam's neck. Adam blocked the shovel, grabbing its handle with one hand, while with the other he punched at the Grottle's face. The Grottle tilted its head to the side, narrowly avoiding the blow, then tore the shovel from Adam's grip. Before it could draw the shovel back for another swing, Adam leaped, hoping to knock the Grottle down, but it spun out of Adam's path with almost balletic grace, and Adam galumphed past, whirling his arms to keep his balance.

By the time he brought himself to a halt and turned around, the Grottle had raised its shovel for a second strike.

A hideous grin cracked its yellow face. It clearly hadn't had this much fun—this much *challenge*—in a long time.

It swung. Adam dodged, but not fast enough. The shovel sliced into the meat of his left deltoid with a *chuck*.

Teeth gritted against the pain, Adam took hold of the shovel before the Grottle could yank it away, and tried to pull it from the Grottle's grasp.

He almost succeeded. The wooden handle slid several inches through the Grottle's hands. The Grottle's eyes widened with almost child-like alarm.

Then fury replaced the alarm, and eyes blazing, it threw all its strength into twisting the shovel free. Adam refused to give an inch. Veins bulged in his hands as he held the shovel in place. The Grottle twisted harder, harder.

Adam let go. The sudden lack of resistance sent the Grottle crashing to the ground.

Before Adam could press his advantage, a streak of orange light struck the street in front of him, sending up a shower of dirt and leaving a small scorched hole in the earth.

Adam realized that for the last few seconds the whine of a motor had been steadily approaching above and behind him. Cursing his inattention, he turned.

Flying over the top of the blacksmith's was the Annihilator, the Marauders' field leader, a sleek shark-like figure in high-tech battle armor with a jetpack on the back. The armor was silvery gray except for the gauntlets, boots, belt, and some ornamental designs on the helmet and breastplate, all of which were a green so dark it was almost black. The helmet had a pair of tinted shatterproof lenses, a pentagonal speaker/air filter over the mouth and nose, and a disk over each ear with an antenna sprouting from the top. A small laser-blaster extended from the back of the gauntlet on his right wrist, and as he descended toward the street, he carefully aimed it at Adam.

Adam sensed movement to his left. He couldn't risk turning away from the Annihilator to look, but he knew what it was anyway: The Grottle had regained its feet and was moving in.

The Annihilator fired his blaster just as Adam made a run for the blacksmith's. More scorched dirt sprayed up.

Adam's path took him directly under the Annihilator, who was able to get in two more shots before he had to stop firing lest he shoot his own foot. Neither shot hit the target, and by the time the Annihilator had spun around in mid-air, Adam had disappeared into the shop.

The Annihilator landed in the middle of the street, face to the blacksmith's, then bent forward at the waist until his upper body was parallel with the ground. It was only then that Maggie noticed a trio of slender red rockets protruding from the top of his jetpack.

"No!" she said.

Ignoring her, the Annihilator fired off a rocket. With a mechanical buzz, it streaked straight through the shop's open doorway, leaving a trail of smoke behind it.

For a moment nothing happened, and Maggie had time to hope that the rocket had been a dud.

The shop exploded. The entire façade split down the center like a double doorway opening, then disintegrated into a rain of glass and wood and nails. The blast shattered the neighboring stores' windows and made the bell in the bell tower above the town hall give off one dolorous *clung*.

Maggie stared in horror at the shattered shop. Through the smoke, all she could see were pale flames flickering among vague, shadowy debris.

The Annihilator turned to the Grottle and the handful of Marauders still in the street.

"We're done here," the Annihilator said, his voice low and tinny through the helmet's speaker. "Let's get moving."

The Grottle cast a leering grin at the ruins of the blacksmith's and then trotted toward the cages.

As the Marauders' caravan thundered away, Anna pressed her face against the bars of the rearmost cage and stretched one arm outside.

"Maggie!" she shouted.

But Maggie could only watch as the Marauders, and Anna, vanished over the brow of a hill.

The moment they were out of sight, she ran toward the wreckage of the shop, but stopped when Adam raced out of a nearby alley, his cloak streaked with dirt and soot.

Maggie threw her arms around him.

"Thank goodness!" she said. "I thought you were still in there when that man blew it up."

"Actually, I was. I had made it to the shop's rear exit and was about to step through the doorway when everything went white around me. The explosion propelled me through the doorway, and I slammed into the back of the building across the alley behind the blacksmith's. It took me a minute to regain my wits." He glared in the direction the Marauders had departed. "A minute too long."

By now the braver residents of Sweetwater had begun slinking from their hiding places—some to eye the monster, others to gather their spilled wares, still others to mourn their dead.

The door of the sheriff's office flew open and a short man with a great round belly and a shaggy handlebar mustache tromped out. A silver badge gleamed upon his black vest. A revolver hung in a holster at his side.

He started to approach Adam and Maggie with the stern and implacable air of a cop, but as he got closer and Adam's features grew clearer, his steps slowed and his eyes widened with dismay. He stopped about ten feet away and swallowed hard.

"You, sir," he said to Adam. "What, uh, what are your intentions here in Sweetwater?" The sweat cascading down his face suggested that he thought Adam's intentions were to pound law enforcement officers into greasy red pulp.

"My intentions *had* been to simply lie low in my wagon while my friends purchased certain items we required and then go on my way. Now, however, I must find a way to rescue one of those friends, since it appears that the job of sheriff in these lands does not involve protecting the lives and livelihoods of his charges—even when he is one of the fortunate few to carry a gun in these desperate times."

Despite his fear, the sheriff scowled. "Now see here, if I'd of come out while those guys were attacking, they would've killed me quicker'n you can say 'Pepperoni'! And I can't very well protect the citizens if I'm dead, now can I?"

Adam rolled his eyes. "Your logic is impeccable. Now tell me who those men are and where they are taking Anna."

Before the sheriff could answer, a middle-aged woman who stood four-foot-ten and couldn't have weighed more than a hundred pounds came running down the street toward them.

"They took my baby!" she cried. "My Nala!"

The sheriff turned to her, grimacing as if he had been punched in the gut. "They took Nala?"

"They took most of the young women," said a skinny bespectacled man as he strolled up to join the group. "Nala, Deirdre, Hari. And they killed about two dozen men." The man gave Adam and Maggie a nervous glance. "I'm Gus Firth, the, um…well, I guess I'm the mayor now."

"What?" the sheriff said. "What happened to Mayor

Depuesto?"

Firth jerked a thumb over his shoulder at a body halfway down the street. "He's there. At least part of him is. We still don't know where his head ended up."

"Forget about that!" the woman said. "What are you going to do about Nala and the other girls?"

"Calm down, Rin," the sheriff told her.

"This is all very tragic," said Adam, "but I need to know where these men are heading so I can begin my pursuit."

Rin looked at him as if seeing him for the first time, hope shining through her tears. "You're going to get our girls back? Really?"

The sheriff now stared at Adam with surprise. "You are?"

Adam shook his head. "I never—"

"Of course he will," Maggie interjected with a sweet smile. She turned to Adam. "Won't you?" The raise of her eyebrows and the precise enunciation of each word told Adam that if he said "no," he would be in for a very unpleasant future.

Adam looked at her in bewilderment. "I...suppose so."

"Oh, thank you!" Rin threw her arms around Adam and sobbed with relief onto his belly.

"Rin!" said the sheriff. "How can you trust him? I mean, just look at him! He looks more like one of them than one of us."

Rin broke away from Adam's cloak and glared the sheriff. "He's doing more than you ever did, Osquin O'Toole!"

"But...but *look* at him. We can't trust his kind. After all our problems with the orcs..."

"I am no orc, or friend of orcs," said Adam.

"Yeah, well, that don't mean much," the sheriff said.

"Way I hear it, those bastards'll eat their own kind if they get the chance."

"I can assure you I have never eaten my own kind. Nor could I, for there are no others like me in all the world. Now for the final time, who are these men, and where are they are going? If we hurry, we might be able to catch up with them before they travel too far."

"And how do you propose to do that, exactly?" the sheriff said with a knowing, almost smug smile.

"We have an old vehicle with horses…" He trailed off, only now noticing that at some point during the battle one of the Marauders had cut the horses loose from the RV and taken off with them. He closed his eyes and inhaled deeply, the way people do when they're trying hard to keep their temper in check. "I do not suppose you have any horses or mules we could use?"

"The Marauders took the only horses we had," Firth said. "And as for mules, well, a few people have mules, but there's no way they'll just give 'em away. You'll have to either trade or buy. And it won't be cheap."

"I see. And what of the Marauders? How do I find them?"

Firth shrugged. "No one knows exactly where their base is except that it's at least a few days' journey west, in the least populated and most dangerous part of Erizan."

"Erizan, then, is the name of this land?" said Adam.

Firth eyed him with fascination. "How far have you traveled?"

Adam glanced at Maggie, clearly at a loss.

"We've been traveling for three months now," she said. "We must have covered at least three hundred miles."

Firth whistled. "Which way've you been traveling?"

"West. Due west."

He nodded. "Well, if you want the Marauders, you can just keep heading that way. But west's bad. Real bad. No one heads west. Heck, when we were having all the trouble with the orcs a few years back, even the orcs wouldn't go into the west country. It's—" He shook his head. "Sometimes folks head that way, and none of them ever come back. The Marauders're the only ones crazy enough to live there."

"What is there that is so terrible?"

"Dunno. Like I said, no one who heads that way ever comes back to tell about it. But you gotta figure, since hardly anyone lives or travels that way, the monsters've gotta be thicker than weeds. And I don't know what it was like where you come from, but the monsters we've had around here make the Marauders look like kittens. We've had spiders as big as horses. We've had black rubbery flying things that ate people—someone named 'em 'night gaunts' and the name kinda fits. We had a little flying metal ball that shot death rays. Heck, we even had a friggin' dinosaur."

"Stegosaurus," said Rin. "It—" Suddenly her eyes lit up. "Oh! The robot!"

"What?" Maggie said. "What robot?"

Rin grabbed the sheriff's shoulder, her face beaming with excitement. "The robot said it came from the west."

"What are you talking about?" Adam said.

The sheriff snorted and said, "A week ago this damnable robot showed up in town and started annoying everyone with all this babble about somethin' called 'sicko analysis.' It wasn't hurtin' anyone and didn't seem like it would, so we let it stay. Which might've been a mistake. There're times I'd love to smash the gabby little bastard to pieces."

"Speak for yourself," Rin said. "I think he's rather charming. But the thing is, he passed through the west country on his way here, so he knows the terrain. He might even know where the Marauders live."

"Where is this robot now?" Adam asked.

Rin looked around the square and up and down the streets leading off it.

"I saw him talking to some folks a few minutes before the Marauders attacked," she said. "I hope he hasn't been killed. I'll hunt around for him, and if I find him, I'll point him your way. He'll be only too happy to help. He always is."

"Thank you," Maggie said. "We would appreciate that."

The sheriff smiled. "So would I. That way the stupid pile of junk can go annoy someone else for a while."

2

An hour later Adam and Maggie sat in the back of the RV with the back door open. The street had already been cleared of bodies and debris, though dark red patches in the dust attested to the afternoon's battle. The citizens of Sweetwater kept looking into the RV as they passed by, which Adam found annoying. But Maggie insisted they keep it open "to air things out."

Adam had stripped to the waist so Maggie could clean and treat his wound with the items from the doctor's bag, which she had retrieved from the street after their talk with Mayor Firth, Sheriff O'Toole, and Rin. It was a miracle no one had made off it with it in all the chaos.

"It's quite fortunate we acquired this when we did," she said as she worked on punching a needle through his unnaturally tough, thick skin to sew up the gash in his shoulder.

"Mm-hmm," said Adam as yet another cluster of women passed the back of the RV, openly staring at him as they went. He seemed to shrink in upon himself every time this happened, clearly embarrassed about letting people see his naked torso, which was broad, wrinkled, and yellow, but not, contrary to popular impression, covered in scars. Dr. Frankenstein's genius had made scars and stitches unnecessary.

"You hardly need to do this, as you well know," he said. "My body heals much faster than a normal man's. The wound would have healed on its own within a day or two."

"This will help you heal faster. Besides, we can't have you bleeding all over yourself, now can we? It's unsightly."

"I am unsightly already," he murmured, watching a little girl peep around the open doorway with eyes as large as dragon eggs. When she saw that he had seen her, she squealed and ducked out of sight. Adam sighed. "Why you insist on displaying my ghastly form for all the town to see is beyond my comprehension. Have you taken it upon yourself to invent new nightmares for the children?"

Without looking up from her work, she said, "People need to see that you are not the monster they fear you are."

He turned his head and looked at her. "What?"

"If they see you receiving the same sort of medical care all men must get, if they see you doing normal things, they will think of you more as a man."

He gave a bitter laugh. "Your attempt at rehabilitating my image is touching but doomed to failure. The merest glimpse of my face is enough to set babes howling in terror and make men reach for their swords. I look like no man alive."

"And the world as it is now looks like no world ever seen before, yet people are learning to accept it as well as they can. They can accept you, too, if you try. If you want them to."

"Why do you waste your time in such a way?"

She stopped sewing and gave him a stern, level,

I'm-only-going-to-say-this-once kind of look. "After the Cataclysm we spent over a decade hiding in that manor because you believed mankind was better off without you. And Anna and I went along with that even though we believed it to be a mistake."

"A mistake? I—"

She shushed him. "So we played the game your way for a while. But now that we have been forced from our home and you walk among mankind once again, we will try a different approach."

"Like what? Parading me naked among the masses?"

"Don't be so melodramatic. Let me ask you one thing: Are you a monster?"

"So the world has named me, so must I—"

"I am not talking about the world. I am talking about you. Do *you* think you are a monster? Because *I* do not."

He was silent for a moment. Maggie waited.

"I—" He faltered, started again. "I believe I understand your point. But things are hardly so simple. It is hard not to feel monstrous when everyone treats you like a monster."

"Then you must prove to them that they are wrong."

"I think I see now why you volunteered me to rescue those other abducted women: You hope that by good deeds I will be accepted into the fraternity of man."

"Somebody has to rescue those women and stop the Marauders from abducting more of them. It is clear that few around here have the means or courage to do so."

He snorted. "I fail to see why it should be my concern. I care only about rescuing Anna. Those other women would undoubtedly spit upon me under any other circumstances, so why should I concern myself with their welfare?"

Maggie didn't reply. She only stared at him with sorrow as he watched the passing villagers. Then she shook her head and resumed sewing.

"This is taking too long," he said. "Every minute we waste here is another minute between us and the Marauders. Why you insist on sewing my wound is unfathomable. She is your sister, for goodness' sake. Aren't you worried about her?"

She glared at him. "Of course I am worried. But we are in no condition to go after them right now. We have no provisions yet, no mules. And you still need to recover from the battle earlier. You are injured and weak and tired, even if you refuse to admit it. It is better to rest and gather our resources and energy for now and begin the hunt tomorrow."

"Perhaps you are right. I—"

"Excuse me," said a deep, refined voice from the doorway at the back of the RV. "I was told that you require my assistance."

It was a humanoid robot with a gunmetal-gray casing and a flexible platinum-white substance serving as its joints. Its eyes were concave circles lit from behind with orange light, its nose a simple wedge-like projection, and its mouth a small rectangular silver grating. A trio of horizontal slits on either side of its head parallel to its eyes seemed to serve as ears or vents or both. As it moved, faint whirs were audible beneath its casing.

"Are you the robot who passed through the lands west of here?" Maggie asked.

"I am indeed," the robot said. "Miss Rin informed me of your plans, and I will be happy to serve you in any way I can."

"Do you know where the Marauders' base is?" Adam asked.

"No, I do not. I do, however, recall passing through an

area about thirty miles due west that showed signs of nearby habitation and the frequent passage of many horses. Perhaps that—"

"That must be it! How do we get there?"

"A simple description would not suffice. The terrain to the west is quite confounding in many places. It would be best if I guide you. I may be of aid in other ways, as well. Like all robots where I am from, I am programmed to protect human life at all costs. Thus, if there is trouble, I shall provide a first line of defense."

Adam shook his head. "I doubt you shall be of much help in that regard; we are more than capable of protecting ourselves. But as a guide, your help would be invaluable." His eyes narrowed in suspicion. "I wonder, though: If the westlands are as dangerous and full of monsters as we have been told, how is it that you were able to pass through unharmed?"

"I imagine it is because I carry no valuables and am completely inedible."

Adam grunted. It made sense. He looked at Maggie. "What do you think?"

She nodded. "I think we should bring him with us."

"I agree."

"Excellent!" the robot said. It paused, then turned its orange eyes upon Adam. "Forgive me if this is an impertinent question, but are you in fact the so-called monster created by Dr. Victor Frankenstein?"

"Why do you ask?" Adam said, though he was pretty sure he knew. He had been through this several times since the Cataclysm.

"Again, forgive any possible impertinence, but according to the *Encyclopedia Galactica* in my internal database, you are in fact a fictional character."

"You are not the first to believe so, but I can assure you, master robot, that I am indeed flesh and blood and as real as anything in this madcap world."

"So my various sensors inform me. But then, since the Cataclysm I have encountered quite a remarkable number of entities that my encyclopedia informs me are fictional, mythical, and/or deceased. I find it most perplexing."

"As do we," said Maggie.

"At any rate," the robot said, "given your story and your unique 'family' situation, I believe that psychoanalysis would be of great value to you."

Adam blinked at him for a moment, then turned to Maggie. "What does 'psychoanalysis' mean?"

She shrugged. "I have never heard the term before."

"Oh, my," said the robot. "I should have known. The great breakthroughs in psychology occurred long after your time! Well, let me explain, for I believe that knowledge of the psychological sciences will be most interesting and helpful to you, as they are to all men."

"I am hardly a man," said Adam.

"And I am a woman," said Maggie.

"Oh, dear," said the robot. "I meant 'men' in the sense of mankind—"

"That might include my cousin here, but it still precludes myself," Adam said.

"Hardly. You have a man's brain, or at least a brain composed of segments of men's brains, am I not correct?"

"Yes…"

"Then your brain functions along the same paths, and thus you are a suitable candidate for psychoanalysis."

"Which you still have failed to explain."

"Because you have not given me the chance. Men who resist psychoanalysis are usually fearful of the results."

"It is hard to be fearful of something I know nothing about."

"Ah, but men naturally fear the unknown, as you yourself must understand firsthand."

For a moment Adam said nothing, his eyes dark with unhappy thoughts. Then he waved a hand for the robot to proceed. "Very well. Explain this...whatever it is."

"Psychoanalysis is the creation of the great Sigmund Freud, after whom I was named."

"Your name is Sigmund?" said Maggie.

"Oh, dear. Perhaps I should tell you about myself first. My name is Freud. I am Mechanical Analyst Number One."

"You mean there are others like you?" said Adam.

"Not exactly like me. Though my eleven 'brothers' and I shared the same boot-up date, the same basic morphology, and the same occupation of instructing and entertaining visitors to the Hall of Psychology on Old Earth, each of us was colored differently and programmed with the complete theories and writings of a different prominent psychologist from the science's long and storied history. There was myself, Jung, Seldon, Ming, Shandra—"

"Pardon my interruption, but I understand very little of what you are saying. 'Boot-up'? 'Programmed'? These terms mean little or nothing to me."

"I apologize," Freud said. "I shall endeavor to explain things in a more comprehensible manner."

"I do not know if I care enough."

"Let him talk," Maggie said. "I, for one, am intrigued."

"Thank you, fair lady," said Freud, giving her a small stiff bow. "Now then, psychoanalysis is a method of helping an individual come to terms with neurotic problems by examining the contents of their unconscious mind via talk therapy."

"Unconscious?" said Adam. "You talk to people who

are asleep or have been incapacitated?"

"Oh, no. You see, all people have mental processes of which they are unaware. In some cases, alas, these processes are neurotic disorders, often stemming from fixations and traumas in an individual's childhood."

"Ha!" said Adam, as if he had just beaten someone at a complex game. "I had no childhood. I was 'born' as you see me now. My consciousness developed quickly, and my education unfolded within a matter of months."

"But it did develop," Maggie said.

He goggled at her. "Whose side are you on?"

"I am on the side of truth."

"Hmp."

"The young lady is correct," Freud said. "A careful reading of my *Encyclopedia Galactica*'s rather detailed synopsis of the novel that recounts your history shows that your overall development did indeed proceed in a manner similar to the average man's, albeit much more rapidly. At first, the world was new and strange to you, and you could not speak, read, or communicate in any meaningful way. You were, in short, in a state similar to infancy. Then, alas, when you sought the love and affection of your creator—your father, if you will—he fled in terror, which is precisely the sort of traumatic event one finds at the root of many neuroses."

Adam scowled and seemed about to say something, but before he could, Freud went on: "But of course your case also presents several highly unusual features, perhaps the most notable being that while your cognitive functions matured rapidly—thanks no doubt to your having a fully grown brain to begin with—your affects, your emotions, developed more slowly, building up through experience. Accordingly, your actions at that time, violent and abhorrent though they were, are about what one would expect from a small child if that child possessed a body and a ratiocinative faculty like yours."

"Bah!" Adam waved a hand at Freud as if dismissing him. "This is absurd. It is infantilizing and insulting. Your work is irrelevant to me."

"I apologize," said Freud. "I did not mean to upset you."

"Were you not necessary to the success of our quest, I would be done with you here and now. Now be on your way. Leave us in peace until it is time for our journey to begin."

"And when will that be, exactly?"

Adam looked uncertainly at Maggie.

"Tomorrow morning," she told Freud.

"Very well. I shall see you then." Freud strode away.

Adam watched him go with slitted eyes.

"Now, now," Maggie said. "We need him to find Anna. We will not regret taking him with us."

"If he continues to be as annoying as he has been so far, I fail to see how I will do anything *but* regret it."

3

After Freud left, Adam and Maggie went in search of a pair of mules. They found only one mule owner in town willing to part with any of his beasts—a decrepit though sly-eyed old man named Thénardier who was completely unphased by Adam's appearance and refused to trade two mules for anything except an atomic flashlight.

"There's no way in hell that snotty little halfling's gonna get one up on me," he said, shaking a withered fist.

"But we have only a single flashlight left," Adam said.

Thénardier eyed him without an iota of sympathy. "Do you want the mules or not?"

Adam and Maggie exchanged a glance. They had hoped to keep the flashlight, but right now they needed the mules more.

"Very well," Adam said with a bitter sigh.

By the time they got back to the RV, night had fallen and the center of town was dark and silent. They tied the mules to the RV's drawpole and climbed into their beds, where they lay awake for hours, their thoughts returning again and again to Anna's empty bunk.

4

Shortly after dawn, three loud raps on the RV's back door jolted them awake. Grumbling, Adam opened the door. Maggie peered around him, squinting sleepily in the bright morning light.

A middle-aged man stood there smiling at them, a gray external-frame backpack on the ground at his feet. He had bright blue eyes and brown hair with white streaks at the temples, and he appeared to be in excellent physical condition: Muscles bulged beneath his safari shirt, and the legs of his faded blue jeans swelled at the quads. The most notable thing about him, though, was a sort of robust cheeriness, which set him apart from the beaten and weary folk of Sweetwater and most everywhere else in these grim days. The smile he beamed at them and the hearty and sincere "Good morning" he addressed to them were artifacts from a distant, nearly forgotten world.

Unfortunately Adam was too tired to reciprocate.

"What do you want at this wretched hour?"

The man smiled quizzically. "It's already seven o'clock."

"As I said, a wretched hour."

The man shrugged. "I'll make this brief, then. I hear you're planning to hunt down the Marauders."

"Yes. What of it?"

"Well, I've spent the last six months on their trail myself, and since we're both after the same goal, I figure it'd make sense if we work together."

Adam regarded the man with surprise. "Am I to understand that you have been hunting the Marauders alone?"

"Yep. I started out hunting only the Annihilator. He's a member of my old rogue's gallery. Now that he's joined the Marauders, I guess I'll have to go through them to get to him." He clapped his hands together with an eager smile. "So, what do you say? You game for a team-up?"

Adam looked dubious.

"It cannot hurt to have another able body," Maggie said.

"I agree," said Adam, "but..."

"But what?" asked the man.

"I am not certain that merely 'able' is good enough. Battling the Marauders is a job for remarkable individuals. I, for instance, am far stronger and more resilient than any normal man. The robot who is accompanying us is, of course, a robot and thus is not prey to the many vulnerabilities of the flesh. And as for Maggie here, in the last fifteen years she has learned the arts of self-defense and can hold her own against all manner of men and monsters. What of you? I see that you sport the musculature of a strongman and the courage of a lion, but those alone will provide little protection against gigantic shovel-wielding brutes and armored madman with laser blasters."

The man chuckled. "I appreciate your concern, but there's more to me than meets the eye. Watch *this.*"

With that, he began removing his clothes. His shirt came off first. Beneath it was a form-fitting top, which was all gray except for a stylized white G on the chest. Next came his jeans, revealing gray form-fitting leggings on top of which he wore a pair of gray trunks held up by a white belt with a round gold buckle. Next he kicked off his hiking boots and pulled from his backpack a pair of gray boots, a pair of gray gloves, and a gray cape that was made of a coarser material than the rest of the outfit. He put these on, affixing the cape to two small clasps on the shirt just below his clavicles. Finally he reached back and pulled on a snug-fitting cowl that was attached to the neck of the shirt. The cowl had two oval holes for his eyes and a larger opening at the bottom, which left the lower half of his face exposed, from halfway down the bridge of his nose to his chin and from mid-cheek to mid-cheek.

When he was done, he spread his arms in show, smiling with obvious pride in his ensemble.

"Well?" he said. "What do you think?"

Adam and Maggie shared a baffled glance.

"I do not understand," Adam said. "Are you an acrobat of some sort? We have little need for—"

"Heh. I'm no acrobat, though I used to be partnered with one. Little fellow named the Contortionist. No, where I'm from I'm what's called a costumed crime-fighter."

"You fight criminals while dressed like that?" Maggie said.

"Yep."

Adam cracked a rare smile. "And do you capture them while they are incapacitated with laughter?"

He half expected an offended response, but the man just chuckled. "Actually the criminals dressed up like this too. I know it seems kinda weird, but that's just the way it was where I'm from."

"I see. Though I confess I am still unsure as to how well

you can acquit yourself in battle against the Marauders."

The man held up a finger. "Watch."

He put his fists on his hips, puffed out his chest, and squared his jaw. Having assumed the prescribed pose, he narrowed his eyes in concentration and his skin immediately took on a grayish cast. As the color deepened, there was a faint crackling sound, and the man's skin and all of his clothes except his cape lost their luster and softness until he appeared to be carved from stone. Even the glistening whites of his eyes turned matte gray. Maggie further noticed that as this transformation occurred his feet sank half an inch into the dirt, as if he had gained several hundred pounds in mere seconds.

When this metamorphosis was done, he looked exactly like an animated statue, except for the cape, which remained fabric.

The man grinned, revealing gray teeth like tiny tombstones.

"Well," he said. "What do you think now?"

"You can turn into stone?" said Maggie.

"Technically it's not real stone. It's something I call organic stone."

Adam frowned. "Is that not an oxymoron?"

The man shrugged. "It's the best I could do. Unique circumstances require unique nomenclature."

Maggie started to extend a hand, then hesitated. "Um, do you mind if I...you know..."

"Touch me?" said the man with breeziness, as if he had been asked that a thousand times before. "Sure."

She lightly laid a hand on his chest, ready to pull it back after a quick feel. But her hand remained there, patting and stroking, while her mouth dropped open in fascination.

"Amazing," she said to Adam with a wondering laugh.

"It feels exactly like stone, yet his muscles still roll and quiver as he moves, and his chest rises with his every breath. Go on, see for youself."

With obvious reluctance, Adam placed a hand on the man's chest. A moment later his eyes went round with wonder. He jabbed a fingertip against the man's chest. Then again, harder. And again, this time with enough force to send a normal man staggering backward. This man, however, didn't move an inch.

"Pretty cool, huh?" the man said with a grin.

"Um, yes."

"So can I join you?"

"I suppose so." He looked at Maggie. "Do you agree?"

"I do," she said.

"Marvelous!" the man said.

"If you are coming with us," said Maggie, "you must tell us your name."

"Oh!" The man looked horrified that he had forgotten this basic social nicety. "My name's Robert. Robert Winston. But everyone calls me Bob. Unless I'm in costume, of course; then my code-name is Granite."

"Well, Mr. Winston, or Bob, or Granite, or what-have-you, I am Magdalena Frankenstein, known as Maggie to my friends, and my overlarge companion is Adam Frankenstein."

"Frankenstein, eh?" Granite eyed the duo with a closed, thoughtful expression. He seemed about to say something more when Freud appeared around the corner of the wagon.

"Is it time to depart yet?" Freud said.

"Yes," said Adam. "And you shall have one more head to probe during our trip."

"I shall?" said Freud.

Adam waved an arm at Granite. "This is Mr. Winston.

Or Mr. Granite, I suppose, since he is wearing his costume."

"Why's the robot coming with us?" Granite asked.

"He recently traveled through the westlands and can show us the way. In return he asks only to subject us to a peculiar custom called psychoanalysis."

"Holy smokes! The robot does psychoanalysis?"

"You are familiar with the practice?"

Granite just sighed. "This is gonna be a long trip."

5

After gathering together whatever provisions they thought they would need for their trip, Adam and Maggie loaded those provisions into packs on the mules. They offered Granite (he was still in costume) use of one of the packs, but he declined. He had been carrying all his belongings in his backpack for years and saw no reason to stop now.

Adam and Maggie didn't want to leave the RV out in the open where unscrupulous folk could break into it, so Adam asked around to find out if there was someplace safe they could put it while they were gone. When Rin found out what he wanted, she told him he could put the RV next to the former bowling alley she lived in on the north edge of town.

"I'll keep a real good watch on it," she said with a crisp nod. "It's the least I can do, seeing as how you folks're taking it upon yourselves to help us out the way you are."

"Thank you."

After Rin gave him directions, Adam returned to the RV, grabbed the drawpole, and pulled. With a groan of metal, the RV rolled forward a foot, then stopped and would budge no more no matter how hard Adam tugged or how red his face got.

"Need a hand there?" asked Granite.

"It's very heavy."

"No prob. In my stone form I can bench press two tons."

"You press benches? For what purpose?"

"Uh, forget it." He concentrated and once again turned to stone. Then he got behind Adam and grabbed hold of the drawpole.

With the two of them pulling together, moving the RV proved much easier, and they slowly made their way along Sweetwater's dusty streets to Rin's home. There was a perfect space for the RV on the stretch of bare dirt between the bowling alley's east side and the field beside it, where Rin and the other six families with whom she shared the building grew most of their food.

When they rejoined Maggie and Freud on Sweetwater's main street, they were surprised to discover that pretty much the whole town had gathered at a safe distance to see them off. Rin stepped out of the crowd and took Adam's hand. He stared at her in surprise.

"Thank you again," she said. Tears glimmered in her eyes. "Thank you for goin' off to save our girls."

"I..." Adam glanced at Maggie, who was looking at him with a cocked eyebrow as if to say, "Don't screw this up."

"I shall do my best." The words felt alien, awkward, as if they were the wrong size or shape for his lips and tongue. Why was Maggie doing this to him?

Rin gave him a big smile and then stepped back into the crowd.

And so the quartet—Adam and Maggie and Granite and Freud—headed west down Sweetwater's main street, a wall of a murmuring residents on either side. Granite grinned and waved at the townsfolk as if he were in a parade. A few of the bolder townsfolk waved back. Maggie watched these exchanges with a smile. Freud's head swiveled this way and that as he observed the various behavioral traits on display among the masses. All three of them were clearly enjoying themselves to one degree or another.

Adam, on the other hand, felt like a condemned man approaching the gallows.

It was the eyes. All those eyes upon him. He wasn't used to being on display in front of so many people in broad daylight. And especially not without inspiring fear and hate and disgust. But few of these eyes harbored such emotions. No, these eyes were guardedly hopeful. They expected things of him. And if he didn't deliver those things, *then* those eyes would fill with that old familiar hatred, and for once they would be right to do so.

In many ways, he decided, their trust was more terrible than their hatred.

Adam fixed his eyes on the ground ahead of him and strode on in silence, eager to leave Sweetwater behind.

Chapter 2

The Old Castle

1

They walked all day, pausing only twice to eat and rest their legs. They crossed fields of tall purple grass teeming with jackalopes and turquoise butterflies as big as bats and beautiful multicolored birds whose calls sounded like circular saws; they passed a high hill where a herd of mastodons wandered with solemn care amid a circle of standing stones; they hurried past the ruins of a sinister basalt temple adorned with carven rows of leering bestial heads; they crossed a rickety bridge over a clear, rushing stream, on the bed of which an army of spidery pale-green crustaceans the size of grapefruit swarmed about with their front legs held over their heads as if they were afraid of dirtying their pincers; they spent three hours traversing an empty asphalt parking lot that stretched away to the horizon like a calm black sea, the monotonous flatness broken only by several rows of sodium arc lamps and a pair of mysterious cinderblock buildings barely larger than outhouses.

The road they had been following, which had gradually dwindled from a ribbon of smooth, hard-packed dirt to a pair of parallel lines nearly invisible amid the weeds, ended at the edge of the parking lot and did not resume on the other side. Fortunately the land beyond the lot was fairly flat and even, and they managed to trek another two miles before the sun got low enough for them to start looking for a place to stop for the night.

Their long, trailing shadows had begun to merge with the growing dimness when they came upon an ancient, crumbling castle that sat on the eastern edge of a thick, dark forest. The castle had once had four towers, one at each corner of its rectangular keep, but time and weather had reduced three of them to heaps of rubble. The fourth looked as if it might join them the minute the next thunderstorm hit: Cracks zigzagged across its surface and it listed precariously away from the rest of the keep.

The castle's front gate lay half buried in mats of decaying leaves just inside the entrance. Beyond was the courtyard, its paving stones heaped and broken where several young sequoias had sprouted up.

"Looks like we found a good place to set up camp," said Bob.

2

They made a fire in the center of the courtyard, well away from any walls that might decide to give up their long and losing battle against gravity during the night. Dinner consisted of salt pork, boiled potatoes, and carrots, all courtesy of Adam and Maggie, plus a bag of dried fruit and some Ho-Hos, both of which Bob had liberated from the ruins of a Bugg's SuperMart a few weeks ago. Freud, of course, ate nothing.

As he herded together the last crumbs on his plate with his fork, Bob said, "That pork was excellent. Where did you get it?"

"We raised it ourselves," Maggie said. "We still have a

good deal of it left if you would care to take some when our job is done."

"Wow. You raised pigs?"

"Yes," said Adam. "For over a decade we lived on an abandoned manor far to the east of here. We were forced to vacate the area three months ago."

"Why? What happened?"

"A peculiar variety of fungus overran the area. It was bright green and slightly slimy to the touch, and it grew in thick shrouds upon anything made of wood, which it ate, dissolving it with a rapidity I would have believed impossible had I not witnessed it myself. So precise and cunning were its responses to our various stratagems to rid ourselves of it that I often wondered if it were sentient. Before long, we decided to flee the now-dilapidated manor and find a new, more hospitable home. It has been hard finding such a place, of course; my gruesome visage makes us undesirable as neighbors. One of the great benefits of the manor was its relative isolation."

"But because of that, it was also very lonely," said Maggie.

"Yes. You and your sister deserve better company than me. You should be out gracing your fellow humans with your charms."

Maggie rolled her eyes. "You should, as well." To Bob she said, "We have these debates all the time. He thinks he is ill-suited to human company simply because his looks are initially fearsome." She turned back to Adam. "But have Anna and I not acclimated ourselves to you appearance? Do we not treat you as the man you are?"

"That is different. We are linked. We are, in a sense, family."

"Yeah," Bob said. He set his plate aside. "That was

something I wanted to ask you about. Are you really the, uh, the *being* created by Dr. Victor Frankenstein?"

"I am. I see you, too, have read this book about which I have heard so much since the Cataclysm."

"Well, yeah. I've seen some of the movies too, though most of them didn't really follow the book too closely. I take it you've never read the book yourself?"

"Alas—or perhaps fortunately—no. After I learned of it, I scoured the ruins of bookstores and libraries whenever we came across them, hoping to find a copy, but I have not yet uncovered one. From what I hear, though, it sounds reasonably accurate. I wonder how this author, this… Shelby, was it?"

"Shelley. Mary Shelley."

"Ah, yes. Shelley. I wonder how she learned my history."

"Well, as far as *I* know, she made it up."

"So others have said. But I am here, am I not? I am no fiction."

"No. Obviously not." Bob stared into the fire, deep in thought. Then his eyes swiveled back to Adam.

"Can I ask something?" he said.

The gravity in his voice made Adam stiffen.

"If you wish," Adam said.

"I have to know: Is it true, what it says in the book? About you murdering all those people? Dr. Frankenstein's wife, and his little brother William, and all them?"

His eyes remained locked on Adam's face as Adam looked away, fixing his gaze upon a rotted wooden door that hung askew in the wall of the keep. Adam had been expecting the question, but that didn't make it any easier to deal with.

"Yes," Adam said in a low voice. "It is all true. Every crime."

Bob glanced at Maggie and saw her eyes shifting back and forth between Adam and himself, her expression tense and uncertain. She was clearly concerned about where the conversation would go. Bob knew he was stomping off into sensitive and possibly dangerous territory, but what else could he do? He was a crime-fighter, and he had to find out if he was in the presence of a criminal.

As if reading Bob's thoughts, Adam said, "I do not act in that manner any longer. I was younger then, and more foolish. I sought to share the pain of my lonely, accursed existence with he who had given me that existence. My goal was to render him as lonely and accursed as myself, which meant stripping him of those dearest to him. They were innocent of any crime against me, of course, yet I cared nothing for that; I was sure that had they but known of me, they would have unthinkingly despised me because of my unfortunate appearance, the way so many other men did. But as I said, I was foolish, immature, my head filled with Miltonic melodrama." He raised his huge, thick hands and held them in front of his face. "Could I take back the hateful work of these hands, I would. But what is done cannot be undone." His hands fell back into his lap and he sighed. "My only goal now is to live out my days without causing further harm. And the only logical way to do that is to isolate myself from mankind, whose blind hate would inspire within me those murderous feelings."

Bob pondered this for a moment, then said, "I thought you died at the end of the book. Or at least it was pretty clear that's what you were planning to do—to burn yourself to death or something like that, up in the Arctic."

Adam nodded. "Yes. After I had destroyed my creator by murdering those dearest to him and then leading him on a round-the-world chase that essentially exhausted him to death, I sought to end my life by building a pyre and setting myself ablaze. And that is nearly what happened, but…"

"But what? What stopped you?"

Adam gave a small, tight, almost rueful smile. "My maker did his work too well. He made me too human, with not only human emotions, but a human will to live. As I knelt, torch in hand, atop the oil-soaked pyre that I had spent most a day constructing, something within me recoiled in terror at the thought of the annihilation of my self. With a wild, animalistic cry, I flung the torch away and hurled myself off the pyre and onto the ice-sheet upon which I had built it. For a long time I lay there on my back in the snow, weeping, cursing my weakness and my creator and the uncaring, unforgiving universe. Eventually, cheeks glazed with frozen tears, I fell asleep.

"The following morning I set out across the ice-sheet in search of dry land, and after several days came to a desolate rocky waste unspoiled by man's ruinous touch. I soon found a large, deep cave, and there I made my home."

"But…" Bob shook his head. "Where do Maggie and her sister fit in? I don't remember them from the book at all. Um, no offense."

This latter comment had been made to Maggie, who dismissed it with a wave of her hand. "No offense is taken. It is impossible for you to remember us from the book since from the sound of things, it ended well before we were ever born."

"They were the daughters of Ernest Frankenstein," Adam said.

Bob thought hard, then gave a wincing, apologetic smile and shook his head. "I don't remember any Ernest. Sorry. Then again, it's been a long time since I read the thing, so I guess it's no surprise I don't remember too much."

"Ernest was Victor's brother and the only surviving member of the family after Victor's death. While I dwelt in Arctic isolation, he remained in Geneva, became a syndic, married, and had twin daughters."

"So did you go back home, or did the girls go in search of you, or what?"

"No, I returned to Geneva."

"Why?"

Adam drew in a breath as if about to speak, paused, then slumped forward a little and let the breath out in a long sigh.

"That is...hard to explain. After ruminating at great length upon my misdeeds and the beliefs that fostered them, I came to see that my rage at my creator and at mankind in general was born of ignorance and childishness. I could not continue blaming my creator for all the ills of my life. He had acted unwisely, yes; but I was here now on this Earth, and the manner of my origin was of little consequence in regard to what I chose to do in the present. And hating men for fearing that which is unpleasant and unfamiliar is pointless. Human nature is what it is. The solution to my problems was to stay exactly where I was, to remain isolated from human society for the rest of my existence.

"But as time wore on, I discerned no change in my body. My mind and muscles remained as strong as ever, my joints flexible, my endurance excellent. No gray hairs intertwined with my familiar black locks; no wrinkles, save those already present, marred my flesh; no haze clouded my vision. The infirmities of man were not mine. The unique circumstances of my creation ensured that I did not age as he did.

"My continued vigor made me realize I could not remain a hermit forever, for eventually my isolation would drive me mad. On the heels of this realization came a nostalgic yearning to see the faces and places of men, particularly those already familiar to me. For a long time I tried to ignore these feelings, but there came a day when they could no longer be denied. Thus I packed up my few belongings and made my way back to Geneva. I was startled to discover that fifteen years had passed since my departure."

"Time flies, huh?" Bob said.

"On the contrary, I believed that I had been away far longer than that. My time in the Arctic had seemed an eternity." He watched the flames leap and snap, his face cast in wavering shades of red and orange, his moist eyes gleaming in the ever-shifting light. He shook his head a little at some private thought or memory.

"So how'd you connect up with Maggie and her sister, then?" Bob asked. "I mean, I can't imagine you just knocked on their door and said, 'Howdy, I'm your long-lost cousin Adam from Amsterdam.'" He had hoped his attempt at levity would lighten Adam's mood, but Adam just moved his head slightly in what might have been a shake, or a nod, or simply an acknowledgement of the feeble joke. Bob glanced at Maggie. Her expression was blank.

"It was an accident," Adam said. "I had no intention of ever again inflicting myself upon that unfortunate family. Although some undeniable urge compelled me to view what remained of the family line, I knew I had no right or reason to do or expect more than that and so I vowed I would only watch them from afar.

"And so I did, grieved to discover that Ernest looked far older than was normal for a man of his years, a condition no doubt caused by my hateful slaughter of his birth family. Fortunately, the kindness and irrepressible good cheer of his young wife helped assuage his sorrows, as did the numerous charms of his twin daughters, upon whom my attention came to focus more and more. Then only seven years old, they were the most delightful creatures I had ever laid eyes on—merry, inquisitive, laughing, full of joy at the world's wonder. Whenever I watched them at their play, my cares and burdens vanished, and I felt my spirits buoyed by a sense of joyful optimism.

"Their favorite pastime, it seemed, was to chase butterflies in a field on the east side of the family estate. Between this field and a road that ran past the property was a stand of pines from which I could observe the girls unseen. One day while I stood ensconced therein, smiling at these two lovely angels as they harassed a hapless pink butterfly, I heard a scream from the road behind me. Afraid that I had been seen, I whirled and peered out through the trees at the road. It proved to be a false alarm: A woman's child had tumbled from the back of a passing cart, and though the mother was in hysterics, the child was unhurt. Seeing that all was well, I turned back around to resume my watch on the girls.

"But the girls were watching me. While I had been distracted, they had pursued the butterfly into the pines, and when I turned, there they stood, staring at me.

"Horror seized me, for I was certain that the sight of my hideous form would scar their delicate minds and send them racing away in fright. Instead, my horror turned to utter bemusement when one of the girls—Maggie here, as I learned later—smiled at me and said, 'You're very tall.'"

She chuckled. "At first, we *were* frightened. When he turned, we thought we had discovered one of the ogres from the books of fairy stories our father sometimes read to us. Yet when we saw the dread that flooded his face upon seeing us, we realized that was impossible. No monster would be so shaken by the sight of two little girls. So extreme was his distress that we were overwhelmed with sympathy for him, and when we spoke, it was to ease that distress.

"For a moment he said nothing. Then he stammered out something along the lines of 'Um, yes, I suppose I am quite tall indeed.'

"'Why is your face all yellow and wrinkly?' Anna then asked. 'Did something bad happen to you?'

"And then…" She glanced at Adam, who was staring fixedly at the campfire.

Without looking up, his voice low and tight, as if he were trying to choke off the words even as he uttered them, he said, "No one had spoken to me in such a friendly manner before. No one, that is, except one poor blind man, who upon learning the truth of my appearance, fled in panic. To hear those well-meant words, to be spoken to as a man rather than a monster—and this by those whose kindness I had most desired yet least expected or deserved—all of that overwhelmed me, and…" He paused, then looked up at Bob, face set, defiant. "I broke down. I wept. I am not ashamed."

"No reason you should be," Bob said.

Adam nodded and looked away, a trace of puzzlement in his eyes, as if he hadn't received the response he had been expecting.

"Anna and I tried to console him," Maggie said, "Too young and ignorant to grasp the real reasons for his sorrow, we feared that *we* had done something to precipitate it. By the end of the day, we had all become fast friends.

"This was the first of many secret meetings between us, meetings that were to continue for over a decade. During these meetings, we would tell him about our family, our lives, our juvenile and ill-formed opinions on anything and everything. He gave us advice and told us stories about the other lands he had visited and the interesting people he had seen.

"When we turned sixteen, he took us aside and told us the truth about himself, leaving out nothing no matter how horrible we might think it. We were understandably aghast. He told us that he could not blame us if we chose to sever all ties with him, but that he thought he owed us the truth no matter how detrimental it might prove to our relationship.

"Indeed as a result of these revelations, the friendship between us chilled to a great degree. But after a time, Anna and I concluded that all people can change and that even the worst criminal can learn to better himself. And Adam had clearly changed. More importantly, he had done so of his own free will. How then could we responsibly reject him?"

Bob nodded. "That's exactly what I've learned from a lifetime of fighting crime. People deserve a second chance, but only if they earn it. No homework, no gold star. But if they do the work and we don't acknowledge it, then, heck, we're no better than the bad guys."

"Exactly." She frowned. "I think. Some of your expressions are rather perplexing."

"So I take it your parents never found out about Adam?"

"No. Never. Had they survived the Cataclysm, no doubt we would have shared the truth with them then. As it was..." She shrugged. "You lived through the Cataclysm. You know what it was like. The earth shook. A hum filled the air."

"And then there was a light," Bob said, his voice soft, his eyes distant, his usual good humor only a memory. "A blinding white light."

"And with it came unconsciousness. And when we awoke, it was to a world altered beyond anyone's wildest imaginings. Unfortunately for us, the Cataclysm occurred at night, after darkness had fallen though not late enough for everyone to be in bed. Thus, lamps were still burning in our house, and the Cataclysm's tremors caused those lamps to fall and break, setting the house aflame. Anna and I managed to escape the blaze; our parents did not."

"I'm sorry."

She gave him a sad smile. "Everyone lost someone or something in the Cataclysm."

"Yeah." Bob opened his mouth, shut it, then shook his head and said, "Geez, I've got all kind of questions I want to ask and stuff I want to say, but it's late. Maybe tomorrow."

Adam grunted. "We can only hope that tomorrow will be quiet and uneventful enough to permit more talk."

"Heh. Amen to *that.*"

As Bob turned to grab his sleeping bag, he noticed that Maggie was looking at him. The moment his eyes met hers, however, hers sidled away. A faint smile curved her lips, and it looked as if she were flushing slightly, though the red and orange hues of the fire made it impossible to tell for sure.

With a small, thoughtful smile of his own, Bob unrolled his sleeping bag.

Chapter 3

Research Lab B

1

After a hurried breakfast of salt pork and dry Count Chocula, they loaded up the mules and entered the forest beyond the castle.

The land sloped gently downward as they headed west. The air was warm and redolent of flora both familiar and unfamiliar. Birds peeped or croaked or gibbered maniacally from the trees. Small animals rustled away through the underbrush at the group's approach.

Sometime around noon, when the sun was at its zenith, its rays shining straight down through the foliage like the trunks of phantom trees, Adam, who was in the lead at that point, fell back until he was walking alongside Freud

"Do you recognize any of this?" Adam said.

"Not specifically," Freud said, "though given the general composition of the flora, this is almost certainly the same forest I passed through on my way east. Barring any significant variation in the thickness of the forest, we should exit it tomorrow afternoon."

"What lies on the other side of the forest?"

"A large valley with a river at the bottom. Beyond that is another forest. And beyond *that,* a long stretch of grassy hills. Very scenic, if one enjoys that sort of thing."

"Did you encounter anything unusual or potentially

dangerous between here and the valley?"

"No. This particular stretch of my journey was singularly uneventful. But since we are traversing a different portion of the forest, I can make no promises."

Adam nodded and quickened his pace to return to the head of the line. Freud matched his speed, staying alongside him. Adam looked at the robot, eyebrows raised questioningly.

"Would you care to talk?" Freud said.

"I beg your pardon?"

"Talk."

"About what?"

"About you. Your feelings. Your thoughts. Given your story last night, I suspect that you have certain psychological issues which talk therapy could help remedy."

"I would prefer not to discuss such matters." He strode faster in an attempt to leave Freud behind.

"I understand, of course," said Freud, the servos in his legs whirring as he matched Adam's pace. Adam strode even faster, it having not yet occurred to him that though he possessed superhuman endurance and would take hours to tire, Freud was a robot and thus did not tire at all. "It is indeed daunting to bare the inner aspects of one's character. Doing so, however, not only unburdens one's mind of dark and weighty matters, but aids in self-knowledge. And it is only by understanding ourselves, our strengths and weaknesses and hidden mental processes, that true personal growth becomes possible."

Freud paused as if expecting a response, but Adam simply kept walking, his watery yellow eyes locked on an invisible point dead ahead.

"For example" Freud went on, "you appear to have some rather substantial abandonment issues that—"

Adam glared at Freud. "I can take you apart with my bare hands, you know."

"You wouldn't!" said Maggie, who had been listening to this exchange with amusement till now. "You know he is the only one of us familiar with this region. We cannot afford to dispense with him."

"I know, I know. And I am sure *he* knows too—knows that he can annoy me all he likes without fear of reprisal."

"I am not trying to annoy you, my good man," said Freud. "I am trying to help you."

"I am not interested in your help, except insofar as you can help us find the Marauders. I cannot believe that this practice of psychoanalysis is a genuine science. It seems silly and childish."

"On the contrary," said Freud. "It is steeped in science, its conclusions and methods having been based upon direct personal observation and a large database of case studies."

"If I may jump in here," Bob said. "Where *I'm* from, psychoanalysis has been around for about seventy years, and although everyone credits it with contributing a lot to the field of psychology, it's not really seen as very useful anymore. Much better theories and techniques have been developed since it came on the scene."

"I am quite aware of that. In my own era, where psychoanalysis is tens of thousands of years old, it is seen as a quaint curiosity from psychology's infancy—a major advance for its time, but no longer of any real relevance."

"But if that's true," said Maggie, "if everyone from your time regards it as such, how can you put so much stock in it?"

"Because I have been programmed to do so."

"Can you not change your programming?"

"Certainly not. But then, neither can you, for what else

are your instincts and elementary thought processes but a form of genetic programming? You can change those no more than I can change mine."

"But…does it not bother you that you adhere to such an antiquated system of thought?"

"It is my peers who regard it as antiquated. *I* maintain that it is still perfectly relevant to all beings with brains."

"But that's only because you're programmed to think that!" Bob said.

"Correct."

"Gah!" Bob spread his arms wide and looked heavenward, as if in search of divine guidance. Maggie giggled.

While they had been talking, bruise-colored clouds had rolled in from the north, and now lightning flashed in the distance. A few seconds later thunder rumbled. A chill breeze swept through the trees, raising goose-bumps on the flesh-and-blood members of the group.

Bob looked up at the clouds, eyes slitted against the rising wind.

"This is gonna be a bad one," he said.

As if to underscore this comment, a lightning bolt arced down into the woods about a mile away. Thunder banged almost simultaneously.

"We had best find shelter," said Adam.

No one disagreed. Storms in this post-Cataclysm world could be severe, with lightning deaths in the hundreds, flash floods that wiped entire towns from the map, and hail the size of hamsters.

They hurried forward, scanning the trees on every side for a cave, a shack, an abandoned wagon—anything that might provide even partial cover.

Five minutes later the rain started, only a few fat drops at first but quickly worsening to a nearly blinding downpour.

With the exception of Freud, whose casing was water-tight, everyone scrambled to get their raingear out of their packs and onto their bodies. It didn't help much; the gusting wind flung rainspray under hats, hoods, and hems.

Lightning struck again, this time half a mile to the south, and as the boom of thunder rolled away through the forest, they heard the crack and crash of a tree falling.

Freud stopped and pointed at something to the northwest.

"If you require shelter, there is a structure of some kind in a large clearing about a quarter of a mile away."

The others looked in the direction he was pointing.

"Where?" Bob said. "I can't see a darn thing."

"Of course not," Freud said. "My optical sensors are superior to those of any human."

"Fortunately I am no human," Adam said. "I can see it, barely, through the trees over there. It appears to be a low, white building."

"Well, what're we waiting for?" Bob said, striding off toward the building. "Let's go!"

The building turned out to be a sprawling, one-storey structure with no windows and only one visible door, which was made of metal and painted brown. A sign on the wall next to the door read "Main Entrance." Chunks of asphalt—probably all that remained of a parking lot or a driveway—littered the grass in front of the building. Between these chunks and the edge of the clearing stood a large white sign with black letters that read "Research Lab B."

"B?" Bob said, looking around. There were no other buildings in sight. "Where's A?"

"Probably yet another casualty of the Cataclysm," said Maggie.

The brown door was unlocked, so they went in, Adam

having to stoop to do so. Fortunately the ceiling inside was high enough for him to stand upright, though just barely; had he risen up on tip-toes, his head would have dislodged ceiling panels.

They were in a reception area with institutional white walls and a white tile floor. A curved white counter stood off to their right. Behind it a wheeled chair lay on its side. A computer, its monitor dark, sat on a shelf on the receptionist's side of the counter along with sundry papers and office supplies. Two doors—one to their right, one straight ahead—led deeper into the building.

Bob tried the light switch on the wall beside the door, but as expected, the overhead fluorescents remained dark. Working quickly in the gloomy light from outside, Maggie tethered the mules to the inner doorknob, while Adam unhooked two lanterns from the mounds of gear on the mules' backs and lit them. Bob likewise lit his.

"I miss our atomic flashlights," Maggie said, wrinkling her nose at the stench of burning oil. Now that outside light was unnecessary, she shut the door. Immediately a gust of wind drove rain against the door so hard it sounded as if someone had pelted the metal with pebbles.

"Actually, the lanterns are unnecessary," Freud said.

"What do you mean?" Adam said.

"My presence obviates the need for lanterns. Watch."

With a faint click, rays of orange light shone from his eyes like twin flashlight beams.

"I didn't know you could do that," Bob said.

"I am equipped with a variety of useful features."

"Well, I appreciate the offer, but those beams are a little too focused. With lanterns, we can light up the whole room. Besides, it's probably not a bad idea if we each have our own individual light. In this world, you can never be too careful."

"I agree," Maggie said.

One of the mules let out a loud snort and stomped its hooves hard enough to crack a tile. The other mule made a series of huffing noises and threw its head about.

"They're awfully skittish all of a sudden," Bob said.

"The thunder must have frightened them" Maggie said.

"Perhaps," said Adam. He sniffed the air and then frowned. "But something smells...*off* in here."

Maggie sniffed the air too, then shook her head. "All I detect is the burning oil. What does it smell like?"

"It is hard to say," he said. "It reminds me a little of raw eggs, of all things."

Meanwhile, Bob, who had been examining the papers behind the desk, said, "Here we go." He held up a sheet of paper and pointed at the letterhead. "This is the Blue Mesa Research Facility. Still no clue what they did here, though."

"Should we explore the building?" asked Maggie. "Or should we wait out the rain right here?"

"I suggest waiting," said Adam. "There is something I do not like about this place."

"I would like to report that my sensors are detecting particles of unidentifiable organic material in the air," Freud said.

"What kind of material?" Bob said. "It's not dangerous, is it?"

"I do not believe so. The particles are not living organisms. They are merely bio-debris, much like dust derived from skin flakes. They do, however, suggest the presence of a life-form that is not in my data base."

"But this appears to have been a human-run facility," said Adam.

"Correct."

Bob heaved a sigh. "Great. This is probably one of those

government facilities where they were doing exotic tests of some kind—breeding mutant monsters or opening worm-holes to other dimensions. And no doubt the experiment went horribly wrong and unleashed hideous beasts on the unsuspecting scientists. That's what always happens in places like this."

"How very reassuring," Maggie muttered.

A flash of blue-white light lit up the cracks around the brown door. A millisecond later a cannonade of thunder shook the building so hard that one of the wheels on the overturned office chair moved enough to produce a faint squeak.

As the thunder faded, a mechanical throb grew audible from the depths of the building. Moments later, the fluo-rescent lights emitted a low hum and a faint wavering glow, while the computer monitor emitted a faint staticky crackle, and screen turned a lighter shade of gray.

"Holy cow!" Bob said. "This place has a generator that still works! Listen."

The throb grew erratic, then died. The fluorescents and the monitor died with it, leaving them once again with only the light from their lanterns and Freud's eye-beams

"Dang," said Granite. "It's not working right, but still, it's *working!* The first electricity I've seen since in over ten years! We should check it out. There might be fuel we can use. And in a place like this there're bound to be plenty of other things that'll come in handy."

Adam shook his head. "What of your earlier concerns about monsters and worms and the like? Freud made it clear that unknown and possibly hostile life-forms dwell here. I say we stay where we are and be on our way once the storm passes."

"I don't like this place either. But there might be guns.

And medicine."

Adam opened his mouth to say no again, then snapped it shut and glanced at Maggie.

"I think we should look around," she said. "But only if we stick together."

"Definitely," Bob said. "Splitting up always ends badly."

"Are you sure about this?" Adam asked Maggie. "It could be dangerous."

"I am hardly incapable of protecting myself," she said. "I know how to use a wide variety of weapons, including my own two hands. Besides, I will be in the company of an eight-foot-tall, nearly immortal being with superhuman strength and endurance, a man who can turn into stone, and a robot. If, despite all that, I will still be in danger, then so will all of you. So I ask *you:* Are you sure you want to go? After all, it could be dangerous."

She said these last two sentences with a gently mocking smile. Adam gave her an amused smile right back and said, "As always, you present an irrefutable argument."

"Let us proceed then," said Maggie.

"Um, I just had a thought," said Granite. It wasn't "Bob" now, for while Maggie and Adam had been talking, he had stripped down to his Granite costume in preparation for the search of the facility. If creepy science-spawned monsters did indeed dwell here, he wanted to have his game-face on. "Maybe we should leave someone here in case something comes after the mules. I mean, we could go through one of these doors, and something else could come out of the other one while we're gone and steal the poor things. Or eat them."

"Maybe Freud could stay—"

"No," said Adam. "We might require his fine sensory apparatus to alert us to things the rest of us would miss."

"Well, *I'm* not staying behind." She folded her hands across her chest with finality.

"Look," said Granite, *"I'll* stay if—"

"No," said Adam. "We might need your knowledge of the technology here." He sighed. "I think we shall have to take our chances and leave the beasts behind. And if some unholy creature should slaughter them, then it can be sure we will pay it back in kind."

He strode to the door opposite the entrance and threw it open. No monsters lurked on the other side. Instead, the lantern-light revealed a bland institutional corridor stretching away into darkness.

They headed down the corridor—Adam first, then Maggie, then Granite, then Freud. Wooden doors passed by on either side, most of them bearing small signs—"Dr. Gooden," "Monitor Room," "Briefing Room." After two hundred feet, a corridor branched off on the right. A large sign on the wall next to it read "Restrooms/Locker Rooms/HES Charging Station."

"Forget that," Granite said. "I wonder where the actual laboratory is."

"I am more concerned with the location of the medicine and fuel," Adam said.

"Don't worry. We'll find 'em."

The corridor ended in a T-junction. They looked down each arm of the T. More doors. More white walls. More white tile floors...

And a man's corpse sprawled in front of an open door halfway down the left arm.

"Yep, science does it again," Granite said.

They approached the body cautiously, concerned that whatever had killed the man might still be nearby. The man had been middle-aged, thin, and almost completely bald, and he wore glasses and a white lab coat. His flesh was dry and shriveled, as though desiccated. His lips were cracked and split and had pulled away from his mouth so much it looked as if he were showing his teeth to a dentist. His eyeballs had collapsed and fallen into their sockets. Dried clumps of a whitish substance clung to his skin and clothes. On the other side of the open doorway a concrete staircase descended into darkness.

Granite crouched and examined the body.

"Hey, check this out," he said.

Adam and Maggie knelt beside him and looked where he was pointing. The body's skin was covered with tiny holes as if someone had driven hundreds of pins into it.

"Do you recognize these marks?" Maggie asked Granite.

"I've never seen anything like them."

While they studied the body, Freud stepped into the open doorway, stood there in silence for a moment, then turned back to the others.

"It may interest you to know," he said, "that my phonic receptors detect faint sounds from below."

Adam stood up. "What kind of sounds?"

"It is hard to say. If pressed, I suppose I would have to characterize them as furtive shuffles."

"So they are presumably sounds made by living beings."

"Most likely. In addition, the concentrations of that odd organic matter I mentioned earlier are thicker in the stairwell than anywhere else we have visited."

Adam joined Freud in the doorway and sniffed the air.

"The smell is a thousand times worse here, too," he said.

Curious, Maggie and Granite stood up and sniffed the air rising from the black depths. Their faces crumpled in disgust.

"What *is* that?" said Maggie, stepping away from the

doorway.

"Nothing good, I bet," Granite said. The smell reminded him more of semen than of raw eggs, but he wasn't about to say that in front of a lady.

"I do not think we should go down there," Adam said. "We know nothing of the nature of the death of this man here, and given the vast assortment of dangerous creatures we have encountered since the Cataclysm, I think—"

In the distance there was a thick, gargling moan, like that of a dying man with a throat full of mud. The sound echoed along the dark corridors, making it difficult to tell exactly where it came from.

"What the heck is that?" said Granite, turning to stone almost without thinking about it. Alas, given the eerie nature of the sound and the horror-movie atmosphere of this place, his stone-form didn't make him feel much safer.

"I believe that something is approaching us from the direction we came," said Freud. "I detect more of those furtive shuffles proceeding toward us down the hallway that connects this hallway with the reception area."

"Lovely," Adam said.

A second moan rose up from the darkness at the bottom of the stairwell, apparently in answer to the first. Seconds later it was joined by dozens more, making it sound as if the lab's lower level were packed with an asylum's-worth of lobotomized men and women drowning in their own phlegm.

"How many of them *are* there?" Maggie said, drawing her dagger.

"I'm sure it's nothing we can't smash and slice our way through," Granite said, trying to sound braver than he felt. Though he was made of organic stone and could hurl a Buick a block and a half, he still got spooked sometimes.

Not that feeling spooked would prevent him from fighting and doing all he could to get them out of here, of course. He was a hero. He had chosen to be a hero. And he had learned long ago that one of the things that made you a hero was refusing to give in to your fears.

"Going downstairs is definitely out of the question," he said, "so our choices are to either keep going down the corridor and hope we find another exit, or go back the way we came and try to get past the one down there."

"The latter choice is the wisest," said Adam. "Continuing down the corridor would take us farther west, and there were no doors on the west side of the lobby."

"Agreed," said Maggie.

They headed back the way they had come, Granite first, then Adam, then Maggie, with Freud trailing last, saying, "Hold on a moment, don't *I* get a vote?"

"The majority's already carried the motion," Granite said.

They stopped just short of the T-junction. Granite motioned for the others to stay put, then took a deep breath and leaped around the corner, cape flapping dramatically. He landed in a crouch, fists and jaw clenched, ready for anything.

His face went slack with surprise. He straightened up. "What *is* that?" he said.

The others joined him. Maggie stifled a gasp at the sight of the creature shambling toward them. Freud said, "How odd." Adam's upper lip curled back in revulsion.

At first glance it appeared to be a faintly luminous, roughly humanoid mass of translucent silvery-white jelly. But a closer look revealed that inside the jelly was a man—or more likely the corpse of a man, given that his skin had the same shriveled look as that of the corpse they had found earlier. This man, too, wore a white lab coat, with a gray suit underneath. His mouth hung open, and his eyes were glazed and half closed. The jelly covering him was over three inches thick in places, and every now and then sections of it oozed languidly, thinning here, thickening there, as if seeking some perfect parasitic equilibrium. The jelly-man advanced in a jerky, stiff-legged shuffle, sliding its feet forward without lifting them from the floor. Its arms hung limp at its sides as if it had forgotten how to use them. The raw-egg/semen smell filled the corridor.

"None of you recognize this variety of creature?" said Adam.

"No," Granite said. "I mean, it kinda reminds me of a zombie from a horror movie. But that doesn't account for the gunk covering it."

"What do we do?" said Maggie. "Can we fight it?"

"Let us find out," said Adam. He strode forward.

The moment he started moving, the jelly-zombie stopped and let out a long, low moan. The jelly covering the man's mouth spun in an inward-turning spiral and sank away like a whirlpool down the man's throat, leaving the open mouth completely exposed. With the muffling jelly out of the way, the moan grew louder and shriller, though the gargling quality remained.

When Adam was barely an arm's-length from the zombie, its moan abruptly ceased and jelly geysered from its throat.

"Ah!" cried Adam as the viscous gunk spattered his chest and arms. He shook his arms in an effort to fling it off, but it stuck like glue. After a second the individual gobs started gliding about on his skin and clothes. When two gobs met they merged into a single mass, and when those larger masses met, they too merged, and so on and so on until it became clear that the blobs of jelly were joining together to form a coating like the one on the zombie.

Maggie started to rush to Adam's aid. Granite grabbed her shoulder.

"Don't," he said. "Let me. I'm stone, remember? It might not be able to hurt me. Besides, no offense, but I doubt a knife's gonna do much good against this thing."

She stepped back with obvious reluctance.

Granite raced forward. Ignoring the zombie, which hadn't moved since it disgorged its jelly-vomit, he tried to grab hold of one of the jellies on Adam's chest. It divided into several smaller jellies, which slipped between his fingers then recombined a few inches away. He tried again and again, with no better success.

"Geez, it's like trying to pick up spilled mercury," he said.

As he tried once more, the jelly-zombie lurched forward and tried to shamble past him, its sights now set on Maggie.

"Oh, no, you don't," Granite said. He snagged it around the neck with the crook of his elbow and slammed it to its back on the floor. He watched it for a few seconds, ready to strike it down again if it tried to get up, but it just rocked about, waving its arms and legs like an overturned beetle. Satisfied it was no longer a threat, he returned to helping Adam, who had set down his lantern and then pulled off his cloak and shirt to get at the jellies that had slipped underneath. His face was tight with pain.

"It feels as if they are puncturing my flesh with tiny needles," Adam said through gritted teeth as he pawed futilely at a jelly on his upper chest.

"That would explain those holes on the corpse we saw," Granite said. "It must attach itself to its host with some kind of wiry cilia."

"Save the scientific analysis for later."

"But analyzing it might help us understand its weaknesses," said Granite. "For instance, why have these things remained in here when they could easily slither out through the cracks around the entry door?"

Adam scowled as he continued tearing at the jelly on his chest. "Am I supposed to answer?"

"No, but maybe they can't abide light. Their luminosity reminds me of deep-sea fish and other things that never see the sun. Maybe the sun'll kill these things."

"Or perhaps the reason they have not escaped is simple stupidity. If we take them outside, we might be unleashing them upon the world."

"Maybe."

Meanwhile, twenty feet away at the T-junction, Freud said, "Oh, no."

"What is it now?" Maggie asked, barely paying the robot any attention. Her eyes were fixed on the zombie Granite had knocked to the floor. Its jelly coating was slowly oozing off it and pooling across the floor. Was it dying? Or was it detaching itself from the compromised host body? She opened her mouth to shout a warning to Granite and Adam, but Freud's next words shot the idea right out of her mind.

"More of those creatures are approaching from the stairwell."

"What?" She turned. Neither the light from her lantern nor Freud's eye-beams extended all the way to the basement door, but they didn't need to: The jelly gave off its own dim luminescence, making the dozen humanoid shapes shuffling toward her and Freud all too visible. She heard a bang down the other arm of the T and whirled around. Another half-dozen zombies were emerging from another doorway about a hundred feet down that arm.

She spun back toward Granite and Adam to alert them to the zombies' approach, then froze. The jelly-zombie Granite had knocked down was no longer a jelly-zombie. Now it was just a desiccated corpse like the one at the top of the basement stairs. The jelly, now free of its host, was gliding across the floor toward Maggie like a giant amoeba.

Freud strode forward and interposed himself between Maggie and the jelly. When it reached his inorganic feet, it flowed around them like water flowing around a rock in the middle of a river. He slammed a foot down on the jelly. The portion of the jelly under his foot slithered out along the crevices in his rubberized treads.

"Ah," he said. "I suppose I should have foreseen that."

Maggie stared at the rapidly approaching jelly in horror, realizing she had nowhere to run and no one to help her. Then she felt something warm bump her thigh and she looked down. It was the lantern. The *burning* lantern.

With a savage cry, she hurled it at the jelly. It struck the jelly dead center and exploded, spraying burning oil in every direction. Trapped in the heart of the blaze, the jelly bubbled and hissed like a pat of butter in a frying pan. Within seconds most of it had been reduced to a black crust on the floor.

"There are more zombies coming!" she shouted to Granite and Adam.

"More?" Granite said.

Maggie nodded. "From both directions. We must flee."

"How will you get through the fire?" Adam asked.

It was a good question. The flames stretched all the way across the corridor, and their tops licked the air four feet above the floor, forming a seemingly impenetrable wall between her and the others.

"Since my casing is fire-proof," Freud said, "I would suggest I carry you across, but I fear I cannot move fast enough to do so without risking your getting burned."

"Maybe not, but *I* can," Granite said, setting his lantern on the floor. He removed his cape, balled it up, and tossed it over the top of the fire. It flumped down next to Maggie. Then he calmly walked through the flames.

He looked back at Adam. "Get close to the fire. Maybe the heat or light or whatever will make the jellies get off of you."

While Granite wrapped his cape around Maggie's head, Adam approached the fire. When he got close enough to feel the waves of heat pulsing across his flesh, the jellies on the front of his body shuddered violently. The sharp pains caused by their cilia digging into his skin suddenly ceased, and as fast as startled cats the jellies darted around to Adam's back, where they immediately began jabbing their cilia into his skin again.

"They simply moved to a less inimical location," he said.

"Get outside," Granite said as he hurriedly tightened Maggie's cloak around her so it wouldn't hang down too much. The two groups of zombies were only twenty feet away.

"Are you sure?" Adam said.

"No, but I can't think of anything better, short of you jumping into the fire. I'll bet money these things don't like sunlight."

"But the sun is not out," Maggie said, her voice thick and muffled beneath Granite's cape. "It's raining."

"It *was*. The rain stopped about five minutes ago. The sun might've come out by now. Even if it hasn't, I suspect even gray cloudy daylight'll weaken those things."

Adam considered this for a moment, then snatched his cloak, shirt, and lantern off the floor and loped away toward the entrance.

As Granite checked the cape one last time, he detected faint movement out of the corner of his eye. The zombie at the head of the group that had come from the basement stood barely ten feet away now. It seemed reluctant to get any closer, probably because of the fire. Still, the jelly over its mouth had started that whirlpool motion. Given the force with which the first zombie had expelled the jelly, Granite suspected the spray could easily travel ten feet. While it posed no threat to him, the jelly would no doubt ooze through the folds in the cape to get to Maggie. They had to leave now and hope the cape was secure enough to protect her from the fire.

He slung Maggie over his shoulder, took a deep breath, and leaped through the fire. Maggie briefly felt intense heat wash over her body, then it was gone and there was a flesh-numbing jounce as Granite landed on the other side of the fire.

Behind them came a pattering noise that reminded Granite of the sound the rain had made hitting the metal door earlier.

"How revolting," Freud said.

Granite glanced back. The zombie had tried to spray them through the flames, but Freud had stepped in front of the zombie, taking the blast of jelly square in the chest. Now a dozen mini-jellies darted back and forth across his casing in search of flesh to cling to.

"This is simply unacceptable," Freud said. He stepped into the fire, stood there a moment while the mini-jellies burned to ash, then stepped back out.

Granite grabbed his lantern with one hand while holding Maggie steady on his shoulder with the other and sprinted down the corridor. His and Maggie's shadow—a long, spidery shape cast by the fire and Freud's orange eye-beams—danced along the floor ahead of them.

"Hurry up," he called back at Freud, who was following at a stiff, jerky trot.

"I was not made to run," Freud said.

"You can put me down now," Maggie protested, barely audible beneath the cape.

"Not till we're outside," Granite said.

Granite turned the corner and saw daylight up ahead. The brown door stood open. The mules, still tethered to the knob, snorted in alarm as he brushed past them and out the door. He set Maggie down on the grass and whisked off the cape. The sheen of sweat on her face quickly dried in the wonderful rain-cooled breeze as she gulped down fresh air.

Freud emerged from the building behind them.

"Oh!" he exclaimed. "This is unexpected!"

Wondering what he was talking about, Maggie looked around. The first thing she saw was Adam sitting on the grass twenty feet to their right. He appeared none the worse for wear and was surrounded by a ring of dead jelly that the daylight had reduced to a fine grayish crust.

The second thing, which was what everyone else was looking at, was a pair of figures who stood next to the Research Lab B sign. One was a young blonde girl, around eleven years old, clad in a dirty pink T-shirt, blue jeans with holes in the knees, and a pair of Keds held together with duct tape. Tucked under her arm was a rolled-up raincoat still dripping from the recent rain, and on her back was an overstuffed navy-blue backpack with red piping.

The second figure was a black jaguar.

"Um," Granite cleared his throat. "Can we help you?"

The blonde girl tilted her head back and regarded them down the length of her nose.

"I am Dagmar," she said, "the queen of this land." She

paused, as if expecting comments or bowing to ensue. When none did, she continued: "My companion is Kukalukl. We will be joining you on your quest to find the Marauders."

There was a long silence.

Finally Maggie managed a smile. "'Kukalukl'?" she said in the most pleasant, conversational manner she could contrive; she wasn't in the mood for another fight or even a minor argument at the moment. "That's an unusual name for a pet. Where did you come across it?"

Dagmar opened her mouth to respond, but the jaguar cut her off: "She heard it from me, cretin. And just so you know, the last person who referred to me as a pet is currently working her way through my small intestine."

Chapter 4

The Field of Colored Cubes

1

That night they camped in a large clearing two miles west of Research Lab B. The east side of the clearing and the adjoining woods were littered with two-foot-high cubes, most of which were the bright primary colors of children's toys: fire-engine red, grass green, banana yellow, royal blue. A few were white. All glowed with a faint but steady light, which made them look simultaneously eerie and festive.

No one knew what they were, but Freud's scanners showed that their surfaces were hard plastic laced with tiny cells that stored solar energy, which was no doubt the source of their luminescence. To make sure nothing was hidden within them, Adam smashed three randomly chosen cubes with a large rock. All three turned out to be hollow, their walls only an inch thick. Despite the cubes' apparent harmlessness, the group set up camp on the western edge of the clearing, as far from the weird glowing boxes as possible.

While the others built a fire, Dagmar and Kukalukl sat off to one side conferring quietly. They hadn't said much about themselves except to explain that they were pursuing the Marauders for reasons of their own and had decided it would be wisest to join forces with Adam's group, whom they had learned of when they arrived in Sweetwater a few hours after the quartet had left. They had spent the next day and a half hurrying to catch up.

"Do you think she's really a queen?" Bob said in a low voice as he fed another twig into the fire.

Adam glanced at the girl, who sat on a log with her back erect as she spoke to Kukalukl.

"She certainly possesses the bearing of one," Adam said. "Very regal and imperious."

"And kinda snotty, if you ask me."

Maggie tutted. "Be nice."

"As opposed to being honest, eh?" Bob said with a grin.

She raised her eyebrows as if to display her lack of amusement, but a hint of a smile broke through anyway. "That is hardly what I meant. I am merely suggesting that there are more polite ways to make your point."

Adam watched this exchange with a frown, noting the brightness and animation in Maggie's eyes as she spoke to Bob and the way Bob's gaze never wavered from Maggie's face. Was something starting to develop between the two of them? If so, he didn't like it. As he got out the pork and potatoes for tonight's dinner, he envisioned a bleak future in which both Maggie and Anna had moved on, having discovered handsome normal humans whom they wished to wed, leaving Adam alone in a world that loathed him. He imagined spending the rest of his days living in a filthy cave far from civilization with nothing to comfort him save the memories of the smiling faces he had known long ago.

This wasn't the first time he had entertained such fears. And while he knew they were selfish and childish (and, irritatingly, corroboration of Freud's diagnosis of "abandonment issues"), this awareness did not make them feel any less real or painful. Besides, his eventual loss of Anna and Maggie was guaranteed, for they aged normally while he seemed not to age at all. One way or another, the twins would someday be gone, and he would no longer know their lovely faces and charming company and most importantly their kindness toward him, a kindness no one else had shown.

No one? That wasn't true, he realized with a start. Despite some initial suspicions—justifiable ones to be sure, given Adam's long shadow in history and literature—Bob seemed to have developed a favorable attitude toward him. Perhaps, then, he should not look too harshly upon the growing closeness between Bob and Maggie...

"Is *that* what we're eating?"

It was Dagmar. She stood next to Adam, her outraged eyes fixed on the pork and potatoes in his hands.

"What is wrong with them?" he asked.

"That *can't* be all we're having. Do you want me to die of boredom?"

"If you insist on behaving in such a manner, that might not be my poorest option."

"How dare you talk to me like that!" she cried. She looked offended and a little scared, as if she feared he might not be kidding. It made him feel sorry for her. Queen or not, she was just a child.

He bowed as much as his kneeling posture would allow. "I apologize for my hasty words. But this is indeed all we have except for some cereal, which we reserve for our breakfasts, and—"

Her eyes lit up. "Cereal? What kind?"

"We have several kinds: Grape Nuts, Chunky Rice Balls, Count Chocula—"

Dagmar squealed with delight and clapped her hands together. "Count Chocula's my *favorite!*" She bestowed a forgiving smile on Adam. "I suppose I can overlook the boring pork and potatoes, then."

"You are most kind," said Adam, hoping the sarcasm he felt wasn't too evident in his tone.

Adam, Granite, and Maggie set to work preparing dinner. Dagmar watched with complacency, not offering to help. Her eyes kept returning to the wedge of Bob's costume visible beneath the half-unbuttoned front of his safari shirt. It seemed to fascinate her for some reason. Kukalukl lay on the edge of the clearing, rhythmically licking his left front paw with his thick pink tongue.

"Um, is he gonna want some of this?" Bob asked Dagmar with a nod at the jaguar.

"No, I am most certainly *not* going to want some of that hideous crap you call food," said Kukalukl, not even deigning to look up from his paw. He extended his claws and turned his paw this way and that as if admiring his ability to gut someone. "Any meat that has been cooked, salted, or in any way modified from its natural state of rawness is an abomination in my sight."

"You know, that's kinda funny," Bob said. "I once got told almost exactly the same thing by this super-villain I fought a couple times. Beastmaster, he called himself. He—"

"I knew it!" Dagmar cried, her eyes alight with excitement. "I knew you were a superhero!" She jabbed a finger at Bob's chest. "That's your costume under there, right?"

"Uh, yeah," said Bob, surprised. So far hardly anyone he had met knew what he was. They generally assumed he was an acrobat, as the Frankensteins had, or worse, a mime. "You've heard of superheroes?"

Dagmar nodded. "Sometimes..." She hesitated, then frowned slightly and looked down at her hands in her lap. "Sometimes my parents—the king and queen—they would give me comic books they'd found somewhere. This was when I was younger, of course. Littler."

"What're comic books?"

She gaped at him in astonishment. "You've never heard of them? They're, like, floppy little cartoon books that tell stories about guys—and sometimes girls—who dress like you and have weird powers and fight bad guys who also dress like that and also have weird powers."

"And...these are fictional?"

She cocked her head. "You mean, like, made-up?"

"Yeah."

"I think so, yeah. Here, hold on." She dug around in her backpack and pulled out a battered comic book. Its cover, which was creased and dirty and attached by a single staple, showed two grotesquely muscular men in skin-tight costumes grappling with each other. One of them wore a brown and white costume with eight-point antlers sprouting from the cowl. The other had four arms and wore a dark gray costume and a slate-gray helmet that tapered to a point on top and sported two black glassy bug eyes. In the background a nubile young woman was tied to a rocket that had started blasting off. The title of the comic was *The Incredible Caribou*. A box in the bottom right-hand corner proclaimed, "The Millipede is back! And this time—it's personal!"

Bob stared at the comic, dumbfounded.

"Are you familiar with anyone named the Caribou?" Adam asked. Though he wouldn't admit it, he felt relieved that Bob now understood the existential uneasiness one experiences upon learning that aspects of your life are believed by others to be fictional.

Bob shook his head. "There were plenty of guys who named themselves after animals—Gray Fox, the Lynx, the Dove—but no Caribou. And no Millipede either, though there *was* a four-armed villain named the Centipede. But he didn't look anything like that. In fact, he was one of the few guys who didn't wear a costume. He was more of a scheming businessman. Always dressed in tailor-made suits. They *had* to be tailor-made, what with his extra arms."

"This is most interesting," Freud said. "Do you mean to tell me that where you come from individuals possessed of remarkable abilities utilized those abilities in gratuitous public displays of altruism or criminality while disguised in colorful skin-tight costumes that often had animal themes?"

"Um, well...yes."

"Fascinating. I must ruminate on this further. I sense a unique psychological complex at work behind it all. Possibly repressed libido energy manifesting as an odd exhibitionistic fetish. A desire to be *seen*. But why the animal themes? Perhaps there is some atavistic totemic significance..."

"Geez, why does everything have to be sexual with you guys? Can't you just say our costumes are a sort of uniform each of us personalizes, and leave it at that?"

"I most certainly cannot 'leave it at that'! Your so-called explanation only begs the question: Why do you choose to personalize them in that particular manner?"

"Yeah, that *is* a good question. Too bad all the psychobabble in the world won't provide a decent answer."

"'Psychobabble'?" The robot's voice rose a few decibels in outrage. "Psychoanalysis is anything but 'babble.' It is based on exacting research and observation, followed by incisive and rigorous reasoning—"

"And virtually none of it's scientifically testable."

Freud remained silent for a moment as he regarded Bob with his orange-litten eyes. Then he said, "I think you are trying to bait me, to rouse my ire in an effort to divert me from performing my analysis. I suppose I shall have to wait until you are in a more receptive frame of mind for my well-meant scientific endeavors."

Bob snorted. "Gimme a break. Most psychology isn't scientific at all. It's a lot of hogwash."

"So I take it wearing skin-tight costumes in public is *not* a form of exhibitionism?" said Maggie with a teasing smile.

His face reddened. "It's…it's just the way we do things. I mean, okay, there might be a *little* exhibitionism involved. But that's not the main reason we do what we do. We do it because it's right. One way or another we received these amazing gifts, and it's only fitting that we share them with the world."

"How *did* you receive your gifts, if you do not mind my asking?"

"Yeah, tell us your secret origin," Dagmar said.

"My *what?*" Bob said.

"Your secret origin. All the superheroes in my old comics had secret origins."

"Well, geez, if I told you, it wouldn't be a secret any-more, now would it?"

"Uh…"

Bob chuckled. "I'm kidding. I mean, the only reason we kept our origins and identities secret was so the bad guys wouldn't find out who we were and come after our families. But now…well, things are different. None of that really matters anymore. So, yeah, I'll tell you.

"Simply put, it was a freak lab accident. I'd just landed a great job right out of grad school, at a geochemical research laboratory in New Jersey, where they were working on a big government-funded project that was trying to find ways to instantly petrify objects. They'd developed some chemicals that looked promising, particularly something called Lot C, which had been whipped up by Dr. Platt, one of their best scientists, right before he got murdered by commie spies. The secret of how he made Lot C died with him. The other scientists studied it like crazy, but no one was able to replicate it.

"Late one night I was working alone in the lab, trying to isolate certain components of Lot C and compare them with other petrifying agents we'd come up with, when a massive electrical storm swept down on the area. I tried to hurry up and get my work done before the power went out, but before I could finish, a bolt of lightning struck the building. For a second I felt a weird tingling sensation throughout my entire body and saw little tendrils of electricity snaking off the ends of my lab equipment, and then everything went nuts—light-bulbs burst, the windows blew out, and every beaker full of chemicals on the table in front of me exploded, drenching me in Lot C and all the other petrifying agents. At the same time, electricity swept through me in one massive surge, and I fell unconscious to the floor.

"When I came to, I found that the combination of chemicals and electricity had had a remarkable effect on my body: My skin appeared to have turned to stone, yet I could still move. You might think I was overjoyed, but the truth is, I was scared out of my wits. I had no idea I could change back to normal. I thought I was stuck like that. And when I tried to pick up a phone to call for help, the receiver shattered into splinters in my hand because I hadn't learned to take my new strength and hardness into account.

"So there I was, freaking out, when dozens of police cars and fire engines screeched into the parking lot. They'd gotten a vague report about an explosion at the lab, and after the murder of Dr. Platt, they weren't taking any chances.

"Thinking they could help me, I raced outside. Not the smartest move on my part. I mean, when the cops saw what looked like a living statue screaming and running right at them with its clothes falling apart from all those stone muscles rubbing against the fabric, they opened fire.

"In a way, that was the best thing for me. When I saw that police officers were shooting at me and that the bullets were ricocheting off my body and could hit someone, I came to my senses. I just stopped right there and held up my hands.

"To make a long story short, I explained to the cops what had happened, and they acted all stern and tough, but frankly I think they were kind of tickled that Heartland City now had its own home-grown super-hero. And as for me, once I started calming down, I discovered that with some concentration I could switch back and forth between my human and stone forms."

"You say that your clothes remained fabric," Maggie said. "How then is it that the costume you wear changes to stone too?"

"Oh, that's because the costume's made of what they call chaotic molecules. I don't entirely understand the science behind it, but the molecules of the fabric somehow recognize the change in the wearer and they change right along with him. It's one of Dr. Prism's inventions. He was a member of the first wave of super-heroes who appeared back in the late 1930s. His body had been turned to crystal by aliens, and as a result he could project and refract energy. He was also a scientific genius. He got filthy rich off the patent to his chaotic molecules. In fact, as soon as he heard of me and my abilities, he called me up, partly to congratulate me on my new powers, partly to make sure I wasn't going to turn out to be a villain, and partly to sell me a costume. I bought one, of course. I kind of had to. By then, after so many years of costumed folk gallivanting around, it was kind of expected for anyone with new powers to adopt that lifestyle.

"And that's exactly what I did. In fact, it wasn't long before I was inducted into the League of Super-Heroes, the first and best supergroup there was. It'd been founded by the original batch of heroes during World War II, and most of them were still involved with the group, which meant I got to pal around with Element Man and Athena and The Gray Fox. Of course, the tightest bonds I formed were with the other guys who entered the biz and the League around the same time I did, especially Lightray and the Contortionist. They were pretty much my best friends ever."

He stared off at the glowing cubes on the other side of the black field as his wistful, reminiscing smile drained away.

"And as far as I can tell," he said, his voice now low and somber, "all those guys disappeared in the Cataclysm." He frowned. "Except..."

"Except what?" Adam asked.

"Well, it's just, for the longest time I thought I was the only surviving super-person from my world. But then late last year, I started hearing about the Marauders, and danged if their field leader didn't sound exactly like a member of my old Rogue's Gallery!"

"The Annihilator," said Maggie. She saw Dagmar stiffen in response to the name.

"Yep," Bob said. "One and the same."

"And if *he* survived..."

Bob nodded. "Then who knows? Maybe others did too. I guess maybe I shouldn't give up hope just yet."

"You shouldn't." Maggie gave him a warm, hopeful smile. He smiled back.

Adam cleared his throat. "Does the Annihilator possess special powers like you?"

"Nah," Bob said. "All he's got is the armor. But that's all he needs. Well, that and no morals whatsoever. His real name's Vincent Vetter. He started out as an illegal arms dealer, but then one day he got hired by a scientist in war-torn Karmovia to help smuggle the scientist's prototype battle armor out of the country. Vetter decided he liked the armor so much he'd keep it for himself, so he killed the scientist and carved himself a new career as a costumed criminal. From what you told me of your encounter with him in Sweetwater, you've already seen everything the armor can do. Well, except for the radio receivers in the earpieces, but I doubt those are much use anymore. What worked in the good old US of A of 1988 A.D. is just so much junk here in the crazy land of Erizan in 15 P.C."

"P.C.?" Maggie asked.

"Post-Cataclysm. Then again, I've also heard people calling it A.C., for 'After the Cataclysm.' I keep wondering which term'll be the one that sticks."

"1988, you said?" Adam asked.

"Uh-huh."

"It was only 1823 for us." He pondered this a moment, then turned to Freud. "What of you? What year was it in your...your world, or whatever one should call it?"

"The exact date was March 19, 1023 F.E."

"'F.E.'?" Bob asked. "What's that stand for?"

"Foundation Era."

"And you?" Adam asked Dagmar. "Obviously you were born after the Cataclysm, but did your parents ever mention the year in which it occurred in their particular world?"

Dagmar frowned. "This *is* their world. They were the king and queen of this land."

"Of course. I apologize."

"'Were'?" Maggie interjected, keeping her tone as gentle as she could. "What happened to them?" She suspected she already knew the answer and that it would explain why the girl was pursuing the Marauders.

Dagmar blinked at her, surprised by the question. "I..."
She glanced at Kukalukl, who simply stared back impassively—or at least with a cat-like feigning of impassivity—and then took a deep breath and said, "The Marauders. They killed them."

"I am sorry."

"Geez," Bob said. "That's awful."

"Indeed," Freud said. "And though I fear that what I am about to say will be interpreted as egregious self-aggrandizement, I would be remiss if I did not mention that psychoanalysis can be of great value when dealing with traumatic events of this nature."

"Oh, put a sock in it already."

"There is no need for snarkiness. I am only trying to help."

"Um, thanks," Dagmar said. She stared down at her battered tennis shoes, lips pursed, then looked up at Adam and said, "2006."

"What?" Adam asked, perplexed by the seeming non-sequitur.

"You wanted to know what year the Cataclysm happened. It was 2006."

"Ah. Of course."

"That leaves you, then," Bob said to Kukalukl. "Everyone else has revealed their year of origin."

Kukalukl let out a small huff to indicate his disinterest in the matter.

"I myself have little use for dates. When you live as long as I have, the years blend together into one great mass of tedium. However, I can tell you that by the reckoning of the Incas who worshipped me the year was 36,016, the seventeenth year in the reign of the mighty (and last) (and, in my

J. S. VOLPE

opinion, vacuous) Incan queen Mango Tutep, all hail her marvelous gloriousness, ho-hum, ho-hum, et cetera."

"Worshipped you?" Freud asked. "You mean they believed you to be a god?"

"No, they didn't *believe* me to be a god. They *knew* I was a god."

"That is preposterous. Gods do not exist."

"Now, I know for a fact that's not true," Bob said. "I've met a few gods. In fact Athena, who I think I mentioned earlier—she was a goddess."

"You mean she was literally the Athena from Greek mythology?" Maggie asked. "The daughter of Zeus?"

"The one and only."

"Bosh," Freud said. "The Greek myths were fictions invented by a primitive society to explain natural processes that were beyond their ability to comprehend."

"Well, according to your databanks, Adam here is a fiction, right? And yet there he is."

Freud looked from Bob to Adam and back again.

"I admit," he said, "that there are apparent discrepancies between my sensory input and the information in my databanks, but I am working to resolve the issue."

Bob laughed. "Well, I have to say I for one am very happy that we got into all this stuff about where we came from, since it allows me to trot out one of my pet theories: that the Cataclysm was simply the merging of a bunch of alternate realities into one."

Maggie shook her head. "I am not sure I understand what you mean by 'alternate realities.'"

"Well, some folks believe that at various points in time, say at moments where an event has a fifty-fifty chance of occurring, that at those points, the event goes *both* ways, creating two realities separated from each other by some kind of dimensional barrier. It might help to think of time as a tree. It starts off with one trunk but at a certain moment, when a certain event could go either way, the trunk divides into two branches. And eventually those branches themselves divide at other points, and so on and so on, down through the eons until we end up with a nearly infinite number of alternate realities, some of which are mindbogglingly different from others further away from them. There might be realities where life never appeared on Earth, or where birds became the dominant intelligent species, or where the native people of the Americas conquered the Europeans—"

"But that *is* what happened," said Kukalukl. Noting the others' surprised looks, he added, "Really. I found it quite amazing that there were so many scientifically advanced pale-skinned people running around after the Cataclysm. I didn't think they had the brain-power to do more than pick lice from their beards and rape their own daughters."

"Uh…that's, um…wow. But, see, that only proves my point."

"But how can it be that our respective times of origin are so wildly different?" asked Adam. "How could it have been 1988 in your world when the Cataclysm struck, but 1823 in ours, and thousands of years later in Freud's?"

"Well, I've heard theories that in some of these different realities, time flows at a different rate." He shrugged. "Nobody knows for sure, though."

"And how can I be real in my own world but fictional in others? The same can be asked, of course, about gods and costumed crime-fighters."

"Again, I don't know. Maybe there's some kind of…of *leakage* between realities, so that Mary Shelley caught a glimpse of what was going on in a different reality, maybe in a dream or something. Or...heck, I don't know."

"Or maybe it was the Cataclysm that made fictions re-alities," said Maggie. "Maybe we are all fictions made real."

And to that strange and sobering thought, no one, not even Freud, had a thing to say.

Chapter 5

Happyvale

1

As they headed west the next morning, the forest gradually changed, growing older and denser, with huge moss-grown oaks and elms and other varieties of tree no one recognized. The foliage above was so thick that much of their journey passed in cool dimness, though when the wind stirred the leaves, spots of sunlight danced upon the forest floor.

An hour of walking brought them to the river valley Freud had mentioned yesterday. It was a mile across at its top and half a mile deep in the middle, and at its bottom a silver river glimmered in the sun. Tall trees lined the sloping sides of the valley, their leafy crowns turbulent with twittering finches. The valley stretched away to the north and south, offering an unobstructed view for many miles in both directions. Far to the south, pterodactyls flew in lazy circles above the river.

A concrete bridge had once crossed the valley a few hundred feet to the north, but most of it now lay strewn up and down the slopes, the chunks of blacktop occasionally brightened by a stretch of a white line or a few yellow dashes. A few of the bridge's support columns still stood, their jagged, broken tops towering over the trees on the slope, as did a small section of the bridge on this side of the valley—a forty-foot-long swath of concrete and asphalt that jutted out over the drop like a diving board. They walked over to it and found that a stretch of four-lane highway extended back from the bridge for about fifty feet before dissolving into rubble. A large faded green sign stood next to this fragment of road. It read "Acalangua Tetso Muta—5 km."

"Anybody recognize the name?" Bob asked, pointing at the sign. "Or the language?"

No one did.

"A better question would be whether or not we can cross the river below," said Adam. "It looks fairly narrow, but deep."

"There must be a bridge somewhere," said Maggie. "The Marauders have to be able to get their wagons across the river."

"There *is* a bridge," said Freud. "All of the original bridges have fallen, of course. But a crude makeshift bridge has since been erected. I crossed it myself."

"Ah, yes," said Kukalukl, peering at the silver thread below. "I see it."

The others peered too but saw nothing.

"Where?" said Bob.

"You have shitty human eyes, so I'm sure you can't make it out. But trust me, it's there. It's a little to our north."

"Then let us proceed," said Adam.

It took them an hour to reach the bottom of the valley and twenty minutes to make their way north along the river to the makeshift bridge, which was made of sliding doors from train-cars lain across sections of tree trunks sunk into the river-bottom. The mud at either end of the bridge was a churned-up mess of hoof- and boot-prints. No one else was in sight.

As they paused for a short rest on the far side of the bridge, Kukalukl sniffed intently at the bridge and the dirt.

"Do you scent the Marauders?" Adam said. "Can you pick up their trail?"

Kukalukl shook his head. "I smell them, yes, but only faintly. Certainly not enough to follow. Something—probably yesterday's downpour—wiped away most of their scent."

Adam frowned. "Which means they passed this way more than twenty-four hours ago." He turned to Freud. "Have you any idea how long it will take us to reach our destination?"

"I cannot be absolutely certain, of course," Freud said, "but if the Marauders' base is, as I suspect, near the signs of habitation I saw on my way east and if we continue traveling at the rate we have been, we will arrive there in approximately three days."

Adam scowled, grabbed his backpack, and started to pull it on. "That is too long. We must hurry to close the gap between us."

The ascent of the western slope took nearly three hours. Halfway up, Dagmar flopped to the dirt and moaned that if she tried to take another step her legs would drop off, so Kukalukl offered to let her ride on his back, which she did. Maggie watched, envious, as the jaguar bore the girl away. Then she armed the sweat from her eyes and plodded after them. She wondered what Dagmar had done to inspire such loyalty and tolerance in the jaded cat.

It was past noon when they reached the top, so they stopped there for a quick lunch. When they resumed their journey, they found that the forest on this side of the river valley was much younger than that on the eastern side. The trees were shorter and slimmer, with smooth gray trunks and delicate leaves almost too green to be natural. As the afternoon wore on and the sun slowly moved ahead of them, the forest thinned out, giving way more and more often to clearings carpeted with thick green grass. Large, colorful flowers dotted the grass like Easter eggs.

"This is so beautiful," said Maggie with a smile when they paused to rest in one such clearing.

"It sure is," Bob said as he filled the water bottles in a clear stream that bubbled along the northern edge of the clearing. "I guess not everything after the Cataclysm is so bad."

Kukalukl, who lay sprawled on his side with his eyes half closed, suddenly shot upright, ears erect and turned slightly back. "What is that infernal noise?"

"What noise?" asked Adam, standing up.

"I hear it as well," said Freud. "It is music of some kind. My *Encyclopedia Galactica* suggests that it might be an old-fashioned march performed by a full marching band."

"What?" said Bob. "A marching band *here?*"

Then the wind shifted and all of them could hear it: The faint strains of brass and woodwinds punctuated by the rhythmic booming of a drum.

"That's not a recording, either," Bob said. "It's live. Somebody's playing."

"Let us learn who," said Adam.

They tethered the mules to a tree on the edge of the clearing, then crept through the woods toward the music. Soon they stood facing a line of trees and bushes too dense to see through. The music, now quite loud and distinct, was coming from the other side.

Adam motioned for the others to stay back, then slunk forward and peeked through the branches. He stood there without moving long enough for the others to start wondering if he was all right. When he finally turned around, his narrow black lips were parted in astonishment, and his moist yellow eyes were large and bewildered. In less uncertain circumstances his nonplussed expression would have been comical.

"What is it?" mouthed Maggie.

He shook his head a little and shrugged, spreading his thick hands. He kept blinking as if he didn't trust his vision. Then he turned and looked through the branches again.

The others came forward and did likewise, and within seconds all of them except Freud and Kukalukl were wearing identical expressions of surprise.

On the other side of the trees was a grassy clearing in the center of which several dozen stuffed animals paraded round and round, many of them playing tiny instruments. A yellow-and-orange striped cat tooted on a trumpet. A green dog puffed away at an oboe. A plaid elephant grasped in its trunk a drumstick which it rhythmically swung over its head to beat a large drum strapped to its back. A lavender teddy bear led the procession, a baton in one paw. The animals without instruments simply bobbed back and forth to the beat as they marched along on their stumpy legs.

Soon the song ended and the animals jumped up and down, cheering and laughing in high-pitched voices, their instruments and their glassy eyes glinting in the sun.

"Ohmigawd!" shrieked Dagmar, bursting from the trees before anyone could stop her. "Look at them! They're so *cute!*"

The animals whirled around. When they saw Dagmar beaming at them, and the others peeping out of the bushes behind her, they jumped and cheered with redoubled vigor.

"Guests!" they cried. "We have guests! Welcome one! Welcome all! Huzzah!"

Adam and the others stepped through the trees and joined Dagmar, who was bouncing up and down with joy, her normally haughty demeanor washed away by a flood of child-like glee. When she looked back at the others, there were tears in her eyes, and Maggie felt a pang of pity for the girl. When, she wondered, was the last time Dagmar had been able to shed the regal airs and the constant cares of survival and act like the child she was?

The lavender teddy bear stepped forward, his blunt arms outstretched.

"Welcome, friends," said the bear. "Welcome to Happy-vale, where every day is a celebration! I am Rumbledum, the mayor and official greeter!"

Maggie glanced at Adam, expecting him to speak, but he was still too rattled by the freakish spectacle of animated toys to formulate anything resembling a coherent thought.

"My name is Magdalena Frankenstein," she said. "And—"

"I'm Dagmar!" the girl said in a voice that was almost a squeal. "This is so awesome!"

"Why, thank you *ever* so much," said Rumbledum. "We strive to fill everything we do with joy and happiness. Now come; you look weary and long-traveled. You must rest and refresh yourselves. Come."

He waddled backward, beckoning them to follow. They did. The other stuffed animals crowded around them, singing nonsense songs full of "lalala"s and "tiddle-di-doo"s. The striped cat, who introduced herself as FooFoo, clambered onto Dagmar's left shoulder and sat there swaying and purring in time to the singing.

Rumbledum led them to a grove of young sycamores next to the stream. In the heart of the grove was a small, cozy clearing with grass so soft and springy you could sleep on it.

"Sit," said Rumbledum. "Relax. Enjoy. It has been ages

since we've had guests and we mean to celebrate your visit to the utmost."

"Please," said Adam. "This is all very lovely, but we—"

"Nonono," said Rumbledum waving a paw. "No 'but's. I insist that you stay, if only for a meal."

"A meal?"

"Oh, yes. We are wonderful cooks. Wait here, and you shall see." He turned to the other animals. "Come! We must prepare a feast!" Cheering, they all hurried away.

When they were gone, Bob turned to the others and said, "You know, just when I think I've seen the weirdest thing this crazy world has to offer, I run into something like this." He shook his head. "This is just…" He couldn't think of a word to satisfactorily end the sentence. He wasn't sure there was one.

"This is so totally awesome!" said Dagmar. "When we're done with our quest, I'm gonna come and live here, like, forever!"

"What about your kingdom?" said Maggie.

"Oh. Yeah. Uh…" She frowned and chewed her lower lip for a moment, then her bubbly demeanor resurfaced. "Maybe the animals can come live with *me!* They can march around and play their instruments in the big garden behind the palace every day! It'll be the best!"

"I don't like them," said Kukalukl.

"Why?" said Bob. "Because they're not the kind of animals you can eat?"

"Ho-ho-ho. Quite amusing, schist-head. No, there's something about their smell I don't care for."

"What, exactly?"

"I don't know. I can't quite put my claw on it. Something tells me I *should* know, but…" He made a small sound halfway between a sigh and a huff. "Ah, well, I must think on it.

Perhaps the answer will come to me."

"I must confess," said Adam, "I myself do not entirely trust them either. This all seems a touch *too* pleasant. Surely in a world as brutal as this, such happy little creatures would have been exterminated by monsters or Marauders long ago."

"Maybe they're just too nice to kill," protested Dagmar. "Or maybe they're really good at hiding."

"Perhaps. But I think we should remain on our guard, and not blindly trust their innocent appearance."

"I suppose that right now would be the most appropriate time to comment that their energy signatures are consistent with their appearance as stuffed animals," said Freud.

"Um, what do you mean, exactly?" said Bob.

"He means they don't emit heat like most living beings," said Kukalukl. "I noticed that too."

"More than that," said Freud. "There appear to be absolutely no biochemical processes occurring within them at all."

"Meaning what?" said Bob. "They're just stuffed animals?"

"So it would appear."

"But they move and talk."

"Magic," said Kukalukl. "It's the only explanation."

"Oh, great," Bob said. "Just what we needed."

"Magic doesn't mean they're evil or anything," Dagmar said. "There's good magic, too, like—like fairy magic or—"

Kukalukl raised his head and let out a long ululating yowl that it took everyone a moment to recognize as laughter.

Dagmar glared at him with wide, outraged eyes. Her chin dimpled slightly as she forced back tears.

As soon as he saw this, Kukalukl stopped laughing and bowed his head at the girl. "I apologize for my rude, thoughtless laughter."

Once again, Maggie was dumbfounded at the jaguar's deferential treatment of the girl. It couldn't be because Dagmar was a queen; Kukalukl wasn't the sort to respect kings and queens. It had to be something else.

"I accept your apology," Dagmar said in a cool, starchy tone, her nose upraised, her queenly manner once more in full force. "But tell me what you found so funny."

"It was your comment about fairy magic being good."

She frowned, this time more in puzzlement than anger. "Why is that funny?"

"I can only assume that you have never actually met a fairy."

"Well…no. I've just heard stories about them."

"Ah. That explains it. You see, I *have* met fairies—quite a few of them over the years—and despite what your books say, they're the most damnably annoying creatures in all existence."

"Really?"

"Oh, yes. Utter pests. The most capricious and self-absorbed creatures you'll ever meet. A lot like debutantes, really. At any rate, you are correct: Just because it's magic doesn't mean it's bad. Like science or religion, magic is simply a tool that can be used for either good or ill. Still, I recommend keeping our guard up until we know more."

"Well, they *seem* nice enough…"

Just then the odor of cooking food filtered into the clearing, and in response their stomachs churned and gurgled, making them realize how hungry they were. They hadn't eaten anything in hours.

After a seemingly eternal wait Rumbledum and a dozen other stuffed animals appeared, bearing silver platters stacked with cuts of meat, flagons of wine, bowls filled with soups and salads and nuts and berries. On one platter that was so heavy four animals had to carry it stood a seven-layer cake covered with white frosting and adorned with flowers made of red and blue icing.

Dagmar gasped. Adam and Maggie exchanged a surprised glance. Bob licked his lips and rubbed his groaning belly. Kukalukl sniffed the cooked meat and harrumphed in disdain. Freud merely commented, "Oh, how lovely."

"Eat!" said Rumbledum. "Drink! Celebrate!"

"Where did you acquire all this wonderful food?" asked Maggie. She tasted one of the salads. It was a mix of spinach and nasturtium leaves topped with tomato slices, pine nuts, and an oil-based dressing that had a mushroomy flavor. "And how did you learn how to prepare it?"

Rumbledum pointed a paw at the green dog, who lowered his head sheepishly. "Slobberjaw there is our master chef. As for the origin of the food, some of it we gathered and caught here in the forest, and some of it we scavenged from some ruined human buildings off that way." He pointed southwest.

"Well you guys did a marvelous job," Bob said in between bites of venison. "My compliments to Slobberjaw, especially."

"Dahr, it was nothin'," said Slobberjaw with an embarrassed shrug. If he had had pockets he would have stuffed his paws into them.

"I notice that you are not eating," Rumbledum said to Adam, his voice full of concern. "Is the food not to your liking?"

"Oh, it looks most delectable. It is simply that I am not currently hungry. My metabolism operates differently than that of a normal human. I will, however, feast later, rest assured."

"I see." He turned to Kukalukl. "And you? Why do you not eat?"

"It's been cooked. I prefer my meat raw and bloody."

Unexpectedly, Rumbledum giggled. "I should have known. We could capture a deer or rabbit or some other animal, if you like. We hate to see our guests unhappy."

"I would be unhappy if you *did* catch something for me. I prefer to hunt my own meals, thank you very much."

Rumbledum glanced at Freud. "I assume the hard shiny one doesn't eat at all?"

"That is correct," Freud said. "All my energy requirements are met by a miniature atomic reactor in my thoracic cavity."

"I see." Rumbledum bowed to the group. "Enjoy the feast. At dusk we will build a bonfire, and there will be singing and dancing. We would be overjoyed if you joined us."

"We will surely consider it," said Adam.

"Splendid! I hope to see you later, then."

With that, he and Slobberjaw and the other stuffed animals scurried out of the clearing.

"Why are you not eating?" Maggie whispered to Adam. "And why did you lie about your metabolism?"

"I refuse to eat until I am certain the food is safe."

Maggie's eyes widened, and her fork, laden with a dripping chunk of rabbit, froze halfway to her lips. Bob spat the berries he had been eating onto his plate. Dagmar gasped and clapped a hand over her mouth.

"You mean it's, like, poisoned or something?" she said, her frightened eyes looking as if they would pop right out of her head.

Adam groaned inwardly. He hadn't meant to scare everyone like this.

"I am not saying it is poisoned. But in this perilous world it is wise to trust only food you make yourself. Or food that you can analyze." He spoke this latter sentence with a pointed look at Freud.

"Oh," said the robot. "Do you wish me to analyze it, then? I am able to identify over seventeen thousand different poisonous compounds."

"Please do."

Freud fixed his gaze upon the meats. His eyes briefly glowed a brighter orange. Then he turned his attention to the soup, then the salads, and so on with each dish until he ended with the cake. The others waited anxiously throughout all this, their own eyes returning to the food again and again as if expecting to spot a telltale hemlock leaf. Only Kukalukl, who hadn't eaten anything, remained blasé. He merely sniffed the food and said, "Well, *I* don't smell anything. Of course, it's hard to be sure, what with the disgusting aroma of de-rawed meat contaminating everything."

Finally Freud said, "I detect nothing that could be considered harmful except to those with violent allergies to milk, eggs, honey, wheat—"

"But there's no poison?" said Bob.

"Probably not."

"*Probably?*"

"There are some molecular structures I cannot identify in the honey and a few other items, but they are trace amounts and are most likely pollen from plants that are not in my database."

"Oh." Bob looked at his food, shrugged, and forked the spat-out, half-chewed berries back into his mouth. "Well, everything sure *tastes* okay."

Everyone nodded in agreement, and they ate.

And they ate.

And they ate.

And an hour later they lay on the grass, groaning.

"Oh, man," said Bob. "I haven't had a meal this large or this rich in...geez, it's been years."

"As with us," said Maggie. "Even the meals I prepared at the manor were never so...so variegated."

"Uhhh," moaned Dagmar. "What does 'fairy-gated' mean?"

"'Variegated.' It means characterized by variety."

"Uh." She clasped her distended belly, her face suddenly turning a pasty green shade. "I think I'm gonna be sick."

Adam snorted. "I told you not to have a third piece of cake."

Dagmar snorted in return. "Oh, right, like I'm gonna do what *you* say. What are you, my dad?"

"No, but you should respect the hard-won wisdom of those older than you."

"Yeah, well, *you* ate too much, too."

Adam started to respond, then belched, swallowed back the hot blob of semi-digested food that had risen halfway up his throat, and turned a shade of green quite similar to Dagmar's.

"What can I say?" he said. "I have a weakness for elk."

Kukalukl had gone out hunting while they ate, and now he returned, his fat pink tongue flapping and slapping noisily as he licked all around his mouth. A drop of blood hung on the end of one whisker.

He took one look at the green, groaning mortals on the grass (Freud stood off to one side in standby mode, resting his processors) and sighed.

"You silly simians have no concept of moderation."

"Please," said Dagmar, "don't talk too much; the vibrations might make me puke."

"Hh. It might be the best thing for you at this point." Chuckling, he lay down near Dagmar.

"I trust your own dinner was satisfactory," Maggie said, not sure if she really wanted to know what the jaguar had killed.

"Oh, it certainly was. That's the marvelous thing about this post-Cataclysm world: There are all manner of tasty beasts roaming about. Today's menu consisted of a plump gopher-like beast the size of a wheelbarrow. It was delightful. Very rich meat. And it put up quite an exhilarating chase. Mmm." He resumed licking his chops. His tongue swiped away the drop of blood. "Mmm. Most delightful indeed."

Half an hour later a bush on the edge of the clearing rustled and Rumbledum appeared.

"Are we well fed?"

"Oh, yes," said Maggie. "The meal was delicious."

"Excellent! The bonfire has been set up and soon we'll have a jolly time with songs and dances and toasted marshmallows!"

"Marshmallows!" Dagmar exclaimed, her post-repast nausea already too dim a memory to have any instructional value. "I love marshmallows!"

"Come, then! Come and celebrate!"

"Are we celebrating anything in particular?" asked Adam.

"The joy of living! The beauty of the day! The wonderfulness of everything! Every day is worthy of celebration! Come, now! Come!"

Adam frowned. "I am not sure we should. We need to resume our hunt for the Marauders. We have been here too long already."

"It is too late to move on now," Maggie said, nodding at

the sun, a bleary red glow behind the tree-trunks to the west. "We would be stopping for the night within an hour anyway. We may as well camp here."

"I suppose so…" He hated that they had wasted so much time in Happyvale. But Maggie was right: There was little sense in packing up and moving on only to have to stop again before they had gotten over the next hill.

They followed Rumbledum out of the clearing, through the trees, and into another, larger clearing where all the stuffed animals stood around a pyramid of logs and branches, their instruments arranged on the grass near by. Torches flickered in holders affixed low on the trees that ringed the clearing. Garlands of flowers had been strung among the branches overhead.

When the stuffed animals saw the group arrive, they cheered and capered about. The elephant raised his trunk and blatted. Slobberjaw raced in circles and barked happily. A shaggy brown monkey chattered and did backflips.

Rumbledum spread his arms wide. "Now we dance!"

Those animals with instruments picked them up and began playing a tune that sounded like Ragtime music to Bob, while the rest of the animals skipped and jumped and do-si-doed.

The monkey approached Dagmar, grabbed her hands, and said, "Eek-eek! I'm Chimparee! Let's dance!" He pulled her toward the merry-making throng. Giggling, she let him.

Rumbledum and a penguin with big orange eyes made of felt approached the others. Rumbledum extended a paw for Maggie to take, while the penguin said, "Hi, I'm Freezy!" and reached out for Adam's hands with his stiff, pointed black wings. Adam yanked his hands away.

"Don't you like me?" Freezy asked Adam in a small, sad voice.

"I am sure you are a wonderful little bird," said Adam. "But I do not dance."

"Oh, go on," Maggie said with a laugh as Rumbledum led her into the crowd. "It might do you good."

"I think not."

Freezy lowered his head, slumped his shoulders, and started to turn away, but then Bob stepped out in front of him and said, "I'll dance with you."

The penguin hopped up and down on his bright orange feet and flapped his wings as fast as a hummingbird's. "Yay!"

He and Bob joined the throng.

"I notice they didn't ask *me* to dance," said Kukalukl. "Not that I'm complaining, mind you. Dancing is a reprehensible activity, fit only for children and fools. It wastes perfectly good energy and makes you look like a spastic idiot."

"They did not ask *me* to dance, either," said Freud.

"No doubt because you already look like a spastic idiot."

"Your insistence on insulting those who have done you no harm betokens a deep-seated dissatisfaction with yourself."

"On the contrary, widget-brain, I am perfectly satisfied with myself. Indeed, in my many millennia of existence I have found nothing else that meets my standards of excellence."

"Millennia?" asked Adam without taking his eyes from Dagmar, Maggie, and Granite, all of whom seemed to be having a wonderful time dancing with the stuffed animals. "You're that old?"

"Certainly. We gods are quite long-lived."

"Again with this ridiculous assertion of godhood," said Freud. "Gods, my good jaguar, do not exist. They are merely the creations of unenlightened minds."

"You *are* an idiot."

"The issue of your godhood aside, one would expect that during such a long life you would have learned good manners."

"Just the opposite. The longer I live the more intolerant I become. It's quite tiresome watching generation after generation commit the same tedious mistakes and espouse the same unthinking opinions. I suppose I should be more sympathetic toward them, seeing as how their lives are so short and they lack any real experience—"

"You should indeed!" said Freud.

"But why bother? Hostility and contempt are more amusing. It provides a sort of entertainment value lacking in most of the rest of the universe."

"I must say, that is quite a peculiar attitude. I am inclined to believe that you are joking, though I cannot be sure, as I have little experience in dealing with theriomorphic entities like yourself."

"Thank goodness for that." Kukalukl realized that Adam still had not taken his eyes from the other three members of their party, who continued to make idiots of themselves in the heart of the clearing. "I think you are too overprotective."

Adam tore his eyes from the dancing throng to look at Kukalukl. "I do not. Fair though they seem, these animated toys have yet to convince me of their trustworthiness."

"Oh, I quite agree. But if they do mean us ill, I don't think they'll do anything for a while yet. Had they planned to simply attack us, they would have done it when we entered this clearing. It was the perfect set-up for an ambush."

"True. But we know nothing of their capabilities. They might be corrupting those they dance with in some subtle manner. I cannot help but worry."

"Ah, but you forget that the converse is true, as well: They know nothing of *our* capabilities. If they do try anything, they'll be in for quite a shock, I assure you."

Adam gave a small, grim smile.

"Yes," he said. "They will."

Twenty minutes later the dance broke up and Dagmar, Maggie, and Bob rejoined the others. They were laughing as best they could through their panting, and their skin shone with sweat.

"Wow," said Bob. "Those little fellas sure like to dance. I guess they're the *real* party animals." He chuckled as if he had made a joke, but if he had, no one else understood it.

Adam couldn't help noticing how close together Bob and Maggie were standing. This, their sweatiness, their panting, their exhausted smiles—all of it melded together to lend them a sated, post-coital air, and in response Adam's heart and mind flashed black with a sickening mix of anger, despair, and jealousy.

He managed to quash these feelings almost immediately. Only a couple of days ago they would have precipitated either a violent outburst or a week-long bout of brooding. But since then things had changed.

He understood now that Maggie and Bob would not simply run off together; Maggie was still his family and would not abandon him, and Bob...well, Adam suspected that, amazingly enough, he and Bob were on the road to becoming friends. What's more, he suspected that Bob valued Adam's companionship as much as, if not more than, Adam was coming to value Bob's. Adam wasn't the only one who had changed over the last few days; improbable as it seemed, Bob had grown happier, more content. And after last night, Adam believed he understood why. When Bob had mentioned the costumed crime-fighters he had worked with, his eyes had grown distant and full of longing. And when he related his inability to find any such people in the aftermath of the Cataclysm, his voice had been tight with remembered frustration. Bob was a team player, most comfortable in the company of other super-powered individuals, and though Adam didn't wear a gaudy costume or use a silly code-name, he was, essentially, a super-powered individual. As such, he filled a fifteen-year-old void in Bob's life.

As Adam watched Maggie and Granite smile at each other, he felt a vague sense of disorientation, as if the world had subtly changed all around him when he hadn't been looking. He felt a pressure in his chest and throat that might have been either incipient laughter or incipient tears.

"What are they doing?" Maggie said, looking off at something.

Adam followed her gaze. The animals had gathered around the pyramid of logs and branches, except Rumbledum, who stood near Adam and the others with one of the torches in his paw.

"Now we light the bonfire!" said the teddy bear, waving his paw at the sky. The sun sat upon the western horizon, its rays thin and weak, and the clearing was growing dim. "Come! Join us! Soon the singing will begin!"

He trotted up to the bonfire and inserted the torch between two of the logs at the base. Within moments milky pennants of fire snapped amid the branches, and streamers of white smoke unfurled into the air.

Adam and the others joined the animals around the fire and all but Freud sat down. Those animals who had instruments played a bouncy tune, and the rest sang their usual nonsense rhymes.

Though only Dagmar joined them in the singing, the rhythm of the music was infectious enough to set most of the rest of the group bobbing their heads and tapping their feet. Freud, of course, simply continued standing there, watching, while Kukalukl took this opportunity to groom his haunches.

The singing went on for over an hour, and by the time it ended, most of the group was half asleep. Maggie's head kept sinking forward only to snap upright again. Dagmar, despite her joy at the music, couldn't keep from yawning every twenty seconds. Even Adam felt his eyelids growing heavy. The mules, however, which Adam had thought to retrieve during the song-fest and now stood tied to a nearby tree, were wide awake and somewhat agitated; perhaps they sensed the magic that Kukalukl said must be at work here.

The stuffed animals were tired, too, and before long they flopped to the grass with a collective sigh and lay there humming sleepily. Rumbledum clambered over many of his prostrate fellows to join their honored guests.

"Now it is sleepy-time," he said in a small, tired voice as he lay down between Dagmar and Adam.

"Do you just sleep here on the grass?" said Maggie. "Don't you have shelter?"

"When it rains we take shelter in the ruined human buildings. But it rarely rains here. Most every day is clear and beautiful."

He yawned and stretched his stumpy limbs.

"I shall sleep here with my new friends," he said, snuggling close to Dagmar.

Beaming, she wrapped her arms around him and held him to her chest as she settled down to sleep.

Adam watched with a soft smile, touched by the scene despite his suspicions. There was something hopeful and reassuring about seeing a happy child curl up at bedtime with a stuffed animal as children did before the world went bad (before all the worlds went bad, if Bob was right about alternate realities). It showed that some of the better aspects of human nature did not—perhaps could not—change.

None of which proved the animals' innocence, of course. Not at all. This might still the beginning of a devious trap.

Yet while he desired to remain awake and vigilant just in case, he was exhausted, and before he knew what was happening, his eyes drifted closed...

2

When he opened his eyes again, the moon shone overhead amid a spray of stars.

He cursed himself for falling asleep. Such sloppiness could get them all killed.

Something had awakened him, but what? A sound? A movement? He didn't know. But something, definitely.

He lay on his side facing Dagmar, who also lay on her side, but with her back to him. Her chest rose and fell with the slow, regular rhythm of her breathing. Rumbledum was still in her arms, but Adam could see only the top of his lavender head protruding above Dagmar's shoulder.

Behind him he heard Maggie snoring—something she vehemently insisted she didn't do, which meant he brought it up whenever possible—and Bob's deep, regular breathing.

Judging by the faint flickers of light and the occasional pop and crack of wood, the fire still burned, but wouldn't last much longer.

Everything looked and sounded all right. Perhaps his natural suspiciousness had overcome his reason. If so, he could live with that. Far better to be unnecessarily suspicious and breathing, than naive and dead.

His eyes had started to drift closed again when he saw a flash of movement.

It was Rumbledum. The little lavender head was moving, stretching upward to peer over Dagmar's shoulder.

Before the bear's button eyes became visible, Adam slitted his own eyes and hoped he looked as if he were still asleep. Through his intertwined eyelashes, he saw Rumbledum's face rise above Dagmar's shoulder like a misshapen lavender moon breaking the horizon. The bear stared at him with its glassy black eyes for so long that Adam wondered if it suspected he was awake. But then it craned its head to look over Adam's body at Maggie and Bob and the others.

Adam waited, muscles tense, ready to spring into action should Rumbledum attempt to harm Dagmar or anyone else.

After nearly a full minute, Rumbledum relaxed back down. Adam himself started to relax, thinking that he had been mistaken, that the bear had simply been looking around to make sure his guests were sleeping peacefully.

What happened next happened very quickly.

With a *sssschrip,* Rumbledum's stitched-on smile tore open, revealing two rows of needle-like teeth, and in one swift movement he plunged those teeth deep into Dagmar's shoulder, sending up a spray of blood.

Before the drops of blood could land, Adam was on his feet. As he threw out a hand to grab Rumbledum, he spotted a brown blur flying toward him in his peripheral vision.

He turned just in time to see what it was, but too late to do anything about it.

It was Chimparee, sailing down toward Adam from a nearby branch. In his open mouth fangs like Rumbledum's glittered in the moonlight. His arms were stretched out in front of him, and in the last millisecond before impact, razor-sharp talons popped out of its paws with a *shnik*.

Chimparee landed on Adam's face with enough force to send him stumbling backward. Simultaneously Adam heard Dagmar scream off to his left, while to his right Bob said, "What? What's—holy cow!"

Adam thudded to his back on the grass. Chimparee chittered and dug his talons deep into Adam's cheeks and temples. Adam felt blood pouring down the sides of his face and plastering his hair to his head.

As he reached up to seize the monkey, more stuffed animals grabbed hold of his arms and sank their teeth into his hands and forearms.

Bellowing with anger and pain, Adam sat up and flung both arms forward as if he were hurling a boulder. Most of the stuffed animals on his arms flew off, and a moment later he heard the distant *chish chish chish* of objects hurtling through foliage.

One animal still held onto his right bicep, its teeth sunk so deep that Adam felt the pain way down in the center of the muscle.

For now, though, he ignored that one. The monkey on his face took priority because it could potentially cause greater damage, though so far it had only gouged furrows across his cheeks and brows. It hadn't gone for his eyes or throat yet.

With his animal-free arm Adam reached up and closed his hand around the monkey's head. Chimparee emitted an outraged squeal that was only a muffled trill through Adam's fist. Adam squeezed, clenching his fist until the veins on his forearm looked like cables and blood gouted from the countless holes and gashes in his arm, but it had no effect on the monkey, whose head just squished beneath the pressure like a tiny pillow. There was no skull inside to crack, no brains to scramble.

Adam decided he hated magic.

In response to Adam's attack, Chimparee dug its claws deeper into Adam's face in an effort to anchor itself more firmly. By now Adam had lost enough chunks of skin not to be concerned about losing a few more, so he just wrenched the monkey off his face. With it came strips of flesh from his left cheek and right temple. Snarling, he hurled Chimparee as hard as he could toward the bonfire, which he hoped was still burning.

It was. There was a clatter of branches followed by the *fwump* of a nearly dead fire seizing upon a new fuel-source.

As Chimparee screeched and thrashed in the heart of the freshly revived bonfire, Adam swiped the blood from his eyes with his free arm, wincing as his sleeve tugged at the edge of a wound on his temple, and then looked down.

The animal on his arm was a green-and-black crocodile that had been introduced earlier as Crocodilly. It glared at Adam with its puffy white tassel eyes, the triangular red felt pupils glowing faintly in the firelight. Adam grabbed it by the tail and pulled it off his arm. The chunk of flesh in its mouth came off with it, and as Adam held out the crocodile at arm's-length, he saw it swallow the chunk and heard a ghastly *glk* from its throat.

Sickened and enraged, he lobbed it at the bonfire. This time the pain in his arm threw off his aim and Crocadilly sailed over the fire and disappeared into a bush.

Adam looked around. Dagmar, still screaming, her shoulder drenched in blood, cowered behind Kukalukl, who was batting away any animal that got too close. Rumbledum lay dismembered on the grass near by. Even in pieces, the bear's limbs wriggled and twisted with hideous life. Rumbledum hadn't gone down without a fight, though; his claws were caked with blood and black fur, and the left side of Kukalukl's mouth was a tattered, bloody mess. Maggie had gotten hold of an unburned log from the edge of the bonfire and was using it to beat back any animal that dared approach. Blood trickled from three parallel gashes on her left calf, and the back of her cloak had been reduced to shredded flaps, but otherwise she appeared untouched. She stood fast beside Granite, whose civilian clothes hung in strips from his uniform-clad stone body (and Adam noted with distant amusement that at some point he had taken the time to pull on his cowl). A crowd of animals scrabbled at Granite's legs, their claws scritching against his stone body as they futilely tried to rip him apart. He calmly picked them up one by one and pitched them into the fire. Freud stalked about grabbing at any animal he came upon. Most of them evaded him with ease. The unlucky few who didn't got their heads and limbs methodically plucked off with a speed and efficiency Adam found rather disturbing.

"This is terrible!" Freud called to Adam. "What shall we do?"

Before Adam could answer, a rustle overhead made him look up just in time to see Slobberjaw drop from a branch directly above him. This time Adam saw the approaching animal early enough to swat it out of the air before it landed on his head. A green blur sailed off toward the creek with a startled yelp.

But Slobberjaw wasn't the only one: Over a dozen more animals were clambering out along the branches to get into position to drop on everyone.

"What shall we do, you ask?" Adam shouted. "Run! Everybody run!"

As the others raced off into the woods, Adam paused to

help Dagmar onto Kukalukl's back. Sobbing softly, eyes clenched shut, she wrapped her arms around the jaguar's neck so tightly she nearly cut off the circulation to his head.

"Thank you," Kukalukl said to Adam in a choked, raspy voice.

They sped after the others. Unsurprisingly, they caught up with Freud first. He was already a hundred yards behind Granite and Maggie and falling farther behind by the second.

"Perhaps I can carry you..." Adam said doubtfully.

"You needn't bother," Freud said. "Since I cannot be eaten, the animals will undoubtedly pass me by in favor of the rest of you. As they do so, however, I shall endeavor to kill or delay as many as I can. I shall catch up with you when I can."

They hurried on and soon caught up with Granite and Maggie. Granite had had the presence of mind to snatch a burning branch from the bonfire before he exited the clearing, and now he held it high above his head, lighting the way through the dark woods. From behind them came yowls and snarls and the rustle of bushes as the animals pursued. A glance back showed Adam that the creatures were faster than their short legs and roly-poly bodies suggested. They were keeping a steady pace behind the group, and as he watched, they streamed around Freud, who managed to snatch and dismember only two of them before they were past him.

After several minutes of steady sprinting, even Adam with his superhuman strength and endurance could feel his energy ebbing away. They would have to find a way to either evade or destroy the animals very soon; otherwise they would just collapse from exhaustion and the animals would swarm over them like ants on spilled sugar.

"Hey, I think there's a building up ahead," said Granite.

"What?" Adam squinted through the trees, and yes, there was indeed a large straight-edged shape in a clearing about two hundred feet ahead.

"I sense something unusual about it," said Kukalukl.

"Like what?" said Adam.

"Magic, I believe. Strong magic."

More damn magic. Unfortunately, they had no other options left.

"We must get inside and try to hold them off from in there," said Adam.

He had only a quick glimpse of the building's exterior as they dashed across the short stretch of clearing between the woods and the building's gaping doorway, but it was enough to show that maybe this wasn't such a good idea after all. Judging by the glass shards fanning out across the clearing from the building's facade, the windows had blown outward with great force. The door had been torn from its hinges and lay partly buried in the dirt. Next to it lay a moldy, nearly illegible cardboard sign that read "Closed." A much larger sign, this one made of wood, stretched across the top of the shop's front. Though streaked and stained and peeling, the painted blue letters were still readable, and they read, "Suzie's Stuffed Animal Emporium."

"Wonderful," muttered Adam.

Once inside, Granite raised the torch and shone it around.

Hundreds of stuffed animals gazed at them from every direction. Maggie yelped. Dagmar screamed. Adam drew in a sharp hiss of breath, sure that this was the end...at least until Granite picked up one of the animals—a smiling cat, its pink fur flecked with dirt—and bounced it up and down on his palm.

"No, see?" said Granite. "They're not like the others.

They're not alive. They're inanimate."

Everyone relaxed a little, except Dagmar, whose screams at least became mercifully muffled as she buried her face in Kukalukl's fur.

"It's okay," said Kukalukl in a surprisingly soft voice. He started purring, a deep rumbling sound quite different than that produced by domestic cats. Dagmar's screams dwindled to gasping sobs.

Granite suddenly turned and frowned into the dark depths of the store.

"What's wrong?" Maggie asked.

"I hear something," Granite said. He raised his torch and strode forward to have a look. "It sounds like—"

He froze, gaping in shock and horror at what the torchlight had revealed.

"What is it?" said Adam. He hurried over to join Granite, the others following close behind. As he drew closer, he heard it too: a susurration barely audible over the snap and crackle of the torch.

Then he saw things moving in the torchlight, and for a second he thought that there were more animated stuffed animals in here after all. But no. At least not animated in the same fashion.

The stuffed animals in this part of the store writhed on the floor like maggots, their limbs tracing aimless trails in the dirt. The shelves that had once held them were empty except for a few where the smaller animals couldn't make it over the shelves' raised rims and so could only twist about in their shallow metal prisons like worms in jars.

"Oh, this is…" Maggie turned away, her hand over her mouth. The soft, incessant rustle as the animals mindlessly squirmed about on the floor made her stomach turn over.

Beyond this section were empty shelves and an empty

floor. Here, then, was where the animals of Happyvale had originated.

And in the center of this empty section, like the bull's-eye at the center of the rings of a dartboard, was the cause of the animals' unnatural animation.

A black stone obelisk stood in the middle of the floor, the rubble heaped around its base indicating it had risen up from below. The stone was of a type no one present could identify, and the very air around it seemed unusually dim, as if light lost its illuminatory power near the obelisk. Letters in some strange language had been carved onto each of the obelisk's four sides. Adam found the shapes of the letters repellent in some inexplicable way, and he discovered he couldn't look at them for too long without feeling dizzy.

"What is this?" said Granite. He held a hand out toward it. "Can you feel it? It's radiating…something."

"Magic," said Kukalukl. Dagmar had finally gotten down off his back and now sat shivering and pale just inside the area free of stuffed animals. Maggie knelt beside her with one arm wrapped around her shoulders.

Kukalukl stepped up to the obelisk, studied the writing, sniffed it.

"As I thought," he said with a derisive snort. "This is Ng'l'xula, one of the languages of the 'Great' Old Ones."

"Meaning what, exactly?" asked Adam.

"Meaning that this must be what they call a T'mazimet. Which means one of the Old Ones is contained within it. Which is infinitely annoying. I hate dealing with those disgusting bastards. The stench alone is appalling. They never bathe, you know. Do you have any idea what eons-old slime smells like?"

"So the Old One is what made all those stuffed animals come alive?" said Granite.

"The Old One's magic, to be precise. The Old One himself is probably slumbering and has no real awareness of any of this."

"Well, then, that ain't a problem." Granite made a fist and cocked his arm back.

"No, you fool!" Kukualukl cried, and leaped in front of Granite's hurtling fist. It slammed into his ribs with a sound like someone stepping on a sack full of sticks.

"Ow," he said as he thudded to the floor. "That'll take a few hours to heal."

"They're here!" cried Maggie.

The others looked around. Crowded against the gaping holes where the door and windows used to be were the animals of Happyvale. Their dark glassy eyes glimmered crimson in the torchlight.

In the center of the doorway stood Slobberjaw, Rumbledum's severed head held in his paws. Grass-stains streaked the teddy bear's face, and a blob of stuffing dangled like a pendulum from his neck-stump.

"Hello, my lovely guests," said Rumbledum, his voice as chipper as when Adam and the others had first arrived in Happyvale. "I think you're cornered!"

The other animals cheered and waved their arms.

"Cornered, cornered," they cried in merry, sing-song voices.

"Now we shall have a beautiful slaughter!"

The animals cheered louder than ever. "Slaughter! Slaughter! Yay!"

"Stall them," Kukalukl hissed at Adam and Maggie. "Stall them for as long as you can. If they attack, protect Dagmar. Hold her over your heads if you have to. If you let them injure her, I shall take incalculable pleasure in flaying both of you alive and then playing with your bones. Are we clear?"

"Yes," Maggie said.

"There is no need for threats," Adam said.

Kukalukl ignored him. "Go."

Adam and Maggie stepped forward to meet the animals.

"What about me?" Granite asked Kukalukl.

"I'll need your help."

"Sorry I hit you. I take it smashing that thing won't help."

"Indeed not. The Old One in question—and if I'm reading the writing on the obelisk correctly, it's name is Oghkhnarakh'gh, not that it matters—the Old One isn't inside the pillar, but is confined by it. It's hard to explain to a being of such limited intellect and perception as yourself, but imagine the pillar as a sort of plug blocking access to or from the infra-dimensional space in which the Old One is slumbering. Destroying the pillar would be like removing the plug, allowing the Old One to pour into this world like a flood. As it is, it's entering in only a trickle at the moment, just enough to corrupt and animate the stuffed animals closest to the obelisk, which leads me to surmise that when the pillar rose up through the floor during the Cataclysm, part of the writing on the stone was damaged."

"So if we can find and fix the damaged writing…"

"It will cut off that trickle of magic which is animating the animals, yes. So help me look for any cracks or chips in the obelisk."

Meanwhile, Adam and Maggie had stridden halfway to the front of the store, then stopped and fixed what they hoped were convincingly forbidding glares on the stuffed animals peering in through the door and windows.

"You may not enter this building," said Adam.

Rumbledum tittered. "Oh, but we may. It is you who are

the interlopers here. This is our birthplace."

With the bear's head held out in front of him like a king's crown on a silken pillow, Slobberjaw stepped through the doorway.

"You are trapped," said Rumbledum.

The other animals giggled and chanted, "Trapped trapped trapped." They began climbing in through the windows and forming a line at the front of the store.

Something bumped Adam's boot. He looked down. It was one of the twitching, semi-alive stuffed animals, a teddy bear with long silver hair. He bent down, grabbed it, and held it up for the other animals to see.

"Stop now, or we shall start destroying your fellows here."

Rumbledum pshawed. "The half-born are of little concern to us. They are feeble, useless things."

Adam gripped either end of the bear and pulled it apart. Stuffing flew in every direction and the half-born bear emitted a short squeak.

Despite Rumbledum's claims, the fully animated animals drew back a little, as if offended.

"That wasn't nice," said Rumbledum in a low, unhappy voice. "Not nice at all."

"They're bad, duh-huh," agreed Slobberjaw. *"Bad."*

With Slobberjaw (and Rumbledum's head) in the lead, the animals trooped forward, teeth and talons gleaming in the torchlight.

Granite glanced back, saw the animals approaching, and said, "They're coming. We've gotta hurry this up."

"Yes," said Kukalukl, "I know. But I'm not seeing any damage to the obelisk at all. It's…ah. There it is."

He nosed a spot on the obelisk. At first Granite didn't see anything there except those weird letters, but as he bent forward and brought the torch in closer for a better look, he saw an oval chip in the stone that had eradicated a single letter of the ancient writing.

"That's *it?*" he said. "Just that one little spot?"

"So it seems. Now shut up; I need to figure out what the missing letter is."

He scanned the writing, then huffed in annoyance.

"Why did they have to construct a language with so many damn cases? Let me see...I think this section is using the ablative..."

Fearing the worst, Granite glanced over his shoulder. Adam and Maggie were slowly backing away from the advancing stuffed animals, a colorful sea of fuzz and fabric that filled the front third of the store from wall to wall. And still more animals were climbing in through the windows. He hadn't realized there were so many of them. Then again, he saw several he didn't recognize, so perhaps some of them had been away from Happyvale for some reason earlier in the day.

"Ah," said Kukalukl. "I think I've got it."

"You *think?*" said Granite.

"I'm mostly certain; let's put it that way. This is one of the most complicated languages in existence. It has seventy cases and twelve genders (though two of them are imaginary) and it often uses adverbs as nouns. At any rate, I'm hoping that your stone finger is strong enough to incise lines in the obelisk."

"It should be." He held up his right index finger. "Tell me what to do."

"Make a vertical line through the spot that's been chipped away."

"You're kidding. All of this happened because of one line?"

"Yes. Are you going to do it, or shall we stand here and get eaten by children's toys?"

"All right, all right."

He jabbed his finger as hard as he could into the top of the chipped-off area. He was half afraid that he would cause even more damage to the obelisk, maybe send a huge chunk flying out. Instead, his finger sank right in. There was a little crumbling around the edges of the hole his finger made, but it was too localized to damage any of the writing. Whatever the obelisk was made of, its physical properties were unlike those of any stone Granite was familiar with. It was somehow soft like butter and hard like steel at the same time. Which was impossible, except...

Well, except that apparently it wasn't.

Far more troubling than that, though, was that while his finger had been strong enough to penetrate the stone, the magic leaking from the stone was also penetrating him: Cold numbness quickly spread up his finger, across his hand, past his wrist. He knew somehow that allowing the numbness to spread over too much of his body would be a very bad thing.

And yet part of him felt an irrational urge to find out what would happen if he let it overwhelm him. It would be so easy. All he would have to do was stand here with his finger in the obelisk. And afterward...well, it didn't matter. It would be just like going to sleep. It would be like when he was a kid all huddled underneath the covers on a cold winter's night, curled up in the warm womb-like blackness without a care in the world. It would be so nice, so cozy...

Adam and Maggie had backed up as far as the section of empty shelves when the stuffed animals finally noticed Granite and Kukalukl next to the obelisk.

"What are they doing?" said Rumbledum, his voice shrill with alarm. "They can't do that! Stop them! Charge!"

Snarling, growling, yowling, yapping, the animals surged forward. Adam squeezed his hands into fists bigger than most of the animals, while Maggie pulled out her dagger, both of them ready to fight and, if need be, die.

Through the veils falling across his mind like black cobwebs, Granite heard Rumbledum shout something. The only word he could make out was, "Charge!" It wasn't important. Happyvale was long in the past. Or was it the future? It didn't matter. All that did was the present, an endless black ocean, silent, blissful...

"Hey, look!" That was Kukalukl's voice. "Isn't that Lightray and the Contortionist over there?"

The veils broke apart in a flash. Granite looked around, blinking like someone jolted out of a dream.

"What? Where?"

"In my ass! Now pull your fucking finger down right fucking now!"

Suddenly it all came back to him. The animals. The obelisk. Granite hoped it wasn't already too late. Rumbledum's voice had sounded close. The darn bear must be almost in the middle of the store. To make matters worse, during his brief trip to la-la land, the numbness had spread well past his elbow.

Lips pressed together in a thin white line, he pulled his finger straight down, cutting a furrow through the chipped-off area. A few tiny fragments of black stone broke off around his finger and clicked to the floor, but none of the writing was damaged and that was what mattered. He yanked his finger out just as the numbness reached his shoulder. While he had been making the line, the black stone had started oozing shut behind his finger in a slow, smooth fashion that reminded him for some reason of Jell-O. But the moment he pulled his finger out, it set.

The charging army of stuffed bears and cats and lizards and birds was only moments away from slamming into Adam and Maggie when the faint crack of stone sounded toward the rear of the store. The animals immediately stopped in their tracks and went rigid as if they were being electrocuted, their backs arched, their arms extended at their sides. Even the half-born animals stopped squirming and stiffened like planks of woods.

And from all of them arose a horrible keening that made everyone cover their ears. It sounded like a million seagulls crying out, their shrill voices combining into one skull-skewering "eeeeeeeeee." Then it abruptly ceased, and the animals collapsed to the floor.

Adam bent down and inspected the nearest animals. No claws. No fangs. They were just toys again.

"I guess we did it," said Granite, joining Adam and Maggie. He kept shaking his arm as if trying to wake it up.

"Are you hurt?" asked Maggie, making no effort to mask her concern.

"Nah. It's just that I had to stick my finger in the obelisk like that little Dutch boy plugging the dike. And let me tell you, that thing's *cold* inside. But it's wearing off now. Slowly."

Kukalukl ignored all this and headed straight for Dagmar.

"How are you?" he asked.

She didn't answer at first, just sat there shivering, her knees drawn up to her chest, her arms wrapped around her legs, her eyes fixed on some distant point beyond the opposite wall. Sweat glistened on her pale, clammy face. Nearly half her shirt was soaked with blood from the wound in her shoulder.

"I wanna go home," she finally said in a tiny voice.

Without responding, Kukalukl turned away and padded over to the others, who were watching with concern.

"She's in shock, and she's lost a lot of blood. We need to clean and mend her wound immediately."

"Agreed," said Adam. "The first aid kit is back with the mules…"

"If the mules are even still there," said Granite. "The stuffed animals might have eaten them."

"But they would not eat the medicine. And right now, that is far more important than two mules."

They retraced their path to the clearing where they had been so rudely awakened less than an hour earlier. Kukalukl carried Dagmar on his back since she was too weak to walk. At about the halfway point, they met up with Freud, still trotting implacably along. He was overjoyed that they had defeated the stuffed animals, though regretful he hadn't been able to do more to help. "We must all learn to work within our preprogrammed limits, I suppose," he concluded stoically.

When they got to the clearing, they discovered that Granite had been right: The mules had been reduced to well-gnawed bones.

The contents of their packs were strewn about the clearing. Though most items were undamaged, several articles of clothing had been torn up, one of the boxes of cereal emptied into a bush, and a strip of salt pork unwrapped and bitten into. The bitten off portion lay nearby in a chewed-up, spat-out wad. Like Kukalukl, the stuffed animals had preferred their meat raw and bloody.

The medicine bag had been opened, then set aside, its contents thankfully of no interest to the animals. While the others repacked their supplies, Maggie treated Dagmar's wound. The chunk of flesh Rumbledum had torn out of her shoulder was too large to be sutured up, so Maggie cleaned it out with alcohol, which produced squawks of pain from Dagmar, then slathered on some antibiotic ointment and covered it with a bandage.

"As it heals, it will itch fiercely, but try not to scratch it. I will help you re-dress the wound every morning if you like. If it looks as if an infection is setting in, we shall give you some Cipro."

Dagmar didn't answer. She just sat on the grass, staring off into space.

"Are you hungry?" asked Maggie.

For a moment Dagmar continued staring at nothing. But then she gave an almost imperceptible shake of her head.

"Thirsty?"

Dagmar nodded.

"Yes, please," she said in a hoarse, weak voice.

Maggie handed her one of the water bottles, and Dagmar gulped down half of it in one go despite Maggie's exasperated calls for her to drink more slowly.

As she handed the bottle back to Maggie, Dagmar gasped and clutched her belly. Her throat bulged as the she struggled to keep the water down. It was a struggle she couldn't win. She turned her head to the side and a stream of soupy liquid shot from her mouth.

"I told you not to drink so fast," Maggie said. She stroked Dagmar's shuddering back as the girl retched up the last few drops. "You should wait a little while before having any more."

"Is she okay?" asked Bob, who had taken off his cowl and put on a fresh shirt and jeans.

"I believe so."

"Good. Um…" He licked his lips and scratched the back of his head, suddenly looking as uneasy as a schoolboy asking a girl to a dance. "Do you, uh, do you need any help dressing your own wound?"

She looked down at the gashes on her calf. In all the excitement, she had forgotten about them. Now that her attention had returned to them, however, she did feel a slight throb of pain. Nothing major, though. They weren't even bleeding anymore. All she needed to do was swab them with alcohol and slap on a bandage. And yet in her mind, she imagined Bob kneeling before her and taking her bare calf in his large, strong hands. Her face reddened. Thank goodness it was too dark for him to see it.

"No, thank you," she said. "It is not necessary."

"Ah. That's, uh, that's good." He sounded a little disappointed.

Adam joined them. "We should try to get some sleep," he said. He glanced at Dagmar. "Not here, though. We should move upstream. Out of Happyvale."

"Good idea," said Bob. "And I was thinking: With the mules gone, there's no way we can carry all our supplies. But since Freud says we're only about three days away from the Marauders' base, it would make the most sense to take only whatever we'll need for, say, a week, and leave the rest hidden away here in a safe place."

"Where would be safe enough?" asked Maggie as she set to work cleaning Adam's numerous wounds. His superhuman biology ensured that they would heal within a few days, but there was still a slight risk of infection.

"I was thinking the stuffed animal store."

At the mention of the place, Dagmar drew her legs up to her chest and buried her head between her knees.

With a guilty grimace, Bob knelt beside her to comfort her, but she drew away from him as if he were radioactive.

"It's okay," he said. "I'm a friend, remember?"

"Pih," Dagmar spat, as if the very idea that anyone could be a friend was too ludicrous for words.

Bob stood up and looked at Adam and Maggie. Adam shrugged. Maggie shook her head at Bob as if to say "leave it alone for now."

"Hiding the supplies in the store sounds like a good idea," Adam said in a low voice. "We should act quickly, though, so we can get at least a few hours of sleep tonight."

Leaving a week's worth of provisions in their packs, Adam, Bob, and Maggie hid the rest in a cabinet under the counter in the store. Adam placed a rock the size of a car's engine against the cabinet door to ensure the more common varieties of wildlife couldn't get inside. The less common varieties, on the other hand, might be a problem, but that would be true no matter where they put the provisions.

After that, they rejoined Kukalukl, Dagmar, and Freud, and the group made their way north along the creek until they were well clear of Happyvale. Dagmar once again rode on Kukalukl's back; he seemed to be the only one she trusted enough to touch her.

They made camp in a meadow next to the creek. Aside from Freud and Kukalukl, none of them got to sleep for a long, long time. They lay awake, in pain, in worriment, in reflection, listening to the wind in the trees and Freud's constant faint hum and Kukalukl's deep, even breathing, until the night was nearly gone.

Chapter 6
Boko Zafendo

1

The following morning all the non-mechanized and non-feline members of the group were groggy from lack of sleep. While Adam and Bob gruntingly worked on breakfast, Maggie shuffled about like a jelly-zombie and examined everyone's wounds.

Dagmar's was still raw and grisly, but this time she didn't make a sound when Maggie poured alcohol on it. She just stiffened, her jaw clenched, her nostrils flaring, her expression simultaneously angry and frightened, as if the anger was a way of keeping the fear in check. She didn't talk at all, not even when Maggie asked her if she wanted any food. She just glared off at the trees in the direction of Happyvale.

Everyone else was healing nicely. Maggie's slashes had scabbed up overnight and required no further treatment. Likewise, the divots in Adam's flesh had already grown crusty with scabs and begun to fill in.

Maggie came last to Kukalukl. She had taken a quick look at his tattered upper lip last night but he had refused to let her treat it, saying only, "I heal quickly."

"Do you wish me to examine your wound?" she asked him now.

"What wound?" he said.

Although she had been looking right at him, she hadn't

realized till he spoke that his lip was completely healed.

"Amazing," she said.

"We gods generally are."

She eyed him appraisively as he walked away. Till now she had regarded his claim of godhood with a great deal of skepticism. And while the fact that he healed ten times faster than Adam didn't prove anything—in the years since the Cataclysm she had met or heard about any number of perfectly mortal beings with all manner of strange powers—it was one big step closer to confirming his assertion.

After breakfast they resumed their trek. Since their backpacks were heavier from the added weight of the goods formerly carried by the mules, they traveled more slowly than before. Fortunately this leg of their journey was quiet and undemanding. They left the forest behind them an hour after setting out, and for the rest of the day the landscape was grassy and flat, the weather was mild and sunny, and they encountered no dangers. They didn't even see many animals. Perhaps the creatures of Happyvale had eaten most of the fauna in these parts.

Dagmar said virtually nothing all day. From her perch on Kukalukl's back, she watched the passing scenery with a pinched, hostile look, as if expecting the trees and bushes to cause trouble. When Kukalukl asked her how she was, she just shrugged.

They camped that night in a shady dell sheltered on every side by dark green ferns that were taller than Adam. After dinner Maggie re-dressed the various wounds, noting with satisfaction that no infections had set in and everyone seemed to be healing well. At least physically. Dagmar remained mute and vaguely hostile. Not even Kukalukl could draw her out.

Everyone was too tired for chitchat that night, so they

crawled into their sleeping bags, and when the moon rose, it was upon a camp wracked with snores.

2

The next day's journey passed just as uneventfully. No monsters. No attacks. The most memorable moment came when they crested a hill, and Freud stopped dead, saying, "Ah. I remember this area. To more accurately retrace my route, we must now adjust our course slightly to the northwest."

The land in that direction sloped generally downward and consisted mostly of meadows thick with wildflowers. The meadows ended about four miles away in a line of trees that blocked the view beyond.

Maggie grabbed Adam's arm. "Look!" she said, her voice high and excited.

He followed her pointing finger and saw a cluster of mountains far to the north, their crisp snow-white crowns contrasting sharply with the hazy, purple-gray slopes beneath them.

"Mountains," he said with a wistful smile.

"The first we've seen since the Cataclysm," Maggie said. "They remind me of home. Of the Alps."

Adam nodded. "Perhaps when our quest is done, we can visit those peaks and compare them with the ones we knew so long ago."

"I would like that." She turned to the others. "The rest of you are welcome to come, as well." As she spoke, she looked mainly at Bob.

"That'd be nice," he said with a smile.

Kukalukl yawned.

They reached the trees when the sun was low and red in the west. The view from the hill had been deceptive, for what had appeared to be a thin line of trees from so far away was in reality much thicker, more like a ribbon of forest.

On the edge of the trees sat a low wooden building with no windows and a single five-foot-high door that slid open on a wooden track. The building's small dimensions led Maggie to wonder if it had been built for children, but Kukalukl asserted the place was clearly of gnomish design. Inside was a long hallway with two dozen doorless stalls opening off it. At the far end of the hallway a broken stool lay on its side. Fourteen crude circles the size of pennies had been scratched into the floor of one of the stalls. Otherwise the place was bare, anonymous.

"I've run into gnomes a few times in my travels," Kukalukl said. "This, I believe, is what they call a *boko za-fendo,* a sort of prison."

"'Sort of'?" Bob asked.

Kukalukl glanced at Dagmar, who was ten feet away inspecting the sliding door. In a voice too low for her to hear, he said, "They tortured prisoners in these places. *Boko zafendo* literally translates as 'corridor of screams.' They're usually built in remote areas, far from civilization. Out of sight, out of mind, I suppose."

"Doesn't *look* too nasty."

"Gnomes tend to be meticulously clean. That doesn't hide all traces, though. Be glad you don't have my keen sense of smell; while it's clear this place hasn't been used in years, it still reeks like a slaughterhouse."

While the others made camp at the edge of the trees a hundred feet north of the *boko zafendo,* Bob scouted ahead to see what lay within and beyond the strip of forest.

He was gone so long that when he returned the others

had already started eating, except for Kukalukl who was still out hunting his own dinner.

"We were growing worried," said Maggie. She was trying to sound casual, but the relief in her eyes was clear to anyone who cared to look. "What kept you?"

"Actually, there was a lot to check out on the other side of the trees."

"Nothing serious, I hope," said Adam.

Bob shrugged as he piled some pork on a plate. "Hard to say. The terrain over there is totally different from anything we've encountered so far. It's gonna be tough going. And slow."

"What is it like?"

"Basically, it's bare stony ground that's full of pits and fissures, with boulders and smaller rocks strewn all over the place. It's like a giant rocky obstacle course that stretches on and on for miles. Beyond it I think there're more trees, but it was too far away and it was getting too dark to tell for sure."

"Ah, yes," said Freud. "I recall that area quite well. It was difficult to navigate."

"Do you recall seeing any potentially hostile life-forms?" Adam asked.

"I do not recall seeing any life-forms at all, aside from a few birds. Though the rocky area is perhaps only three miles wide, it took me nine hours and twenty-six minutes to cross it, for I was continually forced to backtrack in order to seek out new, more accessible paths."

"Should we just go around it, then?"

"Certainly not. For one thing, it extends quite a long distance to the north and south, meaning that even if we possessed no map of the terrain, it would take us far longer to go around it than to cross it. But we do have a map of a sort, for the route I took is saved in my memory. Thus, if I can locate the spot where I exited the maze it will be a simple matter to retrace my steps. Doing so will, in my estimation, enable us to cross this rocky wasteland in only four hours or so."

"Good," Bob said. He sat down near Maggie—close enough to qualify as sitting beside her, but not so close as to appear unseemly—and started to eat. Maggie glanced at him, then returned to her food with a small smile.

Adam watched them with amusement. He wondered if the members of their odd little band would choose to remain together after the quest was done. It was looking more and more likely that he and Maggie and Bob and—assuming all went well—Anna would do so; but what of Dagmar and Kukalukl and Freud? Perhaps all seven of them could become a team not unlike Bob's League of Super-Heroes and travel about this wild world, helping the powerless fight off the monsters that would prey on them...

He s had an image of himself clad in a skin-tight costume similar to Bob's, a blue cowl pulled over his wrinkled face, yellow gloves encasing his huge hands, a stylized F emblazoned on his chest, a cape flapping behind him in the breeze.

No. Absolutely not. They could form a team, they could right wrongs, they could battle evil, they could even call themselves the All-New League of Super-Heroes; but not all the torments of hell could get him to wear such garish apparel.

Besides, what made him think such a scheme would work? People would reject his help no matter how benevolent his intentions, seeing him as just another monster. He knew that. Why, then, was he pretending he could be a hero? What was the use in daydreaming about being something he could never be?

With a small sigh, he returned to his food.

Dinner passed in near silence. The only sounds were chewing and smacking and the crackle of the fire.

When Bob finished eating, he looked around and saw that Dagmar had eaten only a few bites of her food. She was staring down at the plate in her lap and aimlessly moving a strip of pork around with her fork.

"You okay?" he asked.

She didn't respond.

He leaned toward her. "Are you all right?"

Still no answer.

Worried, he laid a hand on her arm. "Do you—"

She shot to her feet so hard and fast her plate flipped over three times and landed in the fire. The pork vanished into the high grass. She glared at Bob, hands clenched into fists, eyes blazing with a volatile mix of fear and fury, chin dimpled and trembling as if she were about to burst into tears.

"Don't touch me!" she screamed. "Don't do *any*thing unless I say so! *I'm* the queen here. *Me.* This is *my* kingdom, and I'm in charge of everyone here. Which means I'm *your* queen, and the stuffed animals' queen, and the Marauders' queen, and *everyone's* queen, so everyone had better do what I say or I'll have you *fucking killed!*" By the end of this speech, her voice had risen to a shriek, her whole body was quaking with rage, and tears were streaming down her cheeks.

For a long moment, everyone just stared at her. Then Bob offered her the sweetest, most disarming smile he could manage (and he could manage it quite well), got down on one knee as if he were being knighted, bowed his head, and said, "I apologize for any unthinking insult on my part, fairest queen."

Dagmar's tears continued streaming unabated and her quaking grew more intense, which led everyone to think she was about to suffer a total psychological meltdown. But then she glanced about at everyone with alarm, as when someone who has been talking to herself suddenly remembers she's in the presence of others, and what she did next shocked everyone: She unballed her hands, took a breath so deep it seemed her lungs must burst, tilted her chin up like a great sage about to deliver a wise and weighty proclamation, and said, "No, *I* apologize for my outburst. It was…childish. It will not happen again."

Everyone gaped at her. Maggie felt a shiver run up her spine. For the first time since meeting Dagmar, she felt— really *felt*—that she was in the presence of genuine royalty.

The bushes at the edge of the clearing rustled and Kukalukl appeared, the front half of a giant squirrel in his jaws. A loop of blood-streaked intestine dangled from its gaping trunk like a slick, slimy noose. He set the half-squirrel on the grass and eyed Dagmar, whose back was to him, then the others, his yellow-green eyes glinting in the firelight.

"Is anything wrong?" he said. A hint of a growl rumbled in the back of his throat as he spoke.

"No," said Dagmar without turning. "Everything is fine. Your concern is appreciated but unnecessary."

Kukalukl gazed at her back for a moment, then said, "Hm," as if he had been given something interesting to ponder. Then he flopped to the grass and started devouring the squirrel.

"I would like some more pork," said Dagmar, "if there is any left."

"There is," said Maggie.

She dished up a fresh plate of food and handed it to Dagmar, who gulped it down as if she hadn't eaten in a week. Everyone watched her out of the corners of their eyes, not daring to look at her directly and run the risk of making her feel like a sideshow freak and thus upset her all over again.

When she finished the pork, she ran her finger all around the plate to catch any crumbs and bits of salt, then stuck the finger in her mouth and licked it clean. She set the plate aside, leaned back against her backpack, and looked contentedly at the others, all of whom pretended they hadn't been watching her the whole time.

Kukalukl, having likewise finished his dinner, padded over and lay down in the grass next to her.

"Again, I apologize," Dagmar said. "I'm still trying to deal with everything that's happened—those awful animals, what happened to my parents, being made a...a vagabond in what's left of my kingdom. But it's still no excuse for such a tantrum."

"You have not spoken much of your kingdom," Maggie said. "What was it like?"

Dagmar blinked at her for a moment as if she didn't understand the question. Then her forehead crumpled into a small frown.

"I...I don't know what it was *really* like. I knew it only as beautiful ruins. It was called Eridia. My parents—King Stevan and Queen Zara—they told me that the royal lands once stretched for over three hundred miles in every direction and had forests full of towering old trees and fat, slow animals perfect for hunting. There were crystal-clear streams with so many fish in them it was said you could walk across the water on their backs. Once in a while you even saw a unicorn or a fairy in the forest, though they'd always vanish if you got too close.

"Tiny villages dotted the land, and the villagers were happy, well-fed folk who grew their crops and paid their taxes and did whatever else villagers do. My father's mighty army kept them safe from monsters and evil men, so they never dreamed of complaining or revolting because they knew they could never protect themselves half as well as he and his army could.

"The royal palace was so huge even the servants sometimes got lost in it. Everywhere you turned there were marble pillars and curving white staircases and fireplaces big enough to fit a wagon inside. It had over two hundred rooms and five towers and a moat.

"Behind the palace was a gigantic garden with a maze made of hedges, and statues carved by the best sculptors in the kingdom, and gazebos with golden roofs, and fountains designed so the falling water sounded like flutes and harps.

"Next to the garden were the stables where we kept the royal horses, which were strong as oxes, pretty as kittens, and fast as hawks. My father and mother would go out hunting on them every weekend, and they'd always come back with deer or elk or buffaloes.

"And that's how it was, and how it had been for many hundreds of years, because my father was only the latest in a long, long line of kings that stretched back as far as anybody could remember. Portraits of the earlier kings filled the longest hallway in the palace, and that didn't even include the earliest kings who didn't have their portraits painted.

"But then came the Cataclysm, and it all got swept away. Earthquakes knocked down half the palace; floods wiped out some villages; other villages just vanished and in their place were monsters and weird buildings and all kinds of other things.

"By the time I was born a few years later, the only people left in the palace were my parents and a single servant—a fat old maid named Nanette. Everyone else was either dead or they'd run away. Nanette usually watched over me since my parents were away a lot, trying to drive the monsters from their land."

"Just the two of them?" Maggie asked in surprise.

"Oh, it wasn't a big deal. They were both great warriors. They battled orcs, trolls, zombies, even a huge black dragon named Klax, and they won every battle. Which isn't to say things never went badly for them on their monster hunts. Once when I was six, they didn't come back by nightfall like they normally did. Nanette and I waited and waited, listening at the window for the hoofbeats of my parents' horses coming up the path, and eventually it got really late, later than I'd ever been up before, and they still weren't back. I was so worried I couldn't stop crying. Nanette kept telling me to hush up and that they'd be back soon enough, they'd just had a little trouble, nothing they hadn't dealt with before. But I didn't believe it, and I could tell *she* didn't believe it either. We both thought they were dead or badly injured, but neither of us wanted to say so because saying it out loud would somehow make it more real.

"A little after dawn the next morning they staggered into the ruins of the palace, exhausted and hungry and looking like they'd been dragged the length of the forest. Their clothes were dirty and torn, and their hair was all wild and knotted, and they were covered head to toe with bruises and scratches.

"When Nanette asked them what happened, my father's eyes got all sad and distant and he said, 'The horses are dead. They were killed by a monster made of clay. We destroyed the monster, but...' And then he just shrugged and he and my mother headed off to their rooms.

"I cried like crazy. I loved those horses. Knowing I'd never see them again made me bawl so hard for so long that Nanette got mad and yelled that I should just shut my mouth and be thankful that my parents got back okay.

"I shut up. It was more because Nanette got mad than because of what she said. I'd never seen her so furious, with her face bright red and spit on her lips. I realized later that the whole thing had shaken *her* up too; that was why she acted like that.

"Nanette died when I was seven, and that stunned me even more than the deaths of the horses. She'd been around all my life. I couldn't imagine things without her. Neither could my parents, and they were so grateful for all she'd done that when we buried her my father read 'The Greatest Never Fall,' a funeral sermon that had been reserved for only the bravest knights of Eridia.

"Since Nanette wasn't around to look after me anymore, my parents didn't go out monster hunting very much after that. But that was okay, because monsters and bandits had pretty much stopped coming through our lands. I guess my parents' years of patrolling had done the job, and the bad guys were scared of entering Eridia…"

Dagmar's face darkened, and her shoulders slumped under the burden of sudden, unwelcome memories.

"Except the Marauders," she said in a toneless voice. "They showed up about a month ago. My parents tried to fight them off, but there were too many of them. My dad managed to take down three of them before they got him, but…"

"Three?" Adam said. "Even with my inhuman strength and speed, I slew only a pair of them in Sweetwater. You father must have been a great warrior indeed."

"Yeah. He was. They both were. They…" She lowered her head and took a deep shaky breath.

"It's okay," Bob said. "You don't need to tell us any more."

She looked up, eyes wet with unshed tears but also

bright and intense with conviction. "No, I should. I have to."

"What? But—"

"I know stuff. Don't you see? They took me prisoner. I mean, I escaped after a day, but I was in their camp. I watched them. I heard what they said. I know more about them than any of you." She paused, considered, then looked at Kukalukl. "Well, except you."

"Yes," the jaguar said. "I can tell them, if you prefer."

She shook her head. "I think this is something I need to do."

"It would provide catharsis," Freud said.

"Cuh-what?"

"He means that talking about it'll help get rid of some of the pain you've got bottled up," Bob said.

"Actually," Freud said, "to be strictly accurate—"

"Isn't necessary. Now pipe down." He motioned for Dagmar to talk.

She looked at them, her expression scared and uncertain, as if they were a jury about to render a verdict on her. Seemingly unconsciously, she laid a hand on Kukalukl's head and stroked his fur. He started purring.

She took a deep breath and said, "After they killed my parents, they threw me into one of their big wheeled cage-things. I don't know if you've seem 'em, but they're like horse-drawn cages with a section attached for a driver to sit on."

Maggie nodded. "They employed such vehicles when they attacked Sweetwater."

"Yeah, so anyway, we traveled all day. I think we were heading west, but I didn't really pay all that much attention. I was pretty out of it. The road was really bumpy and the only thing to sit on was the floor of the cage, which was just bare metal, so by the time we stopped that evening I felt like one big bruise.

"The Marauders made camp in a meadow with a little stream at one end. They parked all the cages in a line near the stream, and mine ended up right next to the only other cage with something in it. That something was a big black lump. It looked like some kind of animal, but its fur was caked with so much dried blood, I doubted it was even alive.

"Anyway, while the Marauders cooked and ate their dinner, which was mostly just meat and ale, I listened to their talk, and I learned stuff about them. I mean, it's not a lot. It might not help much, but…" She shrugged.

"Just tell us whatever you can," Maggie said.

"Well, they talked a little bit about their base. They've got lots of horses and machines of some sort there, and it sounds like it's really big—much bigger than they actually need—like maybe an old factory or something."

Adam turned to Freud. "Did you see any buildings of that sort on your way east?"

"No," Freud said. "At least not in the area in question. But the area is so heavily forested that I could have passed within a couple hundred feet of a large building without noticing."

"How many Marauders were in the group who captured you?" Maggie asked Dagmar.

Dagmar frowned in concentration as she counted with her fingers, the count slowing down the farther it progressed. When she reached a dozen, the count paused for a long time. She lowered her hands.

"Twelve, I think. But there *had* been fifteen, counting the three my dad killed."

"Actually," Kukalukl interjected, "there were originally sixteen. I slashed the throat of one when they captured me."

"Ah," Bob said with a nod. "I figured you had to be the blood-streaked lump."

"Goodness, did you deduce that all by yourself?"

Bob opened his mouth to tell the jaguar not to be so needlessly rude, then realized it would be a waste of breath and just shook his head.

"Do you think you can describe the Marauders you saw?" Adam said to Dagmar. "Their names, their traits, what weapons they used, and so forth?"

"Um, I think so." She hadn't caught all their names but was able to describe them well enough to reveal that all but two had been among those who attacked Sweetwater, which gave Adam and the others hope that the gangs' membership wasn't as large as everyone believed. Perhaps it was only rumor-fed fear that made them seem so numerous.

"I learned some stuff about their leader too," Dagmar said. "It's someone they call M or Big M, and they're all scared to death of the guy. In fact, at one point I heard Schweeliski and Skippy whispering near my cage. Schweeliski had done something with one of their female captives—some sex thing, I guess—and now he was scared out of his wits the boss would find out, because they're not allowed to do stuff like that without permission. Skippy told him that no one'd tell on him, but that he'd better make sure he never did it again. I don't think it made Schweeliski feel any better. I mean, I could actually see his hands shaking as he walked off.

"Oh, and another thing I learned is the leader's got an advisor everyone makes fun of because of some problem with tics or spasms or epilepsy or something. They kept calling him Twitchy." She shrugged. "I guess this isn't really too much help, is it?"

"Even the tiniest scraps of knowledge are invaluable,"

Adam said. "When going into an unknown situation, the things that will prove to be important are likewise unknown."

"I guess..." she said dubiously.

"So how did you manage to escape?" Maggie asked.

"Oh, that was easy. Well...it wasn't exactly *easy*, but it was simple. I waited till everyone was asleep—and they were really deeply asleep; they'd all had so much ale you could probably get drunk just by sniffing 'em—then I just squeezed out through the bars of the cage."

Adam shook his head in disbelief. "If the cage in question was of the same construction as the ones we saw in Sweetwater, I am amazed that even one as diminutive as yourself could fit through those bars."

She blinked at him for a second, then looked at Kukalukl.

"It means 'little,'" he said.

"Oh! Well, yeah. Like I said, it wasn't exactly easy. The worst part was getting my head through the bars. I mean, I could squeeze the rest of me through okay, but my head was just a teensy bit too wide to fit. I tried to force it through, but it hurt so bad I had to stop. It felt like my skull was gonna crack open.

"I was about to give up in despair when I had a brainstorm. They'd given me a bowl of meat for dinner, but even though I was starving I hardly ate any of it. I mean, I tried, but it just made me nauseous. It was all greasy, and it was so underdone it squirted blood the moment you touched it.

"But it turned out that was a good thing, because after sitting there for a while, the bottom of the bowl was a stew of blood and grease, and what I did—and I know this is disgusting, and I was literally gagging as I did it, but it worked—what I did was I smeared this gunk in the bowl all over my head so it'd be slippery enough to get through the bars. Even then, it almost wasn't enough. My head stuck again. I had to pull and pull, and it hurt so much I nearly started screaming. But just then—pop!—I was through."

"It was really quite an impressive display of moxie," Kukalukl said. "I watched the whole thing."

"Yeah, I didn't even realize he'd gotten up until I turned to go and saw the biggest cat I'd ever seen standing there in the next cage over, watching me. I nearly yelped out loud, I was so surprised.

"I was even more surprised when he whispered, 'Hello there, young human. My name is Kukalukl. It's nice to meet you.' I just gawked at him. I mean, I'd never met a talking animal before."

"'Talking animal'?" Kukalukl said. "I'm a *god.*"

"Well, yeah, but I didn't know that *then.*" To the others, she said: "Anyway, he asked me if I'd be so kind as to let him out of the cage. He was very polite and well-spoken and everything, but I didn't think letting him out would be such a good idea because he was, you know, a big meat-eating cat. And I told him that. I asked him, 'How do I know you won't just eat me if I let you out?' That was when he told me he was a god and that if I helped him he'd be in my debt. He swore on his own name he wouldn't hurt me in any way and promised he'd help me and protect me for the rest of my life. He told me that whatever happened, he would always stand by me."

"Wow," Bob said. "That's a pretty nice deal."

"Yeah, well, it sounded good, but for all I knew he might have been a big liar or something. On the other hand, if he wasn't, I couldn't just leave him there to be tortured.

"I guess it was pretty obvious I wasn't sure what to do, because after a few seconds, he suggested I just go get the key and toss it into the cage, and he'd let himself out."

"With no opposable thumbs?" Bob asked Kukalukl.

"It can be done," the jaguar said, "given enough time and ingenuity."

"I thought it over and decided it was a good compromise," Dagmar said. "That way, while he was trying to unlock the cage, I could just run as fast as I could and hopefully be far away by the time he was done.

"I went and got the key—they kept the key to each cage in a leather pouch on a hook above the driver's seat—and came back, being real careful not to make any noise. I mean, all the Marauders were dead asleep, and some of them were snoring loud enough to shatter stone, but I didn't want to take any chances.

"When I got back to the cage door, I stopped and stared at him through the bars for a moment. And then…" She fell silent and gazed off at the pale shape of the *boko zafendo* in the distance.

"I don't know exactly why I did it," she said in a low, musing voice. "I mean, I guess I figured that if he was telling the truth then that'd be fantastic. And if he wasn't…well, I didn't really have much left at that point, you know? My parents were dead. I was in the middle of nowhere with no place to go. I mean, I really had nothing to lose.

"So being real quiet, I unlocked the door and pushed it open. And then I looked at him in there and…well…"

"She ran away," Kukalukl said. "Just turned and fled like a startled deer."

Dagmar shrugged. "I got scared all of a sudden. I mean, there weren't any bars there any more between me and this huge mass of claws and teeth and muscles. I don't know. I guess it seems kind of babyish after everything else…"

"Not at all," Maggie said. "I think you have proven

yourself to be astonishingly brave for one so young."

"Thanks."

"So, what, did you follow her?" Bob asked Kukalukl.

"Of course. But only after I gathered a few items of human food from the Marauders' camp since I assumed (correctly) that she didn't know much about foraging for herself.

"Tracking her down was a simple matter. Though she tried to mask her trail by entering the stream and wading along it for over a mile—a display of cleverness rare in a mortal so young—the lingering stench of the putrid meat-drippings she'd smeared all over her head made her trail impossible to miss."

"And I'd even tried to rinse it off in the stream," Dagmar said.

"Yes, well, with a scent as foul as that, you'd need nothing less than a thermonuclear device to eradicate it so quickly.

"At any rate, I finally found her huddling under the drooping boughs of a huge evergreen. She had traveled over three miles on foot in the middle of the night, leaving me unsure which to admire more: her courage or her endurance. It took me a while to figure out how best to reveal myself to her without sending her screaming for the far side of the world."

Dagmar rolled her eyes. "Yeah, and his great idea was to call out, 'Hello, young human. I brought you some food. And please rest assured, I have no intention of eating you.'"

"I thought it would suffice."

"Well, I guess it wasn't as bad as it could have been, but it was still really scary to hear that deep rumbly cat voice come out of the darkness like that. I didn't answer right away; I guess I thought maybe he was trying to trick me into revealing myself or something. But then he started telling me what food he'd brought. There was bread and potatoes and some Beef Jerky and stuff. And that did the trick. I mean, yeah, I was scared and everything, but I was also starving. It felt like my stomach was trying to eat itself. Plus, I realized that he must know exactly where I was—if he couldn't see me, he could certainly smell me—and if he'd really wanted to eat me, he would've done it already. Of course, even then, it crossed my mind he might be just toying with me, the way cats play with mice. But like I said, I was so hungry I had to take the chance.

"So I crawled out and…" She shrugged. "He wasn't lying. There was a bag full of food, and I ate so much I thought my stomach would burst. And he didn't try to eat me or anything. He was going to protect me and stand by me, like he'd said." She ruffled the fur on Kukalukl's head, eyes shining with sudden, irrepressible tears. "I wasn't alone." She lowered her head, embarrassed.

"That is lovely," Maggie said.

Dagmar shrugged again without looking up.

"Not to be rude," Freud said, "but how is it that a 'god' found himself in a Marauder cage in the first place?"

Kukalukl huffed. "I was wondering when that would come up. And I'm not at all surprised you would be the one to mention it. The sad fact is, being so brilliant and powerful, I sometimes get…lax. My vigilance wavers. Such was the case here. I'd been traveling through an overgrown region for most of the day—lots of vines and bushes and high weeds everywhere. A narrow path wound through it all, covered here and there by thick mats of old leaves. For a while I'd been detecting the scents of men and a couple of creatures I didn't recognize, but since so few beings pose a threat to me, I saw no reason to be concerned.

"Alas, one of the mats of leaves had been quite artfully arranged to conceal a snare, which I stepped into. I later learned the Marauders had been hoping to trap some creature called the Serpicon—whatever that was—and caught me purely by accident. Ah, well. At least I had the satisfaction of killing one of the odious twits as they were trying to get me into the cage."

"The battle must have been fierce, considering the extent your injuries," Adam said.

"Injuries? Oh, you mean when Dagmar first saw me. Actually, the injuries I sustained during my capture were long gone. After all, three days had passed since then, and in that amount of time I can recuperate from practically anything. No, the wounds Dagmar described were born of the Marauders' cretinous sadism. At first they were reluctant to harm me beyond what was necessary to get me into the cage, being under orders to capture 'rare and remarkable beasts,' preferably whole and unharmed."

"What on earth for?" Maggie asked.

"I never found out. Perhaps their leader had plans for a petting zoo. At any rate, when they discovered that my injuries had healed overnight, they saw a new outlet for their cruelty and decided to conduct further 'tests' of my healing powers. And when those injuries, much worse than the first batch, healed nearly as quickly, they did it again the next night, this time ratcheting up the barbarism even more. They pierced me with spears, they burned me with torches, they threw knives at me to see who could get them to stick in my flesh. This time the damage was so severe that I was still healing the next afternoon, when they imprisoned Dagmar. You know the rest, and I am bored with talking."

Bob shook his head. "So the two of you decided to go after the Marauders all by yourselves, huh?"

"Well, why not?" Dagmar asked in a defensive tone. "Somebody had to. And I certainly wasn't gonna leave my parents unavenged, especially now that I had a god on my side."

Bob spread his hands, palms out. "Oh, hey, I'm not saying it was a bad idea or anything. Frankly I think it's gutsy as heck. I doubt most people would even consider it."

"Thanks," she said, wriggling a little with satisfaction as if someone were scratching her back. "Anyway, it's nothing to worry about now; with all of us together, we should be able to deal with the Marauders, no problem."

Bob forced a smile. He glanced at Maggie and saw the same troubled look in her eyes that he was trying to mask in his own, a look born of the belief that Dagmar was being overly optimistic and that dealing with the Marauders would prove far more difficult than any of them could possibly imagine.

Chapter 7

The Badlands

1

They resumed their journey at dawn the next morning and in a little under an hour had crossed the band of trees to the shattered lands beyond.

The terrain was as Bob had described: a vast expanse of rocky ground rent by zigzagging fissures and pocked with deep pits. Barely visible on the horizon were trees and grassy hills.

"Which way should we go?" Adam asked Freud. "You said you could retrace your path."

"Yes, but I shall have to find my exact point of egress from this maze." He turned his head from side to side, then said, "I believe I exited farther north."

They bore north along the edge of the rocky land. After fifteen minutes they came to a weathered wooden sign, merely a painted board nailed to an old broomstick, which read:

Welcome to the Badlands!
Assholes Go In…But They Don't Come Out!

To emphasize the point, a yellowed skull was stuck to the end of the broomstick.

"Lovely," said Maggie.

They walked on. After another twenty minutes, Freud stopped.

"Here we are," he said, pointing to a swath of stony ground that looked exactly like every other swath of stony ground they had seen so far.

"How can you tell?" asked Bob.

"The configuration of the landscape perfectly matches the image stored in my memory."

"What, like photographic recall?"

"In a manner of speaking. I retain every scrap of sensory input until I choose to delete it, which fortunately I have not yet done in this instance."

"Well, then," said Adam, "let us proceed. You, Freud, shall lead the way."

"Of course."

They set out across the Badlands. At first their course was relatively straight, with only occasional and very short detours around small fissures or pits, and some members of the group began to wonder if they needed Freud's help at all.

But after half an hour, the pits grew large enough to swallow houses, and the fissures widened and lengthened and interconnected, necessitating longer, more extensive detours. And eventually the detours ceased to be detours at all as the winding, convoluted path they followed around the rifts and holes and heaps of rock became the only route there was.

They soon found themselves navigating narrow stone walkways with thirty-foot chasms on either side. Against her better judgment, Maggie glanced down into one of these chasms. At its bottom, the dry, white bones of some small animal lay atop a heap of jagged rocks that had eroded from the edges of the walkway above. She drew in a sharp breath as she imagined the seemingly solid rock beneath her feet suddenly crumbling. Would she scream as she fell? Would there be time? Or would her body be dashed to pieces on the stones below before she even knew what was happening?

"Don't look down," Bob said behind her. "It just makes it more difficult."

She gave a nervous laugh. "Easier said than done. When you stand at a precipice, some perverse portion of the mind always insists on taking a look."

"Yeah. It's too bad we can't all do what Dagmar's doing." He jerked his thumb over his shoulder at Dagmar, who rode upon Kukalukl's back, sitting up straight and proud like a queen on parade. It was only upon noticing the way she was gripping fistfuls of skin and hair on Kukalukl's shoulders that Maggie realized the girl's erect posture and upwardly tilted chin were the result of her not wanting to even risk looking down into the sheer drops on either side.

They walked on. Hours passed. The day, already hot, grew hotter as the sun reached its zenith and hung there for what seemed like an abnormally long time. Sweat poured from those who could sweat. Those who drank learned to keep their water bottles near at hand. The chasms grew deeper and deeper until their bottoms were lost in shadow. At times the faint gurgle of water could be heard in the depths. Once, Adam thought he saw a quick, furtive movement in the chasm-shadows, but when he raised a hand to shield the sun from his eyes and took a closer look, he saw nothing that might have accounted for it.

Shortly after the sun began its descent, they stopped to eat at a widening of the path just large enough for them to sit in a tight circle. Freud estimated that they were slightly more than halfway across the Badlands.

"I fail to see how the Marauders can cross this treacherous terrain," Maggie said between bites of pork. She gestured at the stony ground beneath her. "These paths are far too narrow for their wagons."

"Logically, there are only two possibilities," Freud said. "They must either take a route wholly different from ours, or they detour around the Badlands altogether."

"I hope it is the latter," Adam said. "For by cutting straight across the Badlands while they travel far out of the way, we shall considerably reduce the lead they have on us."

Maggie glanced at Kukalukl, who lay next to Dagmar, not eating.

"Are you certain you do not want any of our food?" she said. "I know it is not to your liking, but you must be very hungry.

"Thank you, but I would rather wait," he said. "It will only be a few more hours. I have gone without food far longer than this. Three months, once."

"I find that difficult to believe," said Freud.

"It doesn't matter *what* you believe. It happened. The biology of gods is nothing like those of other creatures."

"But you still require fuel of some kind to power your body. Every action you perform burns energy, and you must replenish that energy when it gets depleted."

Kukalukl sighed. "Has it not occurred to you—and given your mental capacity, I'm sure it hasn't—that perhaps gods can store greater amounts of energy than other creatures, or that they have some means of generating energy that does not require food?"

"I suppose that is possible. Though outwardly you appear identical to the average jaguar (except for your melanism, of course), there may be aspects to your internal biology that are completely different. Even granting that, however, your being a god is a logical impossibility."

Kukalukl, who had laid his chin on his crossed paws with

sleepy satisfaction when Freud conceded his earlier point, now jerked upright.

"What in my own holy name do you mean by *that?*"

"Gods are, by definition, supernatural—that is, they transcend nature. But that is simply not possible. Everything must conform to natural laws; otherwise that thing could not exist in nature."

"How can you say that?" said Maggie. "Surely all the strange and fantastical things we have seen and heard since the Cataclysm prove you wrong. And then there is the fact of the Cataclysm itself…"

"Ah, but simply because something seems strange and fantastical to us does not mean it lacks a perfectly natural explanation. Most of the strange creatures I have seen are simply life-forms with which I am unfamiliar. And the rest, such as the obelisk-bound entity that animated the stuffed animals, are most likely life-forms governed by natural laws of which we are simply ignorant at this time. Gods, by definition, are beings who transcend nature, and I do not believe such a thing is possible."

Kukalukl snorted. "You sound exactly like the Incas in the empire's latter days. Most of them had ceased to believe in gods, having abandoned religion in favor of science and technology. On the rare occasions I allowed them to encounter me they insisted that while I resembled the old mythological creature called Kukalukl, I was probably just a biological oddity—a jaguar blessed with the power of speech and unusual longevity thanks to some ill-defined genetic quirk."

"How can you be certain they were wrong?" Freud said.

"It would be quite a remarkable 'genetic quirk' that enables a life as long as mine. As I told the priests, I recall the days when the Inca were a few dozen frightened savages living in crude huts on the banks of a river."

"That proves nothing in itself. The real question is: How did you come to be? What was your origin?"

"I regret to inform you (well, not really) that the question is unanswerable, for I have no origin, at least not in the sense you mean. The curtain of oblivion rose, and there I was, hunting in the jungle. That is all."

"Or perhaps like all beings your earliest memories have dissipated over time. Given your longevity, it seems reasonable to conclude that the passing years have worn away more of your memories than those of shorter-lived beings, perhaps eradicating all recollection of childhood altogether."

"I think your screws need tightening."

Adam stood up. "We should continue. Your debate, while interesting, is best saved for later. If the Marauders did indeed circle around the Badlands, I would hate to fritter away the opportunity to gain ground on our quarry."

"Of course," said Freud.

Half an hour later, as they made their way along a particularly narrow walkway that formed a tight loop much like a backward C, Freud stopped so abruptly that Adam nearly ran into him.

"What is the problem?" Adam asked. "Why have you stopped?"

"Did you hear that sound?"

"What sound?"

"I heard something large and heavy moving down there," Freud said, indicating the shadow-floored chasm to their right, which, being on the outer side of the C, extended also in front of and behind them. Beyond that, it branched off in dozens of different directions.

As she peered into this abyss, Maggie couldn't help but feel uneasy at the way so many of the chasms had joined together into one sprawling totality. It was even possible that the paths they traveled were not solid all the way down, but contained tunnels that further linked the chasms. Why, the Badlands could really be a vast sunless underworld and the paths they walked merely its riven roof.

Despite the afternoon heat, she shivered.

"There!" said Freud. "I heard it again. Did you?"

Adam frowned. "I heard...*something.*"

"As did I," Kukalukl called from the rear of the line. "It sounded like something heavy sliding against the rocks below."

"I thought you said you saw no living things in these lands," Adam said to Freud, anger rising in his voice. He wasn't angry so much at the robot as at the thought that they might be slowed down yet again.

"I did say that," Freud said. "And it was the truth. I saw and heard no living thing during my crossing of this land, save a few birds overhead."

"*That* means a lot, coming from an unliving, inedible, and completely uninteresting being," said Kukalukl. "Whatever lives down there probably just wisely ignored you."

"Enough talking," said Adam. "We don't have—"

With a wavering hiss, a gigantic head rose up from the chasm ahead of them at the top of the backward C they stood on.

The head was the size of a compact car and reminded Bob of some of the weird, stylized dragons he had seen pictures of in Chinese restaurants. The eggplant-purple face had huge round yellow eyes with small, tight pupils in the centers. Where eyebrows would have been on a man were rows of short, fleshy tentacles that were the same purple as the face at their bases but faded to light pink at their tips. Instead of hair it sported a long, tangled mass of some whitish substance reminiscent of Spanish moss. If it had ears, they were not visible. Its nose was wide and black and spongy-looking like a dog's, and directly below it were two long tentacles that curved out to well beyond the sides of the head like the world's biggest waxed mustache. Rather than lightening to pink like the eyebrow-tentacles, these remained deep purple until their final third, at which point yellowish patches appeared, giving the ends of the tentacles a bruised look. Below the bases of these two tentacles was a wide mouth filled with teeth as long and sharp as butcher's knives. Its chin was a mass of wiry pale-pink worm-like tentacles. The head sat atop another pale-pink tentacle, this one as thick as Adam's torso.

The creature regarded them for a moment, its purple face glistening in the sun like the skin of a grape, its various tentacles waving gently like seaweed.

"Well well, look at you, little walkers," it said in a soft, hissing voice reminiscent of sand slithering down the side of a dune.

"Hello," said Granite. He had already pulled on his cowl and was ready to fight, but figured he should give diplomacy a shot first. "We're just passing through."

The creature's head darted forward for a better look at Granite. Its tire-sized eyes looked him up and down.

"Passing through? Why here, why now, why why?"

"Well, we're on a sort of quest…"

"Ohoho!" it cried with a roll of its eyes. "Questers they are. Fools, more like, yes yes. Only Marauders allowed here. No visitors. No questers. No no." The head trembled slightly as it made a rasping sound that might have been laughter.

"We want no trouble," said Adam. "We merely wished to pass through this land unmolested."

"Why why? To seek the Marauders, I imagine. Silly silly. Think you that the path is unguarded? Or think that Centivert sleeps?"

"Are you Centivert, then?"

"Centivert we are, yes."

"'We'?" said Maggie.

"We," said a deeper but equally snaky voice from behind them. They whirled and saw that a second head identical to the first had risen up from the chasm at the base of the backward C.

"Yes yes, we, us," the second head said. It cocked itself atop its tentacle-stalk and added, "I say eat them."

"Yes yes," said a third voice, which was a little shriller than the first two, and a third head rose up at the midpoint of the C's outer curve.

"Oh, dear," said Freud. "We appear to be surrounded."

The third head snickered. "Surrounded, it says. Surrounded, yes. We are all around. We are everywhere."

"Please let us pass through in peace," said Granite. "We mean you no harm."

"Mean harm to the Marauders, you do, yes yes. No good, no good. Very bad, that is."

"Very bad," agreed the first head.

"Bad bad, bad bad," said the second. "Eat them we must. Enemies they are."

"Gulp their flesh," said the third. "Crunch their bones."

"Am I to take it that you are the Marauders' watchdog?" said Kukalukl.

All three heads reared back as if smacked.

"Watchdog?" spat the second. "No no no, no watchdog, no watchdog. They help us, you see. They feed us old slaves, tired and worn-out ones, yes yes. In exchange we do what we love best, what we would do anyway."

"Eat little men and women, yes yes yes," said the third. "Little walkers, slow walkers, who intrude in our lands. Hate them we do."

"We do," echoed the second.

"Hate Marauders too," said the first with a sly smile. "But they help us for now."

"For now," said the third. "But one day eat *them* as well, we will."

"I think you shall find that eating us will not be as easy as you imagine," said Adam. He was getting sick of the childish chattering of these three creatures. If there was going to be a fight—and it certainly looked inevitable now—he wanted to get it over with. Anna couldn't be helped if they stood here listening to these babbling monsters all day.

The three heads rose up on their respective tentacles and looked at each other over the group.

"Ooh, tough and ruthless, they are," said the first with mock terror. "Quaking I am! Quaking!

"I believe the yellow man is wrong," said the second. "Eating them *will* be easy." His round eyes fixed on Freud. "Except the metal one, perhaps."

"Yes yes," said the third. "Hard to digest he would be, we suspect. Hard to digest, oh yes, oh yes."

"Crush him, then," said the second. "Enjoy the groan of bending metal. Fun fun."

"None of that will happen," growled Adam. "We will pass through this land or *you* shall be crushed."

He pushed past Freud, nearly knocking him into the chasm on the inner side of the C, and said, "Come, my friends. We will leave these fools to prattle to themselves all day. And if they try to stop us, we will rip the tentacles from their faces."

Lightning fast, the first head swooped down and laid its

pink-tentacled chin on the path in front of Adam. Having no other choice, Adam stopped. His hands balled into fists and his massive frame trembled with anger, then he lunged forward to grab one of the mustache-tentacles and rip it from the creature's face.

Centivert opened its mouth and a long, green-black tongue shot out. Its tip, as thick as a man's head, rammed into Adam's chest and sent him flying backward into Freud, who with a squawk banged to the ground with Adam on top of him.

"No escape, no no no," Centivert said once its tongue had slid back into its mouth. "No escape from Centivert."

"If you are Centivert, who are the other two?" asked Maggie. "If we are to be eaten, I should like to know their names."

All three heads blinked at her, then burst out laughing.

"Others?" said the third head. "Others?"

"We are one, silly walker girl-thing," said the first. "We are Centivert. Only one. Only Centivert."

Intrigued, Kukalukl padded to the edge of the chasm and looked down. Dagmar, who still sat on his back, clapped her hands over her eyes and squealed, "Not so close! Not so close!"

"I see," said Kukalukl, backing away from the edge. "It is indeed one single creature."

"Creature?" said the second head. "We are no creature. We are Centivert. Centivert the magnificent. Centivert the unique."

Freud, whom Adam had helped back on his feet, stopped patting the dust from his casing and swiveled his head around to stare at Centivert.

"I can just make out his body in the darkness below," said Kukalukl. "It fills the bottom of the chasm for as far as

I can see. It is vast and pale with darker blotches upon it. Countless tentacles sprout from its back and sides, but only three have heads. The rest are simply tentacles."

"Yes yes," said the second head. "Three heads we have, yes yes."

"And eat three of you at a time we shall," said the first, its wide mouth curling up in a grin that displayed its long, flesh-slicing teeth.

As it spoke, dozens of pale-pink tentacles as thick as a grown man's thigh shot up from the chasm and darted toward the group.

"Oh, crap," said Kukalukl as one grabbed his right front leg. He tried to pull away, but its grip was too strong, and it dragged him across the dusty rock toward the edge of the chasm. Dagmar started to tumble from his back with a yelp, but another tentacle gracefully snatched her by the right leg and lifted her into the air. She screamed for help.

The moment the tentacles appeared, Granite turned to stone. Several tentacles stopped a foot in front of him and hung there, swaying like hypnotized snakes. When one of them glided forward and prodded his stony body, Granite grabbed it and ripped it in two. The rest drew back out of his reach and resumed hovering and swaying, as if waiting for him to make a move. When Dagmar cried for help, Granite glanced over, saw the danger she was in, and started to race toward her. The tentacles, seeing their opportunity, slid between his feet and tripped him. Before he could get up, five tentacles grabbed him, lifted him, and carried him toward the chasm on the inner side of the C. He tried to break free, but without leverage it was impossible; Centivert's tentacles seemed to be made of solid muscle.

Maggie drew her dagger to defend herself, but while she slashed at the three tentacles waving tauntingly in front her, a fourth snaked in on her left side and seized her around the waist. With a savage growl, she plunged the dagger into the tentacle again and again. Then one of the tentacles that had been in front of her snagged her wrist and twisted, producing a bolt of pain so sharp and sudden she dropped the blade. It clattered to the path, only inches from the chasm.

Adam grabbed the first tentacle that dared approach him, and squeezed it until the pink skin burst and a slightly caustic black fluid squirted out across his hands. A moment later two tentacles grasped his arms from behind and tried to pull them apart and back. Adam resisted their pull with all his might, bared teeth grinding together, the cords in his neck looking as if they were about to rip through his yellow skin.

Freud, the only one the tentacles ignored, stepped up to the first head, put his hands to his hips with a *clank*, and said, "You, sir, are a liar!"

All three heads reared up, eyes wide with outrage, and every tentacle stiffened. Those who had been lifted by the tentacles hung in mid-air like riders on a stalled Ferris wheel.

"What?" howled all three of Centivert's heads, which produced a weird and disconcerting stereophonic effect.

"Little tin man dares to call Centivert a liar?" roared the first head.

"Kill it!" snapped the second.

"Crush it!" hissed the third.

"You claim to be unique," said Freud. "But that is impossible. You must have had parents. All things that live have parents of some kind."

The first head cocked itself slightly, as if trying to see Freud from a different perspective.

"Parents we had, yes yes," it said slowly and doubtfully, suspecting a trick. "But then men came, men on horses, men wearing metal clothes—"

"Paladins!" spat the second head.

"Paladins, yes. Paladins came and slaughtered our parents with lances and swords. But Centivert escaped, oh yes, and later slaughtered the paladins and their old fat king, yes yes. Revenge he had. Sweet revenge."

"I see," said Freud. "And were there no others besides you and your parents? No brothers or sisters? No uncles or cousins? No distant tribes of…erm, whatever breed of creature you are?"

"Last of the line we are. Last of the Wurvelims. The nasty paladins wiped all our kind off the face of the Earth. All but Centivert, who spent lonely decades crisscrossing the world in search of others. But none could be found, and now Centivert avenges himself on the horrible walkers who made him alone. Eats them he does. Mmm, tasty tasty flesh they have."

"Interesting," said Freud. "And are you fully grown?"

The first head gasped in exasperation. "No more questions! Silly tin man talks too much. Now is the time for eating, not talking!"

"Aha! You resist my questioning. You attempt to change the subject. Which means, of course, that you fear to continue this line of discussion."

The heads hissed.

"We fear nothing!" said the first.

"Do not listen to the metal man," the second said to the first. "He is tricksy. Wants us to prove we are not afraid by talking more, giving his friends time to find a way to escape."

"Stalling he is," said the third. "Tricksy tricksy."

"Not at all," said Freud. "I would never be so foolish as to put my hope in such a plan, for given the sheer quantity and strength of your tentacles, there is clearly no way for us to escape unless you allow us to do so."

All three heads stared at him for a moment, then looked at each other.

"Flattering us is he?" said the third head.

"Perhaps..." the second said with uncertainty. "But he tells the truth, yes yes. No escape from our tentacles. None at all."

"True true," said the first.

"I merely wish to understand you better," said Freud. "For I think I can help you with your problem."

"We have no problems!" said the first head.

"We will not fall for your tricks," said the second.

"Want to save your friends you do," said the third. "That is your plan, your intention, your goal."

"I am Freud, Mechanical Analyst Number One," said Freud. "My task is to psychoanalyze those who require it, and I believe that you fall into that category."

The heads blinked at him.

"What does it say?" the first head asked the others. The others merely shook themselves.

"So in the interest of helping you," Freud said, "I ask again: Are you fully grown?"

The first head just stared at him for a second, then nodded slowly.

"Yes," it said. "Fully grown, yes. Of course, of course. Well past our two-hundredth year we are."

"And you possess reproductive organs, do you not?"

All three heads shot upward, neck-tentacles stiffening with fury.

"Of course we do!" roared the first.

"Nasty questions he asks," snarled the second.

"Eat him now," said the third in a surly voice. "Before he mocks us more."

"I am not mocking you at all," said Freud. "I asked the question only because I am unfamiliar with your physiognomy. But now that you have confirmed my suspicions, we have reached the crux of your dilemma."

"Dilemma?" said the first, fury giving way to testy confusion. "What dilemma?"

"We have no dilemma" the third said.

"Of course you do," said Freud. "And I am surprised a creature as intelligent as yourself, and possessing a life-span long enough to afford much sober reflection on such important matters, should have failed to perceive it already. I refer, of course, to your desire to slaughter all life-forms other than yourself."

"That is not a dilemma!" protested the first head.

"Perhaps you do not see it as such, but you must at least concede that it *is* unusual. The killing of other creatures to fulfill one's nutritional requirements is normal, of course. Likewise, revenge-killing, while perhaps not something to be encouraged, is certainly normal, as well. You, however, wish to kill everyone and take great glee at the thought of doing so. I cannot help but wonder as to the origin of this gloating hatred and these murderous urges."

"Our hate is all!" said Centivert's first head. "It is born of itself. Pure and perfect it is." It was trying to sound sure and aloof, but a note of uncertainty quavered in its voice.

"On the contrary," said Freud, "nothing causes itself. Your hatred and your homicidal impulses are clearly the result of something else, something other than your parents' death, for any hatred and lust for vengeance inspired by that event should have been satisfied by the deaths of your parents' killers. No, your hatred has grown into a hatred for all living things. Any sane creature would ask *why.*"

There was a long pause. The heads stared at him in expectation. The members of the group, though still ensnared by the now-immobile tentacles, likewise waited for the answer, their own dilemma temporarily forgotten.

Finally, when it became clear that Freud was waiting for a response, the first head cleared its throat a little and in a tiny voice said, "Why?"

"Because although you are an adult of your species and possess fully functioning genitalia and no doubt possess the urge to mate, you lack an outlet for your sexual impulses. In other words, your libido is blocked. And as so often happens in cases where libidinous energy is denied its natural expression in healthy, live-affirming and life-generating sex, it seeks an outlet in the opposite direction, in the affirmation and generation of *death*. In other words, your lust for life has been transformed into a lust for death, a thanatic urge to destroy those who *can* have sex."

"No no no!" said the first head. "Little metal man lies! He lies lies lies!"

"Lies, yes!" said the third. "We are hatred personified. We need nothing. We need no mates. We are sufficient unto ourself."

The second head, which had remained silent while its fellows raved, now shook itself and said, "No, it...it speaks true. We want a *female*. We want to *maaaate*." It spoke this last sentence in a plaintive whine.

"Shut up shut up shut up!" the first head hissed at the second. "You lie lie lie!"

The third said nothing for a moment. It looked back and forth between the other two heads, then hung itself low and sighed and said, "No, he tells the truth."

"Shut up!"

"It is nothing to be ashamed of," said Freud. "All creatures that live possess libidinous urges, which, if blocked, can lead to all manner of neurotic problems. But I believe your urges need not be blocked at all."

All three heads perked up.

"What?" said the first. "What does the little tin man mean?"

"Let me ask you this: You say you searched the world for a mate, but have you done so since the Cataclysm?"

The first head frowned in bafflement. "What is this Cataclysm?"

"Fifteen years ago the Earth underwent a massive upheaval that reshaped geography and threw all manner of unusual beings together, including many believed mythical or extinct."

"Oh-ho. That explains it. Lately many odd creatures have stumbled into our home. Some are tasty. Others…" It stuck out its long, muscular tongue and made a gagging sound.

"Yes," said Freud. "But do you not see that given these events it is quite possible—almost certain, even—that other Wurvelims are now out there somewhere, and have been for over a decade. While you have lurked here in these dark pits, gnawing on your hatred and bitterness as a dog gnaws a bone, the world has changed all around you."

The first head goggled at Freud in amazement. Then a light of realization dawned, and it glanced sheepishly at the other two.

"Told you we did!" the third shouted at the first. "Told you we should investigate after the shaking of the ground and the lights in the sky. But you said no, we should stay here, the outer world concerned us not."

"How were we to know?" the first whined. "How?"

"It matters not anymore," said the second. "We must now seek out a mate."

"What of our feast?" The tentacles shook the members of the group.

"Surely you would not repay our help by eating us," said Freud. "Besides, you should waste no time in starting your search for a mate. The other Wurvelims have a fifteen-year head start on you. And while the Cataclysm most likely made *some* new Wurvelims appear, it might not have made *many* appear. You really should find the females before the competition does."

The three heads shot upright and roared in unison: "No!"

"We will brook no competition!" said the first.

"None!" agreed the second.

"Oh, stop yammering and hurry up," the third snapped at the other two.

Without warning, Centivert dropped everyone, and its many heads and tentacles zipped into the chasm. As the members of the group sat up, rubbing bruised elbows and shins, there was a thick scuffing sound, as of some large, soft mass sliding against hard rock. The sound came first from the entire length of the chasm on the outer edge of the C, then only from the eastern end, then from far away, and then it was gone.

"Is everyone all right?" Adam asked in a gruff voice. Despite the question, he did not look around at anyone. He just sat on the stony ground, staring off into the distance.

"Yes," said Kukalukl. "Aside, of course, from the mortification of having been rescued by the most pathetic robot ever created."

"Speak for yourself," said Maggie. "I thought he performed most admirably."

"Agreed," said Bob, tucking his cowl back under the collar of his shirt. "I mean, I still think psychoanalysis is a bunch of hooey, but it sure got us out of one heck of a jam just now."

"Very true," said Adam. He stood up and patted the rock dust from his clothes. His expression was blank and unreadable, even to Maggie. "But as long as everyone is all right, we should resume our journey immediately. Anna is still imperiled, and to be honest, I am not as certain that Centivert will not return as I would like to be."

"Oh, he will not return," said Freud. "At least not until he finds a mate. One must never underestimate the strength of the libido, especially one that has been repressed for centuries."

Adam eyed the robot in silence for a moment, then waved his arm at the path and said, "Lead on."

With that, they resumed their trek across the Badlands, which with Centivert gone surely weren't all that bad anymore. It took them three tedious hours to reach the wooded hills on the opposite side. By then the sun was low in the west.

"We must be almost there," Adam said, staring up at the hilltop directly ahead of them.

"Indeed," said Freud. "The area in which I saw horse-tracks and other signs of nearby habitation is approximately a three-hour walk due west."

"That close?" said Bob.

Adam continued staring at the hilltop for a moment, then said, "We should rest up there amid the trees tonight. And we should try to rest well, because tomorrow…"

With the unspoken remainder of that sentence hanging over them like a thundercloud, the sextet made their way up the hill.

Chapter 8

The Storage Tank

1

Amid the trees atop the hill was a clearing, in the center of which sat a twenty-foot-high white metal cylindrical structure that reminded Bob of an oil storage tank. A ladder extended up its side to its flat, railing-encircled top. On the side of the tank were symbols or letters in an unknown language, consisting of circles and bars arranged in various configurations. The tank also sported crude spray-painted slogans, like "NO FUTURE" and "Marauders Uber Alles!" Everyone stared at the graffiti in uneasy silence, the inane writing proving beyond all doubt that the journey was nearly over.

Bob climbed the ladder and found that someone—probably the same someones who had sprayed the slogans—had torn off a hatch in the tank's roof. Peering inside, he discovered that whatever the tank had contained had long since evaporated or been siphoned off; only an unidentifiable dark gummy residue remained on the inner walls and floor. From the interior rose a faint scent that reminded Bob of honey.

They set up camp on the west side of the clearing, about halfway between the tank and the woods. As the others got the fire going and prepared dinner, Maggie walked to the treeline and stared west. She couldn't see anything except the trees stretching away downhill into darkness, but she knew

Anna was out there somewhere. Based on what Dagmar had told them, the Marauders weren't supposed to mistreat the female hostages without their leader's approval, which meant that Anna should be safe until the Marauders got back to their base. But even if the Marauders had gone around the Badlands, they had still had a head start and could be at their base already. Yes, Maggie and the others were probably only a few hours' walk away and would, if all went well, arrive there sometime tomorrow morning, but a lot could happen to Anna between now and then. And they couldn't simply charge inside when they got there; they would have to spend more valuable time reconnoitering the area and devising a plan to infiltrate the base to rescue Anna and the other hostages.

Bob appeared beside her. "Food's almost ready."

She nodded.

"You okay?" he asked.

She shook her head. "I was thinking about tomorrow, and hoping Anna will be all right until then."

He placed a hand on her back and said, "She'll be fine. Things have a way of working out okay in the end." The hand began stroking her back in small gentle arcs.

She cocked an eyebrow. "Like they did for the places we came from? Like they did for all your vanished friends?"

He recoiled a little, his hand falling from her back. She was both relieved and saddened to feel it go.

"Whoa, hey, did I do something wrong?" he said. The surprise on his face made him look very young, almost like a little boy.

"No, it…I just…" She sighed. "I do not think such physical contact is appropriate right now. My sister is in peril. Now is not the time for…such things."

"You're right. I'm sorry. That was…I was out of line. I

apologize."

"Besides," she added quickly, before she could stop herself, "if all goes well, there will be time for such things afterward."

"Oh." He smiled. "I see. That seems fair."

Despite herself, she found herself smiling too. She had never met anyone whose smile was so infectious. "I am glad you agree."

"Oh, I sure do agree."

They smiled at each other for a moment. Then she thought of Anna again, of tomorrow, and her smile faded. His faded in response, and together they looked sadly out at the trees and the darkness.

2

At the campfire, Adam knelt in front of the pot containing tonight's meal: a stew containing potatoes, carrots, various herbs, and chunks of a rabbit that Kukalukl had caught for them (he kept a second for himself to eat raw). Adam dragged a ladle through the stew every few seconds but seemed barely aware of it. His eyes were distant, unfocused. His mouth was a thin downturned line.

"Is anything wrong?" Kukalukl said behind him.

Adam whirled in surprise. He hadn't heard the jaguar approach.

"I thought you were helping Dagmar with her sleeping bag."

"I was. That's done. Now I'm here, asking you if anything is wrong. You've been acting annoyingly morose and taciturn ever since the climax of our encounter with that ludicrous Centivert."

"I'm fine."

"Don't lie."

Adam glared at him.

"And don't get all huffy either," Kukalukl said. "Let me guess: What the usually vapid robot said about Centivert skulking in darkness and gnawing its misery—or whatever poetic gibberish he spouted—that particular gibberish hit home with you, didn't it?"

Adam regarded the jaguar in cold silence for a moment, then frowned down the stew as he resumed stirring it.

"Perhaps," Adam said.

"I don't know why. You're clearly not like that any longer."

The ladle paused in mid-stir, then continued its circuit around the pot.

"Perhaps not," said Adam. "But…"

"You can't help but wonder if all of this—the team, the camaraderie, the acceptance of others—is just a pleasant dream from which you'll soon awaken to find yourself back in dark, Arctic isolation."

Adam looked at him sharply, but said nothing.

"If it's any consolation, I doubt it will come to that, considering how your 'cousin' and Mr. Pollyanna have been carrying on. I suspect you three, at least, will stay together."

"Yes, but…"

"But?"

Adam shook his head. "Never mind."

Kukalukl sighed in irritation. "Very well, if you won't talk about it, I will. Unlike the others, you are functionally immortal, and you foresee the day when your cousins and Mr. Rocks-for-brains pass on, leaving you alone once again. Is that it?"

Adam stared at him with his mouth agape. Then he realized he shouldn't be so surprised; the jaguar had been alive thousands of times longer than the rest of them and in that time had no doubt developed an understanding of human nature far beyond that of any sage, scientist, or mechanical analyst.

"It's the burden of immortality, I'm afraid," Kukalukl said. "Sometimes you're alone, sometimes you're not. The only thing that doesn't change is the fact that everything changes. My advice is, make the most of companionship while you have it and cherish the memories of it when you don't. Personally, I prefer not to form lasting relationships with mortals, since they don't exist very long. It would be like a human trying to establish a meaningful relationship with a mayfly. But if that is indeed what you wish to do, I would recommend utilizing your companions' favorable attitudes toward you to help patch up your image problems with the larger public. If you can sway public opinion in your favor, you'll be able to cultivate new companions more easily when the old ones die off."

"Is that not rather manipulative?"

"Definitely. Doesn't make it any less valid, though."

Adam considered this at some length. "No," he said finally. "I guess it doesn't."

"Also, in this world there are plenty of other immortals. You might want to make friends with them, if you can."

Adam's heart began to race with excitement. "You have encountered others? How many are there?"

"I've met nearly a dozen in the last fifteen years, not counting robots."

"I see." Adam swallowed, not really wanting to ask the question he was about to ask, for it would bare aspects of his inner world he preferred to leave dark. But he couldn't *not* ask.

"And were many of these immortals, um…of the female persuasion?"

Kukalukl burst out laughing.

"Ah," he said. "I was wondering if your creator had supplied you with a sex-drive."

Adam scowled at him. "Answer my question or not, as you wish. But do not make light of me."

Kukalukl rolled his eyes. "Touchy touchy. Well, in answer to your question: Yes, since the Cataclysm I have met several female immortals. One was an old crone, and another was a bird, but the rest were rather comely in human terms. At least I think they were. I admit I'm no expert on the pulchritude of hairless primates."

Adam said nothing. He was too busy contemplating the existence of beautiful immortal women. Then he reflected that there were probably beautiful immortal men, too, and that the beautiful immortal women would no doubt prefer the company of beautiful immortal men to that of indescribably ugly immortal men.

When Kukalukl saw the sudden darkening of Adam's formerly brightening expression, he knew immediately what the problem was.

"Bear in mind," he said, "that immortals tend to be less concerned with physical beauty, being all too painfully aware of its transience."

"I hope you are right."

"I am, of course. Anyway, I hope I've helped alleviate your gloominess."

Adam nodded. "You have. I thank you. You have given me much to consider. Especially the question of why you are suddenly so concerned for my welfare. Could it be that I am not the only immortal in this group who secretly yearns for companionship?"

"Actually, I'm afraid you are. I'm helping you only because we go into battle tomorrow, and if you're all broody and distracted you won't be as effective as you could be, and that lowered effectiveness could get Dagmar hurt."

Adam grunted. "I should have known. I must say, though, that your protectiveness toward Dagmar is quite surprising, and possibly even hypocritical, given your dim view of relationships with mortals."

"I explained all that. She helped me get out of an unpleasant situation when she didn't have to. I owe her a debt."

"But to protect her for her whole life…"

The jaguar breathed out a small laugh. "I see you haven't really grasped the whole immortality thing. But that's to be expected; you're still relatively new at this. See, I've lived for tens of thousands of years and expect to live for tens of thousands more, at least. Her whole life will be, at most, a hundred years or so. What is that to me? My accompanying her for a hundred years is no different than a mortal spending an afternoon with someone."

Adam felt a chill run down his spine. He had never before understood the yawning gulfs of time immortal beings faced. He wasn't sure he completely understood them even now. He suspected it was the sort of thing you had to experience to truly understand.

"Incidentally," said Kukalukl, "I think your disgusting stew is about to boil over."

"Damn." With a pair of leather mitts, Adam lifted the pot off the fire before the rising line of froth could reach the lip and then ladled the stew into bowls, all the while ruminating on the inexorable flow of time, and how the mountains they saw the day before they reached the Badlands would eventually erode and be gone, and how strange and terrible it would be to live long enough to see the flat plain where those mountains had once stood.

He decided he didn't want to think about it too much.

3

Midway through dinner, Bob cleared his throat and said, "I was thinking: After all this is over, I think we, or at least some of us, should hunt down Centivert. I mean, his blocked libido and thanatic urges and all that other Freudian claptrap might've made him kill people more often than he would have normally, but his diet's still people. And let's face it, we're responsible for getting him to leave his hidey-hole and prowl the world in search of a mate. If he eats people, that'll be on us."

Adam looked up at Granite in horror. "I…had not thought of that."

"Nor I," said Maggie, equally horrified.

"*I* had," said Kukalukl. "I was wondering when the rest of you would catch up."

"Why didn't you say anything earlier?" Adam said, glaring at the jaguar.

"Would it have mattered? We don't have the time to pursue him right now. We're on a tight schedule, remember?"

Adam glared at him a moment longer, then sighed and resumed eating his stew. "Yes, I remember."

"We'll have to hunt him down," said Bob.

"We shall," said Adam.

Maggie glanced up at him, surprised not only by his words but by the conviction behind them. She smiled. Before this journey, Adam never would have concerned himself with such a thing. Bob's influence—indeed the influence of all of them—had had a profound effect on the previously brooding, self-absorbed patchwork man. It was a change long overdue.

"We'll need to plan it out really well," said Bob. "I mean, we nearly got our butts handed to us by that thing. If it hadn't been for Freud here, most of us probably would've been eaten."

"Yes," Maggie agreed. She bent around to look at Freud. "Thank you again. Your odd knowledge-system saved us all."

"Oh, I was merely doing what I am programmed to do," said Freud. "And I do not mean merely the performance of psychoanalysis on Centivert. As I explained before, I am programmed never to allow injury to human life. In this case, analyzing Centivert permitted me not only to help him but also to prevent him from injuring any of you."

"Well, you did a remarkable job," Maggie said. "Your aid has been invaluable. Prior to this, the only robots we encountered were wild, dangerous things. It is a shame there are not more like you." She cocked her head. "Or are there? I recall your saying when we met that there were eleven other mechanical analysts. Did any of them also survive the Cataclysm?"

"Some did, yes. Others, alas, were less fortunate. Erickson and Skinner were destroyed during the Cataclysm, when part of the Hall of Psychology's roof collapsed. Maslow was destroyed soon thereafter, hurled off a cliff during an altercation with some robophobes. Several others were unaccounted for in the wake of the Cataclysm. They may have ceased to exist, as did so many other things, or they may have wandered off on their own before any of the rest of us could look for them. I do not know. At this point I can confirm the survival of only myself, Jung, Leary, and Adler, though Adler suffered a grievous head injury from falling debris during the Cataclysm, which left him with various motor-control problems, the most noticeable being a compulsion to turn his head to the side every few seconds to the accompaniment of a most distracting clicking sound. His memory circuits were badly affected as well; in the midst of conversation he would quote random lines from his namesake's works. A roboticist could have fixed him in less than a day, but in the wake of the Cataclysm none could be found. It is all quite tragic.

"Where did the other surviving analysts get to?" Bob asked. "I mean, why didn't you guys stay together?"

"We tried. For a short while we traveled about and tried to aid whomever we could, both physically and psychologically. In our own time, most humans were too well-adjusted to require psychological help, and my fellow analysts and I were merely an amusing and educational diversion. But the Cataclysm threw together humans and other species from a wide range of sociocultural conditions, many of which had fostered various neuroses, thus rendering us of great utility. Alas, when we set to work counseling them, we discovered that our theories and methods of treatment were so wildly different that we were, in effect, working against each other. I, for one, did not believe that Jung's or Leary's theories were in any way scientifically valid and so I felt compelled to re-treat those they had already supposedly treated. When they learned of this, they felt compelled to undo *my* treatment—to re-re-treat them, as it were—and so on and so on until the humans gave up on us altogether.

"In the end we decided it was best to split up and go our separate ways. Each of us went in a different direction so as to avoid the possibility of future interaction. I headed southeast and offered the benefits of psychoanalysis to any I considered in need of it, though in most cases those people refused to listen, and that is their right. Indeed, I cannot say I blame them, for in this new world where survival itself is ever in doubt, men have little time to concern themselves with psychological matters, though psychoanalysis would, I am convinced, make their lives vastly better were they to embrace it."

"I find it fascinating that the mind can be studied and understood in the same manner as the body," Maggie said. "Someday I would love to hear more about these various theories of human psychology."

"It would be my pleasure to so enlighten you. Though I warn you, my fellow analysts' theories are in nearly all cases quite crude and unscientific."

"No doubt."

"We should get some sleep," Adam said, gazing up at the moon, which shone white and round through the lattice-work of slender branches above them.

"Yeah," said Bob. He glanced west. "We've got a big day tomorrow."

Chapter 9

Yoyodyne (Outside)

1

Morning dawned warm and clear, with not a single cloud to blot the blue of the sky. Everyone had rested well despite fretting as they settled down to sleep that their anxieties about the following day would keep them awake. So fretting, they had all dozed off.

They ate breakfast in silence. Then, after Maggie treated Dagmar's shoulder-wound—the only injury from their battle in Happyvale that still required attention—they set off on the last leg of their journey.

Before they had gone more than a mile, they began to see evidence they were in the Marauders' territory: Trampled foliage, hoof-prints, empty chewing tobacco tins, a shoebox containing locks of hair, a splintered wooden shield.

"We're almost there," Dagmar said in a soft voice as she stopped to stare at a heap of burnt books, their pages reduced to brittle black flakes. She sounded scared, but also amazed, as if unable to believe she had actually come this far.

Maggie wondered if Dagmar were having second thoughts about confronting the Marauders, so she said, "You could stay here, if you wish."

Dagmar shot her an angry glance. "No, I do *not* wish. I will do exactly what I set out to do."

Head held high, she brushed past Maggie and marched

off after the others.

Maggie watched her with concern. This really wasn't the best place for an eleven-year-old girl. But could anyone dissuade her from her task at this point? If she had come this far, she would almost certainly go the rest of the way, even if it was only to her doom.

Then again, Dagmar had the protection of a god with claws sharp enough to gut a rhino. And she had the rest of the group to watch out for her, too. But what if that wasn't enough? They didn't know all of the Marauders or their capabilities, and more worryingly, the impending confrontation would occur in the Marauders' own lair, which would give the Marauders the advantage. And then there was the Marauders' mysterious leader, about whom virtually nothing was known. Anyone who could inspire the loyalty of a band of criminals and psychopaths and keep them united and organized had to be someone either incredibly powerful or incredibly intelligent. Or, worse, both.

Over the next two hours the horse-tracks grew more numerous and well-defined, and the trash reached epidemic proportions. Graffiti appeared with increasing frequency until every available surface—tree trunks, rocks, the sides of a burned-out armored vehicle—was covered with profanity and belligerent slogans and crude pictures of genitalia.

"We have arrived in the region I passed through on my way east," Freud said. "As I said before, I did not see any actual settlements to which I might direct you, so my guidance must unfortunately end here."

"You have done well," Adam said. "Thank you."

After ten minutes of walking in a direction slightly north of Freud's original route, they came upon a wide dirt path covered in hoof-prints.

Kukalukl sniffed the path and said, "This is it. They've

used this path recently. Probably sometime last night."

They followed the path northwest, staying just within the shelter of the woods so that if anyone appeared, they could quickly duck out of sight.

Soon the trees thinned out enough for them to see glimpses of a gray building up ahead.

They slunk forward and after another minute came to the edge of the woods. They peeked out from behind a screen of branches and bushes at what lay beyond.

After descending a short slope, the dirt path met up with a crumbling asphalt road that ran north-south. To the south the road vanished around a bend a quarter of a mile away. To the north it extended for about three hundred feet, crossed a creek via a short rusting bridge, continued on for another hundred feet, then came to a gateway in a chain-link fence topped with razor-wire. A guardhouse, through the grime-bleared windows of which two figures could be seen sitting, stood in front of the fence on the western side of the road. The original gate had been taken down and was now propped against the inside of the fence to the west of the guardhouse. In its place a line of plywood boards with nails driven through them had been laid across the road, points up.

Beyond the fence, the road ballooned into a huge parking lot that fronted a far-flung network of interconnected buildings, among which were several enormous hangars. On a stretch of withered brown grass between the parking lot and the foremost building, which was clearly the main office, stood a sign that read, "Yoyodyne Propulsion Systems."

Every wall in sight bore more of the same rude graffiti they had been seeing all day. The largest graffito extended across the front of the main office in black letters five feet high and declared: "Marauders Rule!" In the parking lot, a few dozen smashed and burned automobiles sat like black islands amid a sea of garbage and horse droppings.

"I wish we had binoculars," said Granite, squinting at the guardhouse. He had already whisked off his civilian clothes, pulled on his cowl, and slipped on his gloves and cape. He was ready for some heavy-duty super-heroing. "It'd be nice to see who's in there, and how many there are."

"Before we do anything," said Adam, "we should make a circuit of the complex. That way we can get an idea of its size and also see if we can discover anything of value. For all we know, there might be unprotected entrances somewhere."

"I wouldn't count on it, but you're right: We should do a little reconnaissance before anything else."

After stowing all unnecessary items in the heart of a thicket of shrubs—stealth and swiftness were paramount now; cookware and the like would just slow them down and risk making noise—they retreated fifty feet into the woods and bore north. They had to retreat even farther when they came to the creek, for crossing it that close to Yoyodyne would bring them into view of the guardhouse. Luckily the creek bent south not far to the east, and there they waded across it, then headed back northwest until they could once again see the walls of Yoyodyne through the trees.

Twenty minutes later, with the front of the complex far behind them, Kukalukl and Freud stopped simultaneously.

"Do you hear that?" said Kukalukl.

"That is precisely what I was going to say," Freud said.

Adam listened. Off in the distance were voices and metallic clanks and clatters.

"It's coming from Yoyodyne," said Granite.

Maggie crept to the very edge of the line of tall bushes that shielded them from view from Yoyodyne and looked out through a narrow gap.

"See anything?" whispered Granite.

For a moment she didn't respond. Then, without turning around, she beckoned them to come and see.

They did, each of them finding a small gap in the bushes they could peep out of.

The chain-link fence that surrounded the complex was directly on the other side of the bushes, and through its mesh they had a view of a trio of hangars that jutted like piers from the side of the complex. The corrugated steel door of the middle hangar was open, and a peculiar car had been wheeled out onto the tarmac in front of the hangar, about two hundred feet from where Adam and the others stood.

The car was long and low and made of unpainted metal, its front tapering almost to a point, its rear thick and boxy and almost entirely taken up by a wire cage containing a blocky engine with a yellow-and-black radiation symbol on its side. The whole contraption had a rough, unfinished look, like something cobbled together in an eccentric inventor's home workshop.

Five Marauders stood deep in discussion next to the car. One of them, a tall man in a black trench coat and a plastic owl mask, held a fat booklet. A sixth Marauder, his back to Adam and the others, squatted at the rear of the car and examined the engine.

After a moment, the man in the owl mask said something to the Marauder squatting beside the engine.

The squatter stood up, revealing himself to be Tricky Dick, and said something with a shrug. Then he waited while the others consulted the booklet.

"Do you recognize that contraption?" Adam asked Granite.

"Nope. It looks like some kind of prototype jet-car or

something, but I can't really say for sure. They're probably trying to figure how to get it running."

Adam grunted. "Let them tinker. We must move on."

They did. Ten minutes later they reached the northeast corner of Yoyodyne and got their first look at the back of the complex. There, sequestered from view from the road, stood a cluster of dingy, factory-like buildings, their metal sides rusty and soot-streaked. One of them had collapsed, and half buried in the girders and heaps of plaster stood several massive objects that might have been turbines, as well as an industrial metal vat with a staircase winding up around it and a walkway encircling its top. A crusty green substance covered its sides as if it had overflowed at some point. A faint haze of steam rose from its interior.

Here at the rear of the complex, they could no longer follow the fence, for it stood at the top of a wooded slope too steep to climb. They had to walk along the base of the slope, about twenty feet back from the fence and the edge of the woods.

After five minutes of walking they came to a halt. A three-foot-wide metal pipe extended from the slope to their left. From its end a milky, pale-green liquid dripped slowly and steadily into a ten-foot-wide pool that stretched from the bottom of the slope beneath the pipe to the depths of the woods due north.

But a pool of what? The viscous green fluid shone here and there with rainbow colors like an oil slick, every plant within ten feet of it was dead, and the stench rising from it made everyone gag. It smelled as if someone had mixed raw sewage with several dozen industrial chemicals.

Across the pool of ooze was a clearing, on the south side of which stood a mound of twenty-foot-long logs and on the north a wooden shack, a row of corroded metal barrels, and a rusty riding mower. The bare dirt in the clearing was littered with footprints, most of them centering on the pile of logs, which looked as if they had been cut within the last month or two.

"Ugh, can we hurry up?" said Dagmar. It was hard to understand her because she had cupped her hands over her nose and mouth.

"Yes," Adam said. "We *should* hurry up. The Marauders clearly frequent this area, so we mustn't tarry."

A half-submerged log lay across the pool at its narrowest point. It had clearly been meant to be used as a bridge, but the log looked so rotten and spongy everyone was afraid it would either fall apart like wet bread the moment anyone set foot on it, or simply lack the density to support anyone's full body weight.

Maggie headed north along the edge of the ooze-pool to see if the muck thinned out farther away from the pipe, but the opposite was true: After three hundred feet, it widened into a vast fetid lagoon in which dead trees stood like fence-posts in a flooded field.

"It is impassable," she said when she returned. "We shall have to try the log."

Adam stepped forward. "I will go first."

"Not if you have a brain, you won't," Kukalukl said.

Adam glared at him, jaw clenching so hard its ends bulged like eggs beneath his skin. He wanted to grab the obnoxious jaguar, god or not, and squeeze his throat until no more insults would ever come through it.

Then he remembered strangling young William Frankenstein, and his rage vanished, leaving only sick guilt in its wake. Even after all these years of isolation and reflection and, lately, making friends, his first reaction to criticism was anger. Yes, Kukalukl had been unnecessarily rude, but a man—no, a *creature*—of Adam's size and strength should always make anger a last resort. Sometimes bettering himself seemed an impossible task.

Still, he knew what Granite would say to that: Something to the effect of, "You sure as heck won't get anywhere if you don't at least try."

He unclenched his jaw and said, "What do you mean?"

"I mean that you are the heaviest of us all. It's possible that the log will support the weights of those lighter than you, and thus it would make more sense to let those others go first."

"And if you are correct, it will crumble or sink while I am on it, and I will end up flailing about in that reeking muck."

"It's unlikely to sink all at once, which means you'll be able to hurry across before it goes under completely. But if you go first and that happens, then *you* will make it across but no one else will."

Adam considered this for a moment, then nodded. "You are correct."

"Whoa," said Dagmar. "I'm the lightest, but there's no frickin' way I'm going first."

"I wouldn't let you go first anyway," said Kukalukl. He looked at Maggie. "How much do you weigh?"

Maggie instinctively glanced at Granite, then berated herself for being so concerned about what a man might think of her body.

She cleared her throat and said, "One hundred and fifty pounds. More or less. I haven't had an opportunity to weigh myself in...well, a long time."

"I see. And if my back is any judge, I'd say Dagmar weighs around seventy-five pounds. And I weigh about two hundred and ten..."

"And I'm about one seventy," said Granite. "At least in

my flesh form. In my stone form I weigh a lot more than even Adam."

"What about you?" Kukalukl asked Freud. "You must weigh quite a bit. Why, the weight of your stupidity alone could probably crush a giant."

"Your childish insults betray a great discomfort with my always-accurate analyses," Freud said. "At any rate, my weight is three hundred and fifty-two pounds, five ounces."

"Wow!" said Granite. "That's pretty heavy."

"Actually, I am considered light for a robot. Earlier robots were constructed of much heavier materials. In those days, a robot my size would have weighed over five hundred pounds."

"I am only around three hundred," said Adam. "It would appear, then, that Freud here is in fact the heaviest among us, and should thus go last."

"Indeed," said Kukalukl.

Dagmar eyed Kukalukl with suspicion. "So, uh, who's going first, then?"

"I am," he said. Before anyone could reply, he turned and dashed across the log. It sank perhaps a half an inch beneath his weight, but that was all.

Upon arriving on the opposite bank, he whirled around and raced back across. This time the log didn't sink at all.

He lay down on the ground next to Dagmar and said, "Get on my back. I will carry you across."

"Um..." She cast a dubious glance at the log.

"Don't worry," he said. "It will hold both our weights. I could tell as I crossed it."

Still looking concerned, she climbed up on his back and lay flat atop him with her arms wrapped around his neck, her eyes squeezed shut, and her nose buried in his fur. Without waiting for anything else, Kukalukl crossed the log once again, this time a little more slowly than before. The log sank a few millimeters, and halfway across a small piece gave way beneath his paw with a squelching sound and plopped into the ooze. So sure-footed was he, though, that he didn't even break stride.

Maggie crossed next, one arm held out for balance, the other pinching her nostrils shut. The log didn't sink in the slightest.

Granite, in his human form, went next. Again, the log remained immobile.

That left Adam and Freud. Adam stared at the log a moment, then turned to the robot.

"Are you sure you want to go last?" he asked.

"It is satisfactory. If you are concerned, please be advised that submersion in that odiferous admixture of liquids will not damage me at all. My casing is water-tight, and I do not breathe or require outside energy as humans do. Thus, I can exist underwater, or under-ooze as the case may be, for an indefinite period."

"That is good, then. Though if you do end up submerged it might prove difficult to pull you out."

"Fear not. There is almost certainly a way out somewhere."

"All right."

Adam took a deep breath and stepped onto the log. It immediately sank an inch and a half, leaving only a narrow strip six inches wide above the ooze. The sudden motion of its sinking threw him off balance, and he had to extend his arms to steady himself. Once steadied, he walked slowly across with no further problems.

When Freud stepped onto the log, it descended with a *glup* until it was entirely submerged and visible only as a wavering phantom under the ooze. The top half of Freud's metal feet were likewise submerged, but he didn't seem to care. He crossed faster than everyone else except Kukalukl, his sense of balance being precisely calibrated and immune to second-guessing.

Just before Freud reached the halfway point, Kukalukl, who had padded forward to investigate the objects in the clearing, suddenly froze, his ears cocked back.

"Uh-oh," he said.

"What is it?" said Granite.

But then he heard it, too—a high-pitched mechanical whine that he knew all too well: the sound of the Annihilator's jetpack.

"Oh, crud," Granite said.

It was impossible to tell where the sound was coming from. The presence of all the trees and of the large, echo-generating buildings nearby distorted the sound so much that not even Kukalukl's predator's senses could determine its point of origin.

Then the Annihilator flew into view above the treetops a few hundred feet to the west. He was headed toward Yoyodyne and didn't appear to have seen them.

"Stay very still," said Kukalukl. "Any movement might—oh, piss."

While Kukalukl had been speaking, the Annihilator idly glanced over and spotted the group. In his surprise he wobbled a bit in mid-air, then veered sharply toward them, his right arm and its wrist blaster extended.

"What is happening?" said Freud as he stepped onto the western bank. Adam stood directly in front of him, blocking his view of the Annihilator. "Is he coming? I cannot see with you—"

The Annihilator fired off a barrage of laser blasts. Most of the shots hit the earth, sending up showers of dirt. One grazed Kukalukl's right foreleg as he moved in front of Dagmar to protect her. Another blew a hole in the side of the riding mower with a flat metallic *plank*. Another struck the side of the shed, making the whole structure shudder.

Then one hit Adam in the right shoulder and sent him staggering backward. He smashed into Freud, who toppled into the ooze with a great splash that sent the noisome fluid spraying Adam and the shore around him.

At that point everyone scattered, racing for the closest shelter. Granite grabbed Maggie and pulled her against the east side of the shed, out of sight of the Annihilator. Ignoring the pain in his leg, Kukalukl gripped Dagmar's shirt between his teeth and yanked her behind the pile of logs. Adam dove into the bushes to his right. A moment later a series of laser blasts shredded the foliage where he had disappeared.

The Annihilator paused, hovering directly above the center of the clearing. He looked to his left at the shed, then to his right at the pile of logs, then ahead and to his left at the bushes into which Adam had disappeared.

He turned toward the shed, arm raised, blaster ready.

After ducking out of sight, Granite and Maggie had slipped around to the rear of the shed, and now Granite took Maggie's arm and nodded at the woods.

"Go," he said. "Hide. You're no match for him. Heck, I don't think *any* of us are a match for him except me. In my stone form, I'm pretty much invulnerable to his lasers and rockets. The rest of you would just get cut to ribbons or blown to bits."

"But—"

"There's no time to debate it. Just get to safety. I won't be able to fight him if I'm worrying about everyone else. Especially you."

One side of her mouth crept up into a smile.

"It sounds as if you have taken a fancy to me."

He grinned. "Well…yeah."

"Then it may please you to know that the feeling is mutual."

She planted a swift kiss on the corner of his mouth.

"I will do as you ask, but be careful. I shall be very cross if you allow yourself to be injured."

"I'll do my best."

She gave him a nod, then dashed into the trees.

The whine of the Annihilator's jetpack grew louder as he flew down the east side of the shed, advancing toward its rear.

"I know you're there, you superheroic pile of shit," he said in his tinny speaker-transmitted voice. "What're you doing hiding like this? You turned all chicken?"

"Not at all," Granite said behind the Annihilator.

The Annihilator spun around in mid-air as smoothly and swiftly as a weather-vane turning in a high wind.

While the Annihilator had been moving down the east side of the shed toward its rear, Granite had raced up along its west side to its front, transforming into stone as he went. Now he stood at the shed's southeast corner, one of the metal barrels hefted above his head. He hurled it at the Annihilator.

The Annihilator flew straight up, but not quite fast enough to avoid the barrel. It clanged into his shins, sending him wobbling away over the top of the shed with a loud cry of "Shit!"

At the same time, claxons started honking in and around Yoyodyne. Doors banged. Men shouted.

Granite ran toward the rear of the shed, hoping to catch up with the Annihilator and take him down before the rest of the Marauders arrived. It looked like their plan to stealth-ily infiltrate the base was kaput. Instead they were facing a big knock-down, drag-out fight. Which was no big deal to him; he was used to stuff like this, and more importantly, he was nigh-invulnerable. But most of the others—Maggie, Dagmar, even Adam—were much too vulnerable for his lik-ing.

As he reached the rear of the shed, Granite heard the Annihilator's jetpack shut off somewhere on the shed's west side. Had he landed? If so, that was unusual. The Annihilator preferred to stay airborne against a more powerful opponent like Granite. Maybe the barrel had damaged his gyros or something.

When Granite stepped around to the west side of the shed, he found the Annihilator standing ten feet away, one arm raised and pointed at him. Granite started to laugh, thinking that the Annihilator intended to shoot him with his wrist-blaster—the old fool might as well be blowing paper straw wrappers at Granite's stony hide—but then he realized the Annihilator wasn't pointing his wrist-blaster at all. He was pointing some kind of high-tech gun…

The Annihilator fired. Granite felt something strike him hard in the chest and heard a sharp *tink* that sounded like a mountaineer driving a piton into a rock-face.

"What…" He looked down. A metal object the size and shape of a fountain pen protruded from the center of his chest. A small red light at its tip blinked rapidly.

"Found a few new toys to play with after the Cataclysm," cried the Annihilator as he dove for cover behind the row of barrels. "It's called an adamantium-tipped mini-shell, fuck-head!"

As Granite grabbed the metal rod, intending to yank it out, it exploded.

The force of the explosion flattened the shed and blew the metal barrels and the Annihilator halfway across the clearing. The worst damage, though, came from the chunks of organic stone that flew in every direction like bullets. The foliage directly behind the shed dissolved in a rain of green confetti. Gaping holes appeared in the sides of the logs, exposing the smooth pale wood within, and thick splinters and chunks of bark showered down on Kukalukl and Dagmar, who lay huddled behind them.

Adam, who had started to advance through the foliage toward the battle between Granite and the Annihilator, felt his skin punctured and torn in dozens of places as tiny rocks hit him like grapeshot. A larger rock the size of a doorknob passed so close to his head he felt the breeze of its passage on his ear.

Not far away, Maggie, who despite Granite's orders had gone only about two hundred feet into the woods and then turned around and crept back toward the clearing, froze when the explosion lit up the clearing and turned the trees ahead of her into silhouettes. An instant later a flea-sized shard of organic stone grazed her cheek, leaving a thin line across it that quickly filled with blood. Another shard, this one a wedge about six inches long, ricocheted off a tree-trunk to her left, leaving behind a deep gouge, and then thudded to the ground at her feet. She squatted and looked at it, not even aware of the blood that was beginning to trickle down her cheek. It looked like a chunk of regular stone, but she knew it wasn't.

"Oh, no," she whispered. She shook her head back and forth in denial. Several strands of hair struck her blood-streaked cheek and stuck there. "No."

Adam, too, realized what had happened, and burst from the trees, calling, "Granite! Bob!"

But Granite had been reduced to what could only be called a pile of rubble. By some quirk of the explosion, he was intact from the shoulders up, a hideous bust. But beneath and around the bust were only chunks of stone, most no larger than a baseball. Clouds of gray smoke floated over the scene like listless ghosts.

"Bob!" Adam raced forward, barely registering the shell-shocked Annihilator, who was struggling to climb out from underneath the heap of barrels he had found himself under.

When Adam reached Granite, his vision was blurry with tears and his ears were still ringing from the explosion, so it took him a moment to realize that Granite's face was moving and that he was talking.

"You're alive!" he cried, gripping the "bust" by its cracked, crumbling shoulders.

Granite's eyes roved back and forth across Adam's face, apparently unable to fix on one spot for more than a moment.

"Not...for much longer," Granite said. He winced as if struck by great pain. "Boy, I...I sure walked right into that one, duh-didn't I?"

"We can fix you," Adam said, his desire for this to be true so strong that it seemed for a moment it *was* true. "We can—we can piece you back together or—or—"

Granite gave him a rueful smile. "You know that's not...not true."

"But—"

"Take care of Maggie. She's a great girl. I wish..." That rueful smile flashed again, followed by another wince of pain. "Just remember one thing—a hero's a hero even if everyone calls him a villain. It's a guy's actions that count, not...not the labels."

He gasped and his head started to drop backward. Had he been a normal man, his head would have lolled brokenly; instead, as his head descended, his stone body lost its pliability and turned hard and stiff like real stone. As this happened he choked out three final words: "Be...a...hero..." Then there was a faint sound like ice cracking, and all animation left the stone, leaving him nothing more than a shattered statue.

"No!" Adam roared, rage quickly replacing grief. Rage was easier. Rage was a way of putting off dealing with things.

He shot to his feet and whirled around to face the Annihilator, who had just finished dragging himself out from under the heap of barrels.

"Don't—" the Annihilator said and started to raise the gun he had shot Granite with, but it was too late. Adam had already leaped with his long, strong legs, covering the ten feet between them as if it were a single step.

Adam slammed into the Annihilator and pinned him to the ground with one knee on his abdomen. The Annihilator tried to raise the gun again, but Adam smacked it out of his hand. It spun away and vanished into the pool of ooze with a thick *blup*.

"Wretched little man!" snarled Adam. He drove one huge fist into the Annihilator's helmet. It emitted a dull *clonk*, and inside it the Annihilator made a noise like "Guh." Adam hit him with his other fist. This time one of the helmet's sharp corners dug a furrow in his knuckle, but his fury was so great he didn't even notice.

"Fuck!" screamed the Annihilator. "Stop it!"

Adam ignored him and continued pounding on the helmet, a never-ending stream of screams and curses pouring from his throat. His absorption in pounding the crap out of the Annihilator, as well as all the noise he was making, prevented him from seeing or hearing the approach of a group of Marauders from the west. At the head of this group raced the Grottle, shovel in hand, a crazed, homicidal grin on its yellow face.

Maggie saw them, though. After the explosion, she had made her way back toward the clearing, dreading the awful sight she knew awaited her there. When the trees parted and the clearing came into view, she first saw Adam leaping upon the Annihilator, then her eyes fell upon Granite's head and shoulders resting atop the pile of rubble that had been his body.

She drew in a breath, though whether to sob or to scream or to offer Granite's remains some sad last words she never got a chance to discover, for just then the Grottle came racing into the clearing.

"Adam!" she shouted.

He didn't hear her. He just continued pummeling the Annihilator. The Grottle skidded to a halt behind him and raised the shovel, ready to lop off Adam's head.

Maggie snatched a rock from the ground—a piece of Granite, she saw with sorrow, though she was sure he would approve of how she planned to use it—and hurled it at the Grottle at the exact moment it started to bring the shovel down.

As she watched the rock sail toward its target, she thought for sure that she had thrown it too late or too wide, that she had failed and could now only watch helplessly as Adam met his doom.

But no, it struck the Grottle in the side of the neck. The Grottle's resultant flinch threw the shovel off course: Instead of decapitating Adam, its flat edge whacked him in the side of the head hard enough to knock him unconscious. He collapsed atop the likewise unconscious Annihilator.

Lips drawn back in a silent snarl, the Grottle turned, saw Maggie, and pointed its shovel at her.

Skippy and Oscar, who had just zipped into the clearing on their hoverboards, saw where the Grottle was pointing and hooked a sharp left straight toward Maggie.

"Leave the cooz to us!" Oscar said with a leer as they zoomed toward her. "We owe her one." He and his partner pulled out long knives that glinted silver in the sun.

Maggie spun around and ran.

Meanwhile half a dozen more Marauders streamed into the clearing and stopped in a semicircle around the Grottle as it pulled Adam's limp body off the Annihilator so it could decapitate Adam without injuring its fellow Marauder. The Grottle raised its shovel. The Marauders cheered, eyes bright with blood-lust.

With a growl, Kukalukl streaked down from the top of the log-pile and smashed into the Grottle, knocking it to the dirt. Kukalukl clamped his teeth on the Grottle's left arm and raked his claws down the Grottle's belly and thighs. Green blood poured from the gashes and pooled in the dirt.

The Grottle just grinned. As it tried to pull its arm from Kukalukl's teeth, it used its free hand to punch Kukalukl in the face again and again and again. Soon blood was pouring from the jaguar's ear and nose and mouth, his left eye had a reddish cast, and some of his fangs had fallen out and lay on the ground like bloody white thorns. Instead of letting go, Kukalukl bit down harder than ever, bit until his teeth were buried to the gums in the Grottle's flesh and his mouth was filled with green blood that tasted strangely of lead.

Only then did he jerk his head back, narrowly avoiding the Grottle's umpteenth punch. He did not, however, open his mouth as he did so, and a large chunk of the Grottle's flesh came away in his mouth with a wet ripping sound.

Before the Grottle could react, Kukalukl spat out the chunk of flesh and clamped his fangs on the Grottle's arm once more. Now glaring with mute rage, the Grottle curled its lips back from its blotchy teeth and resumed punching the side of Kukalukl's face.

Till now the other Marauders had been content merely to cheer the Grottle on. Now, however, with the clock ticking and the outcome of the battle still uncertain, Tricky Dick decided to sway things in his fellow Marauder's favor. As Kukalukl dug his claws deep into the Grottle's left thigh, ready to kick backward hard enough to slit the Grottle's leg open right down to the muscle, Tricky Dick darted forward and kicked the jaguar square in the ribs. It threw Kukalukl off-balance for only a second, but a second was all the Grottle needed to hurl the big cat off his chest.

By the time the Grottle shot to his feet, Kukalukl had already righted himself and now stood crouched and ready to pounce. Tricky Dick crept up behind him and got ready to kick him in the haunches, hoping to distract him long enough for the Grottle to make its move. It worked, but not in the way he had intended, for Kukalukl heard him approaching and, planting his forepaws firmly in dirt, lashed backward with his hindpaws, his long claws fully extended.

There was a tearing sound as the claws tore through Dick's shirt and belly, followed by a slick slithery sound and a thud as greasy loops of his intestines tumbled out of his torso and onto the ground.

"That...that's not mine, man!" shrieked Dick. "I'm not fuckin' dead! I'm...I'm..." With that, he sank to the ground, dead.

By then the Grottle had sprung forward to take advantage of Kukalukl's momentary distraction. The angle was wrong for decapitation, so instead it swung its shovel like a golfer teeing off and struck the underside of Kukalukl's chin with the flat side.

Kukalukl flew up and back, blood and broken fangs shooting from his mouth, and landed atop the slimy heap of Tricky Dick's intestines. As soon as the Grottle saw where Kukalukl was going land, it leaped so as to land in the same spot a fraction of a second after Kukalukl did.

Kukalukl saw the Grottle coming but was too off-balance to twist out of the way in time, so five hundred pounds of Grottle slammed into his chest. His ribcage shattered. Blood geysered from his mouth.

As the Marauders whooped and cheered, the Grottle raised its shovel in both hands, pointed end down, like a vampire slayer about to stake a vampire, and drove it straight into Kukalukl's neck with a thick wet *shuck*.

"No!" screamed Dagmar, who had been peeking out from behind the pile of logs despite Kukalukl's orders to stay out of sight.

She raced forward to help Kukalukl, but Droke grabbed her arm and pulled her to him in a bear hug. She screamed and punched and kicked at his leathery skin, but it did no good. He only grinned at her blows, revealing his thick fangs.

Kukalukl's forepaws scrabbled at the handle of the shovel as the Grottle placed one foot upon the blade's back edge and pushed it farther and farther into the jaguar's throat. Blood bubbled out around the blade and puddled on the ground. Kukalukl's scrabbles degenerated into spasms, then feeble twitches.

The Grottle gave one final push and with a crack the shovel tore through the vertebrae and the skin on the back of the neck, and Kukalukl's head tumbled to the side.

Dagmar screamed and screamed, her red face streaked

with tears and snot. She wriggled to break free of Droke's grasp, but Droke squeezed his arms tighter and tighter around her chest until her screams trailed off into gasps and wheezes.

The Grottle pulled the shovel from the gory mess on the ground and turned to Adam's limp form. Grinning, it raised the shovel.

"Hold on!" said the Annihilator. During the battle he had regained consciousness and struggled to his feet, grunting and muttering profanities all the while. Now he stood upright, palm held out.

The Grottle stopped, frowning. It looked from Adam to the Annihilator to Adam again like a hungry dog who isn't being allowed to eat the food in his bowl.

The Annihilator switched off the speaker on his helmet, turned away from the crowd in the clearing, and held a conversation with someone on a private channel. At one point he glanced over his shoulder at the others, then at the woods, then shook his head.

Throughout it all, Dagmar watched him and the other Marauders—more had entered the clearing after the melee started and over a dozen of them now stood there waiting for the Annihilator to finish his conversation—her eyes sometimes filling with hatred, sometimes with disgust, but most of all with despair, as if she knew the mission was over and they had failed, and now the Marauders could do whatever they wanted. She did not, however, look at Kukalukl's still, bloody form. If she did, she would start screaming again and probably wouldn't stop until she went mad. "I will always stand by you," he had said. And that was how it was supposed to be. It wasn't supposed to end like this.

Finally the Annihilator turned back to the others and

switched his helmet speaker back on.

"M wants 'em. Tie up the big guy and blindfold both him and the girl. We're gonna lock 'em up for now."

He looked around the clearing. "Dump the bodies in the gunk," he said, gesturing at the ooze. "Especially the big cat. I doubt he can heal from something like this, but I don't want to take any chances. If he *can,* the gunk should dissolve his flesh faster than it can grow back. That stuff'll strip the grease off a wop."

"Vhat about de udder vun?" asked Klaus von Klaus. "De twin girl."

The Annihilator looked out at the woods. "Skippy and Oscar went after her. They should get the job done. But just in case, why don't you stay here and keep an eye out for her in case she manages to dodge 'em and returns to the clearing."

"Vhy me?" whined Klaus.

"'Cause you brought it up," he said.

"Sheisse."

"Now everyone get to work!"

They started rolling the corpses into the ooze. Schweeliski grabbed the bust of Granite and was about to throw it in along with everything else when the Annihilator snatched it from his hands.

"Not that one," he said. "I want that one for myself. That's my trophy. It's—"

"You're all going to die," said Dagmar.

The Annihilator turned to her. "What did you say?"

She flashed a smile so cold and hateful that a few Marauders stirred uncomfortably and looked away. "I said, 'You're all going to die.' You don't think you can do what you did and go unpunished, do you?"

The Annihilator chuckled. "And how are we going to

die, exactly? You gonna drown us in your tears?"

"You haven't caught us all yet, have you? And I escaped from you once before, didn't I? You have no idea what you're dealing with."

He snorted in contempt. "I'm dealing with a couple of beaten-down losers from the look of it." To Droke he said, "Gag her. I don't want to hear any more of her shit."

The Annihilator turned away and gazed into the woods. Despite his bravado, doubt gnawed his mind. The little girl was right: They *hadn't* caught them all yet. And Skippy and Oscar *were* taking too long. They should have been back already. What the hell was keeping them?

2

Half a mile north of the clearing, Maggie hunkered down behind a tree trunk and listened for the whir of hoverboards, the whir that in just ten minutes she had come to fear and hate more than anything she had ever known.

Blood flowed from numerous small gashes on her arms and back. That's what she got for underestimating Skippy and Oscar. She had assumed that the maziness of the woods would slow them down, that if they dared go too fast they would end up wrapped around a tree, but she had been wrong. Their reflexes were incredible, and if they hadn't been sociopathic thugs who were trying to kill her, she would have applauded the grace with which they maneuvered among the trees and bushes.

Before she had run fifty feet, they were upon her, their knives out and ready for blood. If she weren't so nimble herself, she would have been dead in no time. As it was, she hadn't managed to avoid their blades entirely, but had merely turned killing blows into minor wounds by twisting away from their knives as they raced by.

That was how the next ten minutes had gone: They would zip past her, slashing at her as they went, and then circle back and do it all over again. Over and over and over again. Ten times. Twenty. Thirty.

Already she was out of breath and nearly out of strength. She doubted if she could keep this up much longer. Fortunately the last time they had sped toward her, she had dove into a thick stand of bushes, waited there until they zoomed past toward the far side of the bushes, and then run back out in the direction she had entered and hidden behind a tree. It wouldn't fool them for long, but she hoped to come up with a plan during this momentary respite.

She took out her dagger and stared at it. She wasn't sure she would be able to get in even a single blow, given their speed and maneuverability and especially their two-pronged assaults. Still, it was better than nothing.

Her eyes fell on a short, thick section of a tree branch that lay a few feet away. As quickly as she could, she shuffled over to it on her knees, grabbed it, and shuffled back behind the tree.

Great, now she had a dagger and a small club against two men with knives and the ability to travel ten times faster than she could. Lucky her.

She heard the approaching whir of the hoverboards and tensed up, trying to draw herself into as small an area as possible so that no part of her would be sticking out on either side of the tree. Branch and dagger clutched tight, she waited.

The whir stopped.

Maggie strained to hear the slightest sound. They couldn't have stopped more than twenty feet from the tree.

Had they seen her? Were they creeping up on her? They must be.

She heard a faint crackle from the other side of the tree, a crackle like a foot treading on a twig.

She waited another two seconds and then launched herself to her left and swept the dagger in a wide arc across the space to the side of the tree.

"Yowp!" cried Skippy as he leaped back out of the way of the blade. His hoverboard was tucked under his arm, and he held his knife out in front of his like a talisman. "She's here!"

She flung the branch at his face. It hit him in the right eye. He shrieked, dropped his hoverboard, and clapped his now-free hand over his face.

Maggie lunged forward, planning to grab the board and race away, but then heard footsteps thumping up fast behind her, so instead she let herself fall to the ground on top of the board. Even as she fell she heard the swish as Oscar's knife sailed through the empty air where her back had been a millisecond earlier.

She somersaulted forward, somehow managing to grab Skippy's board in the process. Clutching it close so she wouldn't lose it, she shot to her feet and started to sprint away.

But Skippy, still with one hand covering his eye and with blood now seeping out between his fingers, grabbed the back of her shirt with his free hand.

"Gotcha now, you—"

She slashed backward with the dagger and felt it hit something thicker than air.

Skippy screamed. His hand released her shirt.

She raced away, no longer certain which direction she was going. North? East? She thought it might be one of those.

Behind her, Oscar said, "Oh, man! Skippy! That *bitch!*"

Got him, she thought.

But then Skippy said, "Forget about it. She's got my fuckin' board! We gotta get her!" His voice wavered a bit. He was clearly in a lot of pain. But still standing, damn it.

She ran faster than she had ever run in her life, ran until her legs felt like rubber and sweat flew off her face and her pulse banged in her ears, ran until she feared her lungs or heart or brain would burst.

And then she skidded to a halt. Before her stretched the lagoon of ooze, an impassable barrier, its oily green surface undulating languidly.

Now that she had stopped, her exhaustion settled upon her like a waterlogged cloak. She sagged against a tree trunk and gulped the lagoon's reeking, polluted miasma into her lungs, thinking no air had ever tasted sweeter. A moment later she heard the whir of Oscar's board approaching from the opposite side of the tree.

She clutched Skippy's hoverboard with both hands, intending to use it as a club against Oscar. But which way would he go around the tree—left or right? If she picked wrong, she was dead; she didn't have the strength to keep this up any longer.

It was best to pick for him, she realized.

When he was about eighty feet away, she hunched slightly and raised the hoverboard over her shoulder, assuming the posture of a baseball player ready to bat. Then she backed up until the tip of the board and her jeans-clad rump poked out from behind the tree just enough for Oscar to see them. After a moment she moved back out of sight, but slowly, as if she were simply shifting her weight. Once she was out of sight, she whirled around and crouched down, hoping that Oscar had seen her and had fallen for her ruse.

The whir grew louder, and Maggie smiled when she realized that the sound was approaching the side of the tree where she had shown herself. Oscar had taken the bait. He thought he was coming up behind her.

When she saw the first flash of movement as Oscar came around the side of the tree, she swung the hoverboard at his shins. He, meanwhile, thrust his knife at the spot where he thought her back would be. It swept through empty air. Her board didn't. It slammed into his legs hard enough to knock him off the board and send him flipping ass-over-head toward the lagoon. His glasses flew off and snapped in half beneath him. His head struck a rock that protruded from the soil like a skull cap. One of his shoes slipped off and vanished into a bush. At the last possible moment before he tumbled into the ooze, he snagged a thick tree-root with one hand and brought himself to a halt, his feet—one shod, one unshod—in the squishy black mud on the very edge of the lagoon. His hoverboard wasn't so lucky: It continued speeding away above the lagoon until it hit the trunk of a dead tree, at which point its motor stopped and it plopped into the ooze and sank out of sight.

Maggie ran forward, dagger drawn, and reached Oscar as he rolled onto his back with a groan. She dropped down with a knee on either side of his head and plunged the dagger hilt-deep into his chest.

Oscar stiffened. His hands rose toward the dagger as if to try to pluck it out, but then they stopped, quivered, and flopped to the ground at his sides.

His eyes met Maggie's.

"Fuh—first rule...of hoverboarding," he said. "Don't lose...yer fuckin' board."

His head fell to one side. His eyes stared at nothing now.

Maggie tore the dagger from his chest, shook the blood off it, and got to her feet.

She had dropped the hoverboard after she hit Oscar with it. Now she staggered over to it and picked it up. As she did so, she heard footsteps approaching.

"Oscar!" called Skippy.

Maggie ducked behind a bush a moment before Skippy stumbled into view. He was drenched in sweat and gasping for breath and had one hand clutched to his side. His shirt below his hand was slick and shiny with blood. She had wounded him pretty badly after all.

When Skippy saw his partner's body lying beside the lagoon, his eyes bulged and his mouth dropped open, his face taking on such a look of horror and grief that Maggie almost felt sorry for him.

Almost.

"Oscar!" Skippy ran forward as well as he could—it was really more like speed-limping—and threw himself to his knees next to Oscar's body. "Oscar!"

Maggie stepped out from behind the brush, raised her dagger, and crept toward Skippy.

She was almost there when Skippy shot to his feet, saying, "Where the fuck is that bitch?"

He started to turn in her direction, knife raised. There was no more time to be stealthy. She sprang forward and swatted his knife-hand with his own hoverboard. The knife pinwheeled away into the underbrush.

"Ow!" Skippy said. "You—" And then Maggie's dagger plunged into his throat, cutting off his words.

He sank to his knees beside Oscar and goggled up at her, his mouth opening and closing as if he were trying to speak. Then his eyes glazed over, and he fell sideways onto Oscar.

Maggie leaned down and pulled her dagger from his throat. Blood gouted from the wound. It subsided after a moment, but it was enough to make Maggie turn away, her hand over her mouth, swallowing back the bile that had risen in her throat.

She hated killing people. She would do it if she had to, of course, and she had had to a number of times since the Cataclysm. But no matter how evil someone was, killing them always had the stink of failure about it. Though whether that failure was hers, the victim's, or creation's, she was never entirely sure.

She knew if she didn't take a short rest to catch her breath she would collapse from exhaustion, so she sat down against a tree trunk and squirmed about until she found a comfortable position. She wanted to just close her eyes and sleep for a year, but she had to check on the others. They could be in danger, or dead. Or, of course, they could have defeated the Marauders they were fighting just as she had.

She listened intently, but heard nothing. How far away was the clearing? How far had she run? A mile? Two? More?

The thought of a two-mile walk back to the clearing made her feel like weeping. But what choice did she have? She couldn't very well fly back, could she?

Wait...

She looked down at the hoverboard in her lap and smiled.

3

It took her less than five minutes to figure out how to work the hoverboard. On the front half of the board were four narrow pressure-sensitive plates spaced around the spot where you placed your foot. Pressing down on these plates determined your direction. The foremost one moved you forward. The ones on the left and right made the board turn in those respective directions. The rear one moved you backward. The front and rear ones also determined your speed. The longer you kept your foot on the forward plate, the faster you'd go. To slow down, you applied pressure to the rear plate. Keep it pressed down long enough and you'd stop. Keep it pressed even longer and you'd start going backward.

There were two similar pressure plates at the rear of the board, one in front of and one behind the place where your other foot went. These controlled the board's height, the front one making it rise, the rear one descend. The length of time you held one down determined how high or low you'd go.

While it took her only a few minutes to learn *how* to work the board, actually mastering the art of using it was another matter entirely. She kept mixing up the pressure plates, or not activating them fast enough. She hit trees. She tumbled into bushes. At times she wondered if the hoverboard would succeed where Skippy and Oscar had failed, and be the death of her.

As she practiced, she bore ever southward, staying close to the edge of the ooze, since she knew it originated next to the clearing. And while the first half of her trip was an endless succession of wipeouts, bruises, scratches, and outpourings of profanity vile enough to shock a pirate, during the second half, as she started to get the hang of it and her foot started manipulating the controls more and more automatically, she found that she was rather enjoying the whole thing—the wind cooling the sweat on her brow, the smooth fluidity of the board's motions as she wove around trees and bushes, and most importantly the joy of having mastered it, of having power over this thing that reduced your own wearying workload. A few times she even laughed out loud as she sped along.

When the ooze-lagoon narrowed to a mere fifteen feet across, indicating she was about three hundred feet from the clearing, she stopped the board and got off. Tucking the board under her arm, she crept forward to the bushes at the edge of the clearing and peered through them.

Klaus von Klaus stood in the center of the clearing, staring west along the path down which the Marauders had come. His arms were crossed, and his mouth was curled up on one side in a sort of irritated, impatient grimace.

Taking a closer look at the clearing, Maggie saw that the heap of organic stone that had been Granite was gone. Only a coating of dust and a few pebbles remained.

Then she saw dark stains on the ground in several places. Obviously blood. But whose? Some of it was green, which meant it probably belonged one of the more physiologically abnormal Marauders, but the rest was red and could be anybody's. And where were the bodies?

She felt a sick sensation in the pit of her stomach as she realized the Marauders must have won the battle. Otherwise, Klaus would not be standing here now, presumably waiting for Skippy and Oscar. She had to find out what had happened to Adam and the others. And the best way to do that, of course, was to ask Klaus.

Looking around, she found the spot where the edge of the woods was closest to Klaus—a spot about twenty feet west of the ruined shed—then made her way there. Next she headed a hundred feet straight back into the woods, hoping all the while that Klaus didn't move too much. She set the hoverboard on the ground and hunted around for a large rock. When she found one—once again, it turned out to be a piece of Bob—she returned to the board, pumped the plate that made it ascend until it was about three feet off the ground, and then put the rock on the forward-acceleration plate.

The board shot forward, gaining more and more speed as it approached the clearing. Dagger drawn, she raced after it.

When the board was about ten feet from the clearing, she faintly heard Klaus's voice over the whir of the board's motor: *"Dere* you are! I vas vondering—"

The board shot through a bush and into the clearing at forty miles an hour, and Klaus's next words turned into a yelp, followed a moment later by a meaty thud. The board's whirring stopped and Klaus screamed.

When Maggie burst into the clearing, Klaus lay on the ground, curled in a fetal position with his hands clamped to his crotch. His face was bright red, and a high-pitched wheeze was coming from his throat like air escaping from a balloon. The hoverboard lay beside him.

He was so immersed in his pain that he didn't realize she was there until she knelt beside him and placed the edge of the dagger to his throat.

"What happened to my friends?" she said.

Klaus's eyes bugged out at the dagger and he cried, "Ahh!"

"Tell me!" she said, pressing the blade down hard enough to break his flesh. A bead of blood appeared on the edge of the metal and gleamed in the mid-afternoon sunlight.

"De big man und de little girl—dey vere taken inside, taken prisoner. M has plans for dem. De stone man got blowed up, und de big katze got his head cut off by de

Grottle."

Maggie gasped at this last bit of information. Even a god would have trouble healing a severed head.

"What about Freud?" she said.

"De zychologist?"

"The robot! What happened to the robot?"

"Vhat robot?"

Maggie wondered what had become of Freud. Now that she thought about it, she didn't recall seeing him during the battle. For that matter, she hadn't seen him since they crossed the log. Where had he gotten to?

"How do I get inside to rescue them?"

Despite the dagger at his throat, Klaus snickered at her. "You can't, silly girl. Every vay inside is guarded by at least two armed men. Und each entry point has an alarm. De men are instructed to set off de alarm at de first moment of trouble. No vun can break in. No vun."

Maggie pondered this and wondered if there was any way she could use Klaus to get inside. Probably not. The Marauders weren't the type to swap hostages, and it seemed like wishful thinking of the worst kind to hope that Klaus might know of some secret entrance unknown to the other Marauders.

Klaus rendered the whole question moot, however, when, seeing that she was absorbed in her thoughts, he drew a small knife from the top of his boot and tried to plunge it into her neck. The instant she saw his arm shooting up toward her she reflexively whisked her dagger across his throat.

He stiffened and gurgled much as Skippy had done. Momentum carried his arm forward, however, and the knife jabbed her left shoulder.

She bit back a scream and rolled away from Klaus's

corpse, one hand clutching her bleeding shoulder. Great. Another knife wound for her collection. And the first aid kit, which had been in Adam's backpack, was probably inside Yoyodyne. At least her thick shirt had kept the knife from penetrating too deeply.

As she lay there on the ground, she felt her exhaustion returning as the adrenaline rush wore off. She was of no use to anyone in this state. She needed food. Sleep, too, but she didn't have time for that.

She staggered into the woods behind the shed, sat down against a tree trunk, and ate some pork and dried fruit from her backpack. The food only increased her tiredness, and before she knew what was happening, her head sank back against the bark and her eyelids slid shut...

4

"Miss Frankenstein, you should probably wake up now."

Maggie shot awake and nearly shrieked when she saw what appeared to be a swamp monster looming over her. Its smooth gray skin dripped with slime and mud, its eyes burned a baleful orange, and it reeked of the noxious ooze.

But what kind of monster would call her "Miss Frankenstein"? And why did its voice sound so familiar?

Then she noticed that the orange eyes were too perfectly circular to be natural, and she realized that what she had thought was skin was actually metal.

"Freud?" said Maggie. "What happened? Where have you been?"

"When the Annihilator attacked, I was knocked into that foul stew of chemicals. It is, I can assure you, much deeper than it appears. The walls where I fell in were too sheer and too soft for me to climb out, so I started walking north, hoping to find a spot that permitted egress. The going was quite slow, for the pool is floored with thick sludge, and before I had gone more than fifty feet, I sensed items being dumped into the pool near the spot where I had fallen in. I decided to head back to investigate, and it is a good thing I did, for among those objects—which included one of the Marauders, I am happy to add—were Kukalukl's body and head, as well as dozens of chunks of rock that I identified as pieces of Mr. Granite. The latter was clearly beyond my ability to help. As for the former, though doubtful that his healing factor could repair such traumatic injuries, I had to concede that it was nevertheless possible, so I grabbed the body with one hand and the head with the other, and began my journey anew, albeit much more slowly this time, for I had Kukalukl's dead weight slowing me down and forcing my servos to their limit.

"At any rate, after three tedious hours, I finally found a place where the west bank formed a slope instead of a sheer cliff, and there I plodded back into the air once more. I laid Kukalukl's body in the shelter of some bushes where I hoped the Marauders would not find him, and took special care to place his head- and neck-stumps together to facilitate healing, if healing is even possible in a case like this.

"After that I returned to the clearing in hopes of learning what had happened. On the edge of it I found you."

Maggie looked up at the sky, only now realizing that the sun was in the midst of setting, and the woods were growing dim.

"Oh, this is terrible," she said. "I must have been asleep for over two hours…"

"You probably needed the rest."

"No, you do not understand. The Marauders have taken

Adam and Dagmar hostage. We must rescue them as soon as possible. I have no idea what will happen, or when, but when I…interrogated one of the Marauders earlier he said that their leader had plans for them—plans of a decidedly wicked nature, no doubt. We have to find a way inside. We have to find a way to save them."

"I agree. But how?"

"I do not know." She stood up and looked around. The hoverboard and Klaus's body still lay in the middle of the clearing. "First help me dispose of this body. Currently our greatest advantage is that the Marauders do not know that we are coming—indeed, I doubt if they even know you exist—but that advantage will vanish should they return and find the body."

After she and Freud dumped the body into the ooze, she picked up the board and looked at it. Theoretically, they could get on the hoverboard and fly in, but even if they ascended to a great height, they might be spotted flying toward the complex. Besides, she wasn't sure if the board could handle their combined weight, or if she could handle being up so high with nothing but a thin piece of metal between her and a messy death on the ground below.

Her gaze settled on the pipe that jutted from the side of the slope. It no doubt led deep inside the complex, and while it was wide enough for them to crawl through with room to spare, it was slick with the acidic green ooze, which would eat the flesh off her hands before she had gone a hundred feet.

"Come on," she said. "We need to finish reconnoitering the base. Perhaps we will find some other way inside."

They entered the woods just north of the dirt path the Marauders had used, and headed west. After half a mile, the dirt path bent south toward another gate, next to which stood another guardhouse.

"Can you see if anyone is in there?" she asked Freud.

He scrutinized the distant guardhouse. "I see two men. One wears a tuxedo suit, a top hat, a cape, and a domino mask. The other has painted his face in the manner of a skull and wears a black outfit with a tight-fitting hood. They are watching the woods quite closely. No doubt they have been ordered to be on the lookout for us and their missing comrades."

They retreated farther into the woods and passed the guardhouse. When they felt it was safe, they approached the fence again.

During the next half hour, as the sun sank and night spread across the woods, Maggie began to despair of ever finding a way inside. But then she saw something protruding from a cluster of bushes on the slope leading up to the fence. The darkness made it hard to be sure, but...

"Freud, is that what I think it is?" she said, pointing at the object.

Freud looked at it, his eyes like small orange moons in the deepening darkness.

"It is a pipe exactly like the one we encountered earlier."

She strode forward, examined the ground below the pipe, and then peered into the dark bore. "No, not exactly like it. This one does not appear to have been used in years. Indeed, it is clean and dry and free of the burning chemicals that polluted the other one." She smiled. "I think we've found our way in."

Chapter 10

Yoyodyne (Inside)

1

It was pain that brought Adam back to consciousness. The pain was red and pulsing and centered on the side of his head. It scooped him out of the black dreamless unconsciousness within which he had been comfortably ensconced, and hefted him pulse by agonizing pulse toward the waking world.

He didn't want to go there. Everything was bad there. Everything always went wrong there. Everything *had* gone wrong. If he woke up he would have to deal with all kinds of terrible things he didn't want to deal with. Better to just ignore the pain, then. Maybe it would go away.

Despite his wishes, the pain pushed him up and up, and consciousness slowly broke over the darkness like a cruel sun and illuminated piece by piece those things he wished would stay shrouded in shadow—the Marauders' attack, Bob's death, the explosion of pain as something smashed into the side of his head. And then there were fragmentary memories, the products of fleeting moments of semi-consciousness: Dagmar shouting something; cloth pulled tightly across his eyes, rendering everything dark; the smells of sweat and machine oil; large, strong hands gripping him and carrying him somewhere—and his disoriented, dream-like conviction that those hands were his, that he was carrying himself.

He opened his eyes and looked around. He sat with his back against a wall in a metal chamber about thirty feet square. A white hemispherical object attached to the center of the ceiling provided the room's only—and rather dim—light. Adam couldn't tell what this dome was made of, or whether the dome covered the light-source or was itself the light-source.

The chamber was unfurnished except for a metal bench that jutted from the left wall about two feet above the floor. Opposite him was a thick metal door with a wheel-shaped handle in the center. Dagmar sat slumped against the middle of the right wall, her eyes closed and her chin on her chest, asleep. Around her neck and wrists were manacles connected by chains to bolts in the wall behind her. Seeing this made Adam aware of cold metal pressing against his own wrists and neck, and looking down he saw that he too was chained to the wall.

The metal floor sloped gently toward a small round drain in its center. Around the edge of the drain was a thick crust of dried blood. Closer inspection of the floor and walls revealed a few faint streaks of blood that whoever cleaned the room had missed. Worse, on the sharp edge of the bench clung a chunk of flesh with a few strands of mid-length brown hair sprouting from it. The room smelled strongly of some kind of citrus-scented cleaning product, but still faintly detectable underneath that smell were the odors of blood and decaying meat. The odors of death.

Adam tried to stand up, but the chains were too short for him to do so. He grunted in frustration, then twisted around to take a closer look at his restraints. The chains were made of a silver-green metal he wasn't familiar with. The bolts were steel and had been soldered to the wall. Mustering all his strength, and doing his best to ignore the way the pain in his head swelled from pounding to jackhammering with the slightest exertion, he thrust his arms out and forward until the chains were taut, and then pulled as hard as he could. The chains didn't break. The bolts in the wall didn't budge.

The rattle of his chains awakened Dagmar, who jerked her head up with a gasp as if she thought someone had come to kill her. When she saw that Adam was awake, she looked so relieved he thought she would start crying.

"I thought you might be dead," she said.

"No. It will take more than a blow to the head and greater men than these ignorant thugs to kill me."

Dagmar stared at him for a moment, then looked down at the floor, her eyes sad and distant.

"Where are the others?" he asked. "I remember Bob…I remember what happened to him, but what of the others?"

Dagmar heaved a wavering sigh. "Kukalukl—the Grottle cut his head off. It's—I mean, I know he can heal from pretty serious stuff, but…"

"I…I am sorry." Bob *and* Kukalukl? For a moment Adam felt the horrible, devitalizing grip of hopelessness close around his heart. He clenched his teeth and fists and denied it, forced it away. He had to maintain hope at least for Dagmar's sake. "Still, he was a god, and many gods have returned from far worse."

She gave him a small, humorless smile, as if she figured she should at least acknowledge his futile effort to rouse her spirits.

"Yeah," she said, "but even if he can, chances are he probably won't return in time to help us. Besides, they dumped his—they dumped him into that green gunk, and the Annihilator said something about how it'd eat the flesh off him before he could heal it up again."

Adam decided to change the subject. "What about Maggie?"

"She ran off into the woods with those geeks on flying skateboards chasing her. I don't know what happened after that. I just know I haven't seen any of them since then."

"And Freud? Did he find his way out of the ooze?"

She shrugged. "I don't know. I didn't see him at all after the fight started."

"Then it's possible both he and Maggie are still free. Perhaps even Kukalukl as well. What time is it? How long was I unconscious?"

"I don't know. After they captured us, they blindfolded us and tied us up and brought us inside Yoyodyne and threw us in here. After that, I screamed for help for a while, then fell asleep. I figure it's been at least a few hours. Probably more, since I actually feel pretty rested. I must've slept a long time."

Adam realized that aside from his head injury, he, too, felt well-rested. He knew his body and its vicissitudes quite well, and he estimated that he must have been unconscious for at least three hours, probably as long as four or five.

"I, too," he said. "And that is good, for we shall need our strength to finish our task."

She looked at him with her eyebrows raised, as if she couldn't believe he thought she would buy such bluster.

"Surely you do not think this is the end," he said. "We cannot give up now, when we are so close to achieving our goals."

She held up her arms and shook them so that the chains clinked. "Hel-*lo*, chained and captive, remember? How're we supposed to do anything when even *you* can't break your chains?"

"Have you forgotten already that two of our companions are still at large? And Kukalukl may recover and come to our aid as well."

Her face twisted about like melting plastic for a moment, and then she burst into tears.

Adam didn't know what to say or do. He had never been very good at consoling people, especially children. He and Dagmar were chained too far apart for him to hold her, or even touch her. All he could do was stare at her sympathetically and say, "Everything will be all right. You'll see."

"No, it won't!" she spat through her tears. "It *won't!* Kukalukl's dead, and—and—and Granite's dead, and *we'll* probably be dead soon, too."

Adam was about to give up on the seemingly hopeless task of bolstering her spirits, but then he had an idea.

"That is no way for a queen to talk," he said in a low, stern voice.

She looked at him, blinking.

"Do you not owe it to your subjects, to yourself, and to the memory of your parents, the former king and queen, to be strong and righteous?"

She continued blinking for a second, and then her face crumpled up, and she started sobbing again, harder than before.

What the devil had he said to set her off this time? He had thought that his words would remind her of her regal heritage, would straighten her spine and kindle the dignity in her soul as she herself had done after the incident in Happyvale.

After several minutes her sobs died down, and she just sat there, eyes downcast, looking more dejected than ever. Adam said nothing. He had no idea *what* to say anymore.

When several more minutes passed without a word from

her, his thoughts rolled off down a different track, and he began to wonder why they weren't dead yet, why the Marauders hadn't just killed them when they were defenseless. The Marauders must have plans for them. Perhaps they—

"I made it up," said Dagmar.

His train of thought brought to an unexpected halt, Adam stared at her, unsure what she was talking about. Her eyes hadn't moved from the patch of floor they had been fixed on ever since her last crying spree ended.

"What?" he said. "Made what up?"

"The stuff about being a queen."

There was a long silence.

"What?" Adam repeated, convinced he must be misunderstanding her.

She gave him a sheepish look. "I made it up," she said again.

"But…but *how?*"

She jerked her head back a little, frowning, as if it were an odd question, which he supposed it was. "What do you mean? I just made it up."

"No, I mean…your story was so detailed. You…" He shook his head. "I find it hard to believe that none of it was true. So hard, in fact, that I am tempted to think you are lying now."

"I'm not."

"So…so there was no palace?" he said. "No Nanette? No—"

"Oh, well, actually there *was* a palace *and* a Nanette, but they weren't exactly what I said they were. I sort of built the story out of a bunch of little true things, but just changed them around a bit. My parents weren't a king and queen. They were cartoonists before the Cataclysm. And afterward, the village they were living in got attacked by orcs back when the orcs were trying to take over the area. The whole place got burned down and just about everyone got slaughtered, but my parents escaped and after roaming around in the wilderness for a while, they found a ruined palace. It was exactly like I told you about, except it wasn't ours. I don't know whose it was. It was just ruins.

"Anyway, it was really isolated, even from monsters, so they moved in and lived there. And then a few years later I was born."

"What about Nanette?"

"She was a doll my mom gave me. It used to be hers when she was little. She and my dad would draw cartoons for me about the adventures of Nanette." She smiled sadly. "Those were really funny. Since the palace was so isolated and I didn't have any other kids to play with, Nanette was kind of like my only friend. I'd take her out into the garden and come up with my own adventures. I guess that's why I'm so good at making stuff up. I didn't have any real friends, and the world was too dangerous for my parents to take me anywhere, so I was stuck in the old ruined palace with just Nanette and my imagination."

"But...but why did you lie to begin with?"

Her gaze returned to the floor and she heaved a big sigh.

"I don't know. I just...it was just that everyone I met was *some*body, you know? I mean, the Marauders, even though they're a bunch of scumbags, they all had things that made them special—the Annihilator with his armor, and Skippy and Oscar with their flying skateboards, and the Grottle with its Grottleness. And then I met Kukalukl, who was a god. And then Kukalukl and I ended up chasing after you guys, and when you all came stumbling out of that building, I realized that you were all special too. Granite was a superhero. And Freud was a robot. And you were, you know, *you.*"

"Maggie could not have appeared so special."

"Oh, yeah? You should've heard what they were saying about her in Sweetwater after you guys left. They said she was the only woman the Marauders went after who managed to get away. They said she made Skippy eat road-dirt."

One side of Adam's mouth curved up in a smile, and he emitted a soft laughing grunt.

"Anyway," Dagmar went on, "it wasn't even really something I consciously decided on. I just sort of blurted it out when you guys appeared. I don't know, I guess I sort of needed to be someone important. It seemed...safer somehow. And once I started with it, there were times it actually *felt* true. Like I was becoming what I was pretending to be. You know what I mean?"

"I think so. Though I suspect that Freud would have much to say about it."

She rolled her eyes and laughed briefly. "Yeah, I'll bet."

"Did—does Kukalukl know?"

Her smile faded, and sorrow once again clouded her face. She had caught his clumsy change of tense.

"I don't know," she said in a weary voice. "I never talked to him about it. He probably knew I was making it up, since I hadn't mentioned any of it before we met you guys. But he played along because—because he swore he'd help me and protect me and—and—" She started crying again.

Once again, Adam was at a loss for words. He wondered how Bob would have handled this situation. He probably would've said something calm and soothing.

"All will be well," Adam said in what he hoped was a kind, gentle voice. "All will—"

She shook her head so violently he felt her tears spatter his hand.

"Nuh—no it won't. He's *dead!* Just like my mom and dad. Just like everyone else. Everybody I care about always dies, and I can't do anything about it 'cause I'm just—just *nobody.* I'm just a stupid useless loser who can't even help her friends."

She drew her knees up to her chest and buried her face in them as her whole body shuddered with her sobs.

Adam gave a silent sigh of frustration. Kind and gentle wasn't working. If anything, it seemed to be making things worse. Probably because Adam wasn't by nature a kind and gentle person. Time to try something else, something he was better at.

"That is the biggest load of horseshit I have ever heard," he said in a loud, stern voice. The words echoed in the small metal chamber.

It worked. Dagmar's head shot up, and she gaped at him through her tears. Most likely it was only because of the profanity, the tactful use of which always makes a great impression, but at least he had her attention.

"I was not always as I am today," Adam said. "I used to be a normal man. Several of them, in fact. Granite, too, was a normal man before the lab accident that granted him his powers. For that matter, one does not have to possess unusual attributes to be special. Maggie might be tough and courageous, but she was not always like that. She and her sister were little girls no tougher than you when I first met them. My creator was a man like any other, and though he could be too obsessed and short-sighted at times, he was a genius at his work and achieved feats beyond those of any other scientist before or since. And his brother Ernest, Maggie and Anna's father, had a great talent for government, which not only made him and his family wealthy, but improved the lives of everyone in his community. He helped more people and earned more gratitude in ten years than I have in all the years of my existence. And what of your own parents? Would you call *them* 'big losers' because they had no special powers and were unskilled at fighting?"

Dagmar, who had been staring at him with eyes as big as roc's eggs, now frowned as if he had insulted her. "No! They were awesome. They were great parents. And you shoulda seen their cartoons. Those were so cool!"

"Very well, then. That proves my point. It is my belief that everybody has some aptitude or talent that they excel at and can do better than anyone else. But it often takes a long time for a man or woman to discover what that talent is. Once you do, however, you shall know it, and you shall excel at it, and you shall realize that your whining about being a nobody was premature and ill-founded."

She gazed off into space, reflecting on his words. Then a big smile spread across her face, and she said, "You're right!"

He nodded, smiling, happy for her and pleased with himself. His success at bestowing advice and inspiration gave him a wise, fatherly feeling hitherto unknown to him. It was a feeling he did not dislike.

"Yeah!" she continued. "You're totally right! And I know exactly what it is I can do better than anyone else. I know exactly what my special talent is."

"Oh? And what is that?"

For a moment she didn't answer, still too transported by the ecstasy of revelation. But then she turned to him, eyes bright and happy, a huge eager grin on her face, and said, "I'm the best liar in the whole wide world."

Adam just stared at her with his mouth hanging open. This wasn't quite what he had had in mind. He had been thinking in more benevolent terms. But her delight was so pure and strong and such a massive improvement over her previous gloom that he couldn't find it in his heart to rain on her one-girl parade.

Still, she saw the look on his face, and cocked an eyebrow at him. "I had *you* fooled, didn't I? Heck, I had *all* of you fooled. That *has* to take a lot of talent, am I right?"

He had to admit she had a point. But he refused to give her any encouragement beyond a reluctant, "Perhaps."

His lack of enthusiasm didn't matter to her in the slightest. She just kept grinning and grinning.

I may have created a monster, he thought. Then the irony of that idea hit him, and he laughed.

Dagmar, thinking he had finally warmed to the idea of her being the world's number one liar, beamed at him.

"I know!" she said. "Isn't it cool?" And she, too, started laughing.

Footsteps sounded beyond the door, and their laughter stopped. The steps stopped outside the door, and there was a metallic *chack,* as of a bolt or lock. The wheel-shaped handle turned.

Adam glanced at Dagmar. She looked scared, but was doing her best to keep it contained. Good for her. As for himself, he focused his thoughts on possible escape plans. He imagined the visiting Marauder, whichever one it was, getting too close and falling prey to Adam's strong, neck-snapping hands. The Marauder would have the keys to their manacles on his belt, of course, and Adam would free himself and Dagmar from their chains. Then, loose in the complex, they would wreak havoc among the Marauders, and—

The door opened, and there stood a Marauder neither of them had seen before. He wore a white fencing suit and a mesh fencing mask. Two epees hung on his belt, one on either side like a gunslinger's six-guns. In one hand he held an orange plastic cafeteria tray that bore two Tupperware bowls, two dented tin cups, and a pile of mostly clear plastic packages containing pairs of roughly cylindrical yellowish objects.

"Here's your dinner," said the Marauder.

He set the tray on the floor in front of the door, then picked up a wooden mop handle that had been leaning against the wall in the hallway outside, and used it to slide the tray across the floor until one edge was close enough for Adam to grab. It was a smart move, Adam reflected with grudging admiration: The mop handle never once came within Adam's reach.

Adam let the tray sit where it was. He smiled as sweetly as he could—though even his best attempts at smiles wound up looking like hideous leers—and said, "There is really no need to be so afraid. You could have brought it inside by hand. We will not bite you."

The Marauder snorted. "Yeah, right."

He sounded nervous. And young. Adam suspected he was a recent recruit, one of the lowest men on the Marauder totem pole.

"Better eat up," the Marauder said. "You'll need your energy. The boss is planning something extra special for you two."

"What do you mean?" said Adam.

But the Marauder was already pulling the door closed. It boomed shut, the wheel spun, the chack sounded again, and the footsteps receded.

Adam and Dagmar stared at the tray. They couldn't see what was inside the bowls or the tin cups.

"I'm starving," said Dagmar.

"As am I," said Adam. "But the food might be drugged, or poisoned."

"It wouldn't be poisoned," she said. "If they wanted to

kill us, they could've done it while we were unconscious."

"True. But it still might be drugged. They might be planning to put us to sleep the more easily to transport us to this sinister event he mentioned."

"So? We gotta eat sooner or later. I mean, I figure we can either slowly starve to death or go through with this event thing. Frankly, I'd rather take my chances with the event."

Adam nodded. That summed up his own feelings quite well.

He grabbed the tray and pulled it closer. The bowls contained brown broth filled with bits of squishy parsnips, limp greens of some kind, blobs of fat, and shreds of an unknown meat. The tin cups contained water that had an unpleasant mineral smell. The plastic wrappers sported the word "Twinkies" and a picture of an anthropomorphic Twinkie wearing a white cowboy hat and brandishing a lasso.

Having eaten nothing in over twelve hours, Adam and Dagmar were so hungry that every last bite of this questionable dinner tasted absolutely delicious. Especially the Twinkies, spongy cream-filled cakes that seemed amazingly fresh despite having been made and packaged before the Cataclysm.

When not a crumb remained to devour, Adam inspected the tray. He had seen plastic like this before and knew it could be broken into sharp dagger-like shards. He set it on the floor beside him, reserving it for later use.

Dagmar, he noticed, had leaned back against the wall and was quickly falling asleep. For a moment he was convinced that the food had indeed been drugged, but then he realized that he himself felt drowsy in a sated, non-drugged way. It was the normal sort of drowsiness that often came after eating.

He let it carry him off into sleep. After all, if the Marauders were planning some cruel event, he and Dagmar needed to be as well rested as possible if they hoped to have any chance of survival.

They slept.

2

Maggie had never suffered from claustrophobia, but she suspected that might change if she spent much longer in this damnable pipe.

When they had started out, Freud in the lead, his eye-beams lighting the way, Maggie had assumed that even if the pipe proved to be quite long, the journey would be, at worst, rather tedious; she was merely crawling on her hands and knees, after all, not doing anything strenuous.

Her knees started hurting after five minutes, her hands after ten. At that point she called a halt long enough for her to pull an old shirt from her backpack, tear it into strips, and wrap the strips around her hands and knees.

Thinking that now everything would be okay, they crawled on. And on. And on.

The pipe never changed. It stretched constantly onward and upward at a barely perceptible angle of two or three degrees, never curving, never branching, never intersecting with another pipe. Its maddening regularity made her want to scream. She began to wonder if they hadn't been caught in a trap, some clever piece of craft whereby intruders were condemned to retrace the same section of pipe until they went mad.

What made things worse was the smell. Not the smell of the pipe—that was only rust, unpleasant but reassuringly familiar—but the residual odor of the ooze that enveloped

Freud. At first this smell was only a minor annoyance, enough to make her wish she had rinsed him off before they started their journey. But over time the foul chemical stench seemed to accumulate in her nostrils, growing thicker and harsher and making her dizzy and nauseated.

A little while ago, she had asked Freud how long it had been since they entered the pipe. Considering how stiff she was and how much her lower back ached—it felt as if some-one had punched her in the kidneys—she thought the an-swer would be somewhere in the vicinity of two hours, maybe three. She was horrified when he announced that according to his internal clock it had been exactly forty-one minutes.

That was all? Not even three-quarters of an hour? She felt like weeping.

Now, as she continued trying, and failing, to come to terms with the idea that they might be condemned to this cramped metal hell for a few hours more, Freud stopped. Not noticing, head hanging wearily down, she continued forward until her hand banged knuckles-first into his heel.

"Ow," she said, flapping her hand from side to side.

"I apologize," said Freud. "But we have come to a change in the pipe."

She looked up. Ten feet ahead of Freud the pipe ap-peared to end at a blank wall of metal. Maggie's throat tightened, and tears of frustration welled up in her eyes. Then she noticed that it didn't end at all; it bent directly upward.

The question was, how far up did it go before ending? Would they be able to climb out, or had their whole journey been for nothing?

They crawled forward. Freud entered the vertical section and stood upright. Maggie joined him. There was barely enough room for both of them.

Two feet above the tops of their heads was a round metal grate. Freud reached up to push it out of the way, but Maggie suddenly had an image of the Marauders gathered in silence around the grate, the orange glow from beneath it dimly illuminating their grinning faces and their drawn weapons as they waited for the flies to bumble into the web.

"Stop," she whispered. "Turn off your eyebeams for a moment."

He did. The blackness that ensued was absolute and deeply unsettling. Not a glimmer of light shone anywhere.

"Do you hear anything?" she whispered even more quietly than before. The blackness made every sound seem a thousand times louder.

Freud listened for a moment and then, the volume of his voice lowered to near inaudibility, said, "I hear a faint dripping sound, as well as several small insects skittering across a hard surface. That is all."

Relieved, Maggie said, "Turn your eyes back on, and let us leave this awful pipe."

Eye-beams back on, Freud reached up and pushed against the grate. It came up easily, or so it seemed. The way his servos were whining, Maggie suspected that a normal man wouldn't have been able to budge it.

After Freud moved the grate aside, they climbed out and found themselves at the bottom of a metal vat twenty feet across and forty high. Maggie feared that they wouldn't be able to get out of it, but as Freud looked around, his eye-beams fell upon a metal ladder that extended up the side. They climbed it, crossed the vat's five-foot-wide lip, then descended a metal staircase that spiraled down the outside of the vat.

When they were safely down, they looked around and

saw that they were in a nearly empty room the size of a football stadium. The vat, which resembled the one they saw in the ruined building at the northeast corner of the complex, occupied the center of the room. Next to it a huge metal hook hung from the ceiling on a chain. Against one wall stood a rusty metal table atop which sat a smashed computer monitor. A filthy blue tarp lay in a heap in a corner. Beyond that there was only trash scattered across the floor: sheets of decaying and bug-eaten paper, empty plastic wrappers with the word "Twinkies" on them, crushed Styrofoam cups, a pen, and, oddly enough, a single brown shoe. Numerous rectangular patches lighter than the rest of the floor attested to where other objects had once stood.

There were three doors. One, in what Freud said was the south wall (it turned out he had some kind of internal compass in addition to everything else), was large and metal and rolled upward on a track. A second in the west wall led to an office full of broken furniture and more rotting paper.

The third door in the vat-room was in the north wall. Beyond it, a door-lined institutional hallway stretched away to the east and west. They saw nothing to indicate which direction might lead to the Marauders, or more importantly to Adam and Dagmar.

"Well?" Maggie said. "Do your sensors detect any particles or suchlike that might help us decide which way to go?"

Freud turned his head down one arm of the hallway, then down the other, then looked at Maggie.

"I regret to inform you that I detect no meaningful particulates in the air. I can, however, tell you one item of possible importance: Given our approximate distance from Yoyodyne when we entered the pipe, the length of the pipe, and the approximate size of the complex, I estimate that we are roughly in Yoyodyne's center."

Maggie couldn't decide whether that made her feel better or worse. It was good because, being in the center, they were an equal distance from all parts of the complex, which might make finding Adam and Dagmar easier. Unfortunately, it also made it easier for the Marauders to stumble across her and Freud.

"Let us head west," she said.

They headed down the left arm of the hallway.

3

An hour later Maggie threw herself into a chair in a trashed office and said, "How large *is* this place?"

Since leaving the vat-room, they had passed through a variety of labs, storage areas, and offices. They had also run across a dining hall with a sign above the entrance that read "Blue Wing Cafeteria," disheartening evidence that the complex was vast enough to merit multiple cafeterias.

In all that time, they had found no sign of the Marauders. Considering the abundance of graffiti on the way in, logic dictated that the Marauders would express themselves similarly on the inside of the complex. But they had seen nothing. Nor had they seen any indication that anyone had been in this area in years.

"I am beginning to think we should have taken the east branch of the corridor," she told Freud.

"Perhaps."

Her eyelids began to droop. She forced them back open. Sitting down had been foolish. Her body needed rest. Lots of it. Sure, she had had that little nap after her altercation with Klaus von Klaus, but it hadn't been enough. Now her exhaustion was catching up with her again.

She wasn't sure if she could fight it. Should she try? That was the question, wasn't it? What kind of peril were Adam and Dagmar and Anna in anyway?

"I get the impression you wish to sleep, but are concerned that you should remain awake to rescue the others," said Freud.

"That is a very succinct assessment of the situation," she said, hating how drowsy-thick her voice sounded.

"If it helps, my analysis is as follows: Had the Marauders wished to kill Mr. Frankenstein and Ms. Dagmar, they would have done so immediately upon catching them. The fact that they did not suggests that they wished to keep them alive for one reason or another. Torture is, of course, a possibility, as is a showy execution, both of which are precisely the sort of barbarous behavior one would expect from antisocial beings who have almost completely given themselves over to their ids. But the Marauders are nevertheless human and require sleep as all men do. Thus, given the lateness of the hour—it is shortly before midnight—and given that the Marauders appear to be active primarily during the day, it is therefore most likely that either our companions have already been killed by execution or torture, or are currently restrained in some form to await execution or further torture tomorrow. In other words, I suspect that very little will happen one way or another at least until dawn."

"Hmmm," said Maggie, forcing her eyelids up for what seemed like the thousandth time. "But if all the Marauders are asleep, would this not be the best time to…to…"

She fell asleep.

Freud ran a full system scan to make sure nothing had been damaged during the day's activity, set an internal wake-up alert for four-thirty a.m.—four-and-a-half hours of sleep should suffice for Ms. Frankenstein—then entered standby mode to rest his processors for the inevitable confrontation tomorrow, in whatever form it would take.

4

A door banged in the distance. In an instant Maggie was on her feet, her hand flying to the hilt of her dagger. Likewise, Freud exited standby mode. His head swiveled from side to side, trying to pinpoint the direction the sound had come from.

Maggie stood very still, eyes closed, listening. She heard no further sounds.

"Do you hear anything?" she asked.

"No," said Freud. "I believe, though, that the noise came from directly north of us."

She nodded. They had better investigate, but first things first. She zipped open the compartment in her backpack where she kept her meager supply of food, wolfed down a strip of salt pork and a handful of Cap'n Crunch, and drank half her bottle of water. It made her feel marginally more energetic, but did little to alleviate her hunger.

"What time is it?" she asked.

"Four twenty-two. If it is any consolation, you would have slept only another eight minutes anyway."

She sighed. Even only eight minutes of sleep sounded heavenly.

They stepped out of the office and into the east-west hallway they had been traveling down earlier. Fifty feet west of the office door another hallway branched off this one, heading north. They hadn't checked out that hallway yet.

When they looked down it, they saw the glow of

light—*electric* light—shining in the distance. They advanced slowly and quietly down the hallway, and soon discerned that the hallway bent left at a ninety-degree angle about three-hundred feet ahead. The light was coming from around the bend. Faintly they heard muffled sounds and the low tones of a man's voice.

"Turn off your eye-beams," Maggie whispered.

Freud did so. They continued creeping toward the bend, at one point passing a side-corridor on their right that was dimly lit by emergency lights consisting of bars of white luminescence in the angles where the walls met the ceiling. There were also fluorescent light fixtures in the center of the ceiling, but those were dark. Maggie was tempted to investigate this corridor until she noticed the thick, undisturbed layer of dust and dirt on the floor. Clearly no one had gone down there in years.

As they neared the bend in the corridor, Maggie smelled food cooking, which made her mouth water. Was it a kitchen up ahead? If so, she wondered if she could manage to snag a few bites of food. Real food, that is. Something warm and succulent and freshly cooked.

They reached the bend in the corridor. Maggie drew her dagger, held it ready at her side, and peeked around the corner.

The corridor extended due west. Fluorescent lights hummed in fixtures in the ceiling. After so many hours with Freud's relatively weak eye-beams as the main source of light, the fluorescents were so bright Maggie had to squint. On the north side of the corridor, about ten feet down from the bend, were a pair of swinging doors, each with a porthole window that revealed that the lights were on on the other side, too. A sign on the wall above the doors read "Green Wing Kitchen." The smell of food was maddeningly strong.

Maggie detected beef, potatoes, sage, cabbage, and a dozen other scents that made her almost dizzy with hunger. Her stomach gurgled and groaned, and she felt a brief, irrational fear that the sounds were loud enough for the Marauders to hear.

But that was ridiculous, for the noises from the kitchen were far, far louder. She could hear them all quite clearly from where she stood. Pot lids banged. Ladles clattered. Liquids bubbled. Fat sizzled. And throughout it all, one man's low, surly voice rumbled incessantly. His words were clear now, and Maggie was amused to discover that it was one constant monologue of complaint.

"Fuckin' picky little bitches," the man said. "Thinkin' they're all a bunch of tough-ass motherfuckers. Yeah, right. They're fussier than fuckin' old ladies. I mean, holy shit, the Grottle can't eat anything except meat? Sissy bitch. Like if it ever eats a vegetable it'll shrivel up and fuckin' die. And that dumbfuck Viking with his stupid fuckin' venison. You'd think he wants to start dating the shit. Hasn't that lice-ridden stink-pit ever heard of fruit, for fuck's sake? Or whole grains? I guess they're all too retarded to understand the concept of fuckin' nutrition. Well, when they all drop dead of fuckin' heart attacks in the middle of pillaging some dinky-ass village, they'll understand *then*, won't they? They'll think, 'Hey! Asparagus Sam was right!' And then they'll keel right the fuck over. And me? I'll just fuckin' laugh, 'cause I told 'em years before to eat right, and did they fuckin' listen? Fuck, no!"

And so on and so on, without pause.

Maggie tiptoed to the right side of the swinging doors, hunched down below the level of the porthole windows, and crossed to the left side. Then she motioned for Freud to position himself on the right side. When he had done so, she slowly looked through the window in the left door while Freud looked through the one in the right.

The kitchen was huge, stretching over two hundred feet from the door to the far wall and forty feet from side to side. Down its center ran two parallel gleaming metal counters outfitted with sinks and cabinets and drawers and racks. There were counters along parts of the walls, too, but mostly the wall-space was reserved for dozens of electrical appliances: refrigerators, ranges, coolers, microwave ovens. In one section someone had removed the appliances and installed a wood-burning stove and an open fire-pit with a pair of spits above the lapping tongues of flame. Above these new additions a hole had been cut in the ceiling and metal tubing run through it to vent the smoke. A wine-rack and a row of oaken barrels stood to the right of the swinging doors, while to the left was the most well-stocked herb- and spice-rack Maggie had ever seen. The brown glass jars had been meticulously labeled and arranged in alphabetical order on a home-made floor-to-ceiling wooden shelving unit ten feet wide. She saw every culinary herb and spice she had ever heard of and dozens she hadn't. Anise, mint, oregano, saffron—those she knew. But what about eldrim? Or kotch? Or shnozzberry leaves?

Bustling about alone in this vast space, hurrying from pot to counter to spice rack (during which latter trips Maggie and Freud had to duck out of sight for a while), was a thin, stoop-shouldered man, probably in his early forties, with curly dark-brown hair poking out from beneath the bottom of his battered toque, black-rimmed glasses held together with electrician's tape, a blue-and-white plaid shirt with the sleeves rolled up, blue jeans, brown work boots, and a once-white apron now spattered and stained with so much grease and juice and gunk that it looked like an Expressionist painting. His face was pinched and sour as he slaved away on the components of a massive feast: Two dozen pots bubbled on stovetops, some containing what appeared to be stews, others sauces, still others fruit filling for pies. Two huge ovens contained nothing but slowly rising loaves of bread. A wild boar roasted on one spit, a juvenile giant eagle on the other. Venison steaks sizzled in pans. Half-prepared toppings, fillings, dressings, flavorings, and coverings lay on countertops. And throughout his complex one-man dance of food preparation Asparagus Sam grumped on and on and on.

"Ooh, special feast today, special feast today. Holy fuckin' shit, when *isn't* there a special fuckin' feast? Every day's like a faggy-ass holiday around here. But whaddaya expect considering the fucked-up management we got? I mean, shit, last time it was a fuckin' devil's food cake for a mass execution. Who the fuck wants to eat devil's food cake when you're watching neck arteries spraying blood all over everything? I mean, what is this shit? And who the fuck eats devil's food cake anyway? Stuff's fuckin' loaded with enough fat and calories to choke a fuckin' Tyrannosaurus Rex. And do they want the healthy recipe, which I happen to know, and which, in my not-so-fuckin'-humble opinion, tastes just as good as the fuckin' egg-and-butter-loaded version? Of course they don't! They want their arteries plugged up like an old woman who's never heard of prune juice! Fuckin' morons!"

"Someone is coming," Freud said.

Even as he spoke Maggie heard heavy footsteps approaching down a side-corridor that extended north about fifty feet to their left.

"Hide," she whispered, and she and Freud retreated back around the corner to the north-south corridor they had come down earlier.

The footsteps grew louder as whoever it was entered the east-west corridor and advanced toward the kitchen doors. Maggie thought the rhythm of the footsteps sounded familiar in some way. Did she know this person? At the moment there was no way for her to take a look without being seen, but once whoever-it-was entered the kitchen, she and Freud could creep forward again and peep through the porthole windows for a glimpse of the newcomer. Assuming, of course, that the kitchen was where the newcomer was headed. If not, she and Freud had quite a problem.

To her relief, the kitchen doors banged open and the footsteps grew fainter again. They heard Asparagus Sam groan and say, "Well, fuck me! Twitchy's back! What do you want *this* time?"

Twitchy. The Marauders' leader's right-hand man. This certainly deserved a look. She and Freud inched toward the kitchen doors.

As they did so, a tinny voice said, "The Master has"—there was a loud, sharp *click*—"sent me to talk to"—*click*—"talk to you."

Maggie suppressed a gasp. Aside from the clicks the voice sounded just like Freud's. Then she remembered something Freud had said the night before, and she realized who the voice must belong to.

Freud did, too, for as they drew up beside the swinging doors, he said softly, "Well, this is most unexpected."

They looked through the windows. Inside the kitchen, Asparagus Sam, his hands on his hips, watched a robot approach him—a robot that looked exactly like Freud, except that it was copper-colored and its head sported a deep dent on its top left side. Its head kept jerking to the left every few seconds in a motion that made Maggie think of a horse flicking its tail to shoo away a fly. These motions were accompanied by a clicking sound from its neck joint.

"Adler," said Freud. "What is *he* doing here, associating with these uncivilized brutes?"

"Well, what does the most holy fuckin' boss-monster want now?" said Asparagus Sam as Adler stopped in front of him.

"First, our noble leader desires another box of"—Adler's head jerked to the left and that click sounded again—"box of Twinkies."

Asparagus Sam rolled his eyes and raised his hands as if to invoke divine guidance. "Again with the fuckin' Twinkies. How many times down I have to say it: That stuff's artery cement! I mean, shit, I don't care how young and healthy you think you are, you eat that shit, you might as well be drinkin' fuckin' poison."

Adler's only response to this was to say again, "Our noble leader"—jerk; *click*—"desires a new box of Twinkies."

Despite his protestations, Asparagus Sam was already yanking an unopened box of Twinkies from a cabinet that was packed with such boxes.

He thrust the box into Adler's hands.

"What else?" he said with weary resignation.

"I have been instructed to"—jerk; *click*—"instructed to tell you that the feast must be"—jerk; *click*—"must be ready by the end of this morning's festivities, which begin at"—jerk; *click*—"at dawn and are expected to last half an hour at most."

Asparagus Sam goggled at him. "Dawn's only an hour away! There's no fuckin' way this food'll be ready by then!"

"I was told you might say something"—jerk; *click*—"of the sort. That is why I was further instructed to tell you that should you"—jerk; *click*—"should you not have the food ready at that time, then a third"—jerk; *click*—"a third shall enter the arena this day."

Maggie's stomach sank. The two already slated to enter this ominous arena had to be Adam and Dagmar. She dreaded to think what they might face there.

She was about to say something to Freud about how they needed to get moving *now*—after all, they didn't even know where the arena was, much less where Adam and Dagmar were being held—but Freud spoke first.

"I believe I have a plan," he said.

Before he could say more, Asparagus Sam roared, "Damn it! Fuckin' shit! Fine! I'll have it fuckin' ready in time! It'll be shitty, of course, but you fuckin' people like shitty, don't you? You got *no* fuckin' taste whatsoever. Wouldn't know a caper from a rat turd." He made a shooing gesture at Adler. "Now piss off. Leave me the fuck alone to finish this fuckin' garbage-ass meal."

"Conquest of others"—jerk; *click*—"conquest of others"—jerk; *click*—"conquest of others is the goal which directs the activity of most human beings."

Asparagus Sam snorted. "Save your little pearls of wisdom for the big fuckin' kahuna, okay? I got no use for 'em."

Freud sighed. Though he had no lungs and no breath to expel, it sounded just like a real sigh. "It would appear that the Marauders' leader has confused Adler's sayings for great truths, a misunderstanding one can only call tragic, seeing as how Adler's theories are based on countless fallacies, the most egregious being—"

"You said you had a plan?" said Maggie.

"Oh, yes. Come, let us withdraw to our previous position."

They slunk back around the corner.

"My plan," Freud said, "hinges upon two features of the

model of robot of which Adler and I are examples: One, there is an emergency shut-off button on the underside of the back of the head. Take a look at mine, if you wish to see for yourself."

She did. Where the back of the head curved inward toward the spot where it met the neck, there was a round button the size of a fingertip that lay flush with the surrounding metal.

"I see, but—"

The kitchen doors banged open, and Adler's heavy footsteps thumped out into the hallway. As the doors swung shut, Freud stepped around the corner and said, "Why, if it isn't Adler."

Adler whirled around.

"Freud? Is that"—jerk; *click*—"is that you?"

"Yes, indeed. Come over here. I have something interesting for you to see."

Adler strode forward. "You would do well"—jerk; *click*—"do well to join us. The master says that with"—jerk; *click*—"with my invaluable insights, the Marauders are well on the way to becoming"—jerk; *click*—"the superior force in this land."

He reached the corner, looked around it, and saw Maggie.

"Hello," Maggie said, extending a hand but not stepping forward. "It is a great pleasure to meet you. Freud here has told me so much about you."

Adler stepped forward, his free hand rising in response. "Really? I—"

He never got a chance to finish, for Freud, who had been waiting until Adler was out of sight of the kitchen hallway, reached up and pushed Adler's shutoff button. Adler's eyes went dark and his arms fell limp at his sides. The box of Twinkies smacked to the floor, the plastic wrappers inside it emitting one loud rustle.

Maggie and Freud waited in tense silence to see if Asparagus Sam would come storming out into the hallway to see what all the noise was about. Thankfully the swinging doors remained closed.

"Now what?" said Maggie. "We have eliminated Adler from the list of Marauders we must contend with, but I fail to see how that helps us. He hardly seemed dangerous."

"You are missing the point," said Freud. "But that is because I have not yet told you the second pertinent feature of this model of robot."

"And what is that?"

"The casing of such a robot is removable."

Maggie frowned and started to shake her head. "I do not see how that can…"

But then she *did* see, and she grinned like the devil himself.

5

Adam and Dagmar were awakened by a clang down the hall beyond their cell door. As they straightened up, their chains clinking, several sets of footsteps approached.

"What do you think's gonna happen?" Dagmar asked, sounding very much like the frightened child she was.

"Nothing, if I can help it," he said, grabbing the two stakes he had fashioned from the plastic tray during the night. He had split the tray diagonally, then snapped off the upturned edges, ending up with a pair of hard, sharp, right-angled triangles. He held the stakes in his lap and drew his knees up to shield the stakes from view from the door.

The steps stopped at the door, and once again there was a clack, followed by the turning of the wheel in the center of the door. The door swung open.

The Annihilator stepped into the room. Behind him came Schweeliski, the guy in the fencing outfit, and a dour black-haired dwarf who carried a two-headed battle axe and wore a suit of badly tarnished chain mail.

"It's your big day," the Annihilator said with mocking good cheer. "Not only are you gonna provide us with some entertainment in the arena, but you get to meet the boss first. Lucky you."

He raised his blaster at Dagmar, who flinched a little but otherwise just stared at him with steely disdain, jaw set. She was playing queen again. Good. It would help her deal with whatever trials were to come.

"Here's how this is gonna work," the Annihilator said. "I'm gonna keep my blaster on the girlie here while the guys blindfold you, unchain you from the wall, and then tie your hands so we can go meet the boss. You so much as look at me funny and she'll be a bloody, smoking mess from the neck up, got it?"

Adam nodded, outwardly composed but inwardly seething with rage and frustration. The stakes he had made were useless. With his strength behind them, they could probably punch through even the Annihilator's armor, but any attempt to use them would risk Dagmar's life. And that was a risk he was not prepared to make.

The Annihilator looked at his companions. "Schwee', you've got the big guy. Tork, you deal with the girl. Artemis, keep your swords ready, just in case."

"They're not swords," said the man in the fencing costume. "They're *epees.*"

"Whatever. Just get to it, guys."

When Schweeliski bent over to blindfold Adam, he saw the plastic shards in Adam's lap and with a shrill squeal grabbed them and held them up for the Annihilator to see.

"Well, well, well," the Annihilator said. "Looks like somebody was workin' on an escape plan. I oughta blow off the girlie's head for that just on principle."

Adam merely glared at him.

After blindfolding Adam and Dagmar, the Marauders undid the chains that bound them, had them stand, and then bound their hands behind their backs, Dagmar's with a pair of handcuffs, Adam's, because handcuffs would not fit around his thick wrists, with a length of thin but extremely tough rope. Then—and this infuriated Adam more than anything else—they buckled dog collars around their necks, hooked long metal leashes to the collars, and led them along with the leashes.

As they got ready to leave the cell, the Annihilator said, "Just in case you're thinking of some daring last-minute escape, remember: I'll have my blaster pointed at the girlie the whole time."

"You are a brave man to threaten a bound and blindfolded child," Adam said.

"Shut up and get moving."

With Artemis in front, Schweeliski leading Adam, Tork leading Dagmar, and the Annihilator bringing up the rear, they exited the cell, turned left down the corridor, went through another doorway, turned left again, headed down a long corridor that smelled like mold, turned right, went down a tiled corridor, turned left near a room in which large machines hummed and thrummed, then...

Adam stopped keeping track. It was pointless. He had hoped he would be able to get a good grasp of the building's layout, but the place was too large and mazy.

Finally, after what must have been at least fifteen minutes, the procession stopped.

"Wait here," the Annihilator said. A moment later Adam felt him brush past to the head of the line. A door opened and closed, and as it did, Adam caught a strong smell of... was that perfume? He considered breaking the rope that bound his wrists—he had surreptitiously pulled it taut a few times during the walk to test its strength and he was sure he could snap it easily—then whisking off the blindfold to fight the three Marauders remaining in the hallway, but he had no idea if they had their weapons drawn. If they did, they would have plenty of time to wound or kill him and/or Dagmar before he had removed both rope and blindfold. An escape attempt wasn't worth it.

Yet.

A minute later the door opened, and the Annihilator said, "Bring 'em in."

They were led inside. And, yes indeed, the room smelled of perfume or incense or something similar. It was a strong, cloying scent both fruity and floral.

The Marauders had them stand side-by-side in the middle of the room, their backs to the entrance.

"Take off the blindfolds," said the Annihilator.

When the blindfolds were removed, neither Adam nor Dagmar could think of anything to say for several long moments.

They were in a spacious chamber with walls painted bright pink and adorned with streamers of various colors. Against the wall to their right was a red divan littered with pillows and several well-worn stuffed animals (inanimate ones, thankfully). Crystal chandeliers hung from the ceiling, their small oval bulbs blazing with electric light. Several full-length mirrors with ornate gilded frames were spaced strategically about the room to reflect and amplify the chandeliers' light. Against the left wall stood a long table covered with food—fruit, candy, a half-eaten drumstick, a nearly empty box of Twinkies, and a cut-glass punchbowl brimming with punch. Balloons lay in drifts on the floor. Bouquets of fresh flowers exploded from tall porcelain vases set in the room's four corners. The floor had been painted pastel green with pink hearts and yellow stars, and across it a ribbon of red carpet stretched from the entrance to a marble dais in front of them. Atop this dais was a throne of sorts: a tall wooden chair slathered in gold paint, a tiger hide draped over the seat. In an arc across the top half of the seat's backrest sparkling green gems—probably fake, but you never knew—spelled out "Emily."

But neither the garish throne nor the wantonly girlish decor—both of which seemed incongruous and somehow offensive in this brutal world—were what stunned Adam and Dagmar speechless.

No, what reduced them to silence was the girl lounging on the throne with her left leg dangling over the left armrest. Twenty years old at most, she wore a hot-pink belly shirt with the words "Let's Face It, I'm Cute" across the chest in white letters, a mind-bogglingly tight pair of white shorts with virtually no legs at all, and glittery purple wedge sandals with five-inch heels. She had straight black hair, long in the back, cut in bangs in front. Frosty silver eye-shadow accentuated her green eyes. Her lips shone with cherry-red lip gloss. Her fingernails and toenails were painted bubblegum pink. She sported several jeweled rings and bracelets, a plain silver band on the second toe of her left foot, and an anklet of shark's teeth. Lying on the right arm of the chair was an object that looked like a child's idea of a laser gun. It had a plump, bright yellow body like a lemon, with sleek white fins swooping off it. The barrel ended in a glassy rod with a bulbous tip.

The girl grinned at their shock. "Not what you were expecting, am I?"

Adam shook his head slightly, then said, "Is this a joke?" He looked at the Annihilator as he said it. He couldn't help it. In comparison, the Annihilator seemed more like a leader than this…this *teenager.* The Annihilator saw him looking at him, but answered, insofar as he did, only by fixing his gaze upon the girl.

"No joke, dickweed," the girl said. "Though soon enough you'll be hoping it was. You killed members of my army, and for that you'll pay a very big, very unfunny price."

"Your army killed my parents," Dagmar said through clenched teeth. "Which pretty much means *you* killed them."

The girl shrugged. "So? They weren't me, so why should I give a fuck?"

"*Bitch!*"

Adam expected the girl to lash out at Dagmar, but instead she just smiled as if Dagmar had given her a great compliment.

"That's right honey," she said. "I'm the queen bitch of the universe, and don't you fucking forget it."

She turned her attention to Adam. "So are all the rumors true? Are you, like, really Frankenstein?"

Adam frowned in confusion. "No, Frankenstein was my creator. I am called Adam. If we are to be interrogated and ridiculed, I should at least like to know the name of the person responsible."

The girl spread her arms and said, in a manner that was both self-important and gently self-mocking at the same time, as if she were deriding the very institutions she had chosen to embody, "I am Queen Emily the First."

"Queen of what? An abandoned building?"

A light kindled in her eyes, a light that made Adam's blood run cold. It was the same light he recalled seeing in his creator's eyes. It was the light of those who believe they are driven by destiny.

"Queen of everything, dumbshit. This whole fucking world is gonna be mine one day. This is just the beginning."

"What gives you the right to toy with people's lives?"

"*I* give me the right."

As she said it, she jerked a thumb at her chest, which called Adam's attention to her full, round breasts nicely defined by her tight shirt. And that, in turn, made his eyes drop to her equally tight shorts, which boldly displayed the contours of her pudendum. He had never seen a woman dressed like that before. Even the whores he had seen during his travels across Europe dressed more conservatively than this. The sight of it stirred feelings and instincts that had been unfulfilled since his creation decades ago. For one very brief moment he wanted nothing more than to fuck this girl's brains out right there on her throne.

Then he remembered why he was here. He had to rescue Anna and Dagmar. And then there was Bob. His mind flashed back to that ghastly bust sitting atop the pile of rubble, and his lust evaporated in the heat of his hatred for this joke of a girl and her idiot soldiers.

"*I* am the queen here," Dagmar said suddenly, her chin up, her eyes narrow and stony. "This is my land. These are my people. You have no claim to anything here."

Emily stared at Dagmar in surprise for a moment, then shrieked with laughter.

"*You're* a queen?" Emily gasped out between laughs. "You're what, like, eight years old? How the fuck can *you* be a queen?"

"Your men killed my parents, the king and queen of this land. That means I am now the queen." She pointed at the Annihilator and Schweeliski. "Ask *them*. They will tell you they found me in a palace."

Emily looked at the Annihilator, eyebrows raised questioningly.

"It's true," the Annihilator said. "More or less. The palace was in ruins."

"That was because of the Cataclysm." Dagmar looked at the Marauders. "If you kill this false queen now, I will grant you a full pardon for all your crimes."

The Annihilator chuckled. "Yeah, right, kid. If it comes down to a choice of queens, I'm stickin' with Em here."

"My offer does not include you. You were the one who killed my mother, the queen. For that you deserve only a long, lingering death. But the rest of you—none of you care to join me? I will not make this offer again." Her eyes fell on Schweeliski and narrowed. "Except *you*. My offer does not include you, either."

"What's wrong with Schweeliski?" asked Emily with amusement.

"He cannot be trusted to follow orders. Do you not have a rule that says your men must not mistreat the female captives without your permission?"

Adam heard the Annihilator draw in a sharp breath, and sensed the other Marauders stiffen.

Emily said nothing for a moment, only stared at Dagmar with a small smile.

"Yes," she said. "I do have such a policy."

"Well, the night your men had me cooped up in that cage, which I easily escaped from by the way, I overheard Schweeliski confess to Skippy that he had done something he shouldn't have with one of the captives. Something bad."

Schweeliski emitted a squeaking sound.

Emily didn't even look at him. She just continued staring at Dagmar with that deceptively mild smile on her face. If anything, the smile seemed to widen a bit more.

Out of the corner of his eye, Adam noticed the other Marauders edge away from Schweeliski.

"Schweeliski," said Emily, her eyes still fixed on Dagmar, "is this true?" Her voice was soft and gentle. She didn't sound angry at all.

Schweeliski made that squeaky noise again, then said, "I—I—I—I couldn't help it. She's so pretty and—"

What happened next completely dispelled any ideas Adam and Dagmar might have had that Emily was just some self-absorbed teenager with no right or reason to be leading a group like the Marauders.

Moving so fast her hand was a blur, Emily snatched her "toy" laser pistol from the arm of the chair, pointed it at Schweeliski's head, and pulled the trigger.

With a brief, low hum, a purple beam shot from the gun's glassy tip and hit Schweeliski right between the eyes. The beam flared when it struck, briefly casting the room in purple hues and vaporizing ninety percent of Schweeliski's face. His body toppled backward, the front of his head a smoking crater.

Emily cackled and pointed at Schweeliski's corpse as if gold doubloons had just poured from its ass.

"Did you see that?" she cried, her eyes bright with mad glee. "Did you fucking *see* that? His head just went—" she put her hands together in front of her face then flung them wide apart "—*fwoosh!* That was fucking *awesome!*"

Both Adam and Dagmar were stunned into silence by this display. It wasn't simply because Emily had killed one of her men, or even that she enjoyed it; it was how fast she had moved and how accurate she had been at that speed. Whoever or whatever this girl was, she wasn't a normal human. Adam wondered if she were a super-powered survivor from Granite's world, or a world like it.

Emily returned her attention to Adam and Dagmar. "Do you know what I'm gonna do with you two?"

"I heard one of your men mention an arena of some sort," said Adam.

Emily nodded, grinning, as if she were amused to hear someone slated to appear in the arena refer to it so casually.

"That's right," she said. "Do you know what that means?"

"It means, I suspect, that you are a spoiled, selfish child who finds amusement in others' pain." He turned to the Annihilator. "Mark my words, one day you will be on the receiving end of that laser-blaster. She feels no loyalty toward you. You are just a tool to her, and will be discarded as such when you no longer prove useful."

The Annihilator snorted. "Don't talk about shit you don't understand, asshole. Emily here's the future. The old way, it's done and gone. We gotta survive in this shitty new world, and to do that we gotta rally round the people who can best help us do it." He looked Adam up and down. "Damn, it's a shame you're such a fuckin' Boy Scout. You woulda made a damn good Marauder."

"A-*hem!*" said Emily. "Save the male bonding crap for some other time, okay?"

"Sorry, my queen," said the Annihilator with a bow.

"As I was saying," Emily said to Adam and Dagmar, "you guys're heading for the arena, where your lives will quickly go from bad to over. There, the two of you will face two Marauders—Tork here, and the Grottle—" Adam felt a slight surge of hope, for he found it conceivable that he and

Dagmar could defeat two Marauders; but that hope was shattered as Emily continued "—both of whom will be allowed weapons. You two will not only have no weapons, but your hands will remain bound behind your backs." She leaned forward in her throne, smiling. "Won't that be *fun?*"

She waved a hand dismissively. "Get them to the arena. Show's gonna start in half an hour." Her eyes fell on Schweeliski's still-smoking body. "And send someone in to clean that up."

The Marauders re-blindfolded Adam and Dagmar and led them away. As they exited the room, Emily called out, "Oh, and Vic, once you've got everything set up, head down to the kitchen and find out where the hell Twitchy got to with my fuckin' Twinkies."

Chapter 11

The Arena

1

The Marauders led Adam and Dagmar through another maze of corridors. This time, however, there were more signs of life along the way—smells of cooking, sticky patches on the floor, the odors of sweat and dirty clothes and moldering food. The Marauders weren't very good at housekeeping.

After five minutes of walking, they heard the murmur of many voices ahead. The sound had an echoing quality, as if the people making it were in a very large space. The arena, Adam presumed.

The sound grew louder and louder, and then someone up ahead opened a door, and the sound ballooned into a roar. It was the roar of an impatient crowd that wants to be entertained, preferably at the expense of someone's life.

After a few more paces, Adam sensed the walls of the corridor fall away on either side and felt the floor change from smooth tile to something uneven and somewhat granular. Probably dirt.

When the crowd saw Adam and Dagmar, they hooted and hollered and hurled taunts and insults. The Marauders' voices came from every side, and from much higher up than the height of an average man, suggesting they were in tiers of seats like those at the theater.

"Stop," said the Annihilator after they had gone about seventy paces into the room.

They stopped. The Annihilator removed their leashes and collars and then whisked off their blindfolds.

They were in a hangar that the Marauders had converted into a sort of stadium with a dirt floor and wooden bleachers around the periphery. There were dark patches in the dirt, some of them relatively fresh, and Adam detected the faint stink of blood. Several doors led off the hangar, including the door in the west wall they had entered through and wide double doors in both the north and south walls. Metal catwalks crisscrossed the room twenty-five feet up.

In the bleachers sat more Marauders than anyone had thought existed. There had to be close to a hundred of them. Adam saw a few he recognized—Droke, Johnny Circumcision, Big Red—but most were new to him. They were of many races and body types, and their outfits included nearly every fashion Adam was familiar with, and many he wasn't. Most were human, but there were also two dwarves (not counting Tork), four other diminutive humanoids that he later learned were gnomes, a cat-man, a lizard-man, an amphibious creature, and several whose body-types defied easy classification.

All these men and monsters were screaming at Adam and Dagmar. Many pumped weapons or fists above their heads in time to the screams, which slowly evolved into a chant: "Kill 'em all! Kill 'em all! Kill 'em all!"

Adam recalled Dagmar telling him that Skippy and Oscar had taken off in pursuit of Maggie last night. He scanned the crowd, dreading to see them, but they weren't there.

"Where are Skippy and Oscar?" he asked, hoping the Annihilator's response would give him a clue to Maggie's fate.

"Shut up," the Annihilator snapped. He jabbed an armored finger at Adam's chest. "I'll tell you one thing: If your fucking girlfriend did anything to them, when we find her we'll do things to her you can't even imagine."

Tork chuckled at that. His teeth, Adam noted, were dark, rotten stumps.

"I'm off to find Twitchy," the Annihilator told Tork and Artemis. "Make sure these two don't go anywhere."

He headed off through the double doors in the south wall.

"Why do you do these things?" Adam asked Artemis. "Why do you commit acts that are clearly evil?"

Artemis snorted. "There ain't no evil. Not in this world. There's only survival, and the strongest and toughest are the ones who survive."

"How is murdering us in this arena conducive to your survival?"

Artemis just stared at him for a moment, and though Adam couldn't see Artemis's expression behind the tight mesh of the fencing mask, he felt a surge of hope that perhaps his words had gotten through to the Marauder, had sparked some long-dimmed light of reason and fellowship within him.

But then Artemis shook his head and said, "What's 'conducive' mean?"

Adam sighed. "Never mind."

2

"Perfect," said Maggie, looking at Freud's new "outfit."

"I feel distinctly uncomfortable," said Freud. "And copper is decidedly not my color."

"You look fine."

It had taken them twenty minutes to remove both Freud's and Adler's casings and then attach Adler's casing to Freud. Without their smooth gleaming shells, the robots were skeletal figures of dull gray metal with cables and bundles of wires snaking to and fro.

"I cannot guarantee that this will work," said Freud. "Subterfuge is not part of my programming."

"No, but preventing humans from being harmed *is*. If human lives depend on it, you *can* prevaricate, right?"

"I am programmed to do whatever is necessary to ensure the survival of human beings."

"Good. Now, then, can you duplicate Adler's tics?"

"I do not know. Let me try." He jerked his head to the left in a passable imitation of Adler, but as he did so he said, "Click."

"No no no. He did not *say* it."

"I know, but I cannot duplicate the sound in any other way. Adler did it only because his neck joint had been damaged."

Maggie pondered this for a moment, then said, "Perhaps you could merely make the head motions periodically, and if anyone asks why you do not make the sound anymore, tell them that it simply stopped and you do not know why."

"I suppose that would work. But you see? You are much better at prevarication than I am. I fear I am the wrong robot for this job."

"It was *your* idea, do not forget."

"I know, I know." He sighed—Maggie still couldn't get used to the idea of a robot doing that—and said, "I suppose I should be off."

"Do not forget this," she said. She bent down and picked up the dented box of Twinkies. "The Marauders' leader will be expecting it."

"Ah, yes. But I have never seen the Marauders' leader before. How will I identify him?"

Maggie smiled. "I imagine he will be the one shouting at you to give him his Twinkies."

"And what will *you* be doing while I am braving these dangers alone?"

"Sneaking around, trying to accomplish the same objectives as you, but in a different way. I think I should—"

Footsteps echoed down the kitchen hallway.

Maggie and Freud stood as still as stones as they waited to find out whether the footsteps would turn off into the kitchen, or continue toward the bend.

Just when Maggie began to fear that the steps had gone on too long and grown too loud and thus must have passed the kitchen already, the swinging doors banged open, and the Annihilator's tinny voice said, "Where the hell's Twitchy? The boss sent me down to see what's takin' him so long."

The doors closed, cutting off Asaparagus Sam's no doubt long and profanity-laden reply.

"When he cannot find Adler, I hope he does not think to look down this corridor," said Freud.

"If he does—"

Before she could finish, the doors banged open again and the Annihilator stormed out, crying, "And the food'd better be ready *stat*. The show's gonna start in fifteen minutes, and it's gonna take you a while to move everything down to the arena."

"But the pig ain't done yet. Shit, it's still rarer than a fat elf."

"Rare's fine. Now get your ass movin'!"

The footsteps paused outside the kitchen as the door

thumped shut.

Don't come this way, Maggie thought. *Don't come this way.*

The footsteps approached.

Maggie started to reach for her dagger, but then had a better idea and motioned for Freud to move away from Adler's inert, uncased form. She hoped that the Annihilator had never seen Adler without his casing before, and also that he didn't notice the pieces of Freud's casing stacked in the corner. Then again, she didn't plan to give him a chance to assess the situation in any depth.

When the Annihilator rounded the corner, Maggie grabbed Adler's shoulder and shouted at the lifeless robot, "Use your incinerator ray! Now!"

The Annihilator responded automatically. Assuming that the main threat was this strange-looking robot (even though the robot's back was to him), he whipped his arm up and fired his blaster at it three times.

Two of the shots hit Adler in the upper back. The third hit it in the head. Had its casing been on, the robot might have survived the attack, but without that outer armor, it didn't have a chance. Its torso blew apart with such force that its left arm went flipping end over end into the west wall, while its head simply dissolved in a spray of wires and circuits and shards of metal.

The moment the Annihilator had raised his blaster, Maggie had whirled and raced south down the corridor, hoping to lure him after her and away from Freud and the evidence of their deception.

It worked. When the Annihilator peered through the smoke from Adler's burning and popping remains and saw that Maggie was already halfway to the nearest side-corridor, he hissed, "Shit," then glanced back at Freud. "Get moving. The boss wants those Twinkies *now!*"

Without waiting for a response, he leaned forward and activated his jetpack. In a burst of flame, he shot down the corridor in pursuit of Maggie.

Freud didn't start moving right away. Instead he watched Maggie dodge around a corner, followed a few seconds later by the Annihilator.

Then he heard the faint sound of a hoverboard starting up.

"Damn it!" shouted the Annihilator. Three laser blasts rang out in quick succession.

Had he breathed, Freud would have held his breath just then.

And then he would have let it out in relief when the Annihilator roared, "Bitch! You can't get away from me!"

The sounds of the hoverboard and the jetpack faded.

Freud sighed. "This is all quite stressful."

He strode past the kitchen and toward the heart of the Marauders' camp.

3

Maggie had forgotten about the hoverboard until she started running. She had stuffed it into her backpack before the trip through the pipe, though since the board was longer than the pack was tall, the top third of the board jutted from the pack's top. Now, as she ran, this top third whapped against the back of her head with every step.

After she rounded the corner into the side-corridor lit by the emergency lights, she reached back and tore the board from the backpack. She tossed it on the floor in front of her, while behind her the sound of the Annihilator's jetpack swelled from a growl to a roar as he shot around the corner.

She jumped onto the board and slammed one foot onto the elevation button to make it rise a foot above the floor and the other foot onto the forward acceleration button. The board shot forward so fast she almost toppled right off it.

"Damn it!" the Annihilator cried, not only because she was getting away but also because her possession of one of the hoverboards meant things looked bleak for Skippy and Oscar. The Marauders had lost too many good men to these dumbfucks already.

He raised his blaster and fired three times at Maggie as she sped away. She was smart enough to zigzag back and forth as she sped along, and all three shots wound up as scorch marks on the walls.

"Bitch! You can't get away from me." He gunned his jetpack and streaked after her.

Maggie kept her foot pressed on the forward accelerator until she was going so fast she had to squint to keep her eyes from drying out. She hoped she was as good at using the hoverboard as she thought she was, because if she collided with something at this speed they would have to pick her up with the Grottle's shovel.

The corridor ended in a T-junction, and she swept around the corner and down the left arm of the T. Her turn was a little too wide, though, and the right edge of the board bumped against the far wall. The board wobbled, and for a moment Maggie thought that it would tilt far enough to send her tumbling right off. But then it steadied itself, just in time for her to swerve around an empty metal cart sitting in the middle of the corridor.

She continued zigzagging at random to ensure that the Annihilator couldn't predict where she would be at any given moment. Which wasn't to say he didn't try; laser blasts streaked past her every few seconds. Luckily none hit her.

The chase took them down a long corridor littered with fallen ceiling tiles, then down a short hallway with a laundry room off it, then down another long corridor lined with offices. This last section had fully functioning fluorescent lights, and when she discovered how much easier it was to negotiate the often cluttered hallways when everything was brightly lit, she vowed to stick only to areas where the power was on.

As the chase progressed, Maggie was surprised to learn that when it came to banking around corners and dodging objects, she was far more maneuverable with the hoverboard than the Annihilator was with his jetpack. He had to slow down considerably more than she did to turn.

He had her beat on raw speed, though, quickly gaining on her whenever they traveled down a long, straight stretch. During one trip down a particularly long corridor, she heard the whine of his engines growing alarmingly loud, and she looked back just in time to see him not more than ten feet behind her, aiming his blaster at the broadest part of her back. She immediately swerved up and to the right until her hair brushed one of the light fixtures. The blast missed, but just barely; she felt its heat as it passed her left hand. Heart hammering, she upped her speed a notch, kept zigzagging, and swerved down the next side corridor she could find.

She no longer had any idea what section of the complex they were in. She wasn't even sure how far they had traveled or how long the chase had lasted. Five minutes? Ten? Everything was a blur of fear and speed and danger underlain by the whir of her board and the drone of his jetpack.

At one point she heard a sound like the muffled roar of a crowd. Or she thought she did anyway. Before she could focus on it or even get a rough idea of which direction it was coming from, she had sped far past it. She recalled Adler's reference to an arena and felt her guts squirm in helpless dread.

Not long after that, she turned left down a corridor and saw with a start that the corridor ended after about three hundred feet in a pair of doors that resembled the swinging doors to the kitchen but were thicker and had no windows. There were no side corridors in this stretch of hallway, and there was no way she could turn around and go back—the loudness of the Annihilator's jetpack indicated he had already entered the corridor and was closing in fast. She didn't even have time to slow down. All she could do was close her eyes and shield her face with her forearms and hope that the doors did indeed swing and that they weren't locked or barred.

The board hit the doors with a loud, sharp bang. This was followed an instant later by a louder, sharper bang as the doors rebounded off the room's inner walls.

When she opened her eyes again, she found herself streaking down a wide aisle between dark, hulking machines that stretched away toward the concrete room's far wall several hundred feet away. The lights were on in the room— rows of bright white globes suspended by cables from the ceiling—but the towering machines blocked much of that light, leaving everything dim and shadowy down here at floor-level.

She was halfway down the main aisle when she realized that she had seen no doors aside from the ones she had entered through. Panic began to fill her mind like murky water flooding the hold of a sinking ship. Was she trapped? Had she unwittingly fled right into a killing box?

It dawned on her that she hadn't heard the doors bang open again. The Annihilator had been close enough behind her that he should have entered the room by now. She glanced over her shoulder.

The Annihilator stood just inside the doorway, watching her. Somehow she knew that behind the mask he was grinning.

The far wall was coming up fast. Time to turn. But she was going too fast to turn without tumbling right off the board. She had to slow down.

She decreased her speed, zigzagging all the while to make it harder for the Annihilator to hit her with his blaster. When she came to the gap between the last row of machines and the far wall, she banked to the right.

The moment she did, she heard a buzz she remembered hearing in Sweetwater, and her blood froze.

It was one of the Annihilator's rockets. She pressed the board's accelerator as hard as she could and hoped she would be able get out of the way in time.

Before she had gone ten feet the rocket exploded behind her, flinging her from the board. As she sailed through the air, flash-blind, ears ringing, skin and clothes torn by flying chips of concrete, she imagined that this was how a fly felt when someone swatted it.

She crashed to the ground, feeling a sudden, intense flare of pain in her right arm as she landed on it, then skidded along the floor, the concrete abrading rubbery curls of flesh from her face and arms. She came to rest halfway down the length of the machine she had been banking around.

For a moment she couldn't move. Her whole body thrummed with the shock of the explosion. She couldn't catch her breath. Pain radiated along her right arm like an electrical current.

Was the Annihilator coming? She didn't know. She couldn't see through the haze of smoke, and all she could hear was a steady staticky ringing. She had to assume he was, though.

She pushed herself to her feet and staggered to the far end of the machine. When she got there, she noticed the hoverboard lying in the corner where the rear wall met the side wall. She stumbled toward it, discovering as she got closer that it was only the bottom of the board's metal covering. Where was the rest of it? It probably wouldn't work anymore, but it was worth a shot.

As she hunted around for it, a flash of movement at the other end of the machine caught her eye, and she looked up, already knowing what she would see.

The Annihilator stood at the end of the main aisle, wrapped in the smoke that still unfurled from the hole he had blown in the wall, his wrist-blaster pointed right at her.

With a burst of energy she didn't know she still had, she leaped to her left as he fired. The blast hit the wall, while she found herself crashing to the floor once again. This time, however, getting up was much easier. There was nothing like a madman aiming a laser blaster at you to get you motivated.

She ran on weak, wobbly legs down the aisle between the machines and the side wall, heading back toward the entrance. Which way would the Annihilator go? Would he follow her directly, or try to cut her off somewhere? She had no idea. And she couldn't listen for him because her ears were still ringing.

Then she saw a metal door standing ajar about halfway down the side wall. Feeling a surge of hope, she changed course and made straight for it. The moment she did so, another laser blast sizzled straight through the spot she had just vacated, briefly casting her shadow onto the wall to her left.

Maggie ran, zigging and zagging and narrowly avoiding a

series of laser blasts that the Annihilator fired as he raced after her. When she was about ten feet from the door, she veered toward the space between two machines on her right, hoping he would think her movement toward the door had been a feint and that her real goal was the main entrance.

It worked. As she spun around to head back toward the door, she saw out of the corner of her eye that the Annihilator had started to run toward the machines to intercept her and was now skidding to a clumsy halt. While he reversed direction with all the grace of a hippopotamus, she barreled through the open doorway and kicked the door shut behind her.

The door had a deadbolt, so she locked it, knowing full well it wouldn't be much proof against someone with lasers and rockets at his disposal.

The room she had entered turned out to be a maintenance room. It was wider than it was deep, with steel shelving units lining the two long walls. The shelves were laden with tools, tarps, buckets, gloves, bits of wire, a can of paint…

Oh, please, let it not be empty, she thought as she hurried over to this latter item. *Or dry.*

Her hearing was improving. Behind her she faintly heard the doorknob rattle.

"You think this'll stop me for long?" the Annihilator said, his voice muffled by both the door and the ringing in her ears. "I know there's no way out of there. You are so fucked, girlie."

"My name is not 'girlie,'" she hissed through gritted teeth as she pulled the paint can from the shelf with the arm that wasn't twanging with pain. The can was heavy, nearly full. She hadn't prepared herself for the weight, and it started to slip from her grasp. She frantically re-grabbed its handle before it could fall, wincing as the thin band of metal dug into her fingers. Something shifted inside the can. She thought it might be liquid sloshing around, but the way things had been going, she figured she had better make sure before getting her hopes up.

Futilely trying to ignore the bangs and booms as the Annihilator kicked at the door—and the cracks and groans as the door began to give—she snatched a hammer from a nearby shelf to pry up the can's lid. Her hands shook so much that at first she couldn't get the claws under the edge of the lid. When she finally did, she yanked the lid up so hard it went flipping into the air, spraying droplets of white paint everywhere.

Still wet. Perfect.

She slid the hammer into her belt without even being aware she was doing it, then picked up the can and hurried toward the door.

The Annihilator nearly had it open. With each kick, the door shuddered inward several centimeters, and the area around the deadbolt was twisted like sun-warped plastic. It wouldn't hold for more than one or two more kicks.

She was six feet from the door when it flew open and the Annihilator stepped into the room. Clutching the rim of the can with her good arm and supporting its bottom with her injured one, she cast the paint at him as he turned toward her. It splashed across his head and shoulders.

"Wha*fuck?*" he said as he instinctively tried to wipe the paint off his lenses. All he did was smear it around.

Maggie charged forward and slammed the empty paint can into his helmet. It produced a satisfying clang. As she raised it to strike again, he swung his arm in a broad, blind arc. His fist struck her in the right breast and sent her staggering backward.

Lucky shot, she thought as she advanced again, trying to

ignore the pain pulsing in her breast. The important thing was this: He was blind now unless he took his helmet off, which was what she was hoping he would do. Without his helmet he would be vulnerable.

He was too smart for that, though. Instead he said, "Tricky. Very tricky," and then stood very still. She didn't understand why until she moved a little and the can's handle gave a faint creak. He immediately raised his blaster in the direction of the sound and fired.

His aim was off, and the blast streaked harmlessly past her. Before he could do anything else, she tossed the paint can to her right. Its handle rattled as it sailed through the air, and the Annihilator tracked the sound, firing shot after shot, riddling the can with holes.

When the can struck a shelf and clanged to the floor, he realized she had tricked him. He started to turn back toward her, but by then it was too late: While he had been blasting away at the empty paint can, Maggie had slipped the hammer from her belt, and now, clutching the handle in both hands, she swung it as hard as she could at his wrist-blaster.

The force of the impact juddered up her arms. A chunk of the blaster flew away and clattered beneath one of the metal shelves. The bulk of it remained attached, but now its front half was bent to the side at a forty-five degree angle.

Unaware of the extent of the damage, the Annihilator pointed the blaster at where he now knew she was and tried to fire it. The blaster made a faint hissing sound and quivered a little, but that was all.

"Oh, you cunt," he said.

By then she had already brought the hammer up to strike him over the head. Unfortunately he guessed that was exactly what she would do, and raised the arm with the damaged blaster to shield his head. The moment the hammer struck his armored elbow, he punched at Maggie with his other hand and this time landed a solid blow to her stomach. She stumbled backward, slipped in the wet paint on the floor, and landed on her ass.

The Annihilator heard her fall and promptly swung one metal-booted foot at her. It swished past her right ear. Before he could pull his foot back, she kicked at the leg he was standing on, and since, unlike him, she could see clearly, she hit him square in the shin.

Under normal circumstances, it wouldn't have had much of an impact. His armor was thick enough to prevent a simple kick from hurting him, and her position was such that she was unable to put much force behind the blow. But he was off balance, with one leg in the air, and more importantly, he was standing in slick, wet paint, so Maggie's blow sent his foot skidding out from under him. With a startled cry, he crashed face-down on the floor.

The moment he landed, Maggie darted forward and pounded his helmet with the hammer. She landed several solid blows, but they didn't seem to have any effect, for as soon as he had recovered from the shock of falling, he punched at her again. His fist smashed into her right hip hard enough to make her scream and drop the hammer. He must have hit a nerve, because her entire right leg briefly flared with pain and then went tingly and half numb.

She pushed herself backward across the paint-streaked floor with her left foot. The Annihilator scrambled after her, periodically sweeping a hand through the air in front of him in hopes of nabbing her. She evaded him and continued scooting backward until her back thumped against something. She yipped and twisted around to see what it was. It turned out to be only one of the shelving units, but her surprise had stopped her long enough for the Annihilator to catch up to her. Before she knew what was happening, his hand seized her left ankle.

"Gotcha now, bitch," he said.

She couldn't break free, couldn't even slip her foot out of her boot. His grip was too tight.

She grabbed the nearest shelf and tried to pull herself away from him, her injured arm shrieking in pain. The whole shelving unit leaned forward, so she let go before it fell on her. She hadn't realized the units were freestanding.

But that, she realized, could be her salvation. The shelving unit next to her, the one she had nearly brought down, ended at her ankle. At that point a separate unit extended on for about eight feet. And the Annihilator was right in front of that one.

The Annihilator rose to his knees, clearly preparing to stand up. Before he could do so, Maggie grabbed the edge of the shelving unit next to him with both hands, and pulled it away from the wall as hard as she could.

It started leaning immediately, and several items slid of the shelves and thumped on and around the Annihilator. A rusty vise the size of a raccoon rumbled off a shelf about halfway up and crashed onto the Annihilator's jetpack, slamming him to the ground. He screamed. A moment later a motor only slightly smaller than the vise plummeted onto the back of his right knee, producing another, louder scream.

For a moment she didn't think she would be able to pull the unit out far enough for it to fall, but she focused all her energy into one last tug, and with a brief screech of metal on concrete, it tilted forward a little more, hung in mid-air for what seemed like an unusually long time, then boomed down on the Annihilator.

As it fell, a large box full of cans of spray-paint that collectively must have weighed twenty pounds smashed onto her lower left leg. The pain was so bad she couldn't even scream; she just hissed in enough air to fill a blimp.

When the pain receded enough for her to think coherently again, she saw that the Annihilator had let go of her leg and was squirming beneath the shelving unit and its spilled contents. He couldn't find the leverage to push the unit off him.

"I'm gonna kill you, you fucking bitch!" he said.

Maggie tried to stand up, but both legs flared with pain the moment she put any weight on them. The leg the box of spray-paint had fallen on hurt so badly she feared it was broken. It hurt far less to crawl on her hands and knees, so that's what she did, making her way as quickly as she could down the side of the fallen unit, along the unit's top, and toward the still-open doorway.

As she neared the door, she heard a crash behind her and looked back. The Annihilator had gotten halfway out from under the unit and removed his helmet, casting it aside as the useless lump of metal it had become.

He was a thin, rat-faced man, with lank black hair, a long lumpy nose that had obviously been broken many times, and virtually no chin whatsoever.

"You are so dead," he said. Without the mechanical amplification of his helmet, his voice was reedy, almost girlish.

Maggie resumed her crawl. When she reached the doorway, the Annihilator let out a loud grunt. She looked back again, fearing he was on his feet and ready for revenge.

But no: Though he was all way the out from under the unit, he lay on his side clutching his right leg, his eyes squeezed shut, his lips peeled back from his gritted teeth. She realized he had *tried* to stand up, but the motor had injured his leg as badly as or worse than hers.

This development gave her a fresh burst of hope. Maybe she would make it through this after all.

She dragged her herself out the door and toward the nearest aisle between the machines. She kept hoping the pain in her legs would abate enough for her to be able to stand, but though it did let up, it was only a little bit.

When she was less than five feet from the mouth of the aisle, she heard the Annihilator say, "Say 'goodnight,' bitch."

She looked back. He was on his hands and knees in the maintenance room doorway, his rat face made even more so by the sneering, toothy grin he was giving her.

He ducked his head so that the two remaining rockets in his jetpack were pointed right at her.

Her whole body went rigid with horror. Even her heart and lungs seemed to stop working. She had forgotten about the rockets.

There was a click from the jetpack, and she flinched, expecting a rocket to come streaking toward her. But none did. Instead the jetpack kept clicking like a clock.

And then she saw why: The side of the pack had been dented enough to prevent the rockets from leaving their tubes. It must have happened when the vise fell.

"What the fuck?" said the Annihilator, twisting his head around to look at the jetpack.

As he did so, the pack began shaking, and the clicks grew faster and faster until they blended together into a rattle. The rockets started to glow red-hot.

"Oh, you bitch!" cried the Annihilator. "You fucking—"

The pack exploded with a nova-bright flash and a flesh-pummeling boom that left Maggie temporarily blind and deaf for the second time in ten minutes.

When the glare died down and she could see again, she saw that there wasn't much to see. Where the Annihilator had lain a moment ago, there was now a smoking hole in the floor surrounded by bits of twisted metal and charred lumps that reminded her unpleasantly of the pig she had seen roasting on the spit in Asparagus Sam's kitchen.

"That was for Bob," she told the Annihilator's remains.

She rested with her back against the machine for a few minutes, then devoured what little food and water she had left and tried to stand again. This time she was able to do it without falling down. Apparently nothing was broken after all.

Grimacing with every step, she hobbled out of the room and back into the maze of corridors.

4

Jerking his head to the left every five to ten seconds even though he saw no one around (it never hurt to be careful), Freud passed the kitchen and turned right at the first hallway he came to. Immediately he saw signs of Marauder activity—crude slogans and doodles done in marker and spray paint on the walls; smashed-in doors; recent stains and scuff-marks on the floor tiles. He passed a door with "Armory" stenciled over a spot where an earlier sign had been scraped off (Freud determined from a quick analysis of residual traces that it had read "Assistant Director—R&D") and another marked "Loot" (this over an earlier sign that had read "Conference Room").

After about six hundred feet, the corridor ended at a T-junction. He looked down one arm of the T, then the other. Both showed signs of habitation. Indeed, neatly painted upon a nearby door was: "This Is The Cardiac Kid's Room—KEEP OUT OR I'LL SIC THE DAWG POUND

ON YA!" Below it someone had recently scribbled in marker, "The Kid's dawg got pounded first!"

Which way, then?

The kitchen had been to the right. Any logical person would keep the kitchen close to the common areas (a category that included arenas). Therefore those common areas would also be on the right.

But were the Marauders logical people? Definitely not. They were, simply put, barbarians who rejected impositions upon their libidos and gleefully allowed full expression to their basest instincts.

So no, logic had little place here.

Instead he stood very still and listened, trying to detect the faintest sounds with his phonic receptors.

And there it was: a distant susurrus as of a large crowd calling out off to the right (yes, indeed, the right after all, which perhaps indicated that even barbarians such as these still followed the dictates of logic, albeit unconsciously).

He headed toward the sound, bedroom doors passing by on either side, all of them sporting warnings against trespassers, as he knew they would: Even those who proclaim to detest civilization and all its burdens demand a right to privacy and personal property, never realizing the hypocrisy of their attitude, for rights are an artifact of civilization, of law.

After passing numerous bedrooms, a dining hall, and a game room, Freud came to a four-way intersection where arrowed signs pointed the way to various areas. "Living Quarters" pointed west, the direction from which he had come. "Arena" pointed east, the direction he had been heading. "The Big Boss" pointed north. "Harem" pointed south.

No doubt the harem was where the abducted women

were kept. But while those women certainly needed to be freed, the information he and Ms. Frankenstein overheard earlier suggested that Mr. Frankenstein and Ms. Dagmar were to be put to death, or to a challenge that amounted to death, presumably in the arena, where, judging by the noise, such an event was already underway.

His course was clear: He had to rescue those in the most imminent danger.

As he took a step in the direction of the arena, a door down the northern corridor flew open and a black-haired young woman stepped into the hallway. She was dressed in a truly astounding outfit: a diamond-studded black leather bikini top, tight black leather pants with a silver-buckled purple belt, stiletto-heeled black leather boots, enough jewelry to break an elephant's spine, and draped over it all a royal-purple robe with ermine edging. Clipped to her belt was an odd yellow gun in a holster.

There was no way for Freud to duck out of sight before the young lady saw him, so he just continued strolling toward the arena as if he had every right in the world to do so.

But apparently he didn't, for when the woman saw him, her jaw dropped in outrage, and she cried, "There you are! Where the fuck have you been, you fucktard!"

Freud stopped and waited for her to catch up, making sure to jerk his head to the left every few seconds.

"Gimme those!" she snapped, snatching the box of Twinkies from his hand. "When I give you an order, you follow that fucking order, do you fucking understand me?" By the time she had finished this little outpouring, the front of Freud's (actually Adler's, may his operating system rest in peace) casing was flecked with tiny beads of saliva.

"You have my most sincere apologies," said Freud, jerking his head to the left. "The cook is quite…talkative."

Her lip curled back in a sneer, but now her anger seemed divided between the robot and the chef. "He's a fucking whiner. The only reason he's still alive is 'cause he makes a chocolate-cherry cheesecake like nobody else." Without a pause her eyes narrowed and she said, "Why aren't you clicking when you twitch anymore?"

The abrupt change of subject would have rattled a normal person, which perhaps had been this obviously shrewd and suspicious young lady's intention. But Freud was a robot and so answered swiftly and casually: "It stopped happening about half an hour ago."

It wasn't a lie. Adler's clicking had indeed stopped half an hour ago. Permanently.

"Hm," said the woman. "That's good. That fucking clicky shit was really fucking annoying, you know. There were times I wanted to just blow your clicky little head right off."

"Well, it is indeed a delightful thing that it has stopped, then."

"Yeah," she started striding toward the arena, tearing open the box of Twinkies as she went. "Come on. We're running late. By the way, where the hell'd the Annihilator get to?"

"I am not exactly sure."

"Hm."

Freud hurried after her, his processors racing. The weight of the evidence suggested that this profane young lady was the Marauder's leader. Freud found that very surprising for a number of reasons, not the least of which was the fact that most id-possessed men would refuse to be governed by someone smaller and weaker than themselves. The logical conclusion, then, was that this young lady, though smaller than the men, was *not* weaker. She clearly possessed some sort of strength, whether physical, intellectual, or otherwise, that her followers either could not or would not challenge.

Curious, he gave her a quick bio-scan. Physiologically she was human, though she was phenomenally healthy. He had never seen a human, even one as young as she, so problem-free. There was clearly more to her than met the eye. If only he knew what it was.

5

Adam and Dagmar had been standing in the center of the arena for nearly twenty minutes, enduring the jeers and profanities of the Marauders while everyone awaited "Queen" Emily's arrival.

Dagmar was braving the situation quite well, Adam noted with satisfaction. She stood with her back straight, her eyes fixed on the entrance, her expression composed and a little frosty, as if a tardy envoy were about to come through the door rather than her de facto executioner. Though Adam knew Dagmar wasn't a queen after all, right now she looked far more regal than the Marauders' lewd, egocentric mistress could ever dream of being.

Finally the door in the west wall flew open, and Emily strode in. The Marauders cheered and whooped and shouted "Hail, Emily!" She took it all in with a small contented smile, like a sunbather soaking up rays on a tropical beach.

Adam's eyes were immediately drawn to her outfit, which in some ways was far more revealing that the one she had worn in her throne room. He couldn't keep his eyes off her full, round breasts barely contained by their jeweled leather slings; the delicate comma of her navel in the center of her taut belly; the sleek curves of her legs sheathed in her skin-tight pants.

She was an arrogant, self-absorbed, murderous bitch, but he couldn't deny that she aroused in him a primal lust like nothing he had ever felt before. Since abandoning his mad quest for a mate all those years ago, he had consciously suppressed all his sexual instincts. It seemed best to do so, for he knew those instincts were unlikely to ever be fulfilled. But as Freud could no doubt tell him, suppression was far from eradication, and the instincts remained, seething below the surface, caged but as feral as ever. And now this horrid girl had set them free.

Yet while she aroused him, she also filled him with a stew of far less pleasant emotions. Moments ago he had labeled her arrogant, self-absorbed, and murderous—adjectives that could also have described *him* once upon a time. In his youth, he really *had* been a monster, not because of his appearance, but because of his actions. He had been aware of that for many years now; but to see that truth paraded before him in the form of this depraved young beauty brought that knowledge home in an especially sharp and painful way. It shamed and enraged him to think of how much time and energy he had wasted despising the world because it was not his own private paradise and enacting bloody vengeance on people for failing to do what he wished they would. Good lord, if he had met this girl then, what a terror the two of them might have become.

His thoughts broke off as a robot similar in appearance to Freud entered behind Emily. As it looked around the room, its gaze briefly fixed on Adam and Dagmar, then moved on.

"Do you see?" Dagmar said.

"Yes," said Adam. "Judging by its curious head movements, I believe that is the injured analyst Freud told us about the other night. Adler."

Emily made her way to the west side of the arena, where a chair stood in a wide, level area midway up the rows of bleacher seats. Similar to her throne, the chair was large and high-backed and covered with silver paint. "EMILY" was once again written in an arc on the back of the seat, this time with glued-on green glitter. The arm-rests of this seat had holes for cups and a section that could flip inward across her lap to serve as a tray. Atop the chair was a green-and-white striped canopy, which struck Adam as particularly useless, given that the sun never shone in here.

She sat down, setting the Twinkies on an arm-rest. Adler stood at attention at the rear left corner of the seat. Emily picked up a megaphone that sat on a small table to her right. The megaphone was white, and on its side it read, "#1."

"Have we got a fuckin' awesome show today!" she said through the megaphone, her amplified voice echoing throughout the hangar.

The Marauders cheered and stamped their feet and pumped their fists in the air.

"As most of you already know, a bunch of prissy little do-gooders have attacked us in an attempt to shut us down. I could not, of course, allow such aggression to go un-checked. The only aggression I'll tolerate is *our* aggression!"

This inspired another round of shouting and fist-pump-ing.

"Well, we caught the bastards. The Annihilator blew one of 'em up."

More cheers, but Emily didn't notice. She was scanning the bleachers with a slight frown of concern. Adam realized then that the Annihilator wasn't present. Was there trouble somewhere? He hoped so.

"And the Grottle chopped off the head of another!"

A resounding bout of cheering. The Grottle grinned and held up its shovel.

"And Skippy and Oscar are in hot pursuit of another!"

More cheers, but somewhat subdued this time, as if everyone suspected something bad had happened. Even Emily looked unconvinced by what she had said.

"But even if that one gets away, it's no biggie. It's just some skinny, old chick. And as for the other two—they're right here, ready to put on a fuckin' show for us!"

The loudest cheers yet, accompanied by more foot-stamping and fist-pumping. Some of the Marauders even took to banging their weapons on the floor or on nearby seats.

"You all know how the arena works, but I don't think our guests do." She leaned forward and smirked at Adam and Dagmar. "Here's the deal. Each one of you will be pitted against a Marauder. They've got weapons. You don't. Chances are you'll get hacked to ribbons in, like, no time. In fact, most of the guys have made bets on how long you'll last." She focused solely on Dagmar. "You'll be facing Tork. The odds say you won't last more than a minute. Some guys're sayin' you won't even make it past thirty seconds." Her eyes swiveled to Adam. "You'll be up against the Grottle. Considering the little battle you two had a few days ago, everyone's betting this will be the *real* fight. The baby girl's just the warm-up act. Anyway, if either of you manage to defeat your opponent, then you'll face a new challenge: You'll have to take on *two* Marauders." She started to chuckle. "And if by some bizarro miracle you defeat *them,* then you'll face *three* Marauders." She was laughing so hard she could hardly speak now. "And so on and so on until you're totally dead."

The Marauders howled with laughter. The rafters shook with the sound. Adam and Dagmar just stood there, silent and still, refusing to give their captors the satisfaction of a response.

"And so," said Emily, raising her arms, her eyes aglow with demented merriment, "let the games begin!"

Tork with his two-headed battle-axe and the Grottle with its shovel stood up to applause and cheers and cries of "Kill 'em all!" They hopped from the bleachers to the dirt of the arena and without further ado charged at their opponents with their weapons raised, Tork screaming a dwarvish war-cry as he raced toward Dagmar, the Grottle silent but grinning as it loped toward Adam.

"Get behind me," Adam said to Dagmar. She did. He pulled his arms apart and the rope that bound his wrists snapped like frayed string.

Cries of foul went up from the audience, but no one seemed to expect any actual penalty for Adam's rule-breaking. After all, he and Dagmar had no chance of getting out of the arena alive whether their wrists were bound or not.

Tork fell back a little, allowing the Grottle to distract Adam so he could circle around and pick off Dagmar. Adam divined their plan and told Dagmar, "Just run. Stay out of his reach. I will try to defeat the Grottle, then help you."

"Um, okay," said Dagmar, not really convinced of the soundness of his plan. She sprinted for the north end of the arena. Tork raced after her.

Adam nodded when he saw his suspicions confirmed: Tork, with his armor and battle-axe and stocky dwarf body was much slower than Dagmar. He had no hope of catching her unless she did something incredibly stupid.

And then he couldn't think about Dagmar any more, for

the Grottle had reached him.

The Grottle raised its shovel over its head, but before it could strike, Adam grabbed the Grottle's wrists.

It tried to pull its arms free, but Adam held on tight. The Grottle bared its teeth at him. He responded by head-butting it, his forehead smashing into the Grottle's nose. Green blood squirted from its nostrils.

The Grottle shook it off as if it were nothing and swiftly kicked one of Adam's legs out from under him while simultaneously pressing forward, sending both of them crashing to the ground. Adam landed on his back with the Grottle straddling his waist, its wrists still clutched tightly in his hands. The Grottle returned the head-butt, slamming its shiny yellow forehead into Adam's left eye socket. Stunned, Adam let go of the Grottle's wrists. Laughing its distinctive laugh—"hurr hurr hurr!"—it raised the shovel again.

Adam bucked his hips. Thrown off balance, the Grottle stretched out its arms to steady itself, at which point Adam delivered a swift punch to its neck.

Gasping, the Grottle rolled off him and jumped to its feet. Adam rose as well. The two of them faced each other, glaring.

6

Dagmar made it to the north end of the arena before Tork was even halfway there. Seeing that she had plenty of time to do what she wanted to do, she squatted down until her cuffed hands were on the ground and the cuff-chain between them lay in the dirt. Then she moved one foot backward behind the chain, followed by the other foot.

When she stood up, her cuffed hands were now in front

of her. It didn't really improve her chances against a dwarf with a battleaxe, but it was a start. And it made her feel a little better, a little more in control.

Tork was now ten feet away and closing in fast. Well, relatively fast. He lumbered along in his heavy mail, a snarl on his lips, his eyes full of murder.

Dagmar ran to her left, giving Tork a wide berth, and raced toward the south end of the arena.

Behind her she heard Tork groan and say, *"Tukul dim vornot."* She guessed it was some kind of dwarvish curse.

The Marauders in the stands mocked her as she ran past.

"Coward!" shouted one.

"Whaddaya expect," snorted another. "Girls can't fight."

"Don't let Em hear you say that," said a third.

Others started a chant: "Run, bunny, run! Run, bunny, run!"

The chant infuriated her. She wished she didn't have to run. She wished she knew how to fight well enough to leave Tork and the rest of these bastards in little red pieces.

But she didn't, so she ran.

7

Adam and the Grottle eyed each other in silence, the Grottle grinning and turning its shovel round and round in its beefy hands, Adam tense and focused and ready for anything.

This went on for several minutes, neither of them making a move, and the crowd—at least those who weren't criticizing Dagmar's lack of fighting skills—started yelling at Adam and the Grottle to just fucking *do* something already.

Finally the Grottle did. It squatted down until its thighs

were parallel to the floor, and then it sprang into the air.

For a moment Adam just gaped at it. He hadn't thought the bulky creature capable of such a move. But he didn't gape long. As the Grottle sailed toward him, it raised its shovel, ready to lop off Adam's head.

Adam tried to dodge out of the way, but he was too slow; the Grottle swung at him while it was still airborne, and the flat edge of the shovel struck him between the shoulder-blades and knocked him to the ground. At instant later the Grottle landed, whirled toward Adam, and charged.

Ignoring the pain throbbing in his upper back, Adam scraped a fistful of dirt from the arena floor and chucked it in the Grottle's face. The Grottle stopped in its tracks and scrubbed a hand across its eyes.

By the time it had swiped the dirt away, Adam was already barreling toward it. It had no time to dodge or even raise its shovel in defense. Adam slammed shoulder-first into the Grottle's chest. The Grottle crashed to the dirt with Adam atop it in a reversal of their initial melee in the arena.

Adam grabbed the shovel's handle with both hands and yanked it upward, trying to wrest it from the Grottle's grasp. The shovel started to slip from the Grottle's shock-limp fingers, but at the last second the Grottle shook off its daze and tightened its grip.

They pulled at the shovel in a manic tug-of-war. Adam soon realized that he and the Grottle were strong enough and desperate enough to continue the tug-of-war indefinitely, which meant other means of gaining the advantage were necessary. And when Adam noticed their respective hand positions—his own hands in the middle of the shaft, the Grottle's on either side of them—he understood exactly how to do that.

Moving faster than a greased fish, he let go of the shovel

with one hand and swung that arm under the handle and then up until the handle was crooked in the bend of his elbow. Then he let go with the other hand, hoping his elbow was strong enough to counter the Grottle's two-handed pull. It was, so he delivered the coup de grace: He bent the arm not holding the shovel, raised it high, and brought the back of his upper arm down as hard as he could onto the wooden shaft next to the arm that *was* holding it.

With a sharp snap like a bone breaking, the handle split in two.

A shocked silence descended upon the arena. The Marauders gaped at the broken shovel as if it were a defiled holy relic. Even Tork paused in his pursuit of Dagmar to stare at it.

The Grottle took it worst of all. Its eyes widened until it seemed its whole face would slide into them. Its mouth dropped open, and then its lips writhed in a dozen different directions at once, as if it couldn't decide which emotion to express. Anger? Sorrow? Horror? Rage?

Before the Grottle could decide on a response, Adam grabbed the two halves of the shovel, one in each hand, and tried to pull them from the monster's grip. He half succeeded. The all-wood end came away easily, because the Grottle let it go. But the Grottle then switched the hand that been holding it to the blade-end and, pulling with both hands, tore that from Adam's grasp.

Eyes blazing with hate, lips curled so far back from its teeth that Adam could see its black gums, the Grottle let out a bellow so loud it made Adam's ears ring, then swung the shovel's blade at Adam with a speed that surpassed anything it had demonstrated so far. Adam hadn't considered the fact that with the length of the shovel now halved, the Grottle would be able to swing it while lying down.

Instead of trying to block it, Adam just dropped to his left. He felt the sharp edge of the shovel briefly tug at his sleeve, and then he was on the ground, rolling away from the Grottle, the lower end of the shovel's handle held away from his body so he didn't impale himself.

The Grottle shot to its feet and spun around to face Adam. With no time to stand up, Adam scrambled backward across the dirt like a crab.

Again the Grottle squatted and leaped. This time, instead of trying to get out of the way, Adam braced his back and shoulders against the ground, bent his legs until his knees touched his chest, and then kicked straight out at the Grottle.

Adam savored the Grottle's look of mingled surprise and impotent fury as it sailed toward the rising soles of Adam's boots. His boots struck it right in its massive belly, forcing a *whoof* of breath from its throat and pushing it up and back. When the boots stopped rising, the Grottle flew off them like a rock from a catapult and thudded to the ground ten feet away. Adam sprang to his feet, the segment of the shovel's handle clutched in his right hand like a dagger.

Dagmar raced past on his left. He had noticed her and Tork passing by several times during his fight with the Grottle. This was, he estimated, their fourth circuit around the arena.

Dagmar didn't look at him as she passed. She just sprinted by, not even remotely out of breath or tired.

Tork, on the other hand, was glistening with sweat and wheezing for breath as he half ran, half staggered after Dagmar. His face was twisted into a hateful sneer. He had tossed away his horned war-helmet, and his shaggy black hair flopped about as he ran, at least those locks of it that weren't plastered to his sweaty forehead and cheeks.

Every so often he cast an evil glance at the audience, and it took Adam a moment to realize why. Adam had by now grown so accustomed to the roars and calls from the Marauders that he had had ceased to pay them any attention. Now, as he listened, he realized that many of the Marauders were laughing at Tork and his inability to take down one skinny little human girl.

Adam started to smile, but then out of the corner of his eye he saw the Grottle getting to its feet, so he turned his attention back to his opponent.

Though nearly blinded with rage at having its beloved shovel broken, the Grottle had learned enough from fighting Adam not to charge at him again. Instead it stalked forward, eyes never leaving Adam, shovel-half gripped tightly in both hands, until it stood only four feet away from him.

They stood there facing each other for a moment, crouched and ready like wrestlers waiting for the bell, then Adam lunged forward, swinging his left fist toward the Grottle's face. The Grottle swung the shovel-head up to block.

But the punch was a feint, and as the shovel-head rose, Adam plunged the jagged end of the handle into the Grottle's belly. The splintery wood punched through a thick wall of muscle and then slid deep into something soft and greasy.

The Grottle roared in pain. Adam tried to yank the handle out, but it got caught on something inside the Grottle, and while he was distracted with working it free, the Grottle slammed the broad side of the shovel into his face. Adam both felt and heard his nose crunch inward. His upper lip split against his front teeth, and blood squirted down his chin. One of those front teeth wiggled in its socket.

Dazed, Adam staggered backward, then stumbled and fell flat on his back. The Grottle dropped to its knees on Adam's chest, driving the wind from him and cracking a rib. It swiftly raised the shovel over its head, ready to bury it in Adam's brain.

And then the shovel disappeared from its hands. Bewildered, the Grottle looked over its shoulder and saw Dagmar racing away with the shovel held high above her head like an Olympic torch.

"Sucker!" she cried.

Adam forgotten, the Grottle shot to its feet and ran after her. Adam, now recovered from his shock, likewise shot to his feet and set off in pursuit of the Grottle. For a brief interval the quartet formed a line as they ran down the length of the arena—Dagmar in the lead, followed by the Grottle, then Adam, then poor Tork trailing behind everyone.

Sprinting so fast he could hear the air whistling past his ears, Adam caught up with the Grottle and tackled it. They fell to the dirt and fought there like wild dogs, their careful, calculated battle reduced to clawing and punching and growling and biting.

Tork stopped a few feet away from them, then glanced at Dagmar. She was eighty feet away now. There was no way he could catch her. But he might be able to kill the other one if the Grottle could just maneuver the big yellow *muktek* into the right position.

The Grottle rolled onto its back with Adam atop him. Tork stepped forward to sink his axe into Adam's back. But then they rolled away, flipping over so that the Grottle was now on top.

Tork waited impatiently while they beat each other senseless. The Grottle tried to pry out Adam's eyes with its fingers. Adam bit off the end of one of those fingers. The Grottle kneed Adam in the crotch. Adam kneed it back. The Grottle head-butted Adam in the mouth, knocking free the loosened tooth. Adam spat the tooth into the Grottle's eye. And all the while Tork lumbered in when he thought he had a chance to strike at Adam, only to back away when the opportunity quickly passed.

Then in mid-grapple, Adam glanced in Tork's direction and something sparked in his eyes. A smile flitted on his lips.

Tork straightened up, confused.

At that moment several things happened more or less simultaneously.

First, Adam pushed the Grottle off him so hard that it crashed face-down in the dirt six feet away.

Second, something sailed into Tork's field of vision from behind and slightly to the right of his head. It was the blade end of the shovel, and Adam snatched it out of the air with a grin as he sprang to his feet.

Third, Tork became aware that the Marauders in the stands were shouting his name, and had been for some time now. He had been too caught up in the impending kill to hear their cries of "Tork! Look out!"

This third thing led to the fourth thing, which was that he realized he hadn't been keeping track of Dagmar the last few minutes.

He had time to think *dolten tuko*—a dwarvish term which literally translates as "turds galore" and is used to express the feeling that one is surrounded by misfortune—before something else flashed across his field of vision, this time from the top down. He realized too late it was Dagmar's forearms with the handcuff chain pulled taut between them, realized it even as she pulled back with all her might and the chain tightened across his throat.

Had he done the smart thing and swung his axe back over his shoulder to try to bury it in her head, he might have survived. As it was, he foolishly dropped his axe and tried to pull the chain away from his neck. It was hopeless; Dagmar had one foot planted in the middle of his back and was pushing him forward with it while tugging backward with her arms. As Tork's lungs burned, and dark spots filled his sight, he thought *dolten tuko* one last time, and then he didn't think anything ever again.

Meanwhile, the Grottle leaped to its feet, plucked the section of the shovel's handle from his gut, planning to plunge it deep into Adam's eye, and turned around to rejoin the fray.

Adam was right there, teeth bared in fury, upraised arms straining as he brought the shovel-blade down upon the Grottle's head with all his strength.

Chuck!

The Grottle staggered backward three steps, the shovel buried so deep in its head that the handle protruded from between its eyes. Green blood gushed from the cleft in the top of its head, poured down its shirt, puddled on the dirt floor.

It said, "Hurrrrrr," then its eyes rolled up and it toppled backward and crashed dead to the ground.

The arena was completely silent for a moment. Then there was a clink from Dagmar's handcuffs as she released Tork's corpse. It likewise thudded to the ground.

Dagmar strode up beside Adam and glared at Emily, whose eyes and mouth were wide with shock. Adam glanced at Dagmar, noted her look of outraged regality, and decided not to speak as he had been planning to. He figured he had better let her have her say first.

Indeed she was more than outraged. She had just killed

someone. Sure, he had been trying to kill her, but still...*she had killed someone!* She would have to live with it forever, live with the feel of his body convulsing, with the gaspy gurgly sounds he had made, with the small mole she had noticed on the back of his neck as she choked away his life. She knew she had lost something precious she would never get back. And it was all the Marauders' fault.

Well, if they were gonna mess with her, she'd mess with them right back. She couldn't fight worth spit. She couldn't beat them up or hack them to pieces or grapple with them like Adam. But she could lie. Oh, man, could she lie. She was gonna lie like no one had ever lied before. And, no, it probably wouldn't work in the end. But damn it, she'd get her licks in as best she could. She'd go down lying.

"See?" she shouted, her eyes ablaze with indignation. "See what happens when you stand against me and my subjects? Send out more of your men. Send them all, for all I care. Because in the end, I'll be sitting atop a mountain of your corpses and laughing at your stupidity."

All the Marauders were gaping at her now, not sure what to make of this imperious little girl who spoke in tones they had heard before only from Emily. Even Adam gaped at her. Her tone was so convincing that he fleetingly wondered if maybe she had been lying about lying about being a queen. But no: She was just a natural-born bullshitter.

Emily seemed to be the only one not buying it. She just sat there, staring narrow-eyed at the girl with one eyebrow cocked.

She shook her head slightly and opened her mouth to speak, but just then Freud spoke up instead, having seen his opportunity to non-violently cripple the Marauders' belief in their leader—for psychoanalytic theory insisted that a mob like them would become a disorganized mass of egocentric individuals without a strong leader to keep them functioning as a group.

"The girl is correct," he announced. "She is indeed the rightful queen of this land. Emily is a false queen, as has been clearly demonstrated by her repeated failures to vanquish her opponents."

Emily shot to her feet and gawped at Freud with a stunned, hurt expression that made her look no older than Dagmar. Then her face set into a hard, hateful glare and she said, "Shut. Up."

"No, we must face facts. This so-called queen is a fraud whose time is ending, whereas this young girl before us has demonstrated true queenliness. We must—"

"Fuck you!" screamed Emily. She pulled her yellow laser blaster from its holster and pointed it at Dagmar. "You wanna see queenliness? I'll show you her queenly fuckin' brains splatted all over the room."

Dagmar didn't budge. She just glared at Emily, too angry to care that she might be killed. Adam took a step toward Dagmar, thinking to block the shot with his body, but doubting he could make it in time.

And then he saw he didn't have to, because as Emily's finger tightened on the trigger, a black blur streaked down from the catwalk overhead and slammed Emily to the floor. A ray shot from the blaster as she fell and gouged a smoking hole in the dirt twenty feet to Adam's left.

Emily found herself staring into Kukalukl's snarling face.

"If you say another word," he said, "I shall suck your eyeballs from their sockets and pop them between my teeth like grapes." His voice was low and raspy, for his throat and vocal cords had not yet fully regrown. A concave ring of moist pink flesh encircled his neck.

Emily was smart enough to say nothing to this, but she squirmed a little to see if she could break free. She couldn't; she was pinned to the floor by two hundred–plus pounds of angry jaguar, its forepaws on her shoulders, its rear ones on her thighs.

Dagmar felt like sobbing with joy to see that Kukalukl was still alive, but being the best liar in the world, she maintained her regal demeanor. It was difficult, but she did it.

"You see?" she said. "We are undefeatable. My subjects never die. This land and all its creatures are mine to control. The birds of the air and the beasts of the field do my will."

Adam looked around, amazed at how quickly things were turning in their favor. Half the Marauders had drawn their weapons, though they were reluctant to attack while their leader was in such a precarious position. The other half, however, were already inching toward the doors.

Adam and Dagmar started to cross the arena toward the throne. Those Marauders who wanted to fight scowled at them and tightened their grip on their weapons, but made no move to intercept them. Not yet, anyway.

On the floor in front of the throne, Kukalukl sniffed at Emily's face, nose pumping madly.

"What *are* you?"

"Is something wrong?" asked Freud.

Kukalukl squinted up at him. "Freud?"

"Of course!" Freud leaned forward as if to impart a momentous secret and whispered, "I am in disguise."

"Hh. All you robots smell the same to me. Oil and old pennies. As for this bogus queen, she seems human, but there's something else…"

"I noticed she is unusually healthy, even for someone her age."

"Yes. She radiates health like a god, which makes me

wonder if she's another immortal. It's not just that, though. There's a faint odor about her. Something I've never smelled before. It's somehow both organic and artificial at the same time." He lowered his face until his hot breath ruffled Emily's hair. "I ask again: What are you? Where do you come from?"

Emily cocked a mocking eyebrow. "You told me not to talk."

"You will talk when I tell you to. Now talk. Tell me who you are."

"I am Queen Emily the First."

"Your *real* name."

She regarded him with smiling contempt for a moment, then said, "My name is Emily Jane Laramie. I was born in Burlington, Vermont. And that's *all* you're getting out of me, fuckhead!" Moving too fast for Kukalukl to react, her hands shot up and clawed into the soft pink flesh of his half-healed neck. Gouts of blood squirted out between her fingers.

Howling in pain, Kukalukl rolled away from Emily, who jumped to her feet.

The room suddenly became a blur of activity. Adam and Dagmar's walk became a run. The Marauders who had been ready to fight surged forward to attack. Some of the other Marauders changed their minds about fleeing and rejoined their fellows. The rest ran straight for the doors, most of them choosing the double doors in the south wall.

Artemis got there first. As he threw the doors open, something twanged. He said, "Hey, that's—" and then fell over dead, a crossbow bolt buried fletches-deep in his chest.

Quickly fitting a new bolt into the crossbow, Maggie limped into the room. Behind her came Anna, a sword in her hand. Behind Anna came the other eighty-seven women who had been locked in the harem, all of them armed with swords, crossbows, axes, maces, flails, spears, and a variety of other weapons.

"You know," Maggie said to the formerly fleeing Marauders who now stood gaping in a semicircle around the doors, "it was very unwise of you to leave both the harem and the armory unguarded." She raised her crossbow and cried, "Attack!"

The women charged into the arena to vent their long pent-up fury on their captors. The Marauders clustered around the doors fell like saplings in a flood. A few managed to take down a handful of women, but that only made their subsequent deaths much more brutal.

Most of the rest of the Marauders turned to engage the onrush of women. Afraid Dagmar would get trampled in the chaos, Adam grabbed her and set her on his shoulders. Then he proceeded to tear through those Marauders who had chosen to focus their attention on him, punching one—a blond man dressed like the Pope—so hard that with a sickening crack his head turned around one hundred and eighty degrees, kicking another—a four-foot-tall blue-haired gnome—in the chest with such force that his ribcage collapsed and he sailed twelve feet through the air. Adam wanted to get to Emily before she escaped. She was too psychotic and dangerous to be allowed to roam free in the world. He tried to get a glimpse of the throne, but with bodies in motion on every side and the air filled with blood and arrows and other debris, he couldn't see a thing.

What he couldn't see was this: Emily turned to flee, but before she could do so, Kukalukl leaped forward and raked his claws across her outer thigh. The force of the blow sent her tumbling to the floor again.

Kukalukl padded up to her. "You..." He coughed. She had damaged his throat badly, but he wasn't going to let that stop him. Not now. "You will not...get away...so easily."

"Wanna bet, pussycat?" she said. Her eyes flicked over his hunched shoulders.

Kukalukl rolled to the left, narrowly avoiding one of Johnny Circumcision's clipper-hands, which instead punched into the wood of the bleacher.

"Bad kitty," Johnny said as he yanked his clipper free. Smiling, he raised both clipper-hands and opened them wide.

Kukalukl glanced at Emily. She was struggling to her feet despite the blood streaming from the trio of gashes in her left thigh. Damn. He had thought he had hurt her badly enough to incapacitate her for a while. He wasn't about to let her get away, not after she nearly murdered Dagmar, which meant that, mortifying as it was to flee a fight, he had to retreat from this broom-haired fool so he could go after Emily instead.

As if in response to this thought, Big Red stepped between Kukalukl and Emily, battle-axe in hand, a savage grin on his face.

"Your intentions are as plain as my mighty cock," Big Red said, "and I tell you, sir cat, I shall die before I allow you to harm a single hair on my queen's beautiful head."

Kukalukl huffed in frustration. The throne blocked him in on the right, while a battle was raging between several Marauders and several women to his left. In other words, he was stuck between two idiots with extremely large, sharp objects. Worse, he hadn't fully healed and was still quite weak. He had expended most of his energy getting in here and tackling Emily. This was indeed totally sucky, as Dagmar might say. He really didn't want to have to heal another severed appendage. Given his low energy, it might take a week or more.

"Now, my blade-handed brother!" said the Viking in his big, booming voice. He raised his axe. Johnny crouched down, clippers wide open and ready to strike. Kukalukl crouched as well, determined to give at least as well as he got.

And then the amphibious Marauder, dead, neck broken, sailed right into Big Red and sent him smashing into Emily's throne. A moment later Adam came leaping over the bleacher seats, in the process knocking asprawl some of the Marauders who were fighting the women. He held Dagmar in one hand by her shirt, and when he landed a few feet behind Johnny Circumcision, he set her down. Then he turned to face Johnny.

Now it was Johnny who was caught between two enemies. With a loud cry, he swept his arm in a wide arc at Adam's chest. Adam leaped backward and ran right into Dagmar. They fell to the floor.

Johnny whirled toward Kukalukl, who was in mid-leap, having chosen to attack while Johnny's back was turned. Johnny figured the jaguar would do this, however, and was ready for it. He ducked out of the way, jabbing one clipper at Kukalukl as he sailed past.

Kukalukl tried to twist in mid-air to avoid the blow, but it was impossible. The clippers punched deep into his left side. Unfortunately for Johnny, they got caught there and dragged him down with Kukalukl as the big cat crashed to the floor.

Kukalukl tried to slash at Johnny, but the angle was bad and he was too weak to put much force into the blow anyway. Johnny yanked the clippers from Kukalukl's side. Blood streamed out after it. Johnny wanted to finish the kill, but there was still Adam to deal with.

He leaped up and spun around, certain that Adam would be on his feet by now. As he spun, he swung one clipper in an arc. It had worked before.

It didn't work this time. Adam caught Johnny's forearm in both hands, and before Johnny could bring the other clipper into play, Adam twisted Johnny's arm and thrust the clipper up into the soft underside of Johnny's chin with such force the tip of the clipper punched through the top of Johnny's head.

With a high-pitched gurgling sound, Johnny collapsed and died.

Squealing with glee, Dagmar raced out from behind Adam and sank to her knees next to Kukalukl. She started to throw her arms around him, then realized it probably wouldn't be a good idea given his injuries.

"You're alive!" she said, her cheeks wet with tears.

"Yes." He coughed and bright red blood bubbled from the hole in his side.

Dagmar clapped a hand over her mouth as her tears changed from those of glee to those of fright.

"You're hurt so bad!"

He chuckled softly. "I will be fine. If decapitation couldn't kill me, I hardly think a punctured lung will do the job. I told you I would always stand by you, and I will. But right now I just need to rest a little while."

Adam looked around. Emily was nowhere to be seen. Nor was Big Red.

"Damn it!" he growled. He looked down at Kukalukl. "She ran away. We need to hunt her down, but it is clear that you will be unable to bring your keen hunter's senses into play at the moment."

"Sorry about that," said Kukalukl. "Getting hacked up has that effect sometimes."

Freud, who had been staying well out of the fray all this time, now stepped forward. "I may be of assistance. My sensors will surely be able to follow the residue of her hideous perfume." Noting Adam's querying look, he added, "I am Freud. This is Adler's casing. Miss Frankenstein and I—"

"Now is not the time for explanations," said Adam. He took a quick look around the arena. He wasn't needed here any longer. The women, led by Maggie and Anna, had things well in hand. At this point only about two dozen Marauders were still standing and they were quickly being overwhelmed by the women's superior numbers. "If you believe you can track her, then come along," he told Freud.

Adam and Freud hurried out of the arena and into the long corridor they had come down earlier. Far down the hallway, Adam saw faint movement.

"Is that Emily?" he asked.

Freud adjusted the magnification of his optical sensors. "Yes," he said. "Emily and Big Red. Ah, they have seen us. They are running faster. Now they are turning down a side corridor."

The movement up ahead stopped.

"I will run on ahead," said Adam. "Catch up as fast as you can."

He sprinted forward, his long legs helping him reach the side corridor in half the time it had taken Emily and Big Red to get there.

He stopped just short of the corridor and listened, fearing an ambush. He heard nothing, so he swung around the corner, fists raised.

Ahead of him stretched a long, empty hallway lined with doors.

With no idea where Emily and Big Red might have gone, he waited for Freud, who seemed to take eons to arrive even though the robot was hurrying along as fast as he could.

"Which way?" Adam asked.

Freud scanned the corridor. "Follow me."

He walked forward slowly, turning his head from side to side. After about a hundred feet, he stopped and pointed at a door on the right marked "Staff Lounge."

"The perfume-trail leads there," he said, having lowered his volume to a whisper.

Adam motioned for Freud to stay behind him, then crept toward the door.

And then two doors across the hall flew open, Emily springing from one, in her hands a huge high-tech gun she could barely hold aloft, Big Red from the other, axe raised and ready to strike.

Emily pointed the gun at Adam and fired. A metal rod corkscrewed from the yawning barrel, leaving a widening spiral of blue smoke in its wake. But though Emily's aim was dead-on, it didn't hit Adam, because at the last moment Freud pushed him out of the way and took the shot himself. The rod punched straight through his midsection and vanished into the wall further down the corridor. When it exited Freud's back, it took most of his insides with it: Rods and coils and shards of metal clattered away across the floor.

"Ah," said Freud. He wobbled on his feet, then plummeted backward. By the time he hit the ground his orange eye-lights had winked out.

Big Red leaped forward and swung his axe at Adam's head. Adam ducked just in time—as it was, a few locks of hair got cropped—and the axe buried itself in a doorjamb. Before Big Red could prize it free, Adam grabbed him by the collar of his leather vest and threw him as hard as he could at Emily, who was already bringing her gun around to shoot Adam.

When she saw Big Red hurtling toward her, she fired

instinctively. The rod that spiraled from the gun blew a fist-sized hole through Big Red's chest and sent chunks of his right lung, liver, and right kidney splattering all over Adam, who had wisely dodged aside once he had set Big Red in motion and was now racing toward the door Big Red had emerged from.

Big Red's body slammed into Emily, knocking her back through the doorway she stood in. The gun flew from her hands and skidded away down the hall.

Adam burst through the other door and found himself in a small room decorated in a girlish manner reminiscent of Emily's throne room. The pastel-pink walls were covered with posters of half-naked musclemen and images of seashores and sunsets with motivational slogans beneath them such as "You are as great as you allow yourself to be," and "Aim for the stars." Full-length mirrors adorned every wall. A chandelier, a smaller version of the ones in the throne room, hung from the ceiling. Unwashed plates, packs of bubblegum, ceramic knickknacks, and old, pre-Cataclysm magazines with titles like *CosmoGirl* and *Young Mademoiselle* littered the glossy black tabletops. An extra-large T-shirt with a picture of a cartoon frog on it lay draped over the back of a white leather loveseat.

Kicking aside a purple bean-bag chair covered in Twinkie crumbs, Adam hurried toward a door in the south wall that he figured had to lead to the room Emily had just come out of. As he neared the door, he heard a muffled thump on the other side.

He slammed through the door. Beyond it was a bedroom dominated by a four-poster bed with lime-green sheets and a Hello Kitty comforter. On a bedside table sat an open box of Twinkies, an empty pink mug, and, though Adam tried to pretend he hadn't seen it, a foot-long studded black dildo.

Big Red's grisly remains lay in the doorway that connected this room with the corridor. Emily was nowhere to be seen.

But then Adam heard a faint clang from the closet. He rushed over and threw the door open. At first he saw only a wall of clothes—dresses and jeans and bodices and nightgowns—but soon discerned that one of the wooden panels at the back of the closet was askew. Another faint clang rang out from behind it.

Ripping out handfuls of clothes and strewing them across the room behind him, he cleared a path to the back of the closet and tore the panel away. Beyond it was a metal staircase spiraling down a concrete shaft.

It could be a trap. But what choice did he have except to follow her? He couldn't let her get away to further pollute the world with her mad egocentricity.

He raced down the stairs, the banging of his heavy boots on the metal steps surely alerting Emily to his approach. Before he had gone far, he heard a series of mechanical sounds from below—*chack-chack-chack clank.*

At first he assumed she was preparing some sort of trap or weapon, but then a motor started up, and he heard the whine of rusty wheels grinding against equally rusty tracks. No, not a trap and not a weapon. An escape.

He practically flew the rest of the way down the stairs, his feet touching only every fifth step. Even then, even going as fast as he could, something deep inside told him it was already too late.

It was. By the time he reached the bottom of the stairs and stepped out into the end of a dimly lit concrete tunnel down which two pairs of train tracks extended, the little open-topped train-car Emily was in was already a hundred feet away and rapidly gaining speed. A second car sat on the second set of tracks, but its control panel had been ripped off and its wire innards torn out.

Adam glowered at Emily as she receded into the shadows of the tunnel. There was no way he could reach her now.

Emily knew this too, and with a grin she extended one arm and flipped up her middle finger at him.

One day, he vowed to himself, one day he would find her and stop her.

He watched the train-car vanish into the darkness, then listened to the whine of its wheels fade into the distance, and even after that he stood there staring into the black tunnel for a long while.

With a sigh, he ascended the staircase and returned to Freud's shattered remains. He had hoped there was some way to fix the damage, but when he inspected the body more closely, he saw that Freud's torso was essentially nonexistent now. Or rather, it existed as a collection of tiny pieces scattered down the length of the hallway. He doubted if even a roboticist from Freud's own time could repair this damage.

"I am sorry I did not protect you better," Adam said to the inert assemblage of metal and plastic. "And I thank you for protecting me…"

He frowned, realizing the full import of what that meant. Freud had been programmed to prevent humans from coming to harm. His saving Adam meant that according to his cold, rational processors, Adam was to all intents and purposes human, a man.

Adam smiled sadly. "Thank you," he said again.

He returned to the arena. As he neared the closed door, he realized he heard no sounds of fighting from within. And while his heart told him the women had won, his brain perversely concocted a different story: It showed him Maggie and Anna and Dagmar and Kukalukl and all the freed captives lying dead, having been taken by surprise by the last-minute arrival of a crew of Marauders who had been out pillaging and who now sat amid the corpses with smiles on their blood-streaked faces while they waited for Adam to return.

All these fears evaporated when he heard Anna's voice, faint but unmistakable through the door, say, "Gordina, stop mutilating the bodies! I know what they did to you, but that's no reason to be as bad as them!"

"That's easy for you to say," a woman—presumably Gordina—said. "They never got around to you. You don't know what it was like."

Adam tried to open the door, but it would barely budge. Something was blocking it. He planted his shoulder against it and pushed harder. It opened, but very slowly, as if it were moving underwater. Something large and heavy scuffed along the ground on the other side as it opened. When the opening was wide enough, he stepped through and saw what the problem was: Droke's body, now bristling with arrows and crisscrossed with sword cuts, lay sprawled against the door.

He dragged the corpse out of the way. As he straightened up, Anna raced up and threw her arms around him.

"I knew you would come," she said.

"That's the guy you were tellin' us about?" said a woman in a gauzy blue teddy dotted with Marauder blood. "He looks like one of *them.*"

Anna gave her a frosty look. "If you cannot tell the difference, Shona, then you are both blind and stupid."

"Hey, I'm just sayin', is all! He looks like what he looks like."

"Perhaps. But remember: Were it not for him, you would still be…how did you put it? 'Sucking assholes' pipes,' was it not?"

Shona shrugged in defeat. "Thanks," she said to Adam.

He bowed. "My pleasure."

Unused to men bowing to her, she just blinked in bemusement.

Maggie, Dagmar, and Kukalukl joined them.

"Where is Freud?" asked Maggie.

Adam shook his head. "Another one we owe that vile bitch-queen."

"I take it you failed to catch her, then," said Kukalukl.

"Yes. There is a train system underneath the complex. She got to it before I could catch her."

"She is far from the only one," said Maggie. "At least half a dozen Marauders managed to flee during the battle."

"Though the rest are deceased, I am overjoyed to report," added Kukalukl.

"We lost over a dozen ourselves," said Anna. "And a dozen more are wounded."

"We should remain here at Yoyodyne until we have recuperated," said Adam. "That will also give us time to thoroughly inspect the complex and see what sorts of useful items we may find here. It seems that—"

The double doors at the south end of the arena burst open and in rolled a long wheeled cart draped in a white cloth and laden with loaves of bread, tureens of soup, huge platters piled high with cuts of meat, dishes heaped with steaming vegetables, bowls of salt and sugar and spices; and pushing the cart was Asparagus Sam, who froze dead when he saw the Marauders' corpses sprawled all over the arena and the armed angry women clutching bloody weapons and the jaguar that was watching him with an almost human expression of contempt and the eight-foot-tall monster-man with hideous wrinkled yellow skin. And then, seeing how things stood, Asparagus Sam cleared his throat and smiled as best he could and said, "I brought your victory dinner!"

And there was much feasting.

Chapter 12

The Road Home

1

They spent the rest of the day tending the wounded, clearing away the dead, and resting. They slept that night in the Marauders' rooms.

The next morning they began the long task of exploring the complex and cataloguing its contents. There were quite a few surprises.

One cavernous room in the basement was filled with barrels of fuel for the three large generators the Marauders had been using to power the central portion of the complex. There were also a few barrels of a different kind of fuel for the experimental cars in the various hangars ringing the complex. Most of these vehicles had been irreparably damaged by the Cataclysm or the Marauders or simply time and disuse, but a handful still worked.

While stripping down Emily's room preparatory to burning her clothes and furnishings and personal items along with those of the rest of the Marauders, they discovered a small secret room behind her bed that was packed with weapons of much better quality than the swords and spears she allotted her underlings. Among these weapons were a nail-gun, a sniper rifle, a plasma rifle, and a boxy silver gun so large only Adam could lift it without getting a hernia. On the side of this latter item Emily had written in lipstick

"Big Fuckin' Gun 3000!" Adam later tested it on one of the inoperative jet-cars. The car was reduced to a million tiny pieces embedded in the hangar wall, and the muzzle-flash left spots hovering in Adam's vision for over an hour.

On the west side of the complex they found a hangar that had been converted into stables. There were over a hundred horses in there, including the ones stolen from Adam, Maggie, and Anna's RV in Sweetwater. Adam was shocked that the animals were so healthy and well-groomed. Anna told him not to be.

"Girls love horses," she explained. "Even psychotic would-be queens."

A huge walk-in freezer next to the kitchen contained enough food to feed everyone in the complex for years. And Asparagus Sam, who revealed his true name to be Samuel Dolenz, was only too happy to cook that food once he was sure no one was going to kill him. His happiness blossomed into ecstasy when he learned that most of Yoyodyne's new residents preferred much healthier meals than those demanded by the Marauders.

And new residents it had, for although Adam and company planned to escort many of the abducted women back to their homes, twenty-eight of the women had seen their homes destroyed and their families slaughtered by the Marauders. Having nowhere else to go, they decided to stay right there. Which worked out perfectly, because Yoyodyne, with its vast stock of fuel and weapons and other items that would be disastrous in the wrong hands, needed caretakers who would guard and use and distribute those items wisely and well.

Late on the day after they defeated the Marauders, they buried their dead in the woods beyond the fence, including Freud's various pieces and Granite's head and shoulders, which they found resting on a shelf above the Annihilator's bed. They dumped the Marauders' bodies into a mass grave beside the lake of ooze.

Shortly after dawn the next day, Adam, Maggie, Anna, Dagmar, and Kukalukl (who was now fully healed except for a hairless ring around his neck) set out on foot along the train tracks to see if they could determine where Emily went.

The track was over four miles long, and they didn't reach the terminus until mid-afternoon. There they found the train-car sitting at a turn-around next to a cinderblock guardhouse. A flight of stairs behind the guardhouse led up to a small corrugated metal building containing boxes of clothes and toiletries and food and weapons. Some of these boxes were open, and socks and necklaces and tubes of lipstick lay scattered about the floor, as if someone had pulled items from the boxes in a mad rush. Two dust-free rectangles on the floor showed where a pair of suitcases or large bags had stood until recently. On one wall, Emily had written "THIS WORLD IS MINE!" in purple spray-paint. The spray-can lay on the floor beneath the message, next to a much larger dust-free patch. Three wheel-tracks, seemingly from a wedge-shaped vehicle, extended from this patch to the wide roll-up door.

Outside the shed they found themselves in open grassland that stretched away north, west, and east. To the south were the woods that ringed Yoyodyne. A mile due west stood a lone, rusting electricity pylon, its broken black lines trailing in the high grass like guy-ropes. The mountains loomed to the north, larger and clearer now than when Adam and the others had seen them a few days ago.

After hunting around for a while, they finally found a trio of wheel-tracks barely visible in the dry dirt beneath the grass. The tracks led northeast.

Kukalukl sniffed at them.

"Too old for a scent. Back in that building, though, I detected traces of burned fuel."

"A fuel-powered vehicle like those we found at Yoyodyne?" said Adam.

"Almost certainly."

"Then we have no hope of catching up to her." He gazed northeast across the plain. "Not right now, at any rate."

After figuring out how to operate the turn-around, they crammed themselves upon the train car and rode it back to Yoyodyne. The return trip took only half an hour.

2

The following day they left. They couldn't stay any longer. Many of the women who had been abducted by the Marauders were eager to return to their homes and families, and Adam, Maggie, and the others weren't about to let them travel unprotected.

After a final talk with a tall, muscular woman named Elíra who had become the unofficial leader of the women who were remaining at Yoyodyne, and a last visit to the new cemetery in the woods to say their goodbyes to the departed, during which visit Maggie planted some daffodils on Bob's grave, the group of nearly fifty abductees, plus the four remaining members of the rescue party, set out for Sweetwater with a dozen horses laden with food and supplies. The rest of the horses were left for the use of the Yoyodyne Ladies' Army, as it had come to be half jokingly called.

The trip back took nearly twice as long as the trip there. One reason for this was Freud's absence: Without him to guide them across the Badlands, they decided it would be safer and easier to take the extra time to detour around that area. As they did so, they kept watch for any sign of Centivert but saw nothing.

Another reason for the longer trip was their decision to give Happyvale a wide berth, not because they suspected any specific danger still lurked there, but because of the bad memories it held, especially for Dagmar, who was very quiet during that leg of the trip. When they camped that night, Adam headed off alone and returned three hours later bearing the goods the group had stashed under the counter in Suzie's Stuffed Animal Emporium.

Likewise, they avoided coming too close to Research Lab B, but in this case it was because they knew horrors *did* still dwell there, even though those horrors were not likely to spread very far from the darkness of the lab.

And on the evening of the tenth day out from Yoyodyne, they came again to Sweetwater.

As they approached the town, the bell above the town hall rang five times, which one of the women who had been abducted from Sweetwater explained was the signal for "unknown entities approaching."

Adam frowned. "Why was the bell not rung when the Marauders attacked?"

"It was market day," the woman said with a shrug. "Lots of unknown entities show up in town on market day."

Adam shook his head. "Your security system needs improvement."

When they reached the town, they found the streets empty and every window shuttered tight. As the group neared the center of Sweetwater, the door of the general store flew open and Rin ran out, crying "Nala!"

A blonde teenage girl in the group screamed "Mama!"

and leaped from her horse. After two weeks of horror and worry, mother and daughter were reunited.

Other doors opened now as the residents of Sweetwater finally realized what was happening. People poured into the street, and more young women were reunited with their loved ones. Rin barged through the rapidly growing crowd and grasped Adam's and Maggie's hands.

"Thank you!" she said, her eyes wet with tears. "Thank you so much. I can never repay you for this."

Maggie glanced at Adam and was amused by his utterly nonplussed look as he stared at Rin.

"And the Marauders?" Sheriff O'Toole asked, a little suspiciously.

"They will trouble you no more," said Maggie. She dug into her saddle bag, pulled out the Annihilator's scorched and dented helmet, and tossed it to him. He caught it and stared at it with his mouth agape.

At that a great cheer went up. Everyone wanted to know more, but Rin snapped, "Not now. Can't you see how tired they all are? They've been travelin' for two weeks. Why, they're practically fallin' asleep on their horses. Let's get 'em set up with beds and food and save the gabfest for tomorrow."

3

Those who needed lodgings were granted the use of spare beds or couches for the night. Adam, Maggie, and Anna slept in their usual places in their RV. Dagmar set up her sleeping bag next to theirs. Kukalukl went out hunting and had not returned by the time the last of them—Adam, who couldn't stop worrying about the havoc Centivert might be wreaking—fell asleep. When the others awoke the next morning they found the jaguar curled up in a big black ball on the hard floor next to Dagmar.

An hour after dawn, when they were all still picking sleep-crust from their eyes, Rin and Mayor Firth came knocking at the RV.

"Can we help you?" said Maggie.

"You already have," said Mayor Firth. "And in honor of all you've done for us and for Erizan as a whole, and also as a welcome-home party for those you've returned to us, we're holding a celebration tonight at the Community Hall on Pelican Street. The festivities'll start at sundown."

"And you'd all better come," said Rin. "I'm making my famous sweet potato pie. It's got real marshmallows in it."

"That sounds delicious," said Maggie. "We will, of course, be there."

After Rin and Mayor Firth left, Adam shook his head.

"This is insane," he said. "Two weeks ago most of the townspeople thought me no better than the Marauders. Now they are throwing a celebration partly in my honor."

"Is it really something to wonder at?" said Maggie. "You rescued the abductees, you ended the Marauders' reign of terror, and you managed to do it all without being excessively rude and growly."

Adam frowned. "I am never 'rude and growly.' At least not without just cause."

Anna and Maggie looked at each other and then exploded with laughter.

"Of *course* not," Maggie gasped out between guffaws.

"He's always such a patient, cordial fellow," Anna added as she dabbed tears of hilarity from her eyes.

Adam rolled his eyes as if annoyed, but there was a hint of a smile on his lips.

4

Everyone in town turned out for the celebration, and most of them brought food. Indeed there was so much food that the three tables designated for it were deemed insufficient before half the townsfolk had arrived, and more tables were hastily set up. Before long the tables were laden with roasted chicken, beef pies, barbecued rabbit, boiled giant squirrel, athelok burgers, braised chingo wings, boiled potatoes, mashed potatoes, baked potatoes, hash browns, French fries, corn on the cob, Brussels sprouts, green beans, red beans, purple beans, baked beans, yellow eithel, onions, beets, parsnips, cauliflower, apples, pears, stewed prunes, sixteen different casseroles, sweet potato pie (with marshmallows), cherry pie, apple pie, toadberry pie, brownies, rolls, muffins, bread, Cap'n Crunch, Count Chocula, Periwinkle Pops, Chocolate-Frosted Sugar Bombs, Spam, Beef Jerky, Cinnamon Gorka Bugs, Plumtree's Potted Meat, Hoshi's Bubblegum-Flavored Happy Party Crabs, and Twinkies (which everyone who had been at Yoyodyne avoided like the plague).

The finest wine that could be found was brought out, and innumerable toasts were drunk to the abductees and their rescuers, all of whom sat at tables of honor at the front of the packed room.

Rin made the final toast, and she made it especially for Adam.

"Here's to a fella I know darn well probably didn't want to do all he did. But when it came down to it, he did it anyway, and in my book that makes him a hero." She raised her glass. "So here's to my hero."

Everyone boomed their hearty agreement while Adam squirmed.

Maggie nudged him in the ribs.

"Hear that?" she said. "They're talking about *you*. I knew you had it in you."

Adam grunted. "Frankly, I think I would be more comfortable if they were chasing me with pitchforks and torches."

After the feast, half a dozen townsfolk pulled out instruments and started playing, while dozens more got up and danced a peculiar local dance that involved lots of spinning and stomping.

"Ugh," groaned Dagmar. "If I try to dance, I think I'll explode."

Kukalukl sighed. "I see you learned nothing from your horrid feast of pies and cakes in Happyvale."

She frowned. "Oh, don't even talk about that."

"I apologize. I thought you would have put those silly animals behind you by now."

"It's not *that*. I meant don't talk about *food*. Just hearing the word 'cake' makes me feel like puking."

"So," Maggie said to them, "have you two decided what your plans are? Will you travel with us as we escort the other women we rescued back to their hometowns?"

Not caring one way or the other, Kukalukl looked at Dagmar, leaving the decision to her.

Dagmar shrugged. "I dunno. I was thinking of, you know, going home again. To the old palace. Just one last time, to say goodbye. But hopefully we'll be done with that in time to help you hunt down Centivert and Emily and all that."

"And after that?" said Adam. He was thinking of Granite's tales of teams of heroes patrolling the world to protect the defenseless from the wicked.

Dagmar hesitated. "I...I dunno. I thought it might be cool to go back to Yoyodyne. I think I'd like to live there. Besides, they could use a queen's guidance. A proper queen. Not some evil witch."

Adam said nothing. He hadn't told anyone the truth about Dagmar and didn't plan to. Dagmar had done enough, and suffered enough, that he didn't have the heart to reveal her lie.

Still, it would have been nice to be part of a team of heroes. Somebody needed to keep the chaos of this world from overwhelming those who adhered to order. Then again, it seemed likely that sooner or later he would meet others who could help him out with that.

He realized what he was thinking and smiled to himself. Not so long ago, he would have ridiculed such thoughts of heroism. And yet here he was now, the recipient of toasts and food and outpourings of gratitude.

Slowly his smile faded and he found himself staring down at his hands splayed on the tablecloth before him.

"Excuse me," he said brusquely, rising. "I must attend to something I forgot about. I will return shortly."

He strode out of the hall. The others exchanged puzzled glances.

"What's up with that?" said Dagmar.

Maggie just shook her head.

After several minutes had passed, she turned to Anna and said, "Perhaps I should see what's keeping him."

Anna nodded. "I think you should."

Maggie stared at Anna a moment, then said, "You know what he's doing?"

Anna nodded. "I think so."

"Well, then, perhaps *you* should go and talk to him. You

are much better at dealing with people than I am. I lack your innate empathetic instincts."

"No. It should be you."

"Why?"

"Because you were with him during the experiences that changed him. And he *has* changed since last I saw him, even if he refuses to acknowledge it out loud. You know the whys and wherefores of it; I do not, though I suspect some of it has to do with this Mr. Winston you told me about."

Maggie looked down at her plate in silence. The mere mention of Bob's name still tugged at her emotions like a fishhook. She fleetingly wondered what might have been had he lived.

She sighed. "You are right, as usual." She got up and headed out of the hall to look for Adam.

He was where she thought he would be: in their RV. As she approached the back door, she heard the deep, gasping sobs from within. She rapped twice on the door and said, "It's me."

The sobs vanished. After a brief silence, Adam called out, "I am fine. There is no need to—"

But she was already opening the door.

"I am fine," Adam repeated in a low voice. He sat on the edge of one of the two king-sized mattresses that served as his bed. As Maggie shut the door behind her, he wiped at the wet streaks on his cheeks with the back of his hand.

"What is wrong?" Maggie asked.

"Nothing," he said, trying to sound surprised that she might think anything was wrong.

She sat down beside him and waited for him to speak. It was what she thought Anna would do.

He laughed a little too shrilly and turned his face away from her. "I am fine. Perhaps I am just a little tired from all the activity."

Seconds ticked past. Maggie waited. Adam glanced at her, then looked away again with a grimace.

She put her arm around his middle back (he was too tall for her to put it around his shoulders). He stiffened, held that stiff, straight-backed position for a second, then let out a long gust of air in a rush.

"I...I do not deserve this," he said, his voice suddenly shaky. She felt his back shuddering with the unevenness of his breath. He was trying not to start crying again.

"What do you mean?" she asked.

He didn't look at her. He just stared down at his hands, which lay curled and immobile in his lap like dead things.

"You know what I mean," he said. "This celebration. They...they cheer me, they toast me, even the womenfolk look at me with new appreciation, but..."

He turned to her, eyes wet with fresh tears, and raised his hands before his face. "I can think only of William Frankenstein gargling out his death rattle as I choked the life from him. And the others I killed. *I.* With these monstrous hands. This festivity is wrong. I do not deserve it. I am no hero."

She took his hands in her own and lowered them to the mattress between them.

"You have helped countless people. You have saved countless lives. Are you saying that that means nothing?"

"No, not nothing. But no amount of good will make up for the wrongs I have done."

"Does that mean you will not try?"

"Of course I will try, but—"

"Do you not intend to continue helping people? Do you not intend to escort those poor women we rescued back to their homes, and then hunt down Centivert and Emily and the escaped Marauders?"

"Yes, but—"

"But even when you have accomplished all *that,* as I have no doubt you will, and received further accolades for having done it, you will continue to believe that you do not deserve it, is that not right?"

"I…" He thought about it. "Yes."

She nodded and squeezed his hands with a smile. "And all of that is why you are a hero."

He looked at her with his eyebrows raised and his upper lip drawn back—the sort of look you give someone when they've said something completely insane.

She just laughed. She didn't mind his odd looks. Then she let go of his hands and stood up.

"I am returning to this well-earned celebration. I suggest you do, too. If you don't, everyone will miss you."

She headed back to the Community Hall. At the door she paused and gazed up at the crescent moon, which hung clear and white in the sky. Then she smiled softly and whispered, "Thanks, Bob."

She opened the door and rejoined the celebration. Before long, Adam did too.